Two Worlds of Spies

By Anisa Razvi

Two Worlds of Spies
Copyright © 2016 Anisa Razvi

ISBN: 978-1-937251-65-9

Part I

Confederate Spy

Chapter 1

Driving his father's old trailer through the rain to the mechanic's was not exactly Raymond Vincent's idea of a perfect day. However, he whistled cheerfully as he drove along, as it was his practice to make the best of everything.

About five minutes from the mechanic's shop. Raymond pulled to the side of the road to examine the new building that had just finished construction. The outside lot was teeming with people, pouring in and out of doors, carrying boxes and furniture. It looked like a small office building, but there were no signs up yet, so he couldn't tell what the building was meant for.

He drove a little further along, then stopped his truck and leaned out the window to speak to a man on the sidewalk. "Hello! Know what the building's for?" Raymond asked.

The man shook his head, "Nope. 's far as I kin tell, whatever it is, it's top secret," he drawled.

Raymond nodded, then shook his head as he realized his hair had gotten wet. He quickly drew back inside the truck and shut the windows.

~   ~   ~

A few days later, when Raymond went to pick up the trailer, he stepped out of his truck and almost bumped into an old man standing in the parking lot. "I'm so sorry!" he exclaimed.

"Not at all," the old man said, shaking his head, then nodding it, "It was entirely my fault. I wanted to talk to you."

Raymond looked around, wondering if the man was speaking to someone else, but no one was anywhere near them so he said in surprise, "Who, me?"

"You," the old man nodded, "I see you have a big trailer here – or at least, the mechanic said you own it. Let me introduce myself. Bob Elliot's the name." Raymond wondered a little crazily if the man's head would ever fall off from all that nodding. Focusing again, he held out his hand, "Nice to meet you, Mr. Elliot. I'm Raymond Vincent."

"That's right, you are," the man said with a short nod. Raymond was thankful the nodding was slowing down. "I want you for a job, if you'll take it," Mr. Elliot explained.

"What sort of a job?" Raymond asked.

"Just to cart a load of stuff from my house to another property of mine and help me put it together."

Raymond raised his eyebrow, "Well, this is certainly a surprise. Why don't you just get a moving company to do it?"

"I have reasons," Elliot told him vaguely. "Will you do it, or won't you?"

A quarter of an hour later, Raymond had let the old man talk him into carting the stuff for him, and even invited him for dinner to talk it over.

They were both in Raymond's truck driving toward his home when Mr. Elliot suddenly exclaimed, "I forgot to ask if your parents would mind."

"Oh, no! Both Dad and I often bring home unexpected guests. He won't care."

"But it's your mother that's doing the cooking, isn't it? What will she say to an extra mouth to feed?" Mr. Elliot asked with a grin.

A dark cloud passed over Raymond's face and his hands jerked the steering wheel suddenly, startling the old man. "Hey! Watch out," Elliot exclaimed.

"I'm sorry," Raymond forced himself to calm down, in spite of the empty feeling in the pit of his stomach. He explained quietly, "My mother died last year. I guess I still haven't gotten over it."

"Forgive me," Mr. Elliot said with a long glance at the young man and a slow nod, "I didn't mean to – well." And he stopped.

"It's all right," Raymond took a deep breath and directed the conversation back to more neutral subjects, "Anyway, she wouldn't have minded when she was alive. She loved having people over. I think it's nice having more than just a couple people in the house."

"Do you have any siblings?" Mr. Elliot asked.

"Nope. I'm an only child," Raymond grinned, "I guess there are pluses and minuses to everything, but I've often wished I had a larger family."

"Yes. I grew up as one of ten children, and have never regretted it. However, large circles of friends can partially make up for not having a big family."

Raymond laughed, "Not many of those either," he said, "Just me and Dad. Well, here we are!"

Inside the house, Mr. Vincent greeted them, and soon they were eating dinner together. "So what is this stuff you need moved, Mr. Elliot?" Raymond asked, "It must be something important or unusual, or you'd just have a regular moving company do it for you."

"It's an invention of mine, and it is important and unusual," Mr. Elliot said with a nod, "But I'm afraid I can't tell you what it is yet."

"Is it dangerous," Mr. Vincent asked, "Or is it something that could be harmful to anyone? I'm not sure I think we ought to help you if there could be any moral issues attached."

Mr. Elliot looked thoughtful, "I would say it is dangerous, in a way, but I am not planning to use it in a harmful manner."

"In other words, it could be harmful if the wrong people got their hands on it," Raymond stated.

"Yes," Mr. Elliot nodded. He was looking at the Vincents strangely, they thought. "In time I may be able to tell you about it, but I have to be careful."

Raymond spoke in a loud whisper behind his hand, "He means he can't trust us, Dad."

The old man shook his head in protest, "No, no, I didn't mean that – " but eventually gave up and began nodding again, "I guess that is sort of what I mean, but I don't want to give the impression that I think you're untrustworthy."

"Oh, we're not offended!" Mr. Vincent laughed, "We're just curious to know what this strange invention you've been talking about really is."

~   ~   ~

The next day Raymond and his father helped Mr. Elliot move some large pieces of metal and other things – looking like parts of some sort of machine – from his home to a plot of ground near a large brick wall. They then helped him put everything together over a door in the wall. Conversation never lagged, and though the Vincents didn't quite notice it, Mr. Elliot soon found out a lot more about them than they ever did about him. As he put the finishing touches onto his machine, they stepped back and watched eagerly, wondering if he would tell them what it was for.

When he was done, Mr. Elliot looked at them for a moment, then said, "Come with me. I want to show you what's on the other side of this wall."

The Vincents followed him through the door, and saw a one lane road going by directly in front of the wall. A large tree was to the left, and a little hill to the right.

"Remember what you see," Mr. Elliot told them, then he took them back to the other side of the wall. "Watch this," the old man said as Raymond and his father were standing back. He pressed a button on the side of the machine, and it disappeared!

After standing for a few seconds in openmouthed wonder, Mr. Vincent exclaimed, "You can make it invisible?"

"That was the easy part," Mr. Elliot said with a nod.

"If that was easy, what was hard?" Raymond asked in disbelief. He went up to the wall and felt where he had seen the machine before, and his hand touched the metal.

"You'll see," Mr. Elliot said. He was a little breathless. "I hope it actually works. I've been working on it for over sixty years."

"Whew!" Raymond exclaimed, "That's longer than even Dad has been alive."

"You'll know why it took that long when I tell you what it is," Raymond tried to forget the fact that Mr. Elliot was nodding again and pay attention to what he was saying, "I have invented a time-travel machine."

There was silence for a moment, then Raymond asked slowly, "Could you repeat that? I'm not sure I heard right."

"You heard right enough," the old man told him. "Come on with me and I'll show you."

He opened the door and walked through it; the Vincents followed. What they saw there caused them to gasp in surprise. There was the one-lane road in front of them, but now it was made of dirt. The hill on the right side of the door was still much the same, but there was now a tiny stream running along at the foot of it. The huge oak tree they had seen before was now a little sapling. As they looked, a horse-drawn wagon rolled along the dirt road in front of them. They saw a young girl about five years old lean over the side, staring at them as if they were the strangest people she had ever seen. She was wearing a pink flowered dress and a floppy sunbonnet. Her mother, also wearing a sunbonnet, pulled her daughter back into the wagon as it disappeared from the three men's sight.

"Wow," Raymond said in a hushed voice, "it looks like you've really done it!"

"Yes, I have. Now let's see what happens. This door used to be used often. We are in the year eighteen hundred sixty-three. The War Between the States is being fought right in our backyards. I'm going to go back to our side of the door, and wait until someone comes through to come into our town. Then I am going to turn off the machine so that if they go through the door again, it will still be the twenty-first century there. I want to see what they will do about the culture clash, and if they can convince people they are not crazy when they say they were born in the eighteen hundreds."

"Are you going to let them go back sometime?" Raymond asked worriedly.

"Oh of course! I wouldn't make them have to live permanently here, I just want to see what it will be like. But listen, I don't want either of you to breath a word that might get people to suspect there could even possibly be a time machine. It is entirely too dangerous. I don't know what people might do with it if they found out, but I'm not willing to take that chance."

"Oh, we won't, sir!" Raymond assured him, "Don't worry that we will. But what you say about letting some people from the eighteen hundreds come here will be interesting. Are you going to follow them around to see what people say to them?"

"Yes, that is what I'm going to do. And it should be interesting, as you say. I can hardly wait until someone comes through! Let's go behind those bushes. That way we can see if someone comes through that door, but they won't notice us. Then we can go and turn it off, and follow them."

Chapter 2

Lucy looked up at her brother, who was sitting beside her in the stagecoach. She was very tired of riding along the rutted roads in a vehicle which was far from comfortable, but saying so wouldn't help anything, so she kept silent. Richard also was silent, though he gave her a tired smile as he saw her looking at him. She smiled back, and straightened up in the hard seat.

All at once, she heard the driver yell, "Here's your stop!"

The stagecoach came to a halt before a brick wall with a wooden door in the center. Richard jumped out, and reached up a hand for his sister. She stood up and accepted his help to the ground. When she stood on the ground, she wished she could stretch, but, of course, that was out of the question for a young lady of her age. It was times like this that she almost wished she were a young girl again. Then she could have run about on the grass, relieving her cramped muscles.

The coach driver pulled out their trunks and set them on the grass, Richard asked, "Will you help me carry them over there behind that tree? I can't carry them all right now, but I'll have someone come and get them in a few minutes."

The driver was a good-natured fellow, and he picked up a trunk and deposited it at the foot of the sapling Richard had pointed to. After a couple of trips each, from Richard and the driver, they had stacked the trunks at the foot of the tiny tree, and the driver swung up into the high seat in the front of the stage and drove off.

Richard picked up both of their satchels with one hand and offered his other arm to Lucy.

They were about to enter through the door, but Richard suddenly stopped and said, "Look, there's a stream. I'm thirsty, and I don't want to wait until we find someone who will give us a drink."

"How will we drink the water, though?" Lucy asked, "did we bring any glasses?"

Richard laughed, "No, not glasses. I brought two tin cups. One for you and one for me. Those are easier to carry around than glasses."

"I suppose glasses would be a little hard to manage," she agreed, "but *tin* cups? Have I ever drank out of one in my life?"

"I think so," he laughed again, "but I'm sure I have more often than you."

"I know, you travel more than I. But you're right, I am quite thirsty, so if you would get out the cups I would like a drink."

Richard carried the satchels to the stream and Lucy sat down on the grass. Her brother rummaged around in his bag for a moment, then pulled out two tin cups.

"Here's yours," he said, handing it to her, "just dip it into the stream and then drink from it."

She did, and found the water quite cold, "this is good," she said after she had finished drinking, "I'm glad you brought these cups."

"Shall we go into the town now?" he asked, taking her cup from her hand and putting it back into the satchel.

"Yes," she held out her hand and he helped her up, "you said you've been here before, right?"

"Yes, I have. Not more than once or twice, though. We'll be fine. I know you haven't traveled much, but I have, and I know what to do. So let's go through that door, and find a hotel we can sleep in."

"Why don't you just leave the satchels here with the trunks?" Lucy suggested, "you're as tired as I am, aren't you?"

"Not quite," Richard said, "but I'll do that. We must remember to send someone for the trunks immediately when we reach the hotel, though, we shouldn't leave them here for too long," and he placed the satchels on top of the trunks.

Lucy took her brother's arm, and they walked toward the door. Richard pulled on the handle, and opened the wooden door, and the two walked through. Lucy looked around wonderingly, and Richard said, "This doesn't look the way I remembered it for some reason."

"Well you did say you haven't been here for more than a year, didn't you?" his sister said.

"Yes, I did. So I could just be remembering wrong. Let's go to the town."

They walked slowly toward the town, which they could see not far ahead of them. When they reached the road, Richard looked down in surprise, "I wonder what this is made out of? It's not like any road I've ever seen."

Lucy looked down, she was sure that she had never seen anything like that road either.

Richard bent down to get a closer look, "It seems to be made out of tiny rocks, but I don't know exactly what it is."

"The houses look strange too," Lucy said, looking ahead.

"Yes," Richard agreed, and he started walking again. "See," he said as they got closer, "they're not made of wood, or stone, or brick – what *are* they made out of?"

"It looks a little like folds of fabric," Lucy said "but –" she felt the side of a building, "it's very hard."

Richard put out his hand also and felt the strange substance the building was made out of, "I've never seen anything like this!"

Lucy looked around the street, and then started in surprise. After a second she lowered her gaze in embarrassment. She couldn't believe what she was seeing! Across the street, there were two young ladies and a young man walking along. The ladies were wearing trousers! She turned back to her brother so that her back was to them. She did not wish to see such a sight.

"What's the matter?" Richard asked, looking into her face.

"Those young ladies on the other side of the street are dressed so – strangely. I can't believe it! They're wearing trousers like men!"

"Really? That's strange," he turned to look over his shoulder and saw what she was talking about. What was more, a few women and men came out of what he supposed was a store, and though two of the ladies were wearing trousers, one lady had a dress on that was so short it came above her knees. He turned his head away uncomfortably, but not before he saw them give him and his sister strange stares.

He pulled Lucy's hand through his elbow and began to walk along the street. He saw some pictures in one of the shop windows that looked strange. There were pictures of strange creatures and some things he had never seen before.

He saw Lucy looking around and felt her shrinking closer and closer to him as they walked. He looked down at her, and asked, "Lucy? Is there something wrong besides what we've already noticed?"

"Yes!" she said, "everyone seems to be –" and her voice sank to such a low murmur that he had to bend down to hear, "– staring at us!"

Richard straightened and looked around. He saw immediately what she meant. There were several little groups of people on the street, and almost everyone was staring directly at him and his sister. He saw several people pointing, and several others had out little boxes of different shapes and sizes that they were holding up to their faces. He supposed these might be a new kind of eyeglasses that they were looking through in order to see him and Lucy better.

"Richard, can't we go anywhere that no one can see us? I don't like being the subject of so many looks," Lucy pleaded, drawing so close to him that he trampled the hem of her skirt.

"Oh, I'm sorry Lucy, I didn't mean to step on your skirt," he said apologetically. Then, answering her, he said, "I don't know of anywhere to go. This town doesn't seem at all like I remember."

At this moment a large machine on wheels rolled by at an amazing speed. Richard pulled his sister back quickly, afraid of what might happen if they got too close. In a flash, it turned a corner, and was gone.

"Richard, that wasn't pulled by horses?"

"No, it wasn't, Lucy. I'm sorry, I can't answer any of your questions. When I came here, it was a town much like our own. I don't see how these changes could have come about in just a year and a half, but I suppose we will have to ask someone to explain everything to us. Look, maybe we can ask them!" and he directed his gaze ahead of them.

Lucy followed where he was looking and saw a young man and lady coming to meet them. These still were dressed a little strangely, but they looked much nicer than the rest of the people on the street, who, she noticed rather uncomfortably, were still staring at them.

The young man and young lady had now reached Richard and Lucy and stopped in front of them.

"Hi, who are you supposed to be?" the young man asked with a friendly smile.

Richard looked at his sister in confusion, then looked back at the young man and said, "Well, I'm not sure what you mean by that, but I can give you our names if you want."

"No, I didn't mean that, I meant that I would like to know who you're pretending to be."

Richard shook his head, "We're not pretending to be anyone."

"Oh, then you're just dressing up for fun?"

"What do you mean by 'dressing up?'?"

"You know – wearing old-fashioned clothes."

Lucy's eyes grew big, but she quickly dropped them, it wasn't her place to speak out, especially as they had not been properly introduced, but how dare that young man make such rude comments about their apparel? Didn't he know there was a war going on which made it impossible to keep up with the latest fashions? He seemed to have forgotten the rules of conduct, making such rude and ungentlemanly remarks. She clutched her reticule tightly in her gloved hands, but kept her silence. What she really wanted to say was, "Well if those are the latest fashions, I'm glad we haven't kept up with them. Your walking partner's skirt is so short that her ankles can be plainly seen beneath it, and she's not even wearing stockings. Her hands are bare, no gloves to be seen. Even worse, she's not wearing a hat! Your own clothing is hardly acceptable, you haven't got a jacket on . . ." Lucy had to admit, though, that this young man and young woman's outfits were a vast improvement on the clothing of the rest of the people on the street.

Lucy felt her brother's glance at her, but did not look up. She was sure he could tell she was offended, but what was he going to do about it?

Richard looked back at the couple and said, "I am Richard Wilson."

"Thomas Jackson, and this is my sister Susanna," the young man said, holding out his hand, which was accepted by Richard with a firm grasp.

The young lady smiled as she held out her hand, and Richard, as he always did when introduced to a lady, swept off his hat, bent down in a deep bow, and brought her hand to his lips.

Miss Jackson's cheeks tinged a faint pink, and she laughed a little nervously, looking up at her brother. Then she turned back to look at Richard, "My goodness, you do a good job of keeping up your act!" she exclaimed.

Richard looked as confused as Lucy felt, "My – act?" he asked uncertainly.

Mr. Jackson turned to Lucy, "And what is your name?" he asked, holding out his hand as if he would shake hers.

Lucy stared at his hand in utter astonishment then stumbled backward a step with one of her gloved hands to her chest. She clutched Richard's arm tighter and whispered involuntarily, "My name!"

Mr. Jackson looked completely bewildered. He seemed to understand that he had offended her, but in what way, it was obvious he could not tell.

Lucy's mind whirled. A gentleman should always wait until the lady's partner introduced her to him. And he should never offer his hand first, he must wait until the lady held out hers. These people – or at least the young man – had obviously no idea of etiquette!

Richard, as usual, took charge of the situation, "This is my sister, Miss Lucy Wilson," he said, "Lucy, this is Mr. Thomas Jackson, and his sister Miss Susanna Jackson."

Mr. Jackson kept his hand out for a moment longer, but Lucy had no intention of giving hers to him. After a moment, he dropped it, still wearing that confused expression on his face.

Miss Jackson held out her hand, and Lucy placed hers in it. After all, the young lady had as yet not done anything terrible, though it was a bit unusual to shake hands in the middle of the street.

Mr. Jackson smiled as best he could with his confused expression still intact, and said, "Pleased to meet you, Lucy."

For Lucy, that was the last straw. She gasped, and pulled back on Richard's arm. She had no desire to stay here any longer in the company of this rude young man.

Richard stepped forward, partly shielding his sister, his fists clenching and his face hardening in anger, "How dare you, sir? How dare you speak to my sister in that manner?"

Mr. Jackson took a step backward, holding his hands in front of him, palms out, and saying, "I certainly had no desire to offend you! What is wrong? I only said the politest thing that anyone would have said!"

"Miss Jackson," Lucy said, stepping out from behind her brother, "does your brother truly know nothing of the rules of etiquette? Or is he naturally rude and ungentlemanly?"

"Why what in the world do you mean?" Susanna asked in astonishment.

"I mean," Lucy replied as scathingly as she could, "that your brother is either entirely unacquainted with manners, or is being purposefully rude. Either way, I have no desire to stay in your company any longer," her eyes flashed, and her cheeks flushed with anger.

"I am sure I don't know what you mean," Miss Jackson said, her voice calm, "as far as I could tell, Thomas was as polite as anyone could be."

Lucy was not sure what to say, in all her life she had never met anyone such as these two young people.

"Please, Lucy – " but Mr. Jackson got no farther, Richard stepped completely in front of his sister an said in a softly menacing voice, "I will thank you to direct your words to me over the rest of this conversation, sir. I will not permit my sister to be spoken to in such a familiar manner by a man she has only just been introduced to!" His hand went under his coat, and Lucy knew he was reaching for his gun, but strangely, Mr. and Miss Jackson seemed unaware of the fact.

"All right," Thomas Jackson said carefully, "I'm sorry that I still have no idea of what I have done to offend you, but if you would tell me I would thank you."

"I don't suppose my brother shall," Lucy said, stepping out from behind her brother and placing her hand on Richard's arm, gently tugging it, "You, Mr. Jackson, are behaving in such a manner that I do not wish to stay in your company any longer. Please Richard, I should like to go now," and she and her brother turned and began to walk away.

"Richard!" Lucy heard the young man call out from behind them.

Richard turned slowly, his face a picture of distaste, "If you are speaking to me, sir, I would prefer you address me as Mr. Wilson."

The other young man's brow wrinkled in confusion. He started to speak, then stopped. Finally his sister spoke for him, "Mr. Wilson, would you at least tell us what we have done to offend you? I am sure that both Thomas and I would like to fix what we are doing wrong."

Richard hesitated for a moment, then said, "Miss Jackson, you have done nothing that would offend either me of my sister. It is solely your brother we do not wish to spend time with."

"But Rich – Mr. Wilson," the young lady pleaded, and Lucy's eyes widened, Miss Jackson had nearly called Richard by his given name! Susanna Jackson continued, "I can assure you that neither I nor my brother have any idea of what is wrong."

Lucy knew very well her brother's thoughts: Miss Jackson seemed sincere, but how could anyone be so ignorant of proper etiquette? Finally Richard said, "Miss Jackson, I don't know why you or your brother don't know this already, but I'll tell you what you want to know."

"Oh, thank you!" she exclaimed.

"First of all," Richard told her, "your brother said our clothes are old-fashioned. Now we both know that our clothes are not in the latest styles, but I'm sure you at least can understand that there is a war going on, which makes it impossible to keep up with the latest fashions."

He would have gone on, but the Jacksons stopped him. They were obviously shocked at his words. Mr. Jackson spoke first, "What do you mean there is a war going on? Of course, our country is almost always fighting someone else, but how does that affect us here? The fighting is going on over on the other side of the world!" he sounded as if he was starting to get impatient.

Lucy's jaw dropped, but she remembered to shut it almost immediately. A lady's mouth must never hang open. She and Richard looked at each other, then she burst out, "What do you mean that the war is being fought on the other side of the world? Why there was a brigade of bluebellies that came through our town just two days ago! And that was not more than a few miles from here! Surely you haven't been missing all that's going on, have you?"

The Jacksons stared at her for a second, then Miss Jackson gave a relieved laugh and said, "Oh I see! You're still acting! I wish you would stop, though, because I want to really talk to you."

Richard pressed his lips together and then said, "I assure you, Miss Jackson, that we are not putting on an act. I am rather beginning to think you are though. Why do you keep asking us these strange questions? Are you mad?"

"Mad?" Mr. Jackson repeated in a wondering tone, and Miss Jackson quickly explained in a low voice, "He means insane."

"Oh," he said, then looked at Richard and his face suddenly changed into one not quite so friendly, "How could you think we might be crazy?"

"How else would you not know what's going on around you?" Lucy demanded.

Richard touched his sister's hand on his arm, "I think we should move on, Lucy. We are beginning to draw more stares."

"Please," said Susanna Jackson, "couldn't we find a place to sit down so we can try to straighten out this jumble we have gotten into?"

Chapter 3

After the young man and young lady had come through the door, the three men hurried to it, and Mr. Elliot pressed the button that would turn the time-travel machine off. He quickly opened the door and stepped through to make sure everything was in the twenty-first century on the other side. It was, and he came back through, shutting the door behind him.

They followed the two nineteenth-century people at a short distance, and saw them first examine the road, and then the siding on a house.

Mr. Elliot looked at the other two men and laughed softly, "They're surely confused all right," he nodded in satisfaction.

"Yes," Raymond said, watching the two looking around uncomfortably, "look," he said after a minute, "there are two people coming to meet them!"

"I wonder who they are?" Mr. Vincent said, and the three men hurried closer, stepping to the side of a house right near where the foursome had stopped, so that they could hear what was going on, but the others could not see them.

They had a hard time keeping down their laughter as they heard the conversation become confused, but the four young people were so intent on what they were discussing that they didn't even look toward where the men were hiding.

When Susanna Jackson asked that they find a place where they could talk, Raymond's father said, "That girl's trying really hard. She hasn't gotten upset one bit."

"Oh, I think she's frustrated on the inside," Mr. Elliot disagreed, "but you're right that she hasn't shown it. She seems to be pretty good at controlling her temper."

"I wonder where they're going to go?" Raymond said, "I hope it's someplace that we can still be near enough to hear them. If they go into a house or someplace like that, we won't be able to hear the rest of the conversation."

They listened closely again and heard Thomas Jackson say reluctantly, "Well you know, Susanna, there is that large flower garden over behind the post office. We could sit down there and keep talking."

"Oh, that's perfect!" Susanna Jackson was heard to exclaim, "hardly anyone ever goes there, so we won't be disturbed."

Mr. Elliot peeked around the corner of the building the men were hiding behind and said, "They're leaving now, let's go after them."

The three men came out from behind the building, and followed the four young people at a distance. It wasn't a long walk before they turned and left the street, going through an open door. The men waited for a few minutes, so that the others wouldn't notice them coming through, then entered the garden.

Inside the garden, they saw that the little group of young people had entered a small pavilion and were sitting in it, talking.

"I hope we didn't miss much," Raymond whispered.

They went around behind the pavilion, and stood under a low-hanging cherry tree that was still in bloom.

From inside the pavilion, they heard voices rising and falling. Listening closely, they heard the argument growing heated.

~   ~   ~

Lucy looked at Miss Jackson in perplexity, "Why do you keep saying that we are putting on an act?"

Miss Jackson looked back at her with equal perplexity and said, "You're not?"

"No! Certainly not! Why ever would we do such a thing, and what would we act out?"

"Well you're certainly not wearing everyday American clothes, you're not even wearing the same style clothes we are. And you keep talking about the War Between the States as if it's happening right now."

"Why wouldn't we? Do you wish us to pretend, as you are, that there is no war going on?"

"We are not pretending. The War Between the States happened over a hundred fifty years ago!" Mr. Jackson exclaimed, "Would you just stop this strange arguing and talk with us in truth? We want you to tell us how you came to start doing living history, and how you learned so much about everything that happened in the eighteen sixties."

"Sir, we know what happened in the eighteen sixties because we are living in the eighteen sixties," Lucy's brother said, "if you do not stop pretending that you are ignorant of what is going on around you, we will begin to think you are insane."

"I'm beginning to think you are insane," Mr. Jackson said, "*You* are the ones who are saying things that don't make any sense. If you aren't about to tell us anything, or admit that you are acting, we are going to leave. Come on, Susanna, let's get out of here."

"Oh, Thomas," Susanna pleaded, "let's just wait a minute. I don't know what's wrong, but I do want to figure it out."

"What year do you think it is?" Lucy asked, not out of curiosity, but with annoyance at being so many times disagreed with.

"Two thousand twenty-four, of course!" Mr. Jackson answered haughtily.

Lucy and her brother gasped. She and Richard stood up and faced Mr. Jackson, and Susanna rose to stand beside her brother.

"I am sure now, Mr. Jackson, that you are either mad, or the greatest liar I have ever heard!" Richard said, "What nonsense is this?"

"No nonsense at all!"

"Thomas, please calm down. I don't know what's the matter, but I do know something's wrong."

"When were you born?" Mr. Jackson asked.

"I was born," said Richard grandly, "in the year eighteen hundred forty-two."

"No, when were you *really* born?" Miss Jackson asked, "not your pretend birth date."

"Miss Jackson, that *is* the true year of my birth."

"Where do you live?" Susanna Jackson wanted to know.

"We live in Wilkeston, a tiny town several miles north of here," Lucy said.

"I've never heard of it, and I've lived in this town all my life. If it's only a few miles away, we should have visited it once or twice at least," Thomas Jackson said, staring at Richard accusatorily.

"Are you saying that we're lying?" Richard asked.

"Didn't you just say we were lying?" Mr. Jackson asked, "Then what's wrong with us saying you are?"

"Oh Thomas, that's not like you. Usually you're so polite!" Susanna said, "What is wrong?"

"I'm not wrong, these people are wrong!" he exclaimed impatiently, "if they want to say they're not lying, let them prove it!" he turned back to the Wilsons and said, "Take us to your town and introduce us to your family. When we see what it's like there, maybe we'll give more credit to your story."

Lucy was still mulling over Miss Jackson's words, *"you're usually so polite' why would she say that? He's hardly done a single polite thing since we met! This doesn't make any sense. I am sure there is something wrong here."*

Richard pulled her hand through his arm and stepped down from the pavilion saying, "it would be impossible to just take you there like that. It is miles away, and you would have to pack extra clothing, for you would be forced to stay overnight."

"How many hours away is it?" Mr. Jackson asked.

"Hours? It took us about five hours in the stagecoach," Richard told him, "and you won't find a much faster way to travel than that with the ladies."

"What do you mean? You say you came here in a horse-drawn stagecoach?"

"Yes, of course. I couldn't have come here on horseback, could I? Not with my sister."

"Seriously? But that's ridiculous! If it took you five hours with horses, we shouldn't be very long in a car."

"What do you mean? The train does not stop at our town, it is too tiny. If you want to ride in the passenger car of the train, we'd have to go past the town a couple of miles. Better to just take the stage."

"Come on, let's just go in a car. Don't tell me you don't know what *that* is."

"I do know what a car is, and I just gave you my reasons for not riding in one!" Richard said.

"Come with us," Susanna said gently, "and we'll show you what a car is, if you truly don't know. Are you Amish? No, even they know what a car is. And they don't pretend they are living in the eighteen hundreds."

"Stop saying we're pretending!" Richard exclaimed, "You are −" his voice trailed off as he realized he was talking to a young lady, "− I apologize."

"What am I?" she asked with a smile.

"You're a young lady, Miss Jackson, and that is why I didn't finish the sentence."

"Oh, I see. What do you wish to call my brother? I assure you he was not intending to insult you. You've already called him a liar and a mad man, what more do you want to heap on his head? Wouldn't coals of fire be better?"

"Coals of −" Richard nodded slowly as he realized what she had said, "All right, I apologized to you; I suppose I'd better apologize to him, hadn't I."

Richard looked at Mr. Jackson for a moment, then said, "I apologize for calling you a liar and a mad man, Mr. Jackson."

"Oh, that's fine, I said that about you too, so I guess I'll say sorry," Mr. Jackson said, "but can we stop this Mr. Jackson stuff? You're the same age as I am! You don't need to call me mister!"

Richard shook his head, "We've already apologized; I don't want to go over this again. Are you going to show us what you think a car is, or not?"

"What do you mean you don't want to go over this again?" Thomas Jackson demanded, "We haven't said a thing about names."

Lucy sighed, and Richard looked down at her for a split second, then stared at Mr. Jackson, "Are you quite determined to get into another argument?"

"Thomas!" Miss Jackson exclaimed, "can't you just leave it alone please? I would like to see their town, and find out why they believe – well, just see what it's like. So let's stop arguing and go with them."

"You – argue?" her brother laughed, "You haven't argued a bit. You never do, all you do is the peacemaking part. After everyone's all worked up you calm them down."

Susanna Jackson laughed and blushed a bit, "shall I answer that the way I wish to, just to prove you wrong?" she teased, "I don't believe what you said is quite correct. I am afraid it would be impossible for me to never argue, though I do try to keep from it."

"There! You see?" Mr. Jackson said, "you just answered that in the best way you could without arguing. You disagreed, but you didn't argue. That proves I'm right!"

"Oh Thomas! Please! Can't we talk about something else?"

"All right. Let's go home and get my car. Then we can go with them to their town," he nodded to Richard and Lucy and the four started down the walk, and soon were strolling down the street.

Chapter 4

Raymond looked at the other two men who were still standing beside him under the tree. The three had listened with amused interest as the argument had gone on, and when Susanna Jackson had tried to make peace, they had looked at one another with admiration. The young lady didn't seem to become ruffled at anything!

Now Raymond asked, "So what are we going to do?"

The old man who had invented the time machine answered quickly, "I'm wondering how they're going to try to fit a car through that little door."

"*I* was wondering what they're going to do when they find everything in the twenty-first century on the other side of the door," Mr. Vincent said.

"Shall we wait by the door until they get there?" Raymond asked, "I think they might be too far away for us to follow them now."

"I doubt it would be hard to find them," Mr. Elliot said with a smile, "it's likely that everyone they have passed has noticed them particularly. Probably all we'd have to do is ask, and we would be pointed in the direction they had gone."

"That's right!" Raymond laughed, "so then are we going to follow them?"

"No, let's go back to the door. They'll arrive there eventually," the old man decided.

~   ~   ~

Susanna watched her two new friends closely, *"If I can call them friends,"* she thought wryly to herself, *"Thomas and Rich – I mean Mr. Wilson – haven't hit it off very well. I can't imagine why, though. They seem nice enough people, except for the fact that they do seem to have quick tempers. I wonder why they became so angry at the things Thomas said?"*

She glanced at the Wilsons out of the corner of her eye again, as they walked along the sidewalk to her right. *Did* they truly believe what they had told her and her brother? They had said they had been born in the eighteen hundreds – but they *must* be only acting – mustn't they? Maybe they were practicing for a reenactment they would be in, and were trying out their clothes and eighteenth century manners. *"Yes,"* she decided, *"that must be it."*

By this time, they had reached Susanna and Thomas's house, "My car is in the garage," Thomas told them, "I'll get it out, then we'll drive to your town."

"Can you tell us how to get there?" Susanna asked.

"Yes, I'll tell you as we go. First we need to go through the door so we can get to the main road," Richard informed her.

Thomas had headed for the house, but when he heard this, he turned back and asked, "What do you mean?"

"Nothing but what I said."

"Come on, Rich – Mr. Wilson. We don't need to go through any door to get onto the main road. That's ridiculous. All we have to do is keep along this street until we pass the gas station, then turn left and continue around the curve until we get to the highway."

Richard looked disgusted, "Now listen, Mr. Jackson. We are finished arguing. You agreed to that. Now you said that you don't know where my town is, and I told you I'd show you. So let me direct you and don't try to tell me something different than what I know."

"Thomas?" Susanna put as much pleading in her voice as she could. She didn't know what was wrong, usually her brother was extremely polite. But for some reason he seemed out of sorts today, and ready to quarrel at the least bit of spark. She breathed a prayer under her breath that Thomas would not be quite so argumentative the rest of the day.

Thomas nodded, and turned back to the house. He disappeared through the front door. In less than a minute, the garage door opened.

"That's an interesting door," Mr. Wilson said, "Do you have many servants?"

"No, what would we need servants for?" Susanna queried in surprise.

"Oh, I thought you might use them to open that door for you," Mr. Wilson replied, "How is it operated, on pulleys? Who pulls it up?"

"No one pulls it up," Thomas answered, from where he stood behind his car in the garage, "When I push the button on the wall here, it sends a signal for the door to open."

"That's impossible!" Mr. Wilson exclaimed.

"Well, it's not quite impossible," Susanna said slowly, "for you see, it just happened. It's pretty complicated, though, and I'm not quite sure how it works myself. So let's leave it alone right now and get in the car."

"Susanna, Mr. Wilson can sit up front with me, if you ladies will sit in the back," Thomas said, opening the car door and sliding into the driver's seat.

Susanna breathed a sigh of relief, Thomas seemed to be not quite so out of sorts anymore. She opened the car door for Lucy Wilson, motioning for her to get in, and then walked around to the other side of the car, getting in herself.

The other girl moved her eyes over the inside of the car, taking in the strange sight, then asked, "Do you have a carriage?"

"No, just a car. This one is Thomas's, and my father has one too, but he left to go shopping, so his is not here right now."

Susanna noticed that Miss Wilson did not lean back against the comfortable seat in the car. Rather, she sat with her back perfectly straight. Susanna wondered if the other girl was trying to see out the windshield better.

Thomas started the car, and Richard watched his movements with interest, "How does this car move without any horses pulling it?"

"Well, there is a gas tank in the back of the car that I fill up with gas when it gets low. When the gas comes through a –" and Thomas explained as best he could how the car worked.

"I am still not sure I understand all of that," Mr. Wilson said as he finished, "but thank you for explaining it to me. It sounds a lot more complicated than a horse and carriage. You should get one of those."

Thomas laughed, "Those are too slow for me to be able to get to the places I need to be. I think a car is better. It is complicated, I agree, but I don't need to know everything about fixing it. All I have to do is take it to a mechanic."

"A mechanic fixes cars?"

"Yes. I'm going to start driving now," Thomas said.

He slowly pulled out of the garage and into the street. Turning, he followed the other young man's directions as to where to go.

Lucy spoke up from the back seat, "Richard, "I think we won't be able to get home this way."

"Why not?" her brother asked, turning to look at her.

"Because the car can't fit through the door."

"Oh – you're right. I should have thought of that. Well, it's getting late anyway, and we should have supper soon. So perhaps we should just park the car by the door, and show them the road to our town. If we can find a way to get around that wall, we can go home tomorrow."

"But Richard, I don't really – " Miss Wilson paused, "If this town was what we had thought it was, I might have liked to stay here. We must get our trunks, and I suppose we must spend the night, but I'm not extremely excited about going home tomorrow either."

"Why not?" Mr. Wilson asked.

"Oh Richard, you know why. I don't like being right in the path of the war. Soldiers come through the town every couple of days. You said that this town wasn't so often frequented by the troops, and that is why we decided to come here."

"Lucy, that is *one* reason we decided to come here. I had another reason, but I'm not sure I'll be able to carry out what I planned to do anymore," he turned back to Thomas and asked, "Do you know the name of the grocer?"

"Who, the manager or the owner or one of the employees?" Thomas asked in confusion.

"I thought that they were all the same," Mr. Wilson said, "the last time I came here, there was one family, a husband and wife, who owned the store, and they had no one other than themselves working there."

"You must have come a long time ago then!" Thomas laughed, "The store is much too big to have only one couple working there."

"Not too long ago," Richard Wilson shook his head, "only about a year and a half."

It was Thomas's turn to shake his head, "I think you must have come to the wrong town. Nothing you're saying is making sense."

"This is Laurelton, is it not?" Richard asked.

"It is."

"We have not come to the wrong town."

"There is the door," Lucy said, looking up ahead.

"You need to turn off the road here," her brother said, "do you see that door in the brick wall?"

"Yes, but I can't drive there, it's on the grass, and I don't know who owns the property," Thomas said.

Susanna saw the door they were speaking of, "I've been through that door before, Thomas, I went with Adele and Margaret on Sunday after church. We saw an older man there, who seemed to own the place, but when we asked him if he minded us being there, he said no, go ahead."

Thomas looked through the mirror at his sister, "Good, then we can go through the door without any problems, but I'm going to stop the car here anyway. We can walk the rest of the way."

He did as he had said, and stopped the car right off the side of the road. They all got out and walked toward the door.

When they reached the large wooden door, Mr. Wilson stepped forward and opened it. Thomas and Susanna stepped through first, but when Lucy and her brother came through, they gave startled exclamations. Thomas and Susanna turned to look at them in confusion.

"What's the matter?" Susanna asked.

"This doesn't look right," Miss Wilson said.

"Did you come in by a different door?"

"No, we didn't – I don't think," Mr. Wilson said slowly, "see Lucy? There's the hill over there, where we drank from the stream."

"But there isn't any stream there," Thomas said.

"You're right, there isn't. This doesn't make any sense."

"And Richard," that young man's sister began, "we put our trunks under a little sapling, but instead there's a large tree here."

"Do you think you could have been mistaken? I mean, maybe you came through the brick wall at a different point," Susanna suggested.

"I don't think we did, but this doesn't make any sense," Richard Wilson said.

"Well let's go along the wall and see if we can find another door," Thomas said, "that's the only thing we can do. If you say this doesn't look like the place you came through, maybe you got mixed up somehow."

Mr. Wilson lifted a hand from his side, then let it fall back down again, "I don't see how we could have been wrong, but this certainly doesn't look right. It looks similar, but not the same. So I suppose the only thing to do is what you said, walk along the wall until we find another door."

So they went through the door, and turned left, walking along the wall. The foursome walked for a while, but then, finding no other openings in the wall, they decided to turn back.

Chapter 5

While the group of young people was on the other side of the wall, the three men had not been able to hear their conversation, but when they came back through the door, the Vincents and Mr. Elliot listened eagerly to what they said. After their voices had faded in the distance, the men came out from behind the bushes that had concealed them from sight.

The old man spoke first, "I'm going to turn the time-travel machine on now. Raymond, will you go out there into the eighteen hundreds?"

"Yes, but why do you need me to?"

"When they come back, my guess is that they will check this door one more time, to make sure that they didn't miss anything. When they go through, I'm going to turn off the machine. That way, when they decide to come back through, they will not come back into the twenty-first century, but will stay in the nineteenth century."

"Oh my! That will confuse them more than ever!" Mr. Vincent exclaimed.

"But what do you need me for?" Raymond asked.

"You know that I cannot change the settings on the time machine when we are in the eighteen hundreds," Mr. Elliot explained, "I want you to wait until they come through the door, then follow them around for about forty-five minutes. Now, here is the important part *do not forget this.*" He was not nodding now, "I am going to turn the time machine back on in an hour. I will wait exactly an hour from the time I turn it off until the time I turn it on again. So what you must do is make sure that the brother and sister from our time period are on the other side of the door before I turn it on, or else you'll be stuck. That is the only thing that I couldn't get quite right when I was building the machine; if it is turned on when someone is on the wrong side, when they come back to the right side, it won't work anymore. Do not forget that. Do you understand?"

"I think I do," Raymond answered, "if we are not on the other side of the door when you turn it back on, we won't be able to come through to get back into the twenty-first century. But what should I do if I can't convince them to come with me?"

"If you can't convince them in less than an hour, you must not keep going back and forth from one side of the door to the other. That would make it impossible to find you, since I wouldn't be able to tell which side of the door you are on. So find one side of the door, and stay there."

Raymond nodded slowly, "I understand. I will do my best."

"I don't know what I did wrong that made it happen that way," the old man said, "I tried to figure it out, but nothing I did fixed it. I wish that weren't the way it was, but it is. So do the best you can, or else we might have trouble finding you again."

"Now let's pray that nothing goes wrong," Raymond's father said, "God is outside of time, so He can protect you."

They each took a turn praying, and Mr. Elliot ended with, "And, Lord, we ask again that You keep Raymond safe. We are trusting You with this now, for we know that only You have the power to protect him. In the name of Jesus, our Lord and Savior we pray, Amen." Then Mr. Elliot turned on the time machine and Raymond opened the door and stepped through, closing it behind him. The other two men hurried to stand behind the clump of bushes again.

Raymond looked around with interest, surveying his surroundings carefully. He had been to living history sites before, but none had been so real. He felt very out of place; knowing that he had been born more than a hundred years after the time he was in was disconcerting.

He saw a pile of trunks at the base of the sapling they had noticed previously, and guessed correctly that they were owned by the young man and young woman who had been transferred through the time machine into the twenty-first century.

The young man walked over to the little stream and the foot of the hill and sat down on its bank. Then, thinking better of it, he hurried around the hill and lay flat on his stomach so that he wouldn't be noticed by anyone who looked that way.

It wasn't long before the door opened and the four young people came through. He watched as they stopped in wonder, looking around in surprise at the place they had left very different only a few minutes before.

Raymond knew all their names, as he had been listening to most of their conversations since they had met, and now he could see and hear them quite clearly, as they talked of their confusion.

Richard said, "Something is really not right here."

"I agree," Thomas said, nodding his head, "this is not the same place we came to a few minutes ago – and yet it is."

"There are our trunks, Richard!" Lucy exclaimed, loosing her hand from his arm and hurrying over to the little tree.

Susanna followed her and asked, "what do you think could have happened?"

At that moment, a horse-drawn buggy rolled along the dirt road in front of them. Susanna and Thomas turned to stare as it passed.

"You see?" Richard asked, "there are others who use horses. I don't know what you mean when you say that everyone uses cars now. As I said before, I have never seen one in my life until you showed me yours."

"But –" Thomas began, " – there's something wrong here. I don't know what, but this place is strange."

"Let's go back through the door," Susanna said, "and look along the other side of the wall. Maybe this is not the door that we came through before, but is one that we missed when we looked for it along the wall."

"But when we came through I saw my car beside the road," Thomas told her, "so this must be the right one."

"Well, let's see anyway," Richard said.

They opened the door, and walked through. Raymond jumped up and hurried down the hill to follow them. He didn't want to lose sight of the four.

He heard gasps as he stood by the door, just out of sight.

"What in the world?" Thomas exclaimed.

"What happened?" Richard asked.

"I have no idea!" Thomas said.

"Well it's a little strange, wouldn't you think?" Richard said, "But one thing that's interesting is that this town looks much more like the town I came to a year and a half ago than it did before."

Raymond laughed as quietly as he could, *"Now you're finally right, you did come to this town a year and a half ago. Before when you said it, really you had come a hundred fifty years ago."*

"It certainly doesn't look like our town," Thomas said.

"Come on, we should go on into the town and see what it is," Richard said, leading the way with Lucy.

Thomas and Susanna followed a bit more slowly, quite bewildered at what had happened.

Raymond peeked around the edge of the door, and checked the time on his wristwatch, "Five thirteen," he whispered to himself, "so I need to have them back on this side of the wall by five fifty, or we'll be too late."

He hurried after them focusing back on their conversation. Richard said, "Yes, this is exactly how I remember it."

Suddenly all four stopped and stared as an older couple walked across the street in front of them, they were dressed in clothing from the eighteen sixties!

Thomas turned to look accusingly at Richard, "So is this some kind of trick? Is there going to be a reenactment in our town and you're just playing your part so well you won't tell us anything about it?"

"I don't know what you're talking about!" Richard protested, "What would anyone be reenacting?"

"It seems like you are reenacting the War Between the States."

"How can we reenact that, and why would anyone want to?" Richard protested, "We're living in it, so there's no reason to reenact."

"There you go again, telling me things that don't make any sense!"

"Thomas!"

"Richard!"

The girls pulled on their brothers' arms, begging them to calm down.

"Let's go home, Susanna," her brother said, turning and walking down the street. Susanna quickly followed, and Richard and Lucy came up behind them.

Raymond wondered what the Jacksons would do when they found out that their home didn't exist.

Chapter 6

Susanna hurried to Thomas's side, and the two walked down the street in the direction of their home. She looked over her shoulder and saw that the Wilsons were following. Shaking her head in confusion, the girl looked around the street that was once so familiar to her, but now had changed dramatically.

"What do you think happened, Thomas?" she asked.

"I don't know. It could be that some movie company is going to make a production here, and they changed a few things, but I don't see how that could be, since there was almost no time to make the changes in. I didn't see anything strange when I looked back right before we went through the door, and I don't think it was possible to make all this come about in so little time."

Thomas pointed to a store to their right, "What do you make of that?"

Susanna looked, and saw that the store had a wooden signboard above the door that said, 'Martin's Dry Goods.' She looked through the little store window, and saw several people inside, and all were dressed in clothes from the mid eighteen hundreds.

The door opened, and a woman stepped out. She was not dressed as nicely as the Wilsons, but rather, had a plain pink and white dress with no trim, covered in the front by a wide apron. A basket filled with dress making supplies hung over her arm.

As the woman looked around after coming out of the store, she noticed Susanna and Thomas standing looking at her. Her eyes widened, and she marched up to stand right in front of Susanna, saying, "Well, young lady, what do you think you're doing?"

"I'm sure I don't know," Susanna faltered.

"Come here, girl, I think you need a talking to."

Susanna yielded to the woman's grasp on her arm and left Thomas standing by himself in confusion.

"Now," the woman said, when they had gotten around the corner of the building, "what do you think you are doing walking about the street in such attire?"

"I'm sure I don't know," Susanna repeated, "I am quite confused as to what is going on."

"Could you not have put on more suitable clothes before trying to find out?" the woman asked, "look at you, showing your legs well above your ankles for everyone to see!"

"I'm afraid I haven't any clothes much more suitable than these," Susanna said. Her skirt reached halfway down her calf, and she had a few skirts at home that went to her ankles, but she wasn't sure even those would satisfy this woman.

"Well!" the woman said, at loss for a minute.

"If you could find me some better clothes I would be happy to wear them," Susanna suggested slowly.

"Of course," the woman said, taking her arm again and leading her back around the building, past Thomas, and down the street.

Susanna called over her shoulder to Thomas, "I'll be back in a minute if you'll wait there."

He hurried to catch up to them and demanded, "Where are you going?"

Susanna pulled him down to whisper in his ear, "She wants to find me some clothes that are more modest than these."

Thomas looked at her with a raised eyebrow, "I see," he said slowly, and then stopped, letting Susanna and the woman go on without him.

Susanna looked over her shoulder one more time and saw that the Wilsons had joined him and he was talking earnestly with them, "I hope the boys don't get into another fight," she murmured.

The woman's sharp ear caught her words, "Who is going to fight?" she asked.

"My brother and another young man we just met today are confused about a few things," the girl explained, "and they've been arguing ever since we met. I don't say I'm not confused myself."

"Is that what you meant by wanting to find out what was going on?" the woman asked.

"Yes, could you explain to me what happened?" Susanna begged, "I thought I lived in this town, but it's so different that I'm afraid we must have entered the wrong door – though I don't see how we could have, since it was right there all the time."

"Here we are," the woman said, turning toward a tiny house along the street. She and Susanna entered, and Susanna looked around the little house in astonishment, she had never seen living history portrayed so well. In the corner of the room sat a girl a little younger than herself, rocking a baby and singing softly to it. Another girl, a few years younger, was working over a pot, which was hanging over a fire. Still another girl, this one a child of about ten, jumped up as Susanna and the woman entered.

"Mama, could I go and see Pa and Matthew?"

"Come back over here, Alice, and finish peeling the potatoes," the girl at the fire ordered, but her voice was gentle.

"Yes, you may go see your pa – *after* you finish the potatoes," the woman said as the child looked up eagerly.

"Thank you, Mama!" Alice exclaimed, sitting down on the floor and picking up the paring knife.

The woman turned to Susanna and said, "Now wait right here. I'll get you something better than what you've got on.

All three girls looked up as their mother spoke. They had not noticed who was with her until this instant. Now they stared.

Susanna smiled, "Hello," she said.

"Who are you?" Alice asked, "and what are you doing in your petticoat?"

Susanna didn't know exactly what to say, so she looked at the woman for an answer.

"I don't know what she's doing, walking about the streets in that," the woman said, "but I told her I'd get her some better clothes."

"What's she going to wear?" the oldest girl, who was rocking the baby wanted to know.

"I was thinking of giving her your Sunday dress."

Susanna was watching the girl closely, and saw that she pressed her lips together tightly for a second, then smiled and said, "All right, that's a good idea, Ma."

"No, wait a minute," Susanna said, "if I take your Sunday dress, what are you going to have?"

"Doesn't matter," the woman said, "she knows it's better than having you walk around in what you're wearing now."

"Ma," the girl at the fire spoke, "there's Grandmother's dresses."

"Well, you're right about that," the woman said with a relieved smile, "Ma was thinner than Bessie is, and you are too," she said, turning to Susanna, "so it's likely as her dress will fit you better than Bessie's would."

"Grandmother died a while back," Alice looked up from her potatoes as she spoke, "and Bessie couldn't fit her dresses, so we were planning to make them into dresses for me, but you can have one; I don't need all of them."

"Why, thank you dear," Susanna said with a smile, "that's very kind of you."

The woman bustled off into a back room, and left the four girls to themselves.

"Now," Alice said, "what's your name?"

"Susanna."

"Susanna what?"

"Oh – Susanna Wilson."

"We're the Maxwells," Alice said, sweeping her arm about the room to include her sisters, "I'm Alice, she's Bessie, and she's Lily Mae."

Lily Mae looked up from her place at the fire for long enough to nod at their visitor, and Bessie continued singing to the baby, who had begun to fuss.

"What's the baby's name?" Susanna asked.

"His name is Carter," Alice answered, looking over at the infant with a smile.

"We've only got three girls in this family," Alice confided, "we were hoping this baby would be a girl, but it wasn't. I don't care now, anyhow. Carter's sweet as can be."

Susanna laughed and said, "That's just the way my family felt when my little sister was born. We were all hoping for a boy, but now we're glad it was a girl."

Lily Mae turned to look at Susanna, "I think that's how it is with all babies. We hope they'll be one way, but when they turn out to be something else, whether it's a boy or a girl, whether it's got yellow hair or black hair, we like it just the same."

"I agree," Susanna said, "babies are just sweet, no matter what they're like. How many brothers do you have?"

As soon as she spoke, Lily Mae's head dropped, and she turned back to stir the pot again. Susanna looked at Bessie, and saw that she had buried her face in the baby's blanket.

Susanna turned to Alice, who said softly, "We've got two brothers who are off fighting in the war. Lily Mae and Bessie are afraid they're going to get killed, but I'm not!" and the child straightened her shoulders and lifted her chin, "Ben and Jack know how to take care of themselves, they wouldn't ever let anyone hurt them."

Lily Mae turned back and said apologetically, "Alice doesn't understand much about war, Susanna. I'm sorry I acted like that. I usually don't, only today I was out getting water when I saw my best friend outside of the post office. She was crying, and when I asked her what was the matter, she showed me the paper that listed the killed and wounded, and her brother's name was there. That reminded me of what could happen to Ben and Jack."

Susanna stared at her, were these people truly in the War Between the States? No, they couldn't be – but they certainly acted like it.

But Lily Mae continued, "Bessie's sad too, because her sweetheart is gone to fight. So it's even worse for her than it is for us."

Mrs. Maxwell came back into the room at this moment, holding out a dress to Susanna, "Here you go, why don't you go change in the back room right now."

Susanna took the dress, saying, "Thank you very much!" She entered the back room which had a curtain hung in the doorway that separated it from the front room. Examining the dress closely, she decided to keep her own clothes on under it, she thought they would expect her to have a couple of underskirts on anyway. She decided to take off her shirt, though, which might be too bulky, leaving on her thin undershirt. Once she had the dress on, she looked around for a mirror, but saw none except a tiny handheld looking glass which lay on a small table.

"I don't know exactly what I look like," she said to herself, "but I guess this will have to do. I'll just ask the Maxwells if I look all right."

Picking up her shirt, and folding it, she reentered the front room and asked, "Do I look all right now?"

"Yes, that's very nice," the woman said, "That blue is perfect for your pretty blond hair; but now you need a hat."

"If you have an old one, I'd be happy to wear it," Susanna said, "Even if it's very old, and almost ready to fall apart. I can buy a new one when I need to."

"You can have my old one," Lily Mae offered, running into the corner of the room and kneeling down beside a small trunk. The girl pulled out a floppy bonnet, saying, "Ma gave me a new one for my birthday, so I don't need this one anymore."

"Thank you," Susanna said, taking the bonnet from her and setting it on her head, "now I must be getting back to my brother before he starts wondering if something has happened to me."

"If you're strangers to this town," Mrs. Maxwell said, "why don't you and your brother come for supper? We have plenty."

"Thank you, but we're not strangers, I don't think we live too far away from here. We need to be home for supper, Good-bye," she gave them a little wave and a smile, then stepped out the door.

Chapter 7

Raymond watched as the woman guided Susanna down the street. He decided to stay with Thomas and the Wilsons to hear what they said. When Richard and Lucy reached Thomas, he followed the conversation as well as he could from his hiding place several feet away.

"Where did your sister go?" Lucy asked.

"That woman with her wanted to find her some clothes that looked more like what everyone else here is wearing," Thomas answered.

"Oh!" Lucy looked after the two who were walking quickly away from them.

"Lucy," Richard said, "I have something I need to do. May I leave you here, or shall we find a better place for you to wait?"

Lucy looked at Thomas, and Raymond thought she must be considering whether to trust him or not. She had thought he was rude before; Raymond knew it was because manners were different in the twenty-first century then they were in her time period, but Lucy didn't. So Raymond guessed she wasn't sure whether it would be pleasant to stay in his company by herself.

"Does your business have to be taken care of right now, Richard?" she asked.

"Well – it would be better if I could do what I need to do right away, but I suppose I could wait awhile if you'd rather."

"Yes, thank you, I would."

"What type of business do you do?" Thomas asked.

Richard eyed him suspiciously, then said, "I do business for my father."

"What does your father do?" Thomas wanted to know.

Lucy broke in, "He owns a company that used to be quite large, but the war has ruined all his business with the North, and the blockade prevents him from getting supplies from England, so now the company is quite small and we've had to let off most of our workers."

"Not that many of them would have stayed on anyhow, Lucy," Richard reminded her, "Most of the men who used to work for us have joined the army. But you are right that I can take care of most of the business on my own now," he turned back to Thomas, "we only have nine hired workers besides myself."

"Why do you keep talking about the war as if it's going on right now? Will you or will you not explain what is going on?" Thomas exclaimed.

"I don't know what you're talking about!" Richard said.

Raymond had begun to laugh to himself again, when he saw the slight figure of a girl moving along the street until it stopped right behind Thomas. She was dressed as a girl from the eighteen sixties, in a blue dress and a bonnet which shaded her face, and at first he didn't recognize her. But then he saw Lucy turn her way, and suddenly the girl lifted her head and he saw it was Susanna. He bit back a gasp of surprise, and saw Susanna lift a finger to her lips as a gesture of silence to the other girl.

Raymond couldn't see very well from where he was hidden, but it looked to him as if Lucy was about to laugh. Susanna dropped her head again so that the bonnet shaded her face, and stepped between the two young men, slipping her hand into her brother's. Thomas jumped backwards a couple of feet, and Susanna lifted her laughing face to his.

"Susanna!" he exclaimed, "I'm sorry, I didn't recognize you at first!"

The girl laughed, "I meant for you not to," she said, "if you had recognized me, it would have spoiled the trick, but now I don't look quite so different from everyone else, do I?"

"I would say you don't," Thomas said with a laugh, "but I certainly do."

"Oh yes, that polo shirt and khakis you are wearing do stand out!" his sister told him, "are you going to get something to wear, or shall we go straight home?"

"I don't think I'll need something to wear once we get home, will I?" Thomas asked.

"I wouldn't think so, if you want to stay there, but it's fun to wear clothes like this."

"I'm glad you think so," Thomas said, "but I'd rather not. What I'm wearing is good enough for me."

"All right, then let's go home," she said.

"Miss Jackson," Lucy said, "wouldn't you rather wear some more fashionable clothes? I'll lend you some of mine, if we can find a dressmaker to do the adjustments."

"Why thank you, that's very kind of you," Susanna said, "but do you have any idea where a dressmaker would be found?"

"No, I haven't, but of course we could find out by asking around," Lucy told her.

"Wait a minute," Thomas said, "let's go home first, Susanna, maybe Mommy knows what's going on. I tried to text her, but for some reason, my phone's not working. Let's go home first and see what's going on, then you can play all you want to."

"That's fine with me," Susanna said, "do you want to come, Mr. Wilson and Miss Wilson?"

"Yes, let's go with them," Lucy said, "is that all right, Richard?"

"Yes, we can for a little while, but remember, I've some business to attend to that cannot wait long. So soon I'll need to leave you someplace and take care of it."

"All right, maybe I'll stay at the Jackson's house."

"That would be fine," Susanna said, and the four walked down the street.

Soon they arrived at the place where the Jackson's house had been the last time they had come there, but in its place was an old one story house, with a short door in front.

Susanna gasped, and stopped in her tracks. Thomas walked on and opened the door, going up the walk and knocking on the door.

A young woman with a baby on her hip opened it after a moment. Her eyes widened with shock at the sight of the young man standing in front of her. It was obvious she thought he looked strange.

Looking past him, she saw Susanna and the Wilsons coming up the walk. As the other three moved closer, she directed her question at Richard, "What do you need, sir?"

Thomas saw that she was asking Richard, so he waited for that individual to speak. Richard asked, "Do you live here, ma'am?"

"Yes, I do. What is the matter?"

"Is this Laurelton?"

"Yes it is. Would you like to come in?"

"No, that's all right," Richard said.

"Well, if that's all, I've got work to do. My husband is expecting supper at the usual time."

"I'm sorry for bothering you, ma'am," Richard said.

"Oh, that's fine sir, good day!" she backed into the house and closed the door.

Thomas looked at his sister, but her face was turned away so that he couldn't see it.

Raymond, however, could see it, from where he was standing, partially hidden, and noticed that she seemed very confused, but there was something else too, on her face. He couldn't tell what it was, though, and decided to wait and see what they would do next before he told them what had happened.

Richard suggested, "Why don't we ask in the post office if there are any Jacksons living around here?"

"All right, we can try that. But what could have happened to our house? It was right here," Thomas said.

Raymond muttered, "You mean it 'will be' right there. Your house won't be built for another hundred fifty years!"

He followed the others down the street, keeping at a safe distance.

It didn't take them long to find the post office. Raymond had to stay outside of the building, since to go in with them would have been to reveal himself. He watched as the two young men and two young ladies went into the post office and waited to see what they would look like when they came out.

About thirty seconds later, Susanna opened the door of the post office. She came out, then looked back inside, as if to make sure no one had noticed her departure. The girl went slowly down the steps, and walked to a large tree a few feet away. She knelt down on the ground with her back to Raymond and seemed to fuss with her dress. Then, after a moment, she stood up and turned a little toward him so that he could see she had a phone in her hands. She was moving her fingers rapidly across it, but after only a few seconds, she began to frown.

The frown on her face deepened every second, and finally she stopped moving her fingers across the screen and stared at the phone in absolute astonishment and confusion. She tapped the screen a couple more times, and then pressed the buttons on the sides. Finally she dropped the hand that held the phone to her side, and reached her other hand up to her face.

The door to the post office opened again, and Thomas burst out, looking in all directions. He spotted his sister standing by the tree, and ran to her. She jumped as he placed a hand on her shoulder asking, "Susanna! What's wrong?"

She held out her phone to him, and he took it gently from her hand, staring at the screen.

"It says 'Error, unable to find connection,'" he said.

"Yes," she told him, "I was trying to text Mommy, and that didn't work, so I tried to call her, and then the screen went black for a minute. Then it showed that, and it won't do anything else!"

Thomas pulled his phone off his belt, "Mine won't work either," he said.

"So we can't contact Mommy or Daddy. We're lost, and don't know where our house is, and we can't find out how to search for it. The man in the post office said there aren't – any – Jacksons – living here!" the last words were a sob.

"Susanna – " Thomas began.

The Wilsons came up then, and Richard asked, "what happened?"

"You know – we don't know what happened to our house. Our phones won't work, so we can't call our parents and find out where they are."

"You said your *phones* won't work? What are phones?" Richard asked.

Thomas turned to look at him angrily. His fists clenched, and his jaw was set hard. He spoke through clenched teeth, "Now look here. You had better stop this right now. You tell us what is going on or there will be some trouble. Do you not care one bit about my sister having no house to go to? Will you continue to keep up this silly nonsense and refuse to help us – ?"

"Thomas – " Susanna faltered, stumbling to his side and clutching his arm with both her hands.

He turned to her immediately, and pulled her into his arms. She laid her head down on his shoulder and began to cry quietly.

Raymond decided he couldn't wait any longer. He hadn't intended to let things go this far, but it was too late for that. Now he jumped out of his hiding place and ran toward the brother and sister.

"Susanna!" he exclaimed, "let me explain what – "

But he got no farther before she jumped out of her brother's embrace and, dashing the tears from her eyes, gasped, "Who are you, and how do you know my name?"

Thomas stared at Raymond in incredulous amazement, this young man was dressed the same as he was, not in a style from the eighteen sixties!

Raymond repeated, "let me explain what has happened, I know your names because I've been following you around since you met the Wilsons this afternoon."

Richard Wilson jumped forward and grasped Raymond by the arm. Raymond was astonished for a moment, but the other young man's words made him understand, "You're a Yankee, then! A spy! Well, you're not getting away now!" his hand flashed down to his side, and came up with a gun, which he pointed at Raymond's chest. Susanna gasped.

Raymond stood still for a moment, then said, "no, I'm not a Union spy. I will explain what happened if you'll give me a chance. I'll tell you," he said, turning to Thomas and Susanna, "how to get back to your home."

"Oh! Will you?" Susanna pleaded, her eyes filling with tears again.

"Yes, listen. Of course you can tell by the way I'm dressed, that I'm from the twenty-first century like you are."

Richard's hold tightened on Raymond's arm, but Raymond continued, "I met a man yesterday, who told me he needed my help with something. He had invented a machine that he wanted to put together at a different location, but he wanted to have some help to assemble it. So my father and I went with him this morning, and helped him put it together."

All four of the others were listening intently as he continued.

"The machine he had invented was a time-travel machine – "

He broke off as there was a gasp from Susanna and Thomas.

"Yes, a time-travel machine. So you see, you went through it, and that is how you got into the eighteen hundreds."

Thomas stared at Raymond silently, but Susanna asked, "Where is it? Is it right above that door in the wall?"

"Yes, it is. But right now it is turned off. If we go on the other side of the door, we need to wait until five fifty. About then, or a little after, my father and the man who invented the time machine will come through the door to let us know it is on again, so that we can go back into the twenty-first century.

Susanna took her phone back from Thomas and looked at it. After a few seconds, she gave a sigh and asked, "Do you know what time it is? My phone isn't responding very well."

"I brought a watch on purpose," Raymond said, "because I thought that would be the case. Let me see – " after glancing cautiously at the gun which was still pointed at his chest, he lifted his wrist and looked at the watch, "it's five forty right now. So we only have ten minutes to get back there."

"Let's go right now, then," Thomas said, "I don't want to take a chance on getting caught on the wrong side."

Susanna turned to look at the Wilsons, "Do you want to come with us? I don't know if we'll ever be able to find you again if you don't."

"I don't know exactly what you are talking about," Richard said, and Susanna and Thomas saw that he had lowered the gun, but his hand was still on the strange young man's arm.

"Now listen, Mr. Wilson," Raymond began, "I do not wish you to believe I am a Northerner, because I'm not. I was born and raised in South Carolina, and I am definitely a Southern supporter. Now, one way you can tell that I'm not trying to trap you into anything is that I'm not planning to force you to come with me. I am going to take Thomas and Susanna back to the other side of the door, and you can come if you want to."

"No! I am not taking a chance on my sister's safety that way!" Richard exclaimed.

"Very well, let's go," Raymond said to the Jacksons. Richard released the young man's arm and the three headed toward the door.

Richard Wilson watched them leave, then turned to his sister and said, "Lucy, I want to follow them and see if what they are saying is true. Will you stay here by yourself?"

"I will be fine, Richard, but why are you so worried about them following you? We only came here for a rest, and you're not in the Confederate army?"

"Lucy, dearest, I can't explain everything to you right now, but – " and he bent to speak close to her ear in a low voice, "Don't be too sure who's working for the army and who's not. Just because someone doesn't wear a uniform doesn't mean they're not fighting."

Lucy's eyes widened and she turned to look her brother in the eyes, "Richard! Do you mean – ?"

"Hush! Don't say it," he placed a finger on her lips as a gesture to be silent, "Whatever you think, I'd rather not tell you what I'm doing. I will tell you, though, that I'd feel more comfortable if I was sure that the young man who jumped out of nowhere is not a spy. So may I go?"

"Yes, you may go, Richard. But please remember I am alone here, so if at all possible, try to stay out of trouble."

Richard pressed her hand, then released it, turning to hurry in the direction of the door.

Chapter 8

As they neared the door, Susanna wondered how much time they had left before the time machine would be turned on again. She wondered why they would be stuck in the eighteen hundreds if they didn't get there fast enough.

She lifted her gaze inquisitively to the strange young man beside her. He was walking quickly, and so was Thomas, and she had a hard time keeping up with the strides of their long legs.

"I wonder what Mommy will say when she sees me in these clothes!" she thought, *"If we do get to the other side of the door in time, I mean. Oh! What will happen if we don't? Will that mean we will never get back* home?"

It was several seconds before Susanna realized she had spoken the last word aloud. Suddenly she realized both boys were looking at her quizzically.

"What's the matter, Susanna?" Thomas asked, "We are going home, if that's what you're asking."

Susanna dropped her face so that the bonnet she was wearing shaded it. She was embarrassed, but she tried to say cheerfully, "No, that's not what I meant, sorry – I was just thinking aloud."

Her brother dropped a hand on her shoulder for a second, then stiffened. Susanna heard the sound of horses' hooves pounding against the ground and looked up.

They had almost reached the door, but to their right, a group of horsemen were riding towards them. Susanna grasped Thomas's arm, "They're wearing blue!"

"Susanna! There's nothing to be concerned about," Thomas assured her, "I am not in the Confederate army, you know, and I strongly doubt that *he* is," he turned to nod at Raymond with a half smile.

"No, I'm not, of course," Raymond said; but by now the Union horsemen were upon them.

The leading horseman rode up and started to pass them, then suddenly pulled his horse in and faced them.

"Who are you?" he demanded, staring at Thomas and Raymond's strange clothes.

The two boys hesitated for a moment, and the officer asked again, "Who are you?"

"I'm Thomas Jackson," Thomas answered, "and this is my friend – " he paused as he realized he didn't know the other young man's name.

"Your friend?" the colonel asked, as the rest of the soldiers rode up and pulled to a halt. Who is he? Why did you stop?"

Thomas didn't speak. He didn't know the name of his new friend, so he couldn't answer the Union officer's question.

Raymond started, "I'm Raymond – "

"Stop a minute," the officer commanded as his lieutenant leaned toward him to whisper in his ear. His face became sterner than it had been before, and he nodded once, a precise up and down motion, then turned back to the three standing below him.

"What is your *friend's* name?" he asked sarcastically.

This time Thomas answered, "His name is Raymond."

The colonel barked a short laugh, "Is that all you know? He just told us his christian name. What is his surname?"

Thomas opened his mouth, turned to Raymond, and lifted his hands in a shrug. "I don't know. I only met him today," he said.

"You met him you say? Why would he not have told you his name when you met him?"

Thomas was silent. Susanna clutched his arm in alarm, and he placed his other hand on hers, but he couldn't answer to satisfy their interrogator.

"Sir," the lieutenant spoke again, this time loud enough that Susanna could hear him. He had a strong New England accent, which at first was hard to understand, but once the lieutenant's words sank in, Susanna gasped, and felt her knees weaken, but quickly stiffened them and forced herself to stand upright, "he must not be telling the truth. His story doesn't make sense. Perhaps the reason he doesn't know the other man's name is because he is a spy, and they keep their names in secrecy to make it harder to get information."

"But with a girl!" the colonel said in disbelief, "If he is a spy, why would a girl be let in on their secret?"

The lieutenant shook his head wisely, "Don't be too sure sir. I have heard of several young ladies having been caught as spies. It is assumed men will not be as quick to suspect ladies."

"That is true, at least," the officer agreed, "I have a hard time believing such a pretty little girl would be a spy. She looks harmless enough," and he bent down to look closer at Susanna.

Susanna quickly bent her head so that her bonnet shaded her face. Thomas spoke sharply, "My sister is no spy. You are right in that. Now, we must be going, we are going to be late. Please excuse us."

He started forward to walk past the soldiers, but the officer's voice cut sharply through the air, "Not so fast, boy. You can't just leave like that. You say your sister's not a spy, what about yourself and your *friend?*" again he spoke the word 'friend' sarcastically, as if he didn't really believe that Raymond was their friend, "and how can I tell if you are telling me the truth?" Thomas looked at Raymond, and Raymond said, "I know their names, we had only just met when you got here. That's why they didn't know my name. Their names are Thomas and Susanna Jackson."

"Ha!" the lieutenant exclaimed, "that proves nothing! He just told us all his and the girl's names, so of course you know them!"

The officer nodded at his lieutenant, and then said, "thank you, Stephens. That will be all now." The lieutenant backed his horse a step and the colonel turned back to the little group of three on the ground.

"How are you going to prove you are not lying?"

Raymond and Thomas glanced at each other, then Raymond said, "You can search us if you want, to see if we have any messages in our clothes, but I can tell you we don't."

"If you just met these two, and they don't even know your name, how do you know that they're not spies?"

"They just said they're not, didn't they?" Raymond asked.

"Yes, they did, but how does that prove anything?"

"I don't know that it proves anything to you, but I am sure they wouldn't lie."

"How do you know they wouldn't lie, if you just met?"

Raymond felt his stomach turning over. He realized that with each sentence, he was entrapping himself – and what was worse, the Jacksons – more and more. He realized that he couldn't explain how he had followed the Jacksons around for several hours, or how he had listened to their conversations, for that would make the soldiers certain that they were spies.

"Lord, what should I do?" he prayed silently.

Susanna was thinking hard, she realized at the same time Raymond had that saying anything more would only serve to make the soldiers suspect them further. At first, she only thought of how to get away from the soldiers; how to convince them that she and the two young men were not spies. But then she remembered with a start why it was so important they get away quickly.

"Raymond, what time is it?" she asked softly.

Raymond was staring at the ground, and he lifted his head to look at her as she spoke, but his eyes were glazed over and it was obvious he wasn't seeing her.

Thomas clapped a hand on Raymond's shoulder, "Raymond! What's the matter? Susanna wants to know what time it is!"

"Oh!" Raymond shook himself and lifted his hand to look at his watch. He groaned as soon as he saw the face, "We're late!" he exclaimed, "it's already one minute past, so we can't get back until they turn the machine off again!"

Susanna uttered a short cry and felt her knees weaken once again, but this time she was powerless to stop them. She swayed, and would have fallen, but Thomas threw his arm around her waist and held her up.

Thomas set her on her feet and steadied her with one arm, then he grabbed her hand with the other and whispered, "Susanna! You need to be strong right now. I know you can; you know you can. Please, please, Susanna!"

"Pray for me, Thomas," she cried softly, looking up with terror on the stern face of the officer above them.

"I have been," he informed her, "and I'll keep doing it."

"What have you been doing?" Raymond wanted to know.

"Praying."

"I am too."

"Good," Thomas said, "that will help."

"What will help?" the officer caught the last words as he leaned closer.

Thomas hesitated a moment, then Susanna spoke up, to her own surprise and her brother's, "Praying will help," she said, finding the strength to stand on her own feet again and looking the officer in the eyes.

"What will you pray for?" the colonel sneered, "that God will hide from me the fact that you are spies and help you get away?"

"No!" Susanna exclaimed, "If we were spies, I dare say that we might pray for that, but since we are not, there is no need. I pray for strength to stand and not despair or be afraid, and my brother prays for me too."

"Now tell me," the colonel said, sitting up straight again and looking at the three on the ground with narrowed eyes, "do you truly think that God is on your side, and if you pray to Him He will help you win the battle? For my lieutenant here, Johnston," he motioned behind him to the other lieutenant, who had not spoken yet, "thinks the same of the Union. God cannot be on both sides can He?" he challenged the girl.

Susanna took a deep breath and said, "I cannot and do not say whether God is on one side or the other, though I do believe that the Southern cause is just and right."

"You dare say that to my face?" the officer gasped in exaggerated astonishment.

"Please wait a moment, sir," she said, "I have not finished. What I do believe is that there are people of God in both armies, and on both sides of this war. Both believe they are fighting for the right. I believe God protects His own children. Not to say they cannot be wounded or killed, but the comfort of knowing that death is not the end for them is a big thing. God's children will go to heaven when they die, no matter which army in this war they were fighting for. Anyone who is a Christian may ask for God's strength and courage. Those can be given to both armies."

"How can there be people on both sides who are right?" the officer questioned.

"I did not say that there were people on both sides who were right; I said there were people on both sides who think they are right. However, there *are* good points about both sides, and anyone who thinks their side is right probably has a good reason to."

"I don't recall ever hearing a Southerner say the North had good points," the officer said thoughtfully, then he burst out, "Are you sure you're not a double spy? If you think both sides are right – " he paused, looking at Susanna accusatorily.

"I don't really think that both sides are right, but I'm not going to explain and argue everything out right now. All I can say is no, we are not spies. I know of no other way to prove it to you," Susanna said with a stifled sigh as she thought that all her words had gone to no use.

"How many minutes past are we now?" Thomas asked quietly.

Raymond looked at his watch again, "It doesn't really matter now," he said, "It's too late anyway. But let's see – we're five minutes past."

Thomas looked worriedly at his sister, but she gave him a smile, "I'm fine now," she said softly.

"Except for the fact that you're not safe at home with Mommy," he retorted, "why didn't we just decide to take our walk some other day? I would never have brought you with me if I had known what was going to happen."

"But you couldn't have known, Thomas, and I don't blame you. It wasn't your fault that this happened."

"But I'm supposed to protect you. You're my sister."

"How can you protect me from what you don't know of yourself? Stop blaming yourself, Thomas. Please?"

He heaved a sigh and shook his head. "I can try, but I don't know if I'm able to. If I hadn't gotten into a fight with that Wilson guy – "

Susanna looked up and saw that the officer was consulting with his lieutenants. After a few minutes, he turned back to the 'prisoners.'

"We'll let you go now, we have decided to believe you when you say you're not spies."

Thomas grasped his sister's hand tighter. He felt her lean toward him, and steadied her as well as he could.

"Let's go!" Raymond exclaimed.

"Thank you!" Thomas called to the soldiers. The colonel gave him a puzzled look, but nodded curtly, and backed his horse so that the three could go through the door.

Raymond opened the door and they went through. Once on the other side, Raymond told them, "We'll just have to wait now, until Mr. Elliot or my father comes through the door. That way we will know that the time machine is on and working again."

"How long do you think it will be?" Thomas asked, letting Susanna sink to the ground and kneeling beside her.

"I really have no idea. All we can do is wait and see."

So they did that, sitting down on the cool green grass and watching for the door to open.

Chapter 9

After a while, Raymond looked at his watch, "We've been waiting here for ten minutes already."

"Only ten minutes?" Susanna whispered to her brother, "It seems more like an hour!"

"I'm sorry, Susanna," Thomas said, "It seems like a long time to me too."

"What time is it?" the girl asked aloud.

"Where we live, you mean?" Raymond corrected.

"Yes."

"It's five fifty."

Susanna looked at her brother in despair, "Oh no!"

"What?"

"I was supposed to make dinner, since Mommy's not feeling well. I was hoping it wasn't very late; that I could get home and make dinner in time, but now it's too late!"

Thomas threw back his head and let out a laugh. Susanna stared at him as if he had gone out of his mind.

"What is so funny? The children are going to go without food!"

Thomas continued to laugh, and his sister continued to stare at him in confusion. She turned to look at Raymond, and saw that he was chuckling quietly.

"Thomas!" she place a hand on his shoulder and shook him gently, "What is so funny?"

"I'm sorry, Susanna," he said, quieting his laughter until he could talk, "it's just that you looked so upset when Raymond told you it was five fifty that I thought there was something really wrong. Now you say that it's only you were supposed to make dinner!"

"But there *is* something really wrong," she insisted, "if I don't make dinner soon, the children are going to be starved!"

"Not quite that drastic, Susanna," Thomas said, "they'll be all right for an hour or two, and you know that all the children down to Florence – and even Nancy – know how to cook. But that's not what I meant."

"What did you mean?"

"Well, you weren't thinking about yourself, of how you wanted to get home, or that it was late in the day and Mommy would be missing you, or anything like that. All you thought of was that the children needed something to eat, as if that were more important than getting home."

"Isn't it?" she asked in confusion.

Thomas burst out laughing again, "The children are all you can think of now, aren't they?" he asked when he got his voice back, "I really don't know which is more important. But what you just said shows what kind of girl you are, you know."

"What do you mean?" she asked warily.

"Oh, just that you think the needs of others are more important than your own."

Susanna's cheeks flushed, and she shook her head at Thomas, casting a quick guilty glance at Raymond, "Please, Thomas. That's enough."

"Why? It's true."

"That doesn't have anything to do with it."

"You don't care whether or not what I say is true?" he asked, affecting astonishment.

"Thomas!" she exclaimed, her cheeks turning even brighter pink. She leaned toward him and whispered, "I don't mind you saying that kind of thing when we're by ourselves, but – please! Not in front of strangers!"

Thomas opened his mouth, but Susanna was saved by the door opening. Raymond jumped to his feet, and the Jacksons were not much slower. The door seemed to them to open slowly, but as a man stepped out from behind it, Raymond exclaimed, "Dad!" and ran toward him.

His father held out a hand to shake, but Raymond threw his arms around his shoulders and embraced him.

"Well, son, we were a bit worried about you," Mr. Vincent said as they stepped away from each other.

"We were stopped by some Union cavalry who thought we were spies," Raymond explained.

His father's eyes widened, but he didn't say anything. He turned to Thomas and Susanna and said, "So here you are! Let's go back home."

The two Jacksons smiled, and nodded. Mr. Vincent had left the door open, and the four walked through it.

"Raymond! Oh, I'm so thankful that you got back safely!" Mr. Elliot exclaimed as they stepped out on the other side, "When we opened the door and you weren't there, we were afraid something had happened."

"Something did happen, but I'll have to tell you the whole story later," Raymond said, "What's important is that we are back safely."

"Was it interesting," Mr. Vincent asked, "exploring what Laurelton looked like during the War Between the States?"

"Well – we didn't really do too much exploring," Raymond explained, "I, of course, was following the Jacksons around most of the time, but they didn't really explore to see what it was like, since they didn't know they were really in the eighteen sixties."

"Well, we should probably let the Jacksons go home now," Mr. Elliot said. He had been watching Susanna's face closely, and as he was accomplished at reading people's faces, he could tell that she had been stressed or upset.

"Yes," Raymond agreed. He turned to the Jacksons, "Why don't you come here tomorrow at say – ten o'clock. Would that be fine? Then we can go through the time machine again and explore some more. Since we all know now about the machine, we can be back in plenty of time next time."

"No!" Susanna exclaimed, and Thomas looked at her in surprise. His sister hardly ever spoke sharply, and never spoke much above normal voice level. Susanna caught his astonished glance, but continued, barely subdued, "I don't want to go through that thing ever again! I had plenty of that already and I can't believe you did such a thing to us! Thomas, let's go home now!"

Thomas didn't know exactly what to say to Susanna, since he had never experienced such a thing from her, so he continued to stare at her agitated face in silence.

Suddenly Susanna drew in a sharp breath and quickly covered her mouth with her fingers, "I can't believe I spoke like that!" she said with a half sob, "I'm so sorry!" the girl passed the back of her hand over her eyes, then bent her head to stare at the ground.

Thomas couldn't see her face, since she was still wearing the bonnet Lily Mae had given her, so he bent down to look under it, "I'll take you home now, Susanna," he said. Then he added in a whisper, "I'm sorry about what happened. If I could have prevented it, I would have. I know this has been terribly hard for you, so let's hurry home so you can talk to Mommy."

Susanna lifted her head and pulled at the bonnet strings until the hat came off. Then she told her brother quietly, "We can stay here a few more minutes if you want to. I'll be all right. I know it sounded pretty bad when I spoke so sharply just a minute ago, but really, I'm fine now."

Even though she had spoken quietly, Raymond, who was on the other side of Thomas, heard her words, "Why don't you two just go on home now?" he said, "We'll arrange a time to be here tomorrow, and I've got Thomas's phone number, so tomorrow I can call and ask if you want to come with − " the young man broke off as he noticed the look on Susanna's face.

He looked uncertainly at her brother, and Thomas said, "Yes, please call me." He squeezed Susanna's hand as she pulled a little away from him, and told her, "Don't worry, I won't come without telling you," but that wasn't the answer Susanna wanted, and she turned her face away.

Thomas didn't let go of her hand, and finished, "But right now I'm taking Susanna home. Come on," and he turned away from the group and got into his car, which was still parked by the wall.

Thomas parked the car outside the garage, and they walked around the path to the front door. As they opened the door, they saw their thirteen-year-old sister Jennie sitting at the piano in the front room. She got up quickly as they entered and exclaimed, "Where have you two been? We've been waiting and waiting for you, and Mommy tried to call you, but her phone wasn't working, and –" suddenly she broke off and said, "Susanna! What kind of clothes are you wearing? Where did you get them?"

"Oh, I forgot I was wearing this dress," Susanna said.

"Where did you get it?" Jennie asked again.

"Someone thought I would like to have it, and they gave it to me."

"You'll have to tell me about it later," Jennie said, "but first you should go up to Mommy. She's resting in her room; you know she's been resting more and more since she is pregnant; and she might be asleep, but even if she is, I think it would be fine for you to wake her up. She was really worried about you."

"We'll do that, thank you, Jennie," Thomas said, and he and Susanna headed for the stairs.

At the top of the stairs, another sister met them. "Thomas! Susanna! You're back!" Nancy hurled herself into Thomas's arms.

"Careful, Nancy," he laughed, "or you'll knock me down the stairs."

The five-year-old girl giggled, then, as her brother set her down, she burst into their parent's room and exclaimed, "Mommy, Mommy! They're here!"

"Who are here, Nancy?" Mommy asked.

"Thomas and Susanna!" the little girl said, pointing as her older siblings walked into the room.

"Oh Mommy!" Susanna said, running over to the bed and falling on her knees beside it.

"Where have you two been?" Mommy asked, "I tried to call you when you took longer than I expected to come back, but my phone wasn't working."

"Our phones weren't working either, Mommy, so that's why you couldn't call us. We'll have to tell you about it, but it will take a long time," Thomas told her.

"I had Jennie and Edward make dinner since you hadn't come back yet," Mommy told them, "but we haven't eaten yet. I was hoping you would be back in time to eat. Tell me what happened."

Susanna had laid her head down on the bed and showed no signs of interest in talking, so Thomas told their story.

Chapter 10

"We were walking down the street like we had told you we were going to," Thomas said, "when we met two people dressed up in old-fashioned clothes. We asked them who they were pretending to be, but they said they weren't pretending to be anyone. So after we introduced ourselves, we asked them to explain what they meant. We got into an argument because they said they were born in the eighteen hundreds, and of course, we didn't believe that.

"They said they had come through the door in the brick wall at the edge of the town, so we went there to see what they had meant, and the second time we went through, everything was changed. There was a dirt road behind the wall, and horses and wagons passed along it. When we came back through into the town, the town had changed too."

"Thomas, you aren't – making this up – are you?" Mommy asked doubtfully, "I know you would never lie, but this sounds strange."

"No, I'm not making it up, listen. We tried to come home and ask you what had happened, but we couldn't find our house. Someone else was living where we thought our house would be, and we couldn't call you because our phones wouldn't work. Everyone in the town was dressed in clothes from the eighteen sixties – or at least I guess that's it, because they kept talking about the War Between the States. Anyway, finally a boy about my age came up to us, right after Susanna broke down, and said that he knew how to get us home. He was dressed the same as I am, so I knew he didn't have anything to do with whatever everyone else was doing. He told us that a friend of his had invented a time-travel machine, and they were testing it when we walked through it."

"That can't be!" Mommy exclaimed, "How could someone invent a time machine?"

"I don't know, but there really is a time machine, and it really works. We know, because we went through it."

"Did you walk through it by accident?"

"Sort of. Raymond – that's the boy who found us when we were lost in the nineteenth century – said that they wanted someone to come through the door, just to see what their reaction would be. When the two people from the eighteen hundreds came through, they started talking to us. Then when we all went back through the door, the man who invented the time machine decided to block us in there by turning off the machine. He sent Raymond through too, to tell us how to get out."

"How did you get out if the time machine was turned off?"

"At first, we missed the time we were supposed to be back through by, and we were stuck. But finally they had it turned back on so that we could come through, and that was all right."

Mommy still looked confused, and Thomas said, "We can tell you the whole story later," then he pointed to Susanna, who still had her head down on the bed, and mouthed the words, "She's really upset about what happened. Maybe you can – " and he shrugged.

Mommy nodded, and Thomas left the room.

"Susanna," Mommy said softly.

"Yes?" Susanna didn't lift her head.

"Are you all right?"

"I – I don't know."

"Thomas said you were upset about this – and I don't blame you. It must have been really hard to not be able to find our house or contact me. I was worried about you too."

She waited a moment, then saw that her daughter's shoulders and back were shaking slightly. Thinking she was crying, she pulled the girl's head closer and said, "You're fine now, Susanna. You're safe at home."

Susanna looked up, and to her mother's surprise, she was giggling softly. There were still tear stains on her face, but she was smiling, and the shaking was from laughter – not from sobs.

"Why – Susanna!" Mommy exclaimed in astonishment, "what are you laughing about?"

"You – you said," Susanna gasped, "you said that Thomas thought *I* was upset! If you could have seen *him*! I only got upset after we had already been through the time machine and had found out that we couldn't get home. Thomas was arguing with that Mr. Wilson, who lived in the eighteen hundreds, ever since we met! If he thought *I* was upset, *he* was definitely much more upset – and longer."

Mommy laughed, "I understand, Susanna, but there is a difference. I can see why Thomas was worried. You see, Thomas, though he is very good and polite much of the time, is not extremely slow to anger, and gets in arguments almost as often as he tries to keep out of them. You, on the other hand, hardly ever become ruffled, and if you broke down a while ago, I can understand that your brother was worried about you."

"Oh!" Susanna said sadly, "and I spoke very sharply just a few minutes ago to Raymond. I don't know why I did – I just wasn't thinking. I wish I hadn't, but it's too late."

"Who is Raymond?"

"Remember? Thomas told you. He is the boy who ran up to us after I found out that my phone didn't work, and Thomas was about to get into *another* argument with Mr. Wilson," she giggled before she continued, "Raymond knew about the time machine, and helped us find our way back to now."

"If he helped you, then why did you speak sharply to him?" her mother asked.

Susanna looked down, "He asked if Thomas and I wanted to go back through the time machine tomorrow," she said in a low voice, "and I was so upset that I couldn't answer him kindly. I know now that he was not saying anything unkind, but then all I could think about was that I wanted to get home."

"I see," Mommy said slowly.

"I did apologize though," Susanna told her, "I saw Thomas looking at me; he looked so surprised at my words – or my tone of voice; I don't know which, as if he couldn't believe this was his sister talking, and then I realized what I had done. So of course I said I was sorry. But I can't believe I even spoke like that in the first place!"

"So what did Thomas say?" Mommy asked, "Did he want to go back through the time machine tomorrow, or did he have the same aversion to the thought that you seem to have?"

The girl's head dropped lower still, "I think he wants to go tomorrow," she said softly, "he didn't say so, but he almost did, and then I got upset at him too. I think he noticed that I was almost angry with him for even thinking he might want to go again and he decided not to say so exactly. But he did give Raymond his number and Raymond said he would call tomorrow to see if we wanted to come."

"Have you changed your mind? I mean, do you want to go if Thomas goes?"

"I don't know. Right now I want to stay here for just about forever."

A tear dropped onto the blankets, and Susanna's mother decided to end the conversation. She looked across the room and saw that Nancy was still in the room and had her eyes wide open in astonishment.

"Nancy, will you go call everyone into the library to pray?" Mommy asked, "Susanna will be down in a minute, and then you can eat."

"Okay, I will," Nancy said quietly, with none of her usual boisterous five-year-old energy. She started to walk out the door, then turned back and asked, "Is Susanna okay? She's crying."

Susanna looked up, then stood and hurried over to the child, hugging her, "I'm fine, honey. You don't need to worry. I am not crying anymore, see?" and she wiped the tears from her face with her free hand, giving Nancy a smile.

"Good!" Nancy kissed Susanna's tearstained cheek, then ran out the door and down the stairs calling, "Time to eat! Time to eat!"

Susanna turned back to her mother with a worried frown, "I wonder how much she understood?"

"I hope she didn't understand everything," Mommy replied, "I completely forgot she was in here."

"She must not have understood everything," Susanna told her, "She doesn't know much of history yet. And I'm sure she doesn't know what a time-travel machine is."

"That may be true, but she must have understood most of it. She is a smart little girl, you know she's far ahead of most children her age. Are you sure she doesn't know anything about the War Between the States?"

"No, I'm not. Completely the other way – she knows quite a lot. Thomas and I talk of it sometimes, and she's never far away from him if she can help it; so I'm sure she knows much more than we think. But I'm also sure that she *doesn't* know what a time-travel machine is. You know how much I dislike science fiction, and technology in general, and Thomas knows that too. We don't have many conversations about things like time machines – except when he's teasing me."

"I know that, dear, and there's nothing we can do now. Whatever Nancy heard and understood will be impossible to erase from her memory. Now," she changed the subject, "tell Thomas to pray with everyone, because Daddy won't be here until late tonight. I can't come down right now, so tell someone to bring a plate up here for me."

"I will, Mommy, thank you."

Susanna left the room and hurried down the stairs. Once down, she rounded a corner and entered the library to find the rest of the family there waiting.

"Thomas, Mommy said you are to pray with us. She's not coming down right now, and Daddy won't be here for a while."

"Susanna, where did you get those clothes?" Danny exclaimed, staring with wide eyes at his oldest sister.

Susanna lifted her eyes to her older brother's, silently asking if it was fine to tell the whole story. Thomas shook his head at her, so she only said, "Well, I was walking down the street with Thomas, when a woman stopped me. She was dressed in clothes like these, and she wanted to know if I would like some. I agreed, so she took me to her house and gave me these."

"Oh, that was perfect for you, wasn't it?" Edward, who was Jennie's twin, exclaimed with a hearty laugh, "You're always saying how you like old-fashioned clothes and old-fashioned ways of doing things. Too bad you couldn't have lived back then! You seem to like that kind of thing a lot!"

Susanna bit her lip, then forced a smile, "I'm not sure it was very fun to live back then," she said, "You're right, I do like some of the ways people used to do things, but I'm glad I live now." She looked up at Thomas again, and he nodded at her with a smile, mixing approval and pity on his face.

"Shall we pray?" he asked, looking around the room to make sure all his siblings were present.

"Yes," Susanna nodded at him.

~   ~   ~

When the rest of the family was in bed, Susanna slowly climbed up the stairs to her room. She was the oldest girl, and so often had to stay up later than the rest of the family. Now she was tired from her long eventful day. When she reached the top of the stairs, she caught a glimpse of Thomas going into the boys' room. She gave him a tired smile, and he blew her a kiss before closing the door. Susanna switched off the hall light and entered the room all the girls shared.

She lay down on her bed and pulled the covers up tight under her chin. At first she thought she would never get to sleep, with all the thoughts going through her head, but finally she did, and being extremely tired, slept soundly until morning, troubled only by a quick dream or two that were soon forgotten.

Chapter 11

When the Jacksons and the strange young man left together, and her brother Richard decided to follow them, Lucy was left to herself, not knowing exactly what to do. She watched Richard until he disappeared around a corner and then walked over to a little bench near the post office and, after dusting it with her handkerchief, sat down.

"I don't suppose he'll be back any time soon," she said to herself, "I do hope he knows what he's doing. Oh, but it is silly of me to say such a thing, for Richard always knows what he does; I needn't worry about him.

"What did he mean when he said – no, he didn't say anything. It only seemed like he said things – but I'm not getting anywhere. Is he really a – " and she stopped short, not daring to say it aloud for fear of being overheard. She finished the thought in her head, though, *"Is he a spy? I had no idea of such a thing. If he really is, he did a good job of hiding it from me – well, actually, that's what spies are supposed to do, isn't it? Not let people know they're spies."*

She continued to wonder and think, and didn't notice when Richard came back. He sat down on the bench beside her and placed a hand on her shoulder, making her start in surprise.

"You're thinking quite deeply," he said with a smile, "what is it that's troubling that pretty little head of yours?"

"Oh, well – "

"Well what?" he asked.

"First shall we find the inn?" she suggested, "I'll tell you what I was thinking about when we get to our rooms."

"Fine," he agreed, getting to his feet, "but I hope it wasn't anything very serious."

He reached out a hand to help her up, and she accepted it and stood. They walked down the street until they reached an inn.

"This looks like a good place," Richard said, opening the door and leading her inside.

He paid for their rooms in Confederate bills, much to the disappointment of the man at the desk, who hoped they might have some gold, or at least Union greenbacks.

Richard sent a man to bring their trunks, and then they were shown up to their rooms. Once there, Richard seated his sister and pulled up a chair beside her for himself.

"So, Lucy, what was it you were thinking so deeply about?" he asked.

"What do you think?" she asked laughingly.

"How can I know?" he smiled.

"You truly cannot guess?" she asked playfully.

"I'm sure I don't know."

"I was thinking about what you told me – or didn't tell me – right before you went to see what happened to the Jacksons."

"Oh! You mean –?"

"Yes, can't you tell me any more than you did, now that we can't be overheard?"

"Let me tell you what happened to the Jacksons," he avoided her question.

Lucy sighed, then jerked her head up to look at him, "something happened to them?" she asked, worried, "are they all right? What happened? Did you help them? Was that young man with them a spy? Did he get them into trouble? Are we safe?"

"Whoa!" he exclaimed with a laugh, "one question at a time please, I can't keep all of those straight. First of all, your most important question: are we safe? Yes, we are fairly safe. As safe as we have been for the past few years," he hesitated, "I wish I didn't have to tell you, but it's better you should know."

"What is the matter, Richard? Why can't you just tell me?"

"I will. A Union cavalry unit just rode into town."

"Oh Richard! Please don't tell me that!" she cried in horror, "I thought we came here because it wasn't frequented by Union soldiers!"

"I'm sorry, Lucy. I thought it wasn't, but it appears we came at a bad time. I don't know what to say."

"Then don't say anything," she whispered, then said in a stronger voice, "I will be fine," her chin went up, "A Southern woman can stand in the face of her enemies."

"Now that is my sister talking," Richard said with a smile, "We can't go home right away, because I've some things I need to take care of. But in a couple of days, we can go back home, and at least you'll have your own place to live in."

"That is fine, Richard. Thank you."

There was a knock on the door, and Richard stood up to answer it, "Now, Lucy, here are the trunks," he said, letting in a few men with their arms loaded, "Yes, thank you. Set them over there," he told the men.

When all the trunks were stacked neatly on the floor of their rooms, Richard paid the men for their work, and closed the door after them.

"Do you wish to eat now," he asked, "or wait until later?"

"I would like to eat now," his sister replied, "I am hungry, but I am afraid if I wait any longer, I will fall asleep before I can eat. It has been a long, tiring day."

"You are right about that!" Richard agreed heartily.

"Are you tired too?" she asked in surprise, "I shouldn't have thought you would be, since you travel all the time!"

The corners of her brother's mouth twitched upward in amusement, "Why Lucy," he said, "surely you didn't think that because one does something often one must like a thing?"

"Well!" she said, "I hardly ever do something over and over again that I dislike."

"But you see, Lucy, I can't simply pick what I wish to do and only do those things. I must work, you know."

"And you truly don't like to?" she queried.

"It is not so much that I dislike to as it is that I would rather be doing something else," he explained, "I often would like to go places with you when you ask me, but I've told you there is work I need to do. Do you remember that?"

"I do, Richard, but I thought it was only because you liked working – though I couldn't see why."

"I see! I'm sorry I never explained things to you. The real reason was because there was work that needed to be done, and I was the one who needed to do it. Let's see, how can I explain it to you? Have you ever felt that you wished to stay home and read or sew instead of going calling, or to a party?"

"Oh, yes, many times."

"Well, but you dressed in your nice clothes anyway, and went where you needed to go, didn't you?"

"Yes, of course! I couldn't stay home without calling on anyone. It is my duty to return the call of anyone who calls on me."

"Even if it is someone you don't particularly like?"

"Yes; do you mean someone like Mrs. Dixon?"

Richard laughed, "Do you dislike her? I didn't know."

"Oh, most definitely! She is a horrid bore. But I see what you mean, I know I must return her call, and suffer through her conversation with a smile on my face. It is duty, and I suppose that is what you are going to say about your work."

"Yes, you do understand. But we have gotten off the subject. Where did we come from?"

"I was wishing the Union soldiers hadn't come into town."

"Yes, but before that we were talking about what I saw when I followed the Jacksons."

"Oh yes, please do tell me."

So Richard told her what he had seen. He was a very good storyteller, and Lucy got a good idea of what had happened.

"What would you have done if the Yankees hadn't believed them?" Lucy asked.

"I am not sure, since the officer did believe them and let them go, but I did have my gun with me."

"And would you have shot them?"

"I couldn't have gotten all of them with one gun," he told her, "And I'm sure that neither Mr. Jackson, nor the other man had guns on. So I suppose I would have had to wait."

Chapter 12

Both Vincents slept in pretty late the next morning. Raymond had been very tired the night before, but when he did wake up, he was refreshed and feeling ready for whatever happened that day.

"Breakfast is ready, Dad!" he called from the kitchen half an hour later, "are you ready to eat?"

"I'm coming," his father called back, "don't eat it all before I get there!"

Raymond laughed, and set the dishes on the table. After they had been eating for a few minutes, Mr. Vincent asked his son, "well, what time did you figure to go over to Mr. Elliot's place?"

"He said he'd call me when he's ready for us to pick him up," Raymond answered.

"Okay, do you have any idea of what time that will be?"

"Well, I would think that he'd want to go as soon as possible, so it shouldn't be very long. Do you think the Jacksons will come?"

Mr. Vincent thought for a moment, "That depends on the girl, I guess. Thomas might come by himself, but I don't think it's likely."

"She didn't seem to think much of the time-travel machine."

"No, but she did have a bad experience, I don't blame her," his father replied.

"Why don't you think that Thomas might come without his sister?" Raymond wanted to know.

"She'd be scared to let him go by himself," Mr. Vincent answered, "She knows she won't be able to contact him the whole time he's in the past. I'll bet she won't want to have to worry the whole time he's gone, and so will come with him."

"But do you think he will come?"

"That I can't say. All I can say is that if he does come, I'm pretty sure Susanna will come with him."

Raymond's cell phone rang, and he stood up, "It's Mr. Elliot," he told his father, "He's probably ready to go."

He answered the phone and said, "hello? Hello, Mr. Elliot! – no, we're not quite ready to go yet. Give us about a half an hour, okay? – thanks, bye!"

"Sit back down and finish eating," Mr. Vincent said, "there's no big hurry. It's only ten forty-five. We'll have all the rest of the day."

"Mr. Elliot said the same thing," Raymond said, sitting back down in his seat.

After breakfast had been eaten and cleaned up, it had been about half an hour, as Raymond had said.

"Should I call Thomas right now, or wait 'til later?" Raymond asked.

"Why don't you call Mr. Elliot and tell him we're on our way, then call Thomas."

"All right."

The two men walked out to the truck and got in. Raymond was already on the phone with Mr. Elliot, "Hi, we're on our way – okay – good-bye," he looked at his father, who was driving, "Now I'll call Thomas," he said.

The young man skimmed through his contacts until he found Thomas's name. He tapped it, then waited for his new friend to pick up, "Hello, this is Raymond," he said when he heard Thomas's voice, "How are you doing? - good, we're heading for the time machine, are you coming? – okay, that's fine – give me a call when you decide, all right? – thanks."

"So they haven't decided yet?" Mr. Vincent asked.

"That's what he said. I hope they do decide to come, but of course, I have no idea if they have anything else to do today."

~   ~   ~

"Susanna, where are you?" Thomas called, putting his phone back in his pocket.

"I'm at my desk," she called from the room behind him. He hurried over to where she sat writing.

"Is that a letter?" he asked.

"Yes."

"Who are you sending it to?"

"Margret."

"Margaret!" he exclaimed in surprise, "she lives only on the next street!"

"No, no!" she laughed, "Margret Horton, our cousin."

"Oh! I should have known. The one who traded homing pigeons with you."

"Yes, but you know we don't use them every time we write. Only for things that are really important. But I'm surprised you forgot, are you thinking of something else?"

"Yes, I am, Susanna," Thomas said gravely.

"What is it?"

Thomas lowered his head and toyed with an eraser lying on her desk, "Raymond called," he said quietly.

Susanna took a long breath – a very long breath, then said, "And he wants us to go with him again?"

Thomas nodded.

"Do you – do you want to?" she asked.

"You don't want to, do you?" he asked, instead of answering her question.

"I – I – no, I don't really," she said.

"You don't have to come," he told her, "I'll go by myself if you wouldn't like to come with me."

"No, I could never do that, Thomas," she shook her head, "I'd be afraid the whole time you were gone. If you go, I'm coming with you."

"Would you be fine with going again if we waited a few days before trying?" he wanted to know.

"No, Thomas. I don't think I'll ever be used to the idea of a time machine. I just – can't like it. But I could never let you go by yourself. Not after what happened to us yesterday."

"What should I tell Raymond, then?" he wondered, "I told him we hadn't decided yet, and that I'd call back when we had."

"This is really important to you, isn't it."

Thomas looked at his sister. Her head was down, her arm still in the position of writing, but her pencil was not moving across the paper. He knew pretty well what she was thinking, and knew that the question she had just asked was an important one. But he had lived with his sister too long to try to avoid the question again. She would want a direct, true answer. And he also knew what she would say when he gave it.

"Yes."

Susanna rolled her chair back and stood. "All right," she said, she looked in his eyes for a brief second, then away, "I'll be ready in about ten minutes. You can call Raymond and tell him we're coming."

She started to leave, but Thomas stopped her, "Susanna, please! I don't want you to – "

"But you do want to go, Thomas," she said quietly, "I'll be fine." She looked straight at him and smiled. It looked real, but he couldn't be sure, "See you in ten minutes!" she sang as she left the room.

Thomas watched her leave, then thought for several minutes. Finally, he slowly reached into his pocket and pulled out his phone. Still slowly, he found Raymond's name and called him.

"Hello – yes – yes, we're coming." He paused as he heard a whoop come through the phone, then said, "We'll be on our way in about fifteen minutes. – yes, I did say we – okay – bye."

He slid the phone back into his pocket, then looked at the clock hanging on the wall. "What time was it that Susanna left?" he wondered, "I don't think I checked. Oh well, it's probably been almost ten minutes by now, I'll see if she's ready."

He walked out into the hallway, and then turned up the stairs. When he got upstairs, he went over to the girls' room. He was about to call his sister when he saw her by her bed, kneeling on the floor. "Is she crying?" he asked himself, "no, she's praying. I'll leave her alone right now. She can come when she's ready."

Thomas turned around and softly walked away. He entered the boys' room and brought out his backpack. He tried not to get too excited, since Susanna was so upset, but he had a bounce in his step as he hurried downstairs, and a happy grin of anticipation played around his lips.

He sat down on the sofa in the library, where he could see the stairs, and waited for his sister to come down.

"Oh! I forgot to tell Mommy we're going!" he exclaimed, and leaving his heavy backpack next to the sofa, he bounded up the stairs two at a time and entered his mother's room.

"How are you doing, Mommy?" he asked.

"Oh, I'm fine. This baby's been kicking like crazy all night, though, so I haven't gotten much sleep. The little girl – or boy – has calmed down a bit now, so I should be able to catch a nap in a few minutes."

"I'm sorry."

"I'll be fine. Now what do you need?"

"I just wanted to tell you that Susanna and I are going to see the time machine again, so don't be worried if our phones don't pick up. We'll try to be back in plenty of time, though. I'll tell Raymond and the others that we can't stay long. Do you need anything before we go?"

"No, nothing. But Thomas, are you sure it's safe to be taking Susanna in there?"

"Well, I can't be sure of anything," he told her, "but I don't think it's really that dangerous. I'll take care of her; don't worry please."

"I'll try not to. But don't get into any arguments, and if you see any soldiers, walk the other way."

"I'll do my best, Mommy," he took her hand, pressed it, then went out and down the stairs to sit on the sofa again.

It wasn't long before he heard footsteps overhead. Through the balcony railing he saw a swish of skirts, and then Susanna flew down the stairs, one hand on the railing and the skirt of her dress held off the floor in the other.

He jumped up and swung his backpack onto his shoulder, "Ready?"

"I'm ready, Thomas! Sorry I took longer than I intended," she said with a big smile. Her step was light as she opened the front door before he could get there. Her older brother wondered at the sudden change, though this was much more like the sister he knew.

Thomas suddenly realized she was wearing the dress the woman had given her the day before, "Are you trying not to make yourself conspicuous?" he asked.

"Of course! I don't want everyone who sees me with my ankles showing to think I'm a shameless girl with no idea of modesty!" she laughed.

"Do you want to ride in the car, or walk?" he asked.

"Let's walk," she suggested, "it's such a nice day."

"Yes it is," he agreed, and so they turned down the street and soon arrived at the door in the brick wall. The others were there waiting for them.

"Hi, Thomas and Susanna!" Raymond exclaimed as he ran up to them, "I'm so glad you could come! Are you ready to go through now?"

"Yes, I think so, but first: we can't stay very long. So let's come back after half an hour, okay?" Thomas said.

"That's fine with me," Raymond said, "but who's going to stay out here and turn the machine on and off?"

Thomas turned to his sister, "You could stay," he whispered, "since you don't want to go through."

She shook her head, "I'm going with you," she told him with a smile, "I won't be able to contact you once you're through the door, and I don't want to be waiting out here not knowing what's happening to you. I don't want to stay out here unless you do too."

Thomas nodded, then looked around to see if anyone volunteered to stay out. After exchanging a few words with his son, Mr. Vincent decided to stay. "I don't particularly care to go through the machine," he told them, "And I know the rest of you do. So I'll stay here."

Susanna looked up at Thomas as Mr. Vincent said, 'I know the rest of you do,' and laughed. Thomas laughed with her. He knew his sister wasn't extremely excited about the time machine, but he also knew that she wasn't about to explain that to the others. And since she wasn't, he wouldn't either.

"Mr. Elliot," Raymond asked, "Is the time machine going to take us to the same time period we were in yesterday? Or is it going to be the next day, or will you set it to a different period?"

"Let me explain a few more details about my machine," the old man said, "first, as I told you yesterday, the door can only be opened twice each time that the time machine is turned off, then it will stop working."

"I understand that," Raymond nodded.

"Secondly," Mr. Elliot continued, "I didn't quite perfect the machine, so once I set it at a certain time period, it can't be changed without dissembling the entire machine."

"What exactly do you mean?" Mr. Vincent wanted to know.

"Well, I set it for a certain day in eighteen sixty-three yesterday, and today it will be the day after that. So next year if we go through the machine we will end up in eighteen sixty-four. Do you understand?"

"Yes, I think so. So if we meet the Wilsons today they will remember what happened yesterday?"

"As well as you remember it."

"I see."

"Is everyone ready to go now?" the old man asked.

Raymond and Thomas nodded. Susanna didn't move. Now that the time had come, she was even more terrified of the machine than she had been. She struggled to keep the smile on her face and prayed earnestly for strength.

As the four started walking closer to the door, she forced herself to keep up with her brother. Thomas forgot to look at his sister's face as they neared the door, and she was glad he did, for though to the others she looked as if she was smiling, Thomas knew her too well. She let her long blond hair fall forward a bit, in hopes that he wouldn't notice her slightly stiff features.

Mr. Elliot, however, could read faces better than Susanna had counted on, and while she turned away from Thomas, her face was fully exposed to the old man. He couldn't know for sure what was the trouble, but it was obvious to him that she wasn't all too excited about going through the door.

"Thomas, Susanna, wait a minute," he said as Raymond put his hand on the door's handle.

The Jacksons looked at him questioningly, and he asked, "I want to tell you something."

Thomas and Susanna stepped closer to the old man and he said gently, "I just wanted to say I'm very sorry about what happened yesterday, and I wish I hadn't acted the way I did."

"What do you mean?" Thomas asked.

"I mean that I was testing the machine on you, and wanted to see what happened with the culture clash, and didn't think of how it might affect you.

I'm very sorry that we didn't inform you of what we were going to do, and that I turned off the machine so you couldn't get back home."

Thomas held out his hand, "that's all right, we accept your apology."

Mr. Elliot took the younger man's hand, but then looked at Susanna. "And what about you, Susanna? I'm very sorry I hurt you and frightened you in that way."

Susanna smiled, "I forgive you, Mr. Elliot," she said softly, "I know you didn't mean for everything to happen as it did."

Thomas nodded, then said, "let's go now."

So they joined Raymond at the door, and he opened it. As they stepped through, Mr. Vincent called, "I'm supposed to turn it off when the door closes, right?"

"Yes," Mr. Elliot called back, "and then turn it on in a half hour."

"Okay, good-bye!"

Raymond closed the door, and Susanna shivered, then forced herself to smile. It was now impossible to go home for half an hour, no matter how badly they needed to go. Thomas seemed to read her thoughts, for he said quietly, "it's only half an hour."

"Yes," she whispered.

Chapter 13

They began walking down the street, and soon saw that there were blue-coated soldiers all over the town. There really weren't too many, but there seemed to be a lot, since there weren't many other people on the streets.

"Where do you want to go?" Mr. Elliot asked his younger companions, "I don't know what it's like here, so you tell me where you want to go and we'll go there."

Susanna looked around at the Union soldiers, then noticed a girl on the street, "There's Lily Mae!" she exclaimed softly.

"Who's Lily Mae?" Thomas asked.

"Remember the woman who gave me this dress?" Susanna asked, gesturing toward her clothing, "that's one of her daughters."

"Really? You didn't tell me much about them," Thomas told her, "do you want to go say hi?"

"Yes, I would like to," Susanna said, and she hurried across the street to the other girl.

Lily Mae smiled when she saw Susanna, "Hello, Susanna, how are you?"

"I am well, and you?"

"As well as can be expected," Lily Mae sighed, her face turning into a frown.

"What do you mean?"

"Haven't you seen the bluebellies in the streets? What can be more awful than that, except hearing that my brothers have been killed?"

"Oh, yes I see. It must be very uncomfortable."

Thomas, Raymond, and Mr. Elliot came up at that moment, and Susanna said, "Thomas, this is Lily Mae Maxwell. Lily Mae, this is my brother Thomas Jackson."

Lily Mae held out her hand and said, "I'm very pleased to meet you, Mr. Jackson."

"And I am pleased to meet you, Miss Maxwell," Thomas replied with a glance at his sister. Susanna was thankful that he had remembered to call her friend 'miss' instead of 'Lily Mae.'

"This is Raymond Vincent, and this is Mr. Elliot," Susanna continued, motioning to the two other men. Lily Mae dropped a curtsy, and then said to Susanna, "will you come to my house?"

Susanna looked at Thomas, who said, "You go, Susanna, we'll find something else to do."

"All right, I'll come," she told Lily Mae, and the younger girl smiled with delight.

Lucy jumped out of bed as she realized how late she had slept, "My goodness! I know most ladies sleep late, but *I've* never slept *this* late before! What will Richard think?"

She quickly dressed, having learned that skill herself when her nurse had died, and they had trouble finding another maid. Now she didn't long for a helper anymore, though sometimes she called in one of the cook's girls to assist her with buttons she couldn't reach. This trip she had taken good care not to pack anything she couldn't dress herself into.

She opened the door and walked over to Richard's room, knocking lightly on the door when she reached it.

She received no answer, and said out loud, "Richard could never have slept this late, so he must be downstairs or out somewhere. I will go down and see."

The young lady stepped lightly down the stairs, holding her full skirts up to her ankles so she wouldn't fall. As she reached the bottom of the stairs she saw the form of her brother leaning against the wall staring at something across the room.

Following his gaze, she saw two union officers standing talking at the other side of the room. She did not do more than sigh, for she had been used to this scene over the past couple of years while the two countries had been at war. As she had discussed with her brother the day before, their hometown was quite often frequented by soldiers of the Union army.

As the girl stepped down from the last stair, the two men turned to look at her. Each nodded politely, and she returned a cold, stiff bow. "Be polite and ladylike no matter to whom," her mother had often told her before she had died, and Lucy tried to follow that advice, though now, as she had done her duty, she lifted her chin proudly and went to her brother, not favoring the officers with another glance.

A step sounded behind her, and she glanced back for a moment. Her shoulders jerked as she saw, coming down the stairs, another man dressed in the hated blue. *"Three officers in the same hotel we are staying at!"* she thought with an inward groan, *"why didn't we stay home? At least there I can stay inside without having soldiers going through the house!"*

"Lucy, here you are!" Richard said, "I am glad to see you."

As the two girls neared the Maxwells' house, Susanna heard the sound of humming coming from around the side of the small building.

She looked at Lily Mae questioningly, "Is that Bessie?"

"Yes, she has a beautiful voice," Lily Mae answered, "do you want to listen? She won't mind."

Susanna nodded, and the two walked closer and rounded the corner of the house to see Bessie sitting in a chair, having taken her brother outside, sewing and watching him.

She was still humming, and Susanna listened closely. She didn't recognize the tune and was about to ask Bessie to sing the words when she opened her mouth and did just what Susanna was hoping for.

In a low alto, the girl sang the words to the beautiful tune:

> *Dearest love, do you remember,*
> *When we last did meet,*
> *How you told me that you loved me,*
> *Kneeling at my feet?"*

Bessie' voice swelled louder with pride as she continued,

> *Oh! How proud you stood before me,*
> *In your suit of gray,*
> *And you vowed to me and country*
> *To be true throughout the fray!*

> *Weeping sad and lonely,*
> *Hopes and fears how vain,*

The girl's voice faltered, and Lily Mae's soprano chimed in as her sister tried to hold the note: "Yet praying..."

Then Bessie grew stronger, and finished,

> *When this cruel war is over,*
> *Praying that we meet again.*

Susanna remembered that Lily Mae had said Bessie's fiancé was fighting, and realized this song meant more to her than it would otherwise.

"I have never heard that song before," she told them, "it was beautiful."

"Would you like me to bring a chair out here for you?" Lily Mae offered.

"Oh, no thank you. I'll sit on the ground for a moment, but I can't stay long."

"How old are you?" Bessie asked, "I'm eighteen."

"I'm seventeen," Susanna answered, she looked at Lily Mae questioningly and Lily Mae said, "I'm fifteen."

"Where do you live?" was the next question.

Susanna thought a moment; this was a hard one. "I don't exactly live near here," she said slowly, "And I don't know how many times I'll be able to come visit you again over the next few days, but I think that in a few days we will never see each other again."

Lily Mae' brow wrinkled in a confused frown, but she directed another question at her new friend, "do you have a beau?"

Now it was Susanna's turn to be confused, "A bow? I don't think so. Not today – well I have this ribbon in my pocket. You can use it to make a bow if you want."

Lily Mae and Bessie both burst into giggles, "Oh, Susanna!" Lily Mae exclaimed, "That's not what I meant! I wanted to know if you have a beau; meaning a young man."

"Oh!" now Susanna understood, and laughed with them. Then she shook her head, "no, I'm nowhere near old enough to get married yet."

"What do you mean?" Bessie asked in surprise, "My Paul started beauing me when I was fifteen. We would have gotten married last year if he hadn't gone to fight. And Lily Mae here is pretty enough that she might have gotten a young man this year if only they hadn't all gone off to war."

"Oh! Yes, but my family believes we should wait until we are older until we marry," Susanna explained hesitantly, "I probably won't even start courting until I'm nineteen at least."

Both of the Maxwell girls looked taken aback at this. They could understand a girl not getting married until she was nineteen or even a little older if she happened not to have anyone interested in her, but to purposefully avoid marriage until that age was not something they had ever considered.

Lily Mae changed the subject, "Why hasn't your brother joined up – Oh! Please don't take that as an insult, I truly want to know."

"Where we live most of the young men have not joined the army," Susanna said quietly. She wondered whether they would ever find something to talk about that wouldn't show the drastic differences in the cultures each lived in. Suddenly she remembered, "Oh!" she exclaimed, jumping up, "Thomas will be wondering what happened to me. I must go back and find him now."

"You – you aren't angry with me for asking you about your brother, are you?" Lily Mae faltered uncertainly, "I – I – "

"Oh, no. I am not angry about that at all. I would love to stay and talk some more if I could, but Thomas really will be wondering what happened to me if I don't find him soon."

The younger girl breathed a sigh of relief, "I'm glad. I'll go with you to find your brother."

"Thank you," Susanna agreed, and the two girls left Bessie to her sewing and went back to the street.

"Your brother isn't where he was when we left him," Lily Mae observed, scanning the street on both sides.

"No, he isn't. I hope he hasn't gone far away."

"I'm sure we'll find him soon," Lily Mae reassured the older girl, "You don't think he would have gone far without having told you, do you?"

"I don't think so," Susanna shook her head, "Thomas is usually careful of what he does when he's out with me."

"Then let's – " Lily Mae's eyes widened, "oh no!" she whispered.

"What?" Susanna asked. She looked in the direction the other girl was staring and saw that one of the blue-coated soldiers was headed their way.

Chapter 14

The soldier drew nearer to the two girls, and took off his hat, bowing slightly as he saw they noticed him. Lily Mae recoiled in terror as he came close, and Susanna wasn't sure exactly what to do.

Before the man could speak, Lily Mae found her voice, "Please excuse us, sir," she begged, "We are in a hurry."

"Wait a moment, if you please, miss," he held out his hand, "are you looking for the men you were with a few minutes ago?"

Lily Mae looked even more frightened, and Susanna finally answered, "Yes, we are. Do you know where they went?"

"Yes. They are behind the post office."

"Thank you," Susanna said, and Lily, recovering a little from her fright, nodded.

The Union soldier bowed again, replaced his hat, and strode away.

"Oh!" Lily Mae gasped as the two started to walk toward the post office, "I thought he was going to be insolent."

"I don't think all Union soldiers are rude," Susanna told the younger girl gently, "As you can see, there was no cause to be afraid of this one. But that does not mean you should not avoid them if possible. I don't have any way of knowing what the rest of them are like, and I don't plan on introducing myself to any."

Lily Mae laughed; she was fully recovered from her fright now. "Oh, certainly not, Susanna, but I am thankful that the man who spoke to us was not offensive."

"So am I. Let's see if we can find my brother where he said he was."

The two girls hurried back around the post office, and saw Thomas, Raymond, and Mr. Elliot there talking.

As the girls came into sight, Thomas looked at them, then hurried toward his sister, "Susanna!" he said, "I didn't know you would be back so soon. I'm sorry I wasn't where you left me. Were you worried when you didn't see us? Did you have trouble finding us?"

"It's really okay, Thomas," Susanna reassured him, "Yes, I was a bit worried when I didn't see you, but one of the soldiers in the street had seen you leave and he told us where you were."

"You asked a Union soldier where we were?" Thomas exclaimed in astonishment, "I wouldn't have thought you would do such a thing!"

"No, I didn't," his sister answered, shaking her head, "he saw us looking around and came up. I guess he'd seen us with you when we first came up the street, because he asked us if we were looking for you. Then he told us you were here and left."

"That was nice of him," Thomas said, "but I am sorry we weren't there to meet you."

"It's been about twenty minutes," Mr. Elliot said, "I think we should go back now."

"All right," Thomas agreed.

Susanna waved a hand to Lily Mae. "It was nice to see you again," she said.

"Good-bye," Lily Mae answered, nodding. The girl hurried back around the post office and was gone from sight. After a few seconds, the whole group followed in the direction she had gone, but she was far ahead, and they didn't see her again.

They walked back up the street toward the door they had to go through, and Thomas looked at a small church they hadn't noticed before. Beside it was a little graveyard, and he gave a sudden snort of laughter.

Everyone turned to look at him, and he explained, "I was just thinking: what if I died while we were still on this side of the time machine – what a funny looking gravestone that would make! 'Thomas Steinwand Jackson, Born two thousand five, Died eighteen sixty-three!"

All three men burst into laughter – and Susanna burst into tears. She quickly turned away so that Thomas wouldn't see her. It was just a little too much. She had tried hard, drawing on the strength the Lord gave her throughout this trip, but this time she hadn't been able to keep from giving way to her feelings. She didn't let herself continue to cry, however, she forced herself to think of the funny side of Thomas's idea and finally was able to laugh with the others.

She waited until the three men had calmed down a bit, then turned and looked her brother in the face, saying, "Let's see – that would mean you lived – negative one hundred forty-two years, wouldn't it?"

This sent the men off into another shout of laughter, in which the girl was able to join, chasing off all of the morbid thoughts of her brother's previous statement.

By the time they reached the door, they had calmed down to a point where only a few chuckles were heard here and there. Once they had gotten through the door and thrown themselves down on the grass to wait for it to open again, Raymond asked, "What did you say your middle name was, Thomas?"

"Steinwand," his friend answered with a laugh.

"Sh-tein-vandt," Raymond pronounced slowly, stumbling a bit over the unfamiliar sounds, "I don't think I've ever heard that name before. What does it mean?"

Thomas laughed again, "I'm not surprised you've never heard it before," he said, "Susanna, why don't you tell them how I happened to get a name like that? You're better at storytelling then I am."

Susanna laughed too, then began, "When Mommy was a girl, she always thought Thomas was the nicest boy's name in the world, and when she married Philip Jackson, our daddy, and found out she was about to have a boy, she told him that she wanted to name her baby Thomas.

"Daddy thought a moment, then looked at her with some amusement and asked, 'why do you want to name him Thomas?'

"'Because I've always liked that name best, since I was a little girl,' she explained.

"Daddy looked at her curiously, then asked again, 'there's really no other reason? You don't care what it means, and you're not naming him after anyone?'

"Mommy didn't have any idea why he was asking these questions, and she got kind of confused, but still, she answered 'no,' and he nodded and left the room."

Susanna paused and looked at her companions, "Neither of you can guess what Daddy was thinking of?" she asked.

Raymond and Mr. Elliot shook their heads. Thomas's lips twitched.

"Well," she continued, "Daddy came back a few minutes later with an excited look on his face. 'I've found the perfect middle name for him!' he told Mommy.

"'What is it?' she asked. Daddy told her he thought that Steinwand would make a good middle name, and this time it was her turn to ask why."

Mr. Elliot and Raymond listened closely. They were sure that now they would hear what Thomas's middle name meant.

"Daddy told her that Steinwand is a German word, and asked her if she wanted to know what the English meaning was. She did, of course, so he explained, 'Well you see, my dear, you want to name our son Thomas Jackson, so of course he has to have a middle name that means Stonewall!'" Susanna looked at her listeners to see if they understood what she was trying to say.

"Oh!" Mr. Elliot exclaimed, comprehension downing over his wrinkled face.

Raymond said, "Now I remember, Stonewall Jackson's real name was Thomas! I wonder why I didn't think of that before?"

"You've only known us for two days," Thomas laughed, "I'm not surprised that you didn't make the connection."

"Oh well, so you're named after that famous general! I think he was a great general, but of course, no offence," Raymond laughingly asked for pardon, "I do like General Lee better."

"*I* don't," Susanna made a small face and Raymond looked at her in surprise, "What's wrong with Robert E. Lee?" he asked, "why don't you like him?"

"He fought for something he didn't believe in," she explained. He thought that the Northern cause was right, but he fought for the South anyway. He said that he didn't want to fight against his family, and so he couldn't fight for what he believed in."

Thomas wasn't surprised at his sister's outburst. If there was one subject she was passionate about, it was the War Between the States. He had discussed this point of the subject with her several times, but they agreed, so there was nothing really to discuss anymore. He nodded when Raymond looked at him to see whether he agreed with Susanna's words.

"But why don't you like Lee?" Raymond asked. He still wasn't sure what Susanna was trying to say.

She looked at her brother, and he said, "You know in the Bible where Jesus says 'If any man come to me, and hate not his father, and mother, and wife, and children, and brethren, and sisters, yea, and his own life also, he cannot be my disciple'?"

Raymond shook his head, "I don't remember that particular passage, but I do remember the place where He says, 'He that loveth father or mother more than me is not worthy of me,' and that refers to a similar principle, I guess."

Thomas nodded, "well we believe that those passages work for everything, not just being a Christian. I think that if our family or friends – or anything else for that matter – are more important to us than doing what's right, we have a problem. While I am glad General Lee fought for the South in that it helped us a lot, I believe he shouldn't have, since he believed the Northern cause was right."

"Are you sure he believed that?" Raymond asked.

"Pretty sure – I mean, I wasn't alive at the time to hear him say it." Thomas laughed.

"You know, we do have a time travel machine here," Mr. Elliot murmured, and everyone burst into a laugh.

"But seriously, Thomas," Mr. Elliot said, after the laughter had calmed down, "I think you're right. If Robert E. Lee really thought that the Union was in the right, he shouldn't have fought for the Confederacy."

Raymond nodded slowly, "I can see what you're getting at, but I'm going to have a hard time giving up my hero. I've loved General Lee since I was a little boy."

"Oh!" Thomas exclaimed, "I didn't mean you shouldn't like him anymore, only that I thought that one choice he made was wrong. He was a wonderful general and a Christian, so there's nothing wrong with liking him. Susanna was just saying that she doesn't like him as well as she likes Stonewall Jackson."

"I'm sure she doesn't like him as well as she likes Steinwand Jackson either," Mr. Elliot added with a smile.

"No I don't," Susanna laughed, "I don't even like Stonewall Jackson as much as I like his namesake."

At this point the door opened, and Mr. Vincent stepped through, calling, "So you had a good time?"

"We certainly did, Dad!" Raymond answered, springing to his feet. All four of the explorers hurried through the door.

"Well, I guess from the looks of you that you had no misadventures?" Mr. Vincent queried, looking around at the faces of those who had gone through the machine.

"No, none this time," Mr. Elliot shook his head, "Everything went well."

"We've got to go home now," Thomas announced, "Thank you for inviting us, we had a good time, but we have things to do at home and if we don't get there soon, Mommy's going to worry that something happened to us again."

"Well, good-bye, General!" Raymond called as they turned away.

Thomas turned back to look at him in surprise, then recognition dawned as he realized his new friend was referring back to the conversation they had had about his middle name. He laughed and waved his hand.

The two Jacksons headed back home, and soon Susanna was helping her sister Florence with a math problem she hadn't been able to understand while Thomas was in the kitchen helping Danny finish cooking lunch.

~ ~ ~

The next day, as she and Richard walked down the street Lucy was sure she saw the bluecoated soldiers throw covert glances toward the pair.

"Why are they watching us?" she whispered as her brother leaned down in answer to her pull on his arm.

"Who?" he asked.

"The Union soldiers."

Richard gave a start, then quickly composed himself and shook his head at her, "They have nothing to do today," he told her, "so they're probably only trying to find something interesting to look at." She searched his face, but finally accepted his explanation.

That night, however, he left her in her room, and was about to go downstairs. "Where are you going?" she called.

"I have some things I need to take care of," he told her.

"This late?" she asked, "It's almost ten o'clock!"

Richard merely nodded, and headed down the stairs, leaving her standing in her doorway, gazing after him. A few minutes later, she was still standing in her doorway when one of the Union officers came out of his own room and headed down the hall. As he was about to pass her door, he bowed slightly, and she returned it coldly, as she had before. Then quickly turning, she entered her room and closed the door. Hearing the man's footsteps on the stairs, she remembered her brother and wondered once again why he had wanted to go out so late at night.

"It's not his habit at home," she said to herself, "to stay up very late, unless there's a ball – and there haven't been many of those since the war started. He doesn't drink much, so he can't be going to do that, and – " she broke off, not having any more ideas.

Chapter 15

On Sunday, everyone went to church, and though the Vincents could have gone with Mr. Elliot through the time machine after church if they wanted to and Mr. Elliot had been free, the Jacksons hosted evening services at their house. So Susanna was relieved from going to the place she still was wary of, even after her good experience the second time she had gone.

Though some people would hardly think that hosting a group of fifty guests or more was restful, Susanna had assisted in the job for years, and now, though her mother was still not feeling extremely well and couldn't help much, the girl felt glad that everything was going back to normal after the stressful moments of the past few days, and none of the work she had to do was tiring for her.

That afternoon and evening as her friends came with their families for fellowship, she was careful not to mention anything that had happened in the past two days, and instead talked of other subjects of interest.

Thomas also, though he would hardly admit it, was glad for the restful day instead of the challenging moments he and his dear sister had gone through two days before. He was not in any way tired of the time machine, and hoped for many more chances to learn about it and explore behind it, but to be thrown unexpectedly into circumstances he had no idea how to control, and his sister breaking down, were things he thought he would rather not have happen often. He too guarded his conversation to make sure he didn't say anything the young men he talked with would notice as unusual.

Other than exchanging a few text messages with his new friend Raymond, no mention of the time machine was made by him that day.

When the last guest left, it was nearing midnight. Susanna and Thomas assisted their younger siblings and father in cleaning up, which took only about twenty minutes, and then everyone got ready for bed as quickly as possible. After family worship, the whole family was asleep almost instantly, with the exception of Jennie, who still preferred to read a few chapters of her book no matter how late it was.

~   ~   ~

When Lucy woke up the next morning, she got ready as quickly as possible and then hurried to her brother's room to knock on the door. She was eager to know the answer to her questions of the previous night. No answer, however, was made to her knock, and she laughed to herself, shaking her head, "how Richard can stay up so late and still be up in the morning so early is beyond me. Oh well, I suppose I'll go downstairs and see if he's there."

She hurried down the stairs and looked around the room where she had found her brother before. Richard was nowhere to be seen. Lucy slowly let her gaze fall on every corner of the room again, but still no Richard. "Where could he be?" she asked herself, "Why would he leave without telling me? He knows that I won't know what to do without him, I've never travelled before, and without my brother – " she walked up to the desk and inquired of the man sitting behind it, "Do you know where my brother went?"

The man she addressed stood and shook his head, "I'm sorry, Miss Wilson, all I can tell you is that your brother went out an hour ago, and I haven't seen him since."

"Thank you," Lucy nodded, and turned to go upstairs again. She would never venture out into the street without her brother as an escort in such a strange town with Union soldiers lining the streets.

Another hour passed. Lucy Wilson had eaten breakfast, and then tried to read for a while, but after the hour had gone, she became restless, and finally went down again to see if Richard had returned.

Once again, however, the man at the desk shook his head and apologized, having no news of her brother. So Lucy went back to her room once more to wait. "What am I going to say to Richard when he comes back?" she asked herself, "I can't believe he would go off and leave me like this. At home, such a thing wouldn't matter, but here? He knows I don't know what to do."

She took out again her well-worn volume of Shakespeare's Midsummer Night's Dream, and opened it to read. "I've always liked this one best of all his plays," she said aloud, "I suppose it's because I like the fact that many of the lines rhyme instead of the blank verse of most of his other plays. Though the blank verse *is* pretty sometimes."

Lucy laughed softly to herself as she read. Though she had read the play so many times that she had most of the lines memorized, she never tired of reading how Puck – mischievous boy – led Demetrius around the forest, pretending to be his enemy, Lysander. She read the little elf's lines aloud as he taunted Demetrius,

> "Thou coward, art thou bragging to the stars,
>
> Telling the bushes that thou look'st for wars,
>
> And wilt not come? Come, recreant; come, thou child;
>
> I'll whip thee with a rod: he is defiled
>
> That draws a sword on thee."

The girl forgot her troubles as she lost herself in the old story. For an hour she read, murmuring aloud some lines that she loved, and skipping over some passages in her hurry to reach favorites.

Then, suddenly, starting up, she closed the book, tossed it on the bed, and was at the door in an instant. She had heard footsteps on the stairs, and remembered that she was waiting for her brother.

Lucy opened the door eagerly, but her face fell as she saw an elderly man tapping his gold-tipped cane in front of him as he slowly maneuvered his way up the narrow steps.

She closed the door again, but only for a moment. Then, as she heard the gentleman step into his room, which was next to hers, she opened the door again and hurried downstairs, as fast as she could without losing her lady-like manner, and eagerly inquired of the man at the desk once again, whether he had any news of her brother.

"No, Miss Wilson," he began, looking kindly at the young anxious face before him, "I am very sorry, but I have been asking everyone who comes through, and none has heard of Mr. Wilson."

The hotel door opened, and Lucy turned hopefully to look, but it was only one of the Union lieutenants. He bowed slightly, taking his hat off as he did so, and she gave a nod that she had to work hard at to keep from being frigid. Turning back to the hotel manager, she said politely, "Thank you, If you find out anything – Anything! – please send up a note to my room."

She was about to leave when the soft voice of the officer behind her was heard, "Miss Wilson."

Lucy turned slowly, and looked at him questioningly. His brother officer threw open the door and strode into the entryway.

"Miss Wilson, I have something to tell you," the first officer spoke gently, and Lucy began to feel alarmed. The manager came out from behind the desk and stood slightly behind and to the side of her.

"Is it – is it about my brother?" she asked slowly, her head whirling with pictures of what could have happened.

"Well – yes, it's – " but he was interrupted by the other lieutenant who burst out, "*Your brother,* Miss, has been arrested as a spy, and is being held in prison."

Lucy felt dizzy, and realized vaguely that she was going down. The hotel manager caught her and through a haze she heard the officer who had come in first exclaim angrily, "How *could* you, Stephens!" then all went black.

A few drops of cool water sprinkled Lucy's forehead, and then she felt a motherly hand place itself on that part of her face. She forced her eyes open and heard once again the angry tones of the lieutenant who had entered first.

"Stephens! I told you not to do that! If you had listened to me we might not have a fainting case on our hands. I want you to get out and stay out."

Lucy stiffened as she remembered all that had happened, and heard a gentle woman's voice murmur, "That's all right, honey. You'll be fine. Don't worry about anything."

The girl turned her eyes upward, and beheld the face of a woman she had seen but briefly working around the hotel. She supposed she was the housekeeper.

"Is she all right, dear?" a man behind her asked. Lucy couldn't turn her head to look at him, as she was lying in a sofa, but she recognized the voice of the manager, and guessed correctly that the woman was his wife.

"Oh yes, of course she's all right," the woman reassured him, "in just a few minutes she'll be as well as ever."

Lucy shifted her position so that she was more upright, leaning against the back of the couch, and saw the two Union officers standing across the room.

"Richard!" she whispered.

Sullenly, the officer who had broken the news on her so harshly left the hotel, closing the door with a bang. The other lieutenant came nearer the couch and looked at the girl anxiously.

"My brother!" she exclaimed, sitting up straight now, "What has happened?"

The officer dropped his gaze to the floor, "I'm sorry to tell you, Miss Wilson," he said quietly, "but everything Stephens told you is true. We caught your brother doing some spy work, and of course, had to take him. I – I'm sorry that – " and he stumbled to a halt.

Lucy bent her head and turned a little away from him. "Where is he?" she asked.

The lieutenant sat in a chair next to the sofa, then answered, "he's in the prison. We have taken some of the cells for our own use."

"Like you have everything else in this town," the woman next to Lucy exclaimed indignantly.

"I hope not everything," the young man said with a faint smile.

"What is going to happen to – to him?" Lucy faltered, turning still farther away as she bit her lip and clenched her hands tightly together.

"Do you know what the usual sentence for spies is?" the lieutenant asked in a very low voice.

"N-no, at least, I don't think so – Oh! Don't tell me! I can't – bear – it!" and she bounded off the couch, lifted her skirts, and almost ran to the stairs.

In ascending the stairs, Lucy did not hold her skirts quite high enough, and so narrowly escaped from several falls by catching hold of the railing. However, she reached her room safely, and closing and locking the door, she quickly shed her hoops and flung herself down on the bed in a fit of sobs.

Awaking several hours later, she realized she must have cried herself to sleep, and wondered if the officer was still downstairs. Looking at a small clock, however, she shook her head, knowing it was very improbable after so long a time.

But not wanting to remain by herself in her room, tormented by thoughts of her brother in prison, the girl washed her face, straightened her clothes, and smoothed back her long black hair, then went slowly downstairs. To her surprise, the officer was there, and he stood as she entered, holding out his hand to seat her.

Lucy hesitated, then uncertainly accepted his assistance, and as she settled into a chair, she managed to say a bit teasingly, "I've always heard that all Northerners were rough and unmannerly. Are you the exception that proves the rule?"

The corner of his mouth went up, and he shook his head, "I wouldn't say that all Northerners are unpolished," he told her, "but I cannot truly say I am a Northerner, though I do fight for their cause. I was born and raised in Georgia."

Lucy's back became straighter than before, if that were possible, and her face drew into an angry frown. "Traitor!" she hissed, turning away from him, her fists clenching.

The young officer was not startled. He had expected a reaction like this, but had found no reason to keep his birthplace a secret.

"How can you – how *dare* you desert your own family like that!" she exclaimed, "Even General Lee wishes that we had stayed with the Union, but *he* wouldn't fight against his family!"

"That is where I believe General Lee is wrong," the young man said quietly.

"Of *course* you believe General Lee is wrong, you – you Northerner!" Lucy said as scathingly as possible.

She stood up, and the officer jumped to his feet. "Family," she said, "family honor is far more important than anything else. No matter what you believe yourself, there should be no cause to turn against your own relatives. If you cannot stand and uphold your family's beliefs, you are a traitor."

Lucy had not looked him in the eyes once during this speech, and now she turned without looking to see the effect of her words on him. her back straight as a ramrod, she marched up the stairs without looking back.

Once she had reached her room, however, she remembered that she had not asked him what would happen to Richard. "It is too late to go back down now," she told herself, "I'll have to ask him some other time – that is, if he isn't too angry with me for speaking out like that. I can't ask the other lieutenant. He would be – " and she shivered, "I'm afraid of him. He is too harsh – no, more than harsh, he is cruel. Maybe the Colonel in charge? I'll have to find him some day when he's not out."

She asked for her supper to be sent up, and soon it came, brought by the same woman who had helped her when she had fainted. "How are you doing, dear?" the woman asked kindly, "I hope you are feeling better."

"Yes, thank you," Lucy replied, softening under the gentle gaze of the motherly woman.

"Do you know that Lieutenant Johnston has been waiting downstairs for you? He said that he wanted to be there in case you had any more questions about your brother."

"Is his name Lieutenant Johnston?" Lucy asked, "I didn't know. But I do know he was down there, for I was also down only five minutes ago. Is he still there now?"

"No, he left just as I was coming up. I saw him go out the door. Was he able to answer all of your questions?"

"No, I forgot to ask. You see, I became angry over something he said, and left without remembering the reason I came."

"Indeed! He doesn't seem to be a man who would say unkind things," the woman said in surprise.

"No, he said nothing unkind or ungentlemanly," Lucy hastened to say, afraid of putting the wrong impression on the hostess.

At this the woman seemed even more confused, but she did not ask any more questions. Leaving the tray with Lucy, she left the room and her steps were heard heavily on the stairs.

Lucy ate her supper slowly, but when she had eaten most of it, thoughts of her beloved brother choked her so much that she couldn't finish. So she sent the tray down, and quickly got ready for bed, hoping sleep would cut off her unhappy thoughts.

Chapter 16

Waking up early had never been so easy for Raymond as it was on that Monday morning. His eyes flew wide open, and he jumped out of bed at the first sound of his alarm. Stretching, he took a long drink of water before sitting back down on top of his blankets to read his Bible.

After reading a good portion of the Scriptures, he got ready for the day as quickly as possible and hurried downstairs to make breakfast. Soon his father was beside him, assisting in the final preparations before they sat down to eat.

"You seem extremely excited today, son," Mr. Vincent commented, his eyes searching Raymond's face, "what is it?"

"Do you think Mr. Elliot will let us go through the time machine today?" Raymond asked eagerly.

Mr. Vincent shook his head smilingly, "Raymond," he said with a chuckle, "you seem to have completely forgotten that today is Monday."

"What does that have to do with it?" Raymond asked confusedly.

"What do we usually do on Mondays?" his father returned, still smiling.

"I don't know – nothing important, I don't think. We just work, and – Oh!" Raymond broke off with a gasp and a laugh, "You're right, Dad. I completely forgot that we've got to work today. Too bad, I guess we won't get to go all week."

"Couldn't we go in the evenings, after work?" Mr. Vincent suggested.

"I guess we could," Raymond nodded, "but I don't think Thomas and Susanna will be able to come then. I know we still don't know much about their family. But it seems to me from what they said that their mother isn't – " he paused and took a deep breath, an expression of pain quickly flitting across his face, "isn't feeling too well, for whatever reason, and Susanna has to take care of their younger siblings."

Mr. Vincent nodded. He had understood his son's pause at the thought of a mother not feeling well, for that was how it had started with his own wife, the year before. He knew his son was still suffering from the effects of her death – not to say that he himself wasn't.

"I think you're right," he agreed, "but why don't you want to go without the Jacksons?"

"I don't know," Raymond admitted, "it just seems that since they're the ones we started going through the machine with, they should be the ones to share it with us all along."

"Good-bye, Daddy!" Nancy called, running down the hall and into her father's arms as he squatted down for a hug, "are you going too, Thomas? Why? You never used to."

"That was two whole years ago, that I didn't go to work with Daddy," Thomas laughed, catching his baby sister as she launched herself at him, "I'm surprised you even remember all the way back then. You were only three!"

"I'm almost six, Thomas," Nancy reminded him importantly.

"Oh yes, that's right!" he said, setting her on the floor again, "Well, I'll be back before dinner."

"But that's such a lo-ong time!" the five-year-old said sorrowfully, turning her dark eyes on her big brother reproachfully.

"I'm sorry, Nancy. I'll miss you," he told her, "but I'll make sure to play with you when I get back."

"Good!"

"Bye, Susanna!" Thomas called, looking past the little girl to the older one standing in the hall behind her.

"See you later," she called back, and as Danny peeked around the corner to wave, the father and son went out the door.

Nancy ran to the window and looked longingly out. Susanna, seeing this, ran up behind her and placed her arms around the child's shoulders, saying, "Nancy, sweetheart, won't you help me make lunch?"

Nancy's face immediately brightened at the thought of being allowed to cook. She took hold of her big sister's hand and marched into the kitchen.

The two girls were just in time to see Danny flash a soft punch at Edward's shoulder, and then turn and flee for his life. Edward absolutely *could* not keep studying his math lesson after that attack, so he pushed back his chair so fast it would have turned over had not his twin Jennie caught it, and whizzed around the corner in hot pursuit of his younger brother.

"Come on, Danny!" Florence called eagerly, looking for any sign of the mischievous boy, "don't let Edward catch you!"

"Get him, Edward, Get him!" Jennie laughingly called out, as Danny burst into the school room, followed by a growling Edward.

Charles laughed and skipped out of the way of his brothers before he was trampled.

Danny tried his best, and managed to get out of the school room once more without knocking more than two books and three chairs out of their places, but on the second time around the house, Edward reached out and grasped the younger boy by the arm.

"Now I've got you!" he exclaimed triumphantly, twirling Danny around, tripping him up, and lowering him to the floor. He sat on the younger boy, and growled in his most menacing tones, "Will you surrender?"

"I surrender!" Danny cried mournfully, after struggling unsuccessfully to throw off Edward's weight, "you're bigger than me, and you've got me – *now* – but I'll get you – SOMEDAY!"

Edward laughed good-naturedly, and let his little brother up.

Susanna and the other girls joined in the laugh, then Susanna said, "Now boys, it's time to study. Please wait until after lunch when school is over before you play any more wild games like that."

"All right, Susanna. Sorry."

"That's all right. One chase isn't too big a problem, especially since we are just starting school time now. But please – " and she lifted a hand, pointing to their desks, "don't forget that now it's time for school."

Both boys nodded and grinned, heading back to their desks. Their two sisters Jennie and Florence had fixed the books and chairs they had knocked out of place, and Charles was already at his desk. All five paid close attention to their work.

~   ~   ~

Lucy went downstairs as soon as she could the next morning and saw to her surprise that Lieutenant Johnston was there, and it seemed as if he had been waiting for her. He again rose as she entered, and seated her on a chair, himself sitting on another close by and looking at her closely.

She searched his face for any signs of resentment for the words she had spoken the day before, but saw none. Dropping her eyes to the restless hands in her lap, she asked in a low voice, "Can you tell me anything about my brother?"

The lieutenant now dropped his own eyes, though Lucy didn't notice since her own were down. "What do you want to know?" he asked carefully.

"I want to know anything – anything that has to do with him!" she exclaimed.

"I can tell you that he is being held in the prison in the town here."

"I know that already."

"Oh! Yes, you do. I told you."

"Well?" she asked, as he didn't say anything else for several seconds, "can't you tell me anything?"

"The reason we are keeping him there is because we caught him with spy papers."

Lucy drew a long breath and said, "I knew that too. You told me, but I had forgotten. I was too upset. But I should have guessed it anyway, from something he said – or really, something he didn't say."

"So you are not surprised."

"No, but this is not getting me anywhere. Please, if you can, tell me what is going to happen to him."

"He hasn't been tried yet."

"So you don't have any idea?"

Lieutenant Johnston waited several seconds, then, instead of answering, he asked, "Miss Wilson, do you want to send a note to your brother?"

"Oh, yes please! Would you take it to him?"

"Yes, I will, but Miss Wilson, please don't forget that your letter will most likely be read before it is delivered to him."

"I understand. Will you wait here while I write it, or shall I give it to you later when I see you again?"

"I'll wait here. I haven't anything to do yet today for another couple of hours."

Lucy went upstairs to her room and got out her writing case. After pausing for a moment to think, she wrote a message she knew her brother would understand and be grateful for, but one that she had no objection to anyone else reading. She folded it, she went back down to the room where the lieutenant was waiting.

"Here it is," she said, handing him the note, "who is going to read it?"

"I or Lieutenant Stephens will read it to make sure there is nothing important you are telling him, unless the colonel wants to read it."

"Oh, I am telling him some important things," Lucy said with a little smile.

He looked startled, then smiled, "I didn't mean that. I meant something that has to do with the war or spy information."

"I knew that was what you meant, but I couldn't say I'm not writing anything important to him."

He smiled again, then asked, "shall I take it to him now?"

"If you would. Oh, no wait a minute. Please would you read it yourself or have the colonel read it? I don't want Lieutenant Stephens to see it," she pleaded.

"Then I will. Have a nice day, Miss Wilson."

"Have a nice day? How?" her lower lip quivered, and she fled to her room. He shook his head, pulled his hat on firmly, and went out the door.

Once outside, he paused for a moment to read the girl's swirling handwriting.

Dearest Richard,

I miss you so! Never forget that I love you, dear brother. Please tell me if there is anything I can do for you. I have no ideas of anything that would help, and 'Alas, I am a woman, friendless, hopeless!' Do not worry about me, though, for I am safe in the hotel. Do not blame yourself for what has happened; I am proud to have a brother who is willing to serve his country. Will you tell me what you wish me to do while I am waiting for you?

Your Loving Sister,
Lucy

P. S. Do you wish me to write Father? L. W.

Lieutenant Johnston pressed his lips together tightly twice during the reading of the little note. The first time was when he read the quote from Shakespeare, 'Alas, I am a woman, friendless, hopeless!' and the second was when he read the last sentence. He knew that if the trial of her brother went the way those things normally did, she would not wait for her brother much longer. Spies were shot almost without exception.

Chapter 17

It was not until the next day that Lucy saw Lieutenant Johnston again. She wondered what Richard had said when he had been given the note, and hoped that he would write back, but the lieutenant was not to be seen until the afternoon of that day.

When she saw him, Lucy almost ran up to him. She had come downstairs on purpose to see if he would be there, and hoped he could tell her more of what she wanted to know.

"Miss Wilson! How are you doing?"

"I – I am fine, but what about my brother?"

"Your brother?" he pulled a paper out of his pocket and held it out to her, "here, you may see for yourself what he says."

"Oh thank you, sir! Please excuse me. I must go read it right away."

"Of course."

He bowed, and she ran back upstairs.

Dear Lucy,

I am sorry this happened. Please forgive me for putting you in this situation. Thank you for your kind words, saying that you are proud I was willing to serve my country. If you feel you must write our father, you may, I do not care. Are you sure you are not uncomfortable, darling? If you are, do not hesitate to send for some of the servants from home to take you back. You cannot do anything to help me, except keep brave and pray. Oh, dearest little sister! I love you so, and I wish for your sake this had never happened. But I know you will be brave.

Your Brother,
Richard

P.S. To counter your former quote from Shakespeare, dear sister, I recall another to show the first quote is not quite true: 'Yet know, my master, God omnipotent/Is mustering in his clouds on our behalf/armies of pestilence.' I am praying for you. R.W.

Lucy's tears were streaming down her cheeks as she finished reading the letter. She pressed his signature to her lips, then folded the paper, and kissed it again. Then she slipped it into the dresser drawer and, after washing and drying her face, she went slowly down the stairs, hoping the Union officer would still be there.

As the girl walked, she thought of the words in her brother's letter. "He says he knows God will help us. I don't feel that way. He is praying for me? Why? I should be the one praying for him, but I cannot. I never understood the way Richard felt about being a Christian. I wish I did, but how can I? I had forgotten that quote he found. I – I think – " but she had reached the bottom of the stairs and was in the doorway of the entry room, so her thought was left unfinished.

The lieutenant was gone, and she saw no one but an elderly gentleman in the room. In fact, he was the same one she had seen on the day she had discovered her brother missing. He nodded politely to her as she entered, but as she turned aside to speak to the manager, he continued reading his book.

"Excuse me, sir," she said.

"Yes, Miss Wilson? Is there anything I can do for you?"

"Yes, there is, if you would be so kind."

"What is it? Let me tell you," he went on, speaking in a lower tone and looking around the room to make sure no one overheard, "I and my wife would do anything for you now. We are staunch Confederates, and you with your brother in prison for spy work, we will help you all we can. Now," he continued, resuming his normal tone of voice as Lucy gave him a grateful look, "what do you need help with?"

"I would like to send a telegram to my father."

"Of course. Here – " he searched around the desk for a moment, then placed a paper before her, "is a piece of paper and here is a pencil. I will take it to the post office as soon as possible. I wish I could take it right away, but I have no one to leave at the desk at present."

"Thank you, sir. I don't need to have it sent right away. You are very kind."

Lucy bent slightly and picked up the pencil.

Dear Father, Richard has been put in prison by Union. Supposed to be spy. Will write letter. Love Lucy.

"There," she said, "thank you so much. I – " she stopped, unable to go on. Tears began to form in her eyes, and she lifted her head to look at the ceiling so that they might drain back behind her eyes and not fall. Finally she finished simply, "- thank you." Then she went back upstairs to her room.

Once in her room, she shut the door carefully and sat down on a chair to think. After a moment, she remembered Richard's note and pulled it out to read it again. Reaching the place where he had said all she could do was keep brave and pray, she said to herself, "I will try to keep brave for his sake, yes I will, but I do not know how to pray for him. Why did I never listen more closely when he tried to explain to me? Well I will try to see what I can find."

She reached into the bottom of her trunk and pulled out her Bible. Flipping through the pages aimlessly, she found nothing that would help, and finally closed the Book with a sigh.

~   ~   ~

After Lieutenant Johnston handed Miss Wilson her brother's note, he had left as quickly as possible. As he walked down the street he recalled the conversation he had had with her brother the day before.

"Richard Wilson," he had said, "a note from your sister."

Swinging open the door as he heard a short, quick breath from within, he handed the letter over into the eager hands that reached for it.

"I will be back in fifteen minutes with paper and a pencil in case you wish to send a return note."

"Thank you," Wilson had said, to his surprise, as he turned away and shut the door.

When he came back, he saw the prisoner sitting on the bed with his elbow on his knee and his hand over his eyes. After waiting a moment to see if he would look up, Johnston cleared his throat.

The man in front of him looked up then, and as the lieutenant handed him the papers and pencil he had brought, Richard Wilson nodded, saying, "thank you" again.

Lieutenant Johnston stayed just outside the door as the prisoner wrote his message. Then he heard Wilson call, "Lieutenant?"

"Yes?"

"Does my sister speak to you?"

"Sometimes."

"She asks you about me?"

"Yes."

"Would you mind – " he waited a moment, and finally Lieutenant Johnston made a motion for him to go on.

"Well, I know that at my trial if I am convicted, which of course I will be, I will be shot. That is always the sentence for spies."

Johnston nodded, "Yes, and?"

"And I am afraid for my sister. Would you mind not telling her that fact until I ask you to?"

Lieutenant Johnston thought of the girl who was waiting for her brother at the hotel. He hesitated a moment, and Richard Wilson lifted a hand beseechingly, then let it fall back to his side.

Finally the lieutenant spoke, "I will try. I cannot say for sure, because Miss Wilson has asked me that very question already, and I am sure she will ask again. When she asked, I avoided the question, and made her think of something else, but I do not know how many times I will be able to do that. Then again, I cannot speak for the colonel or the other lieutenant."

Richard handed him the note, "here. I know you will read it, but I do not mind. Thank you again for your kindness."

"Of course."

This was the reason Lieutenant Johnson left as soon as he had given Miss Wilson the note from her brother. He hoped to avoid a conversation concerning the fate of her brother.

"Miss Wilson! Telegram!" a voice sounded outside her door the next evening.

Lucy ran to open it, and took the envelope quickly from the messenger. Then she sat back down on the bed and opened the envelope quickly. Pulling the slip of paper out, she read,

Miss Lucy STOP Your father very ill STOP Did not tell him STOP What should I do STOP Lolly

Lucy let the telegram fall to her lap as she gazed off into the distance. She had thought nothing could get worse, but now? Lolly's telegram banished all hope she had left. Her father could do nothing to help his son as long as he was ill.

"I must ask Richard right away," she told herself, "but how can I get word to him? I cannot go out into the streets by myself, especially not with all of these soldiers around, and I don't know when Lieutenant Johnston will be back. I will write a letter, then go down and wait."

So she did. After writing a simple letter composed of only a few sentences that would tell her brother exactly what the situation was, she went downstairs to wait.

After waiting for half an hour, she decided to go upstairs to fetch her knitting. She sat back down on the chair when she had gotten it, and set her workbasket at her feet. After so many years of using fine embroidery thread, and expensive yarn, the girl was still not used to the coarse woolen yarn used for the soldiers' socks she had learned to knit as one way to support the war effort.

However, she stuck to her task, and soon was knitting mechanically as her thoughts flew off to her home where her father lay ill, and to the prison where her brother was being kept.

Before she knew it, the finished sock lay in her hands, and she realized she must start another. As she began to cast on, she heard the door open and close. Hopefully, she looked up, but was disappointed when she saw the colonel enter.

"At least it's not Lieutenant Stephens," she thought to herself, but at that moment, the dreaded lieutenant did enter. Lucy drew in a deep breath, and then hurriedly stuffed her knitting back into her basket. Hoping neither would speak to her, she stood up and walked to the stairs, trying not to show her fright.

Lucy breathed a sigh of relief as she reached her room safely without hearing a sound behind her. "I might as well eat and go to bed," she said to herself, "I won't dare go down for another hour, and by then it will be too late to ask him to take my letter. I will get up early tomorrow to see if I can catch him before he goes out."

~ ~ ~

The next day was Sunday, to Lucy's surprise. She had forgotten to keep track of the days of the week, and when she got downstairs, the motherly housekeeper asked, "Would you like to come to church with us, dear? I know you don't have anyone to go with."

Lucy hesitated, and the woman quickly explained, "Oh, I know you won't want to sit with us in the back, but we'll walk with you to church so you won't have to go alone."

"Yes, thank you. I would appreciate that," Lucy nodded, then she went back upstairs to change into more suitable clothes for going to church in.

At church, Lucy sat by herself in an empty pew. She tried to listen to the sermon, but didn't hear more than a few words at a time, for she was still thinking of her brother – and now her father too.

When the service was over, after the final hymn, Lucy turned around and saw Lieutenant Johnston in the back. He met her eyes, and she made a little motion with her hand, signifying she wanted to speak with him.

He nodded, and then turned away. Lucy understood that he couldn't reach her yet, but was sure that he would wait until she got outside before leaving.

When Lucy finally reached the door, the pastor reached out his hand to shake hers, and she placed her own within it. He bent nearer and spoke so only she could hear, "We are praying for you, Miss Wilson."

Lucy started, and stared at him in astonishment. What was he talking about? How did he know her name? Did he mean – but no, how could he have heard?

"Yes, I do know of your troubles, Miss Wilson," the pastor explained, "We are praying for your brother, and also for you."

Lucy gave him one more incredulous look, then smiled slightly and nodded.

The smile stayed in place as she walked across the grass in front of the church, where people were milling about, talking. A moment later, she felt a presence at her side, and heard a male voice saying, "Miss Wilson, did you wish to speak with me?"

Lucy looked up to see Lieutenant Johnston standing near her. The smile she had been wearing died from her lips as she remembered what she had needed to ask him.

He was waiting, and she forced herself to nod, and hold out her hand for him to take. "How do you do, Lieutenant Johnston," she said, "yes, I did wish to ask you something."

She thought she saw something that looked like worry in his eye, and he released her hand.

"But if it isn't possible – " she began quickly and apologetically.

He held up his hand, "No, forgive me. I didn't mean anything. What can I do for you?"

Lucy pulled the note to her brother out of her reticule. She had brought it with her in hopes of finding the lieutenant at church.

"Would you mind taking another note to my brother?"

"Certainly not!"

"Oh, thank you! If it is not too much trouble, couldn't you take it to him at the earliest convenience? I need his advice about something, and it is very urgent. You see – but no, you will read the note anyway, then you will understand. Please excuse me, sir."

"May I walk you back to the hotel?"

"No, thank you, but I will walk with a friend," Lucy said, drawing a little farther away from him. "I hope you have a nice day."

"I will take the note to your brother right away," he promised.

Friday morning, even before breakfast, Thomas called Susanna into his room. She came quickly, wondering what he wanted to say.

"Good morning, Susanna," he said, "Raymond texted me today – " he broke off for a moment as his sister caught her breath, but she motioned for him to go on, so he finished, "he wants to know if we can come this afternoon."

"Come – where? Through the time machine?"

"Yes. What do you think?"

Susanna couldn't say no. Not with her adored brother sitting there in front of her looking so eager, so she nodded her head slowly and said, "Let's go then, if Mommy and Daddy say we may."

"Oh Susanna! Do you mean that?"

"Yes, I'll be happy to go with you," she said with a smile. Somehow the idea of the time machine didn't seem so forbidding just now.

"That's great! Then we'll ask Mommy and Daddy and go this afternoon."

"If they say yes."

Thomas nodded, "If they say yes."

Chapter 18

Their parents did say 'yes,' and Thomas was elated. He came home from work to eat lunch, and decided he could take the rest of the day off. So as soon as the family was done eating, he hurried Susanna out of the house before she had a chance to protest.

Raymond met them at the door, and explained that his father and Mr. Elliot would be there in a few minutes. In fact, right as he said that, Mr. Vincent's car pulled up near the door, and the two men jumped out.

"Let's hurry," Raymond pleaded, "I can't wait!"

"I feel the same way," Thomas nodded, "I'm just starved for the time machine."

Mr. Elliot and Mr. Vincent laughed, but they did hurry. "You go this time," Mr. Elliot nodded at Raymond's dad, "I'll stay out and work the machine."

"All right, that's fine with me. How long are we going to stay there?"

"Oh – say half an hour again," Mr. Elliot proposed, "It isn't a good idea to stay too long without having any contact with me."

"Okay. We'll do that."

Mr. Elliot pressed the button on the time machine, and then swung the door open. The group of four went through the door, and Susanna turned to see as it closed behind them. She could not repress a shiver, but told herself, *"it's too late to do anything now. I must keep going and not think about it."*

As they neared the graveyard on their way through the town, Raymond told his father of Thomas's joke of the day before. This time Susanna was able to laugh with the others from the very beginning.

When they got closer to the little church that was beside the graveyard, they saw a few people standing out on the lawn talking.

"I wonder if there is some event today," Thomas said, half to himself.

No one answered, and they walked farther into town, passing a few blue-coated soldiers standing in the streets. Then, up ahead of them, they saw a crowd of people in front of the church. "This is interesting," Raymond commented, "I wonder why both churches had people in front of them?"

"I don't know," Mr. Vincent answered, "but we can find out."

"You mean we could ask someone?" Raymond questioned.

"Yes."

Thomas had already gone, with Susanna at his side, up to a woman who was standing alone.

"Why are there people at the church?" he asked.

The woman gave him a strange look, "it's Sunday, that's why, young man. If you don't know what good Christian people do on Sundays, you'd do well to find out!" she turned with a huff, and walked away.

Thomas stared after her, then he regarded his sister in perplexity, "It's not Sunday, Susanna, it's Friday! What did she mean?"

"You didn't seem to have much success," Mr. Vincent chuckled, as he and Raymond joined the brother and sister.

"I don't understand," Thomas said in confusion, "she said it was Sunday."

The Vincents stared at him, "that doesn't make sense," Raymond began.

"I think it might," Susanna said slowly, and they all looked at her in surprise, "You all must know that every year the days of the week are different than they were the year before. I mean, one year you might have your birthday on a Tuesday, and the next year it would be on a Wednesday. I guess in eighteen sixty-three, the days of the week were two days ahead of those in two thousand twenty-four."

"Hey, you're right!" Thomas exclaimed, "now it makes sense. I never thought of that."

Susanna laughed, "you didn't have much time to think of it, Thomas. I'm sure if you had waited a while, you would have figured it out."

"Maybe, but I'm not so sure about that."

"Look, there's Lucy Wilson!" Raymond exclaimed, nodding in the direction of the girl.

His companions followed his gaze, and saw their acquaintance standing next to a Union lieutenant.

"That's strange," Thomas murmured, "why would she be talking to a Union soldier?"

"I have no idea," Raymond said, "Oh!"

"What?" his father asked.

"Look! She's giving him something!"

"Yes, she is," Susanna said, "it looks like a piece of paper."

"What do you think it could be?" Thomas questioned.

"Maybe she's a spy," Raymond suggested.

"Seriously? That's ridiculous!" Thomas exclaimed, "if you had heard how she talked about the Union soldiers as if she hated them!"

"We did," Raymond reminded him.

"Oh! Yes, you did. I forgot."

"See? She's leaving him now," Susanna said.

"He's watching her," Raymond noticed.

"Neither of them are smiling," Mr. Vincent commented.

"Do you want to go talk to her?" Thomas suggested.

"Oh, yes, lets!" Susanna agreed.

So the foursome walked in the direction of the girl. She was evidently looking for someone; scanning the crowd of churchgoers, and didn't notice them until they were almost beside her.

"Miss Wilson," Susanna said, "how nice to see you again."

"Oh! Miss Jackson. I didn't see you before."

"No, we – go to a different church," Susanna hesitated, not wanting to go into the whole discussion in public. She held out her hand, "we came up when you were talking to the Union officer and recognized you, so we decided to say hello before moving on."

"Hello Miss Wilson," Thomas said, "here are two people you haven't met before – at least, you haven't been introduced, though you have seen Raymond here. Do you remember him? He's the one your brother thought was a spy, and his father – " he broke off as Miss Wilson drew in a breath at the word 'spy.' Her lip began to tremble, and her eyes had just a suspicion of tears in them.

"Oh, forgive me," she said, "I don't mean to be so – well – but my brother has just been captured by the Union soldiers as a spy, and – " she bit her lip and then finished, "well, that is why I was talking to Lieutenant Johnston. He is going to take a note to Richard. Oh, I don't know why I ran on like that, telling you everything; please excuse me, I must go." And she walked quickly away.

The Jacksons and Vincents stared at each other without a word. Then Susanna looked behind her at Lucy Wilson's retreating figure and suddenly her own eyes filled with tears. Thomas looked down at his sister and saw, and then threw an arm around her waist, "what's the matter, Susanna?" he murmured.

"I'm – sorry, it's – just that I was thinking – you know what happens to spies!"

Thomas nodded seriously, "they're shot."

"Yes, and then Lucy Wilson – Oh Thomas, if it were you!"

"But it's not me, Susanna."

But then, suddenly, a heavy hand grasped Thomas's shoulder and dragged him away from his sister.

"Spy!" a hard voice exclaimed, and they all turned to behold Lieutenant Stephens, who had been so suspicious of the three young people on the first day they had been through the time machine.

The lieutenant had a firm hold on Thomas's shoulder and was saying, "Now, all of you! Come with me or it will be the worse for you! I knew you must be spies on the very first day I saw you, and now I'm sure of it. Why else would you be talking to the spy Wilson's sister? March now! In front of me, straight to the prison!" The man began to draw his gun.

Thomas shot a look at his sister, and fought to break free, but at nineteen he had not yet gained his full strength, and Lieutenant Stephens was a man in his mid-thirties with strong muscles, hardened by years of army training.

Suddenly Raymond's fist shot out and hit the man on the forehead. That loosened his grip, but soon he had a firm hold again, using both hands, instead of his gun, which he seemed to have forgotten for the moment.

Thomas threw a look over his shoulder for a split second, then panted out, "Mr. Vincent! Take – Susanna – " Mr. Vincent caught Susanna by the arm and started to hurry her away, but she pulled back and gasped out, "Thomas!"

"Susanna, you must come with me!" Mr. Vincent ordered, "right away. It will be easier for the boys if you aren't there to slow them down." He pulled harder on her arm, and finally she fled with him.

A young boy of about thirteen suddenly appeared in front of them and held up his hand, "Come!" he exclaimed, "you can't go down the street with the bluebellies all around! I'll show you the back way, and you can tell me where you want to go."

Mr. Vincent nodded, "thank you," and pulling Susanna along with him, he followed the boy behind a few buildings into a back street that was empty.

~   ~   ~

Lieutenant Stephens was shouting, "Someone help me with these spies!" but the crowd of churchgoers was silent. They moved in closer around the three struggling men and watched, but did not do anything to help either way.

A couple of blue-coated soldiers came running, but the crowd thickened purposely and made it hard for them to get closer. They began to push and shove their way through the throng in answer to the cries of their officer.

Thomas had broken free, only to see that Raymond was caught instead. Both boys fought hard, and finally Thomas put his leg behind the lieutenant's legs, and Raymond wrenched himself free, both boys giving the officer a hard shove that sent him tumbling onto the grass, tripped over Thomas's leg.

The crowd parted for the two young men to run away, and then closed as Lieutenant Stephens leaped to his feet and tried to run after them.

"Let me through!" he shouted angrily, "I'll have you all arrested for this!"

A ripple of laughter flowed over the crowd; there were too many of them to hold in the prison of the town, and so many that it would hamper the movements of a small cavalry unit that hoped to move quickly.

As Thomas and Raymond ran out of the crowd, there were several quiet cheers for them. Once they were completely free, they slowed and looked around, "Where did your dad and Susanna go?" Thomas asked as he gasped for breath.

"I don't know, but here come some soldiers after us!" Raymond exclaimed, "we've got to go somewhere."

"Not down the street! There are too many soldiers there."

A boy leaped out from behind a house and exclaimed, "quick, come with me! I'll show you where your pa and sister are!"

Raymond and Thomas quickly jumped after him, and he led them around several houses and through a couple of tight places until they found themselves face to face with Mr. Vincent and Susanna.

Susanna ran to her brother and he hugged her tightly, "Oh Thomas!" she cried, "I'm so glad!"

"What are you glad about?" he asked teasingly, "that we got into a fight?"

"No, that you got out of it!" she said. And she did smile a little.

"Now where d'you want to go?" the boy asked.

"We want to get to that door in the brick wall just on the outside of the town," Mr. Vincent told him.

"I know where you mean. I'll get you there right enough."

"Thank you."

The boy turned abruptly and led them off around corners and across a couple of open places, finally reaching a point where they could see the door.

"Now I guess you can find your way just fine from here," the boy laughed, as he turned to go.

"Wait," Mr. Vincent stopped him, and the boy turned around questioningly, "I just wanted to thank you for what you did."

"Aw, it weren't nothing," the boy said, "When I saw you trying to get away from that soldier, I just had to help. I've got two brothers in the army – Confederate of course – or you could count it three, as my sister's got a sweetheart fighting too, and he'll be my brother sometime if he ain't killed. Anyhow, I'd do anything to help whip those bluebellies. I just wisht I could be a soldier too," he finished wistfully.

"What's your name?" Susanna asked.

"Matthew Maxwell," he answered, grinning at her.

"Maxwell!" she exclaimed, "you're Lily and Bessie's brother?"

"Yeah, and Alice's brother too, and Ben and Jack's, and Carter's – and almost Paul's," he added with a chuckle.

"Paul is Bessie's fiancé, right?" Susanna said.

"Yeah, he is. What's fee-ahn-say mean, anyhow?"

They all burst out laughing, "Fiancé means the one she's going to marry," Susanna told him, "but how did you know to say yes, if you didn't know what it meant?"

"Oh, he's Bessie's everything," Matthew informed her, "Bessie and Lily call him all sorts of names. Sometimes he's her sweetheart, sometimes he's her beau, sometimes he's her young man – why can't a fellow be his own self instead of being called a girl's something? Oh, they have lots of names for him. When he first started seeing Bessie they called him Mr. Finn, and a couple o' times Pa's called him a spark; 'course, he does look like one. He's got the reddest hair you ever seen on anyone. But never mind. You'd better light out before those soldiers decide to search these here parts for you. So long!" and he ran away.

"Oh! Isn't he funny?" Susanna giggled.

"Yeah, Paul sure does look like a spark," Thomas imitated, "his hair is red as fire!"

"Thomas, you know that 'sparking' is another word for courting."

"Yes I do, but I like Matthew's way of putting it better," he laughed again.

"Sorry to interrupt," Mr. Vincent said, "but Matthew was right, we'd better get back through the door before anyone decides to come here to look for us."

The three young people sobered down, and they all hurried to the door. Raymond opened it, and this time they didn't throw themselves down on the grass as before. Instead, they stood near the door, eagerly waiting for it to open.

It was barely thirty seconds before it did open, and the inventor's smiling face was seen.

"So you're back safely," he said.

"Barely," Raymond told him, "we almost got captured as Confederate spies."

"Really! Well 'all's well that ends well,' I'm glad you're all right."

"We've got to get home," Thomas said, "good-bye."

"Good-bye, General," Raymond said, as he had the other day.

Thomas laughed, waved a hand, and walked with his sister back toward their home.

Chapter 19

Lieutenant Johnston did not hear any of the uproar. After Lucy left him, he watched her walk away for a few seconds, then he made his way back to the prison. On the way he read the girl's note to her brother and realized what an urgent situation she was in.

Dear Richard, she wrote,

I sent a telegram to Father, and Lolly sent one back saying Father is very ill. Lolly asked what he should do, and I ask the same. I do not know any more than that Father is very ill, but Lolly asked if he should even tell Father, so I am afraid it might be dangerous. I am very worried, Richard, with both you and Father in danger. Please tell me what you wish me to do and what I should tell Lolly.

Your Loving Sister,

Lucy

The lieutenant frowned. The poor girl. This was much more trouble than she should be forced to handle. The colonel would say that it was war, but still, Johnston couldn't help but feel sorry for the young girl who was compelled to carry the load thrust upon her. At least she still was able to send notes to her brother and ask for his advice, but how long would it be before she was brotherless? And perhaps fatherless too.

He had reached the prison by this time, and entered. "Wilson!" he said, "a note from your sister. It is very important, and I will take back a reply right away if you will write one."

Richard quickly took the paper held out to him and read it. He groaned, and reached for the paper and pencil the lieutenant had given him before. He scribbled down a message and held it out to Lieutenant Johnston, "Please, take it to her as soon as possible."

"Right away."

"Thank you."

Dear Lucy,

Telegraph Lolly to tell us exactly what is wrong with Father. Stay at the hotel for now. When we have learned about Father, I will know what you should do. I am still praying for you,

With Love,
Your Brother,
Richard

Lieutenant Johnston read as he walked quickly back to the hotel where he and Miss Wilson were both staying. He found her waiting for him in the entrance room.

"Do you have an answer?" Lucy asked eagerly.

He held it out to her silently and waited while she read it, then asked, "Is there anything else I can help you with, Miss Wilson?"

"No, not right now. You have already done so much, thank you."

"You are welcome to any poor assistance I can give, Miss Wilson."

~ ~ ~

After Thomas and Susanna left, Raymond and his father told their friend all that had happened while they had been in the nineteenth century.

"Whew!" Mr. Elliot exclaimed as they finished, "that sure was a close call. I'm really thankful you got through safely."

"Yes," Mr. Vincent agreed, "let's thank God right now for protecting us." The three men bowed their heads for a brief moment of thankfulness.

When they raised them again Raymond said worriedly, "I'm afraid that the Jacksons won't come anymore, after those two terrible experiences."

"Maybe not, but Susanna didn't seem as upset over this one as she was the first time," his father reminded him.

"That's right, Dad. I think Matthew helped a lot with that," he chuckled, "you should have heard him, Mr. Elliot, he was – oh! So funny."

That night, however, as Raymond got into bed, he lay awake for a while, thinking. "Dad was right, she didn't seem to be as upset this time," he said aloud, "but what Matthew said probably took her mind off the scary parts of our visit. Once we mention going through the machine again, she'll remember, and refuse."

He rolled over on his side, "Now, just when I found two wonderful friends who prove that Dad and I are not the only ones out there who believe the way we do, am I going to lose them? I never knew anyone like them." His thoughts suddenly took a slightly different turn, "I haven't even met their mother. Maybe she'll be nice – like – Mom."

The young man's eyes filled with tears as he thought of his beloved mother. He closed them, and lay quietly, finally drifting to sleep.

~   ~   ~

Saturday morning, Raymond received a text from Thomas that asked, "Are we going through the time-travel machine today?"

"No," Raymond texted back, "Dad says it's too dangerous, after our last experience. He is sure the whole brigade of soldiers will be looking for us, and we'll be too easily found in these strange twenty-first century clothes!"

"I understand. He's right."

"I think so too," Raymond agreed.

After that, no more texts passed between the two friends for several hours. Later in the day, however, Raymond received a message from Thomas that made him shout excitedly and run to find his dad.

"Dad, Dad!" he called, "where are you?"

"I'm upstairs, Raymond. What do you need?"

Raymond ran up the stairs three at a time and burst into his father's room where he found the man sitting at the computer.

He turned as his son entered and said with a smile, "hello, Raymond, you certainly seem excited about something. What is it?"

"I just got a text from Thomas asking if we can go to church with them tomorrow," Raymond explained.

"Really! I wouldn't mind going, but I suppose it's no use asking if you want to go," he said with a straight face, "you like the church we go to fine."

"Dad!" Raymond knew his father was joking.

"I know, don't worry, of course we can go."

"Oh Dad! Thank you so much!"

"Well I'm glad you want to go, because I would like to go too," Mr. Vincent said seriously, "but would you mind telling me why you are so extremely excited about it? I mean, I know the church we go to isn't as good as we wish it were, but it seems like there's more to it than that, isn't there?"

Raymond walked over and sat on the corner of his father's desk. "Dad," he said, "you understand, don't you? I've never known anyone like Thomas and Susanna. I always thought we were the only ones in the whole world who believe the way we do – well maybe not the only ones – but you know what I mean. I've never known any other Christians who are as much like us as the Jacksons are. Even if their church isn't any better than ours, we can at least get to know the whole family."

Mr. Vincent stood up and put a hand on his son's shoulder, "I understand, son. You don't need to try to explain it any better than you already did. It's the fellowship you're longing for – fellowship of other believers. I knew what it was like once, when I was young, and I miss it badly; but I know you have been starved for it. I am sorry. I can't tell you how many times I've tried to find other families like us and have failed. Maybe you're right. Maybe the Jacksons are the right ones. Please, tell Thomas yes, we will come."

Raymond's arms went around his father in a bear hug, and they stayed clasped together for several seconds, then the young man stepped back with a smile, "thanks Dad. I knew you would understand."

Chapter 20

So on Sunday, at the time Thomas had told them to be there, the Vincents drove into the Jacksons' driveway and walked up to the front door. Raymond caught a glimpse of a child's face peeking through the window, and when his father knocked, the door was opened by a boy of about eleven.

"Hello," he said, "I'm Danny!"

"Well, hello Danny!" Raymond said, "where are Thomas and Susanna?"

"Here I am," Thomas answered, coming out of the library, which was to the right of the door.

"Hi, Thomas! Thanks for inviting us to church with you," Mr. Vincent said.

"Hello, Mr. Vincent; hello, Raymond. Thank you for coming. You are going to stay for evening services also, aren't you?"

"Of course!"

"Hello, Susanna!" Mr. Vincent called, as he spotted the girl leading a five-year-old by the hand as she entered the hallway.

"Hello, Mr. Vincent; hi, Raymond. This is Nancy. I assume Danny has already introduced himself."

"He has," Raymond's father said with a smile, "and how old are you, Nancy?"

Nancy grinned, "five!"

"Five! Really?"

"Yes!"

"Wow!"

Another girl came rushing through the library, "Susanna! I – oh! Sorry," and she cowered back a little, hiding behind one of the two tall pillars that bordered the entrance to the library.

"It's all right, Florence," Susanna reassured her, "this is Mr. Vincent and Raymond. Remember, we told you they were coming to church with us. Now what did you need me for?" and she placed an arm around her sister, who was about eight years old, and led her out of the room.

A boy and a girl in their very early teens peeked around the wall that connected the hallway to the kitchen, then walked slowly into the foyer, smiling at the newcomers.

"These are Jennie and Edward," Thomas explained, "they're twins," the two nodded and smiled.

Thomas turned to Jennie and asked quietly, "are you two ready to go?"

"Yes, we are," her twin answered for her.

"Okay, then Jennie, could you go check on Mommy please? Ask her if she's almost ready, and help her if she needs anything."

"All right," she skipped up the stairs, leaving Edward beside his oldest brother.

"Are you staying for evening church too?" the boy asked.

"Yes we are," Mr. Vincent answered.

"Great!"

Danny, who was still looking on, spoke up, "and you'd better like it, or – "

"Or what?" Raymond asked.

"Or you won't, that's all!" Danny finished, grinning.

This made everyone laugh, and then Thomas invited the Vincents to sit in the library until the rest of the family was ready.

As soon as they were seated, the father of the family came in.

"Daddy," Raymond said, "this is Mr. Vincent and Raymond."

The Vincents stood up and shook hands with Mr. Jackson, then all the men sat down to talk.

A few minutes later, Susanna came back with Florence, another boy a little older than Florence, who was introduced as Charles, and Nancy, who had run off almost as soon as her sisters had left. Then Jennie came downstairs and placed herself on a floor cushion next to her twin, nodding to Thomas's silent question.

Less than a minute later, Mrs. Jackson came slowly down the stairs and smiled a greeting to everyone in the library.

Thomas went through the introductions again, and as Raymond clasped the hand of Thomas and Susanna's mother he looked into her eyes and saw the same gentle look he had seen in his own mother's eyes a thousand times or more.

Thomas turned to look at his mother, "Everyone's ready to go, Mommy," he told her.

"Good," she replied, "let's get into the car then."

Raymond's eyes followed every move the woman made. He couldn't stop thinking how much she was like his own mother. He realized everyone was standing up and going to the door, but he couldn't make himself move.

Finally he dropped his eyes and rested his chin on his hand. Then he heard a voice close by, "You coming, Raymond?"

"Yes, I'm coming," he replied, as Thomas reached out a hand to pull him up.

"Good. We're ready to go."

The drive to church was short, and then the Vincents walked into the little church building with their friends. Before they had any chance to meet anyone, a man at the pulpit announced the opening hymn, and the Jacksons quickly found their seats, nodding right and left as their friends greeted them.

As the singing began, Raymond was once more amazed. He had never heard such singing except when he and his father went to a concert to see professional singers. He knew the song fairly well, as his mother had sung it to him when he was a child, and he and his father sang it together once in a while, but when he tried to sing the melody, he was thrown off a couple of times at the sound of Thomas, who was beside him, singing bass.

After a couple of songs, the song leader read the passage that day's text would be taken from, and then, after another song and a prayer, the pastor launched into his sermon, which was entirely based on the Bible.

After two and a half hours of church, there came a time for announcements, and another man, different from the song leader, the pastor, and the man who led the Lord's Supper, asked if there were any visitors. The man looked around the congregation, and then asked that a mike be taken to the Jacksons.

Raymond was somewhat surprised, but then Mr. Jackson passed the microphone to his oldest son and Thomas stood up, saying, "These are some friends of mine and Susanna's, Mr. Vincent, and his son Raymond."

Thomas sat back down as the rest clapped a welcome. Then followed a few more announcements, some prayer requests, and then a long prayer.

After that, they sang one more song and were finished. Thomas and Raymond were immediately besieged by young men who greeted the visitor and welcomed him enthusiastically.

"Are you staying for lunch?" one asked Thomas.

"We are, Jack. Are you coming for church at our house?"

"Well, I haven't asked Mom and Dad, but I didn't think there was a need. Don't we usually come?"

"Yes, but I hope nothing turns out you won't be able to come."

"So do I."

"Hey! You're Raymond, aren't you?" someone asked at Raymond's side.

"Yes," he turned with a smile.

"Welcome! I'm Noah McKeith."

"Hello, Noah; nice to meet you."

The two shook hands, and Noah asked, "So are you going to be at the Jacksons' for fellowship tonight?"

"Yes, we are."

"Good, then I'll see you there. Right now I've got to go. See? My sister's calling," and he nodded to a girl who was standing near the door waving at her brother.

"See you later, then," Raymond said, as Noah hurried away.

A few minutes later Jennie appeared at Thomas's elbow and pulled gently. She waited until he looked at her, then said, "It's time to eat."

"All right. Come on, Raymond."

After lunch was over and they got into the Jacksons' van, which the Vincents had ridden over in, Raymond sat quietly for a few minutes. Thomas was beside him in one of the middle seats, with Susanna on Thomas's other side, and the younger children were in the back seats.

Suddenly Raymond looked up and quoted,

"The little church of Long Ago was not a structure huge,

It had no hired singers or no other subterfuge

To get the people to attend, 'twas just a simple place

Where every Sunday we were told about God's saving grace."

Susanna leaned forward so she could see him around her brother and exclaimed, "that's Edgar A. Guest, isn't it? He's one of my favorite poets."

"Yes it is," Raymond nodded, "and you know, when I first read it, I thought all churches like that were long gone and impossible in today's world. Now I know I was wrong."

Mr. Vincent looked back from the front seat where he was sitting with Mr. Jackson, "You're right, Raymond. The Jacksons' church seems like the one my mother told me about when I was a boy – the one she said she used to go to when she was a girl. I also thought that kind of church was lost."

"I am glad we can prove it's not," Mrs. Jackson smiled, "but there actually are other churches with a simple, Christ-centered service around the country. We often travel around the states, and have been able to visit some of those churches."

Chapter 21

W hen they reached the Jacksons' house, everyone got out of the car quickly and rushed into the house. At least, all of the Jackson children did. Raymond didn't realize what was happening until almost everyone was inside. Mr. and Mrs. Jackson and his father were talking, still outside, but when he reached the house, all of the Jackson children were already in the house with their shoes off and their Bibles away. He heard sounds of pots and pans in the kitchen and saw the Jacksons rushing to and fro, so he walked down the hall toward that room.

"I'll put the lentils on!" Danny said, and for a moment Raymond couldn't see him, because he had disappeared behind the counter, but soon the boy came up again with a pot in his hands, and hurried to the pantry.

"I'll do the onions for you, ok Danny?" Jennie called after him.

"Okay!"

"Where's the lettuce?" one of the others asked no one in particular. Raymond couldn't tell exactly who was talking every time, but there were comments and questions and answers, banter and laughter, really every kind of conversation possible was heard in that kitchen.

"The lettuce? Check outside. It might be in the garage fridge."

"All right, I will!"

"Do you need help, Florence?"

"No thanks, I'm fine."

"Hey Thomas! Could you move out of the way for a second so I can get a knife?"

"Sure, for five dollars!"

"Don't have any with me today, couldn't you give me a knife on the house?"

"Oh Charles! A *knife* on the house? What in the world?"

"You told me 'on the house' meant for free, Jennie."

"Yes," and she burst into a giggle, "But – but – I didn't – didn't mean for anything except for food. 'On the house' usually is for restaurants."

"Well, you didn't tell me *that*."

"Sorry."

"Here, Charles. You can't have your knife 'on the house,' but I'll give it to you 'on the garage.'"

"Thanks."

"Susanna! Susanna? Thomas, where is she?"

"I think Nancy needed help with something. She should be here in a few minutes. What did you need?"

"Which kind of chicken are we supposed to make today?"

"Just pick something. I don't think she'll care. Did Mommy get inside yet?"

"Yes, but Susanna said not to ask her if possible."

"That's right. Anyway, I think she's going to rest for a bit so she'll be feeling fine when everyone gets here – Oh! Raymond, hello! Sorry, I forgot you were here."

Raymond shook his head. Once again he had heard the dreaded words saying that Mrs. Jackson was not feeling well. He pushed the thought out of his mind and smiled at his friend, "That's all right, Thomas. Is there anything I can help with?"

"I don't think so, we've done this so many times that we almost work automatically."

"Yes there is something he can do," Edward said, "He can get that glass bowl down for Florence. He ought to be tall enough. I can't because I'm cutting chicken and my hands are all messy. Why in the world did we put those bowls way up there anyway?"

"Because there wasn't any other space for them," Jennie reminded him, "all of the other cabinets are full."

Raymond saw Florence behind the island in the center of the kitchen. She was standing on a chair, but the little eight-year-old was still unable to reach the top shelves of the cabinets along the wall. He walked over to where she stood and she hopped off the chair, backing up several steps until she bumped into Charles.

"What's the matter, Florrie?" Charles asked in surprise.

"Nothing," she murmured, but stood staring at Raymond with wide, dark eyes as he reached for the bowl she had been trying to get.

"Is this the one you want?" he asked, handing it down to her. She reached for it timidly, nodding, then turned and hurried to the other side of the kitchen.

Edward leaned a little toward Raymond and whispered, "don't worry, she's just shy. In a couple of weeks she won't mind talking to you."

Raymond had already figured that was the case, but he shook his head and said, "What do you mean 'a couple of weeks?'"

"Well by then we'll have seen you several times, and she'll be used to your being here," the younger boy answered, a bit surprised.

"How do you know I'll be coming again?"

"Aren't you? What do you normally do on Sunday evenings?"

"Nothing really, but we were only invited this once. Maybe we can have your family over to our house sometime though."

Edward dropped his knife in astonishment and turned to fully face Raymond. He stared at him for a moment incredulously, then went off into a shout of laughter.

Raymond was confused. What had he said that was funny? But Edward calmed down after a few seconds and asked, "Do you really think you have to be invited to come to our house? What an idea! Don't you know that anyone can come on Sundays for church, and then drop in any other day, whether we're home or not?"

Raymond shook his head. "I see," he said, but he didn't really – not quite, "well, if Dad wants to I'd love to come again."

"Raymond!" Thomas called his friend over to where he was working and occupied his attention for a few minutes. Then the two young men heard a loud laugh and turned to look as Jennie's plaintive voice rent the air.

"Thomas!" she cried, and to Raymond's astonishment, her eyes were full of tears, several of which were coursing down her face. Her lips were in a pout, and she pointed accusatorily at her twin. "Edward was – he was laughing at me!" she said, her voice breaking.

Now, Raymond had been astonished before, but he was even more so when he saw Thomas's face break into a grin, and heard him give a chuckle.

"Was he, Jennie?" Thomas asked, "I don't blame him. I expect you asked him to in the first place anyhow." He looked at his guest's surprised face and laughed again. "Introducing Jennie, the actress of our family," he said, waving a hand in the girl's direction, "it's amazing to see what a couple of onions will do to making very real tears. Edward is her accomplice in this plot, as usual. I would guess she was trying to trick you, since that joke is too old to work on the rest of us."

Raymond looked back at Jennie and saw she was wiping away the tears on her sleeve. Beneath was a big smile, and a couple of giggles escaped loud enough for him to hear. He laughed, and the others joined in.

~   ~   ~

"The Davises are here!" Charles shouted, running into the kitchen where the older children were still talking.

"Nancy, could you go tell Mommy that someone's here, please?" Susanna asked. The child nodded, and climbed up the stairs.

Thomas and Susanna, Charles, Raymond, and the twins went out into the foyer to greet the guests.

Florence had her hand on the doorknob already, and turned to look as the others came in. "It's just Jack and Margaret," she said in a disappointed voice.

She opened the door before they even knocked, and then stood a little back as the came in, with her hands on her hips and her feet a little apart. She looked up at the brother and sister accusatorily. "Where are your mom and dad and Trevor and Cyril and Harold and Billy and Sophie and Rob and Wagon and – and – are Mr. Luke and Miss Angie and the baby coming too?"

Raymond's eyes widened as he heard the little girl reel off the long string of names with hardly a break. Everyone burst out laughing except Florence, and after a moment Jack Davis asked, "why didn't you just say 'the rest of the family,' Florrie? That would have been much easier."

"I don't know," a little crease of confusion appearing between her brows, "I just got started and couldn't stop."

They laughed again, and then Raymond asked, "are those all the names of the rest of your family?"

"Yes," Margaret nodded, "except Angie, she's Luke's wife, so she's in our family now, but she's not exactly one of our siblings. The baby Florence mentioned is theirs."

"But – what about the wagon?" Raymond questioned.

A chuckle passed over the group, and Jack laughed outright. Edward explained, "Oh, his real name is Carter, he's about my age. We called him Carter for a while, but a couple of years ago we boys started to shorten it to Cart, and then, well, you can see where Wagon came from."

Raymond grinned and nodded.

"So?" Florence asked, "what about *the rest of the family?*" she looked at Jack as she said this, and he laughed at her imitation.

"They'll be coming later. Dad's taking Mr. Lloyd to the airport. He has to fly to D.C. for a business meeting, and Mrs. Lloyd doesn't want to drive him because she's eight months pregnant, you know. Harold and Carter could have come, but they were in the middle of something at home, and by the time they're done Dad'll be back. Mama wanted the rest of the kids to wait, but she said we could come if we wanted. I don't know about Luke and Angie."

"The Hostlers are here!"

"So are the Starrs!"

"A-a-and now the Wallaces are too!"

"Is that the Wallaces? It looks like Mr. Anders' car."

"No, that's the Wallaces, see it has their bumper sticker."

"You're right."

From then on, people kept pouring into the Jacksons' house. The young men went downstairs to play the table games the Jacksons had there, and Raymond was soon in the midst of a challenging game of table tennis with a boy in his teens, who was named Steve Pitt.

The younger girls disappeared upstairs, and the older girls sat down in the library to talk.

"Okay, Susanna," Adele Hostler said, turning to her hostess demandingly, "who is this new boy?"

"Yes, Thomas didn't say anything about them in church, except that you were friends," Kitty McKeith nodded.

"How long have you known him?" Ann Starr asked.

"Where does he live?" Margaret wanted to know.

"How did you meet him?" Ann's younger sister Crystal questioned.

This was the question Susanna had been expecting, but she was still not prepared for it. In a panic, her mind roved over possible truthful answers. She heard pounding noises on the stairs and looked around, "here come the boys," she said.

A couple of younger boys accompanied by Edward and Danny turned away from the library and entered the kitchen, but the greater part of the group came into the library where the girls were sitting and Noah McKeith asked, "may we come in?"

"Of course!" came the chorus of girls' voices, greeting the boys and welcoming them. Most of the boys and young men stood leaning against the walls or pillars; a couple of them sat down on the floor, and one or two sat next to their sisters on the sofas. As Thomas was settling himself onto the arm of Susanna's chair, Margaret asked again the question, "Susanna was about to tell us how you met Raymond Vincent."

Thomas looked at his sister questioningly, and she tilted her head to the side murmuring pleadingly, "you tell, Thomas. I don't know what to say. We can't tell them everything."

"Stop whispering!" Ann teased, "we want to hear too."

Thomas looked at her, laughing. He glanced around the room and then leaned back so that the rocking armchair he was perched on tipped back alarmingly and Susanna sat up quickly, saying, "Thomas, please sit up, you'll tip us over!"

"Sorry," he laughed, leaning forward again, "well, in answer to the question of how we met Raymond," he paused for a moment, smiling teasingly around the room until several of his friends made impatient gestures, "well," he said again, "Susanna and I were walking down the street and she started crying – "

"Thomas!" Susanna exclaimed in horrified tones.

He grinned at her and continued, "she was upset because we were lost, and Raymond appeared out of the middle of nowhere and showed us the way home. So of course we were friends after that."

Exclamations of disbelief rippled across the room. Finally one of the girls voiced hers aloud, "Thomas," Margaret said, "what do you mean telling us such a story as that? First of all, Susanna would never cry over such a little thing as being lost in the streets, because you would be certain to get home sometime, and in the second place, you couldn't have possibly been truly lost. That sort of thing doesn't happen nowadays, what with all the GPS and map apps that I know you have on your phones."

Thomas was answering the girl, but Susanna barely heard, because at that moment Raymond, who was leaning against the bookshelf behind her chair murmured out of the corner of his mouth just loud enough for her to hear, "she's right, it didn't happen 'nowadays'."

Susanna turned to look at him to see if she had heard right, and when she saw she had, she turned back quickly, and bit her lip to keep from giggling.

"What did he –?" began Kitty, who had watched this little byplay, but then both girls' attentions returned to Kitty's brother, Noah McKeith, who exclaimed, "both of your phones at the same time? Impossible!"

"'Fact is stranger than fiction,' you know," Thomas shrugged.

"There wasn't any – " Susanna hesitated, trying to find the right word, "any frequency where we were. Our phones wouldn't do much at all. We couldn't call Mommy or Daddy either," she explained.

"My guess," Raymond broke in, "Is that their phones started working too hard, trying to find a signal, and then ran out of battery."

"Strange," Adele paused, "anyway, I've always wondered what it was like living back in the old days when there weren't any phones, and people had to rely on letters to be able to communicate. I guess for a few minutes, it was that way with you two."

Thomas and Susanna looked at each other, then at Raymond. Adele didn't know how close she was to guessing the truth.

"One thing I'm wondering," Steve Pitt began, "is how did Raymond know you were lost? I mean, you don't just walk up to someone in the street who looks – worried – and ask if they are lost."

This was a poser. What could they say to that? It would lead to even more uncomfortable questions if they were to tell how Raymond had followed the brother and sister around, listening to their conversations and virtually spying on them.

"Steve is right," Frank Garrold nodded, he was the oldest young man in the room, and was often looked to for an opinion on important questions. Just now, though, he was as confused as the rest of them.

Thomas looked at his sister, and in his eyes she read as plainly as words, "why did I ever even try to explain?"

They were rescued, then, though unintentionally, by Jennie, who came into the library and announced, "Daddy says 'time to eat,' everyone please come into the kitchen to pray."

This broke up the conversation effectively, and the whole group of young people stood and hurried to wash up and enter the kitchen as directed.

With a decided effort, Susanna, Thomas, and Raymond were able to keep the conversation away from the question of how they met for the rest of the day.

Chapter 22

During the week, while she was waiting for the letter from Lolly which would explain her father's condition, Lucy had several conversations with the Lieutenant Johnston. The first took place on the day after she sent the telegram Richard had requested.

"May I ask you a question, sir?" she asked, seeing Lieutenant Johnston sitting downstairs as she came up to him.

He jumped up, not having seen her as she entered, and seated her before answering.

"Most certainly, Miss Wilson," he replied, "though I cannot promise to be able to answer it."

"I wish to know – how it happened that you allowed yourself to be drawn away from your family and join the other side of the war?"

For some reason, looking into his eyes, Lucy felt that he seemed relieved. She wondered why, but didn't think any more about it as she listened to his answer.

"Why Miss Wilson," he said in faint surprise, "I had supposed I had answered that already. It was because I believed the Northern cause was more just. Was I not explicit enough? I am sorry."

"But I do not understand, sir. Have you so low an idea of family honor that you could walk away from your home to fight against them? How can you go against your family in such a manner?"

"It was hard. It was very hard, but I cannot go against what I believe. I have read in the Bible how Jesus said, 'He that loveth father or mother more than me is not worthy of me.' Since I believe that the Union is right, I ought not fight against it."

"I do not understand how the verse illustrates that, the Union is not God."

"No, most certainly not. What I mean is, God wishes me to do what is right. Another verse says 'If you love me, you will keep my commandments.' If I choose to do as my parents wish, even though I believe they are wrong, that means I love them more than what is right."

"It is impossible to love one's parents too much," Lucy demurred.

"In a way, yes. But I did not mean that. What I meant was, if I am so attached to my parents that I must turn from what is right to follow them, I would be doing wrong."

"But surely it is not such a great sin to fight for the Southern Cause, sir?" Lucy asked, looking up at him with a small, teasing smile.

He gave her a half grin, but it was obvious he was serious. "No, Miss Wilson, I think it is not a sin for you or anyone else who really believes the South is right, but for me it would be. Romans fourteen says – well, here, I will show you," and he pulled a New Testament out of his pocket and opened it.

As he flipped through the well-worn pages Lucy reflected that he must use the Book often. The young man found the place he had mentioned; then got up from his chair, kneeling on one knee beside hers, and held out the Bible for her to see.

The girl bent forward to see as he pointed to the lines, then looked at him questioningly.

"This seems to be talking more about food than about disagreeing with one's parents," she said.

"Yes, but see here where Paul writes that if one man believes something to be wrong, it is a sin for him? That is not necessarily confined to clean and unclean food. I believe Paul is meaning that if at any time a man believes something to be wrong for him to do in the eyes of God, it is wrong *for him.* But if someone else believes that same thing is something God wishes him to do, *for that man* it is not a sin."

"I am sorry – " she began, then stopped.

"You do not understand?"

She shook her head, then nodded, "I think I do, partly. But I am not sure. Are you meaning to say that since you believe that fighting for the South is wrong, it is wrong for you, but since I and my – brother believe fighting for the South is right, it is right for us?"

"Yes, in a way."

"But how can both be right?"

"You see, Miss Wilson, that this war is not a question of religion. Both sides have a little right on them and a little wrong. Some believe one side is more right than another, but fighting for either side would be no sin – unless one is fighting against his conscience."

"I believe I understand you now, sir, but since we have that question settled, would you mind discussing the fact that you believe the Union to be right?"

"Not at all. Are you asking for my reasons?"

"I suppose."

"Well, to begin with, our country's forefathers created the government to hold all of the states together. I think it strange that because of a little disagreement some would wish to separate."

"A *little* disagreement, sir?"

He smiled, "I suppose most would think it a large one. I don't see why it couldn't be resolved, though."

"Perhaps it could have been, if the Northern-minded government hadn't been so set on having its own way."

"On the issue of slavery?"

"Partly; I mean, that was the issue in question, but on any other issue I believe the result would have been the same."

"How do you say that?"

"Well, the united States Government was designed to do no more than to hold the states together. Each state was originally intended to make her own laws. Understand, please, that I do not condone the practice of slavery. My father freed all his servants years ago. However, I do believe that each state would eventually have outlawed the custom for themselves if the Union government had kept out of the question," Lucy explained slowly.

The lieutenant raised his eyebrows, "Truly, Miss Wilson, you amaze me. I had never heard the question explained from that point of view before. However, do you not think that our – I mean the United States' founding fathers, would wish the government they established had lasted longer without breaking up?"

"We are not trying to break up the Union government, sir, we are only trying to form our own, which we would have done in peace had you Northerners allowed us," Lucy kept her voice moderated as well as she could. It was impossible to discuss the subject in question without animation, but she tried to control it so it wouldn't be noticeable.

The door opened and a private soldier entered, saluting the lieutenant and handing him a note.

Lieutenant Johnston returned the salute and then said to Lucy, "Excuse me, Miss Wilson, the colonel has sent for me."

She nodded, and then went back upstairs.

It was not until Friday morning that Lucy received the letter she had asked Lolly for. She took it quickly, barely remembering to thank the manager, and went upstairs to her room. Closing the door securely, she seated herself and opened the envelope. Her father had educated Lolly, even though the laws said he wasn't supposed to, since no negroes were allowed to be taught to read and write; so the servant had been able to write the letter for himself.

Miss Lucy, the letter ran,

I am very sorry for the news I must write you, but your father is very ill. He fell sick with a fever on the very day after you left, and had to go to bed then. We could not find a doctor for three days, because, as you know, Miss Lucy, the doctors are all fixing up the soldiers and even our own Doc Peters too. After we got a doctor he said that he would try to help Mister Wilson, but he was not sure if he could. Then he said the sickness is very dangerous and your father doesn't have much chance. We all were very sorry about that and very sad and my wife Lindy, has been nursing him very nice the doctor says. I sent you a telegram when I received yours saying that Mister Richard is in jail as you already know and I am still waiting for an answer but I will get that before you get this letter. I think we have some very bad trouble for our family at this time and I am not sure as to what we should do, but keep praying.

Respectfully Yours,

Mahalaleel Wilson

Lucy didn't cry, it seemed as if she couldn't. She sat still, almost numb. What was she to do now? Ought she to go to her father? Or stay with Richard?

A few minutes later, she broke from her reverie and slowly descended the stairs. The sitting room was empty, and she sat down on one of the couches to wait.

"Miss Wilson," she heard a soft voice a few minutes later.

"Lieutenant Johnston."

"May I?" he indicated a chair near her.

She nodded, and he seated himself; then she handed him the letter.

"It's from my father's head servant, Lolly, who stayed with us when my father freed him," she explained.

He read through it silently, and then looked up. To the girl's surprise, she thought he looked worried, but she refused to allow herself to wonder, and asked, "Will you take that to my brother?"

"Yes, I will. Do you need anything else?"

"No, but why do you ask? I am just a Southern girl, on the opposite side of the war from you. The only reason I even speak to you is so that I may hear about my brother," Lucy started in confusion, and finished a little defiantly.

"Miss Wilson," the soldier spoke so soberly, almost sternly, that she looked quickly up at his face, nearly frightened, "I am not fighting against you," he continued, "I do not war with women. The reason I am helping you to the best of my abilities is that I am a Christian man, and a gentleman. I cannot do otherwise than assist any woman or child to whom I can render the least of aid."

Lucy smiled suddenly, and asked, "Which category do I come under, sir? Am I a woman or a child? Of late, I have not been sure I am either."

The lieutenant opened his mouth, then closed it again, looking embarrassed. Finally he said slowly, "I will change my words, then, a little Miss Wilson. Any female or child whom I am able to help, I will aid."

Lucy laughed softly, and curtseyed, "thank you, sir. Adieu!" and she went back upstairs.

~   ~   ~

As Lieutenant Johnston went out his thoughts were busy. "Is she a woman or a child I wonder? She is neither fully, but seems to be at times one or the other. I think she is almost a child still, or would be at least, if this trouble had not come upon her. Oh, if it only had not! The poor little girl. But she is very intelligent. Do you know, Johnston, I almost think she has convinced you to desert your ideals and turn Rebel! Her arguments are very convincing. But she does not seem to be as strong a Christian as her brother obviously is. Perhaps I will be able to teach her in time for her to have a support before her brother is – killed. For of course he will be. I don't know why we have even waited this long. But if her father dies, she will be wholly unprotected. Oh! Be quiet, Johnston," he told himself angrily, "there is nothing you can do, and it's not even your duty!" but suddenly a Bible verse flashed through his head, "'defend the fatherless,' how can I do that?" he exclaimed aloud, "I suppose all I can do is keep doing as I have been, passing messages between her and her brother. I will ask Wilson if there is anything else I can help with, though. Maybe her father will get well after all."

By this time he had reached the prison and handed Richard the letter.

"This is not from your sister," he told the prisoner, "it is a letter sent to her from your father's servant. I believe you have been expecting it. She asked me to bring it to you."

"Thank you, Johnston."

Richard read through Lolly's letter quickly, and then dropped the paper to his lap, staring into space for several minutes. Finally he looked up, seeming surprised that the lieutenant was still there.

"You know?" the prisoner asked.

"Of course."

"Yes, you must read all of our letters. Well, what shall I tell her? She ought to have sent for one of our servants before this, as she has no protector."

"The hotel manager and his wife are very good to her."

"Are they? But I think I will send for her maid, if she stays here – but should she stay here? If she goes to our father, he may be dead before she reaches him. Then, if she tries to come back, I will probably have already been shot."

"I agree with you, Wilson, it is a hard choice. I am afraid I cannot advise you at all, except to pray about it."

"I have been praying almost all the time. I would not mind anything, if it weren't for Lucy. Why did I ever bring her with me!" he groaned.

Johnston shook his head and turned to gaze out at the hallway. Then he looked again at the prisoner and said quietly, "I just want you to know, Wilson, that I am praying for you too. You, your father, and your sister."

As Richard looked up, Johnston stepped closer and bent down, speaking in a hushed voice, "I am not sure I wish you to be shot anymore, I'll tell you, Miss Wilson has almost converted me to the Southern point of view."

Without even looking at Richard's shocked face, the lieutenant straightened up quickly and left the cell, saying as he went, "I've something I need to do, Wilson. I will be back for an answer to the letter in a few hours."

Richard stared at the closed cell door for several minutes. *"Was he telling the truth, or was he lying?"*

When Lieutenant Johnston came back, Lucy was disappointed that he had no word of advice from her brother.

"He needs time to think and pray," the lieutenant told her, "He isn't sure what to do."

Lucy sighed, "I understand. I wish I were able to see him and talk with him."

~   ~   ~

A few days later, Lucy approached the lieutenant with a question. She had tried to ask him the same before, but for some reason, she didn't remember getting an answer.

"May I speak with you for a moment, sir?"

"Certainly, Miss Wilson."

"Do you know when my brother will be tried, and what the sentence will be? Is it possible that I might bail him out until then? Will he be kept in prison until the war is over?"

"A telegram for Miss Wilson!" a voice interrupted them.

Lucy reached out her hand for the envelope, and quickly tore it open. Then she staggered backward, and the paper fell from her hands.

Lieutenant Johnston put a hand under her elbow to support her, and asked, "what is it, Miss Wilson?"

The manager's wife came to them and picked up the slip of paper from the floor. "'Your father is dead, what shall we do?'" she read, "Oh, Miss Lucy! You poor little girl!" and the kind woman took Lucy in her arms. Lucy laid her head down on the woman's shoulder and began to cry.

Lieutenant Johnston took the telegram from the woman and went over to the manager's desk. "If Miss Wilson asks where I went, tell her I took the telegram to her brother please," he said quietly.

The manager nodded, and Johnston went out.

On the way to the prison, he thought to himself, "well, this may solve the question Wilson had over what to do with his sister, but it may not. I wonder what he will say? I don't think he will be surprised, but – " he stopped, and shook his head, then quickened his steps to reach the prison.

When he got there, he handed the telegram to Richard silently, and then waited, watching the prisoner's bowed head. Finally Richard looked up, "What did Lucy say?"

"The news staggered her, as I suppose it would anyone. She actually didn't say a word while I was there, but the manager's wife took her and she started to cry right before I left."

Wilson nodded, "Well, I will have to ask Lucy what she wants to do before I decide anything."

"What do you think she will say?"

"I really don't know," Richard answered. Then he quoted softly, "'the Lord gave, and the Lord hath taken away," then he jumped up and said fiercely to Johnston, "but do you understand how hard it is to say 'blessed be the name of the Lord?"

Johnston bowed his head, "yes," he said quietly, "I think I do."

Wilson jerked away and strode to the other side of the cell. He gazed out into the bare hallway.

Johnston spoke softly. "My sister – " he choked, then continued, "my little sister died five years ago. It was very – hard." The lieutenant paused for a moment, wondering if it was really necessary that he tell this man everything. *"If it might help him – even a little bit – I really ought to. Well, I will.* She was my only sister," he said aloud, "and after her death I wandered aimlessly through life for almost a year. I finally came across a poem of Tennyson's which ended, 'From the sod/ She will not rise again;/ But this sweet thought, "She rests with God,"/ Relieves a brother's pain.'"

Richard turned and stared at him, "I realize that, Johnston," he said in a low voice filled with pain and anger, "and that would be all right if it were simply that my father had died and I was grieving. That is not the problem. I know my father is in heaven now, I am not grieving for him, but for my sister. She does NOT rest with God, and that is why it will be so hard to leave her. If I were free, I would be able to support her in her grief for our father, but soon I will be dead, and she will be all alone."

He took a step closer to Johnston and stared into the other man's face for a few seconds, then said, "Do you understand me? My sister will be completely lost without anyone to support her. Oh, why did we ever begin this horrible war?" Richard groaned.

Johnston turned and leaned his arm against the bars of the cell. Wilson walked to the back of the tiny place and sat down on the bed, leaning his head on his hand.

Finally Johnston straightened, and opened the door of the cell to go out. "Wilson," he said, "I just want you to know that I think your sister is closer to God than she was before. I don't know how long it will be before she puts her full trust in Him, but I believe it will not be long."

Then he stepped out of the cell and locked it.

Chapter 23

At the sound of the door opening, Lucy looked up. It was Lieutenant Johnston again, and she greeted him with a trembling smile. The manager had told her that the lieutenant had taken the telegram to Richard.

He came over to where she was seated on the sofa, "How are you, Miss Wilson?"

"I'm doing all right, sir," she answered.

"I suppose you know I took the telegram to your brother," he said, asking with a motion of his hand if he might sit down.

She nodded, then said, "Yes, thank you very much."

"He has no advice for you as yet," the young man told her, "he first wants to know what you would like to do."

Lucy bowed her head in thought for a moment. "I don't know," she finally said, then quoted, "'God for his mercy! what a tide of woes/ Comes rushing on this woeful land at once!/ I know not what to do.'" She looked up at the lieutenant, "I can't think very well just now."

"I understand; would you like to be by yourself for a while?"

"I think so. I will go up to my room. Thank you, sir."

"When you go up, I wish you would look up in your Bible these verses," and he handed her a slip of paper on which he had written several references.

"I will."

When Lucy reached her room, she curiously examined the paper Lieutenant Johnston had given her. The first reference on it was Romans 15:13. She picked up her Bible and sat down on the bed. Turning through the pages until she found the place mentioned, she read, "Now the God of hope fill you with all joy and peace in believing, that ye may abound in hope, through the power of the Holy Ghost."

"'That ye may abound in hope,'" she repeated, "How can I? it says 'through the power of the Holy Ghost.' I don't understand. I suppose the only thing I can do is look up the other references."

The next one was Matthew 14:30. When she had found it, she read, "But when he saw the wind was boisterous, he was afraid; and beginning to sink, he cried, saying. Lord, save me."

"Well, it is true that the winds of life are boisterous now, and I am afraid, and beginning to sink," she said to herself, "Ought I cry out to the Lord to save me? That is what Lieutenant Johnston meant when he gave me this verse, I do believe. I will read the rest of the verses first, though. The next one is Matthew 11:28. Ah, here it is. It says 'Come unto me, all ye that labour and are heavy laden, and I will give you rest.' Let me see . . . yes, that is Jesus talking. Come unto him? That is almost the same meaning as the last verse I suppose. What shall I do?"

She sat there for several minutes, thinking. Finally she bowed her head, "Lord, my father said Thou knowest what is happening in my life right now. I come to Thee as Thou hast said in Thy Book. Thou saidst if I come to Thee, Thou wilt give me rest; and that is what I need now, Lord. I do not know very well how to pray, but I believe what Thou hast said is true, so I cry out to Thee as Peter did, 'Lord, save me."

She sat for several more minutes, then looked at the paper in her hand and saw the next reference was Luke 8:48. Slowly, almost listlessly, she turned the pages until she reached the correct chapter. She read it silently first, then a great smile broke over her face, and she read it again aloud. "'And he said unto her, Daughter, be of good comfort: thy faith hath made thee whole.'" A single tear made its way down her face, "I thank Thee, Lord."

When Lieutenant Johnston left the hotel, he went directly to find the Colonel. As he entered the office, saluting, Colonel Martin looked up and returned the salute, then asked "What have you to report, Johnston?"

"Nothing, sir. I am sorry, but we can't seem to find any information as to who Wilson's contact was. He probably was in this town, but we can't even be certain about that, since the contact would most likely have fled when he found that Wilson was captured."

"That's right, Johnston, but we'll keep looking. Maybe something will come up. Was there anything else?"

"Yes, sir."

"What is it?"

"I have been delivering notes between Wilson and his sister, as I told you. It seems that the young lady had simply come to this town to be with her brother, and was not involved in the spy work he was doing – and indeed was not certain of it until he was captured."

"Yes, I had an idea that was the case."

"Well, their father just died, and Miss Wilson and her brother are trying to figure out what would be best for her to do. She doesn't know yet that her brother will probably be shot, but of course he does, and he is worried that she will be left without a protector."

"I can understand that, Johnston, but why come to me with this? I don't see that I can do anything to help. Of course I am sorry for the young lady, but war is war, and I don't see that it's my duty to help these people."

"Yes, sir," Johnston said, but his jaw clenched for a moment at the callous words of his commander.

Colonel Martin saw and chuckled, "I know you don't agree with me, Johnston, but you should just be glad I'm not as bad as Stephens. If he were in charge now – "

Johnston nodded, "you're right, Colonel Martin, and you *are* a good colonel. What I really came to ask you, though, was if Miss Wilson might be permitted to see her brother. I will stay with them the whole time to make sure he will not escape."

"Oh, that will be all right. You just do what you wish as to that. As long as Wilson doesn't escape and continue spying for the Confederacy, which I am certain you will ensure will not happen, I am perfectly fine with him receiving his sister into that cell of his, if she will consent to enter it."

"I am sure she will, sir." He saluted, and went out.

~   ~   ~

"Miss Wilson!"

"Goodness, Lieutenant, you sound extremely excited! What is the matter?"

"Colonel Martin just gave me permission to take you to see your brother."

Lucy looked at him with shining eyes, "Did he really? Oh!" she clasped her hands in front of her and smiled radiantly. "It is true, then, those verses you gave me," she said softly.

His smile had been simply happy before; now it grew gentler, "'The God of hope fill you with joy and peace in believing,'" he quoted.

"'That ye may abound in hope,'" she finished, "yes, it was hard, but I understand it now. He said 'Come unto me,' and I did, and He did give me rest. Now you have brought me the news that I may see Richard! How soon may I go?"

"I will take you right now, if you wish," Lieutenant Johnston told her.

"As soon as I get my hat."

She hurried upstairs, and was soon back again, ready to leave for the prison. He offered her his arm, and she took it; then he led her down the street.

The Union soldiers were still standing around the streets of the town, but Lucy barely noticed them, filled with ecstasy at the thought that she would soon see her beloved brother again.

However, she was not unnoticed by the soldiers, who at first made a few jeering remarks, until Lieutenant Johnston suddenly turned and barked an order that hushed them for a few minutes until he and Lucy reached the prison.

"Your brother's cell is the third on the right," he told her, as they stepped inside the long hallway.

Lucy could not repress a small shiver as she looked around the cold, bare hall, but nodded once, and walked along with him until they reached the cell indicated.

"Wilson," the lieutenant said, as they reached the door. He pushed the key into the lock and swung the door open.

Richard looked up, murmuring, "yes?" then suddenly he saw his sister.

"Lucy!" he cried.

"Richard!" she exclaimed with a half sob, and threw herself into his arms.

Lieutenant Johnston leaned against the wall outside the cell and waited, after witnessing this first fond reunion.

Richard Wilson held his sister tightly in his embrace and kissed her, then released her and held her off and looked at her. Finally he crushed her to him again and whispered tenderly, "Oh, Lucy, little sister! Are you all right? How have you been doing?"

"I-I'm fine, Richard," she murmured, resting her head on his chest, "I just wanted to see you again."

He sat down on the bed and pulled her down beside him, keeping his arm around her, then asked, "What have you been doing, though? Johnston said that the hotel manager and his wife have been taking care of you."

"Yes, everyone has been very kind," she told him, "the people I meet at church, the manager and his wife, and – Lieutenant Johnston."

"I am glad, little sister. Now what do you want to do about yourself?" you can't stay here alone anymore. We will either send for your maid, or find someone to take you back home."

"Oh, Richard! If those are the only two choices, I want to send for Lizzie. I must stay here."

"'Must' is a hard word, Lucy."

"I know, but I just can't leave you alone here. Father is – gone – and I haven't any reason to go back home now. You are my only living relation. I will stay with you."

Richard leaned his cheek on her head for a moment, then said gently, "Don't you want to go back for our father's funeral?"

"No. I want to stay here for you," she repeated.

"Oh, Lucy!" he groaned, "If I could only be sure what I should do with you!"

"Please don't tell me to go home!"

"I don't know what's best!"

"Then let me stay here until you have prayed some more about it," Lucy pleaded.

Richard jerked his head up and stared at her, "Do you mean that?"

"Of course! I want to stay."

"No, do you mean that you want me to pray?"

"Yes."

"Oh, Lucy, do you really understand now, what I've been trying to tell you all these years?"

"Yes. The lieutenant gave me some Bible verses to look up today, and I finally came to understand what you and Father had been talking about for so long."

"I'm so glad. Now you will have a support when – " he hesitated.

"Yes, when things go wrong I know where to turn."

That had not been what Richard had meant, but he could not bring himself to explain to his sister just now what would eventually happen to him.

"Did you say Johnston gave you the verses?"

"Yes. He and I have talked many times in the past couple of weeks, he trying to convince me to put my trust in God, and I trying to convince him that the Confederates are right."

Richard chuckled, "Well, he succeeded; will you be able to?"

Lucy laughed, "I don't know; I am getting closer to my goal!"

"Lieutenant!" Richard called, "won't you come back in?"

"Certainly," Johnston replied, stepping back into the cell.

Richard stood and held out his hand, "I want to thank you for what you have done for Lucy and me since I was captured."

Johnston reached out and grasped the prisoner's hand, then looked over at the girl, wondering what she had told her brother about him.

"I am glad I can help," he said slowly, then opened his mouth as if he were about to say more, but hesitated. Wilson had already turned away.

"Now, Lucy," Richard said, "I want you to go back to the hotel with Lieutenant Johnston. I will think and pray over what we were talking about, and I want you to also."

"Oh, I will, Richard," his sister replied. He hugged her one more time, and then released her after murmuring in her ear, "I love you."

As she left the cell with the lieutenant, Richard sat down on the bed and rested his face in his hands. "I have just sent my sister away," he said to himself, "and it may well be the last time I will see her on earth. I ought to have told her what will happen to me, but somehow I couldn't. Oh, Lord God, tell me what I should do!"

~ ~ ~

Lieutenant Johnston had thought many times of the discussions he and Miss Wilson had had over which side of the War was more right. Late one evening he paced up and down in his room, praying, and trying to make once more the awful choice which had divided many families. "Lord, I cannot bear this estrangement from my family much longer!" he groaned, "I do not know how my mother must feel. If I could find one good reason to 'turn rebel' as Stephens calls it, how gladly I would do so!" Johnston sat down on his bed and pulled off his long cavalry boots, then lay back with a sigh, *"Could it be that the Lord has put Miss Wilson into my life to show me how the South could be right?"* he wondered. He mulled over the arguments she had used, and as he had over the past couple of weeks, continued to marvel at their reasonability. "The Southern States joined the union voluntarily; why shouldn't they leave voluntarily?" he asked himself. Eventually he drifted off to sleep, his thoughts still on the morals of the secession.

Chapter 24

The following Saturday Johnston was summoned by the colonel and told the news he had been expecting for the past three weeks, but it still staggered him. Though he had known it was coming, and even agreed that it was the only course to take at first, his ideas had changed, and now the thought of it gave him hard work at keeping his face composed in the presence of his superior officer.

"Johnston, I have come to a decision. Wilson is to be shot on Wednesday. I would have said Monday, but you will be happy that I remembered what you said about his having to make arrangements for his sister. Remember, most officers would not be so lenient."

Johnston turned aside for a moment, thinking, *"Would that you were more lenient!"*

"So that is all, do what is required. I have other business to attend now."

Johnston saluted automatically, then went out of the room, stumbling slightly. He walked slowly to the prison, trying to reunite his dizzying thoughts.

Wilson read the news in his face as he entered the cell.

"When?" the prisoner asked.

"Wednesday," the lieutenant replied dully.

"Poor Lucy," Richard said softly, then was silent for a few moments. A little later he looked up. Johnston was still there. "I heard a song, Johnston, a couple of months ago. It didn't affect me as it should have, I suppose, when I heard it first, because it was about a mother, and mine had died several years before, but now the song has come back strongly into my head, only with my sister's name in the place of 'Mother.'"

The young prisoner sighed, then began to sing quietly, with much feeling.

Why am I so weak and weary,
See how faint my heated breath,
All around to me seems darkness,
Tell me, comrades, is this death?
Ah! How well I know your answer!
To my fate I meekly bow –

Richard stood suddenly and clenched his fists, sending out the next words with anguished force,

If you'll only tell me truly
Who will care for Lucy now?

Soon with angels I'll be marching
With bright laurels on my brow;
I have for my country fallen,
Who will care for Lucy now?

Johnston looked out into the hall. He could not control the choking sensation that rushed into his throat. Finally he said in a low voice, "I – I'd like to."

Richard came to him quickly and placed a hand on his shoulder, turning him to face him. "What did you say?" he asked.

Lieutenant Johnston's lips tightened, then he said slowly, "I would like to care for your sister."

"What exactly do you mean?"

"You know what I mean, Wilson. You are her only living family member, and soon – you won't be."

"I am and have been aware of that."

"Enough, Wilson! Stop deliberately misunderstanding me. As her protector, will you give her to me?"

"Gladly." Richard's hand reached out and grasped Johnston's. "But what will Lucy say?"

Johnston turned away again, "That's what I don't know."

"And now we must tell her that I'll be leaving her."

Johnston gave a half smile at the "we," which showed that Richard considered him one of them now, but frowned again at the thought the prisoner had called up.

"Yes. Do you want me to bring her here and let you tell her? I think that will be best. Did I ever tell you what she did when Stephens told her you had been captured?"

Wilson looked up, startled, "No, did you say *Lieutenant Stephens* told her?"

"Yes."

"Why – he's – "

Johnston nodded, "That's why he took such pleasure in the telling. I had just entered the hotel and was about to tell her when he burst in and shocked her so much that she fainted."

"Fainted!"

"Yes."

"Has he heard the news of the colonel's decision about my fate yet?"

"I don't know."

"Just in case he has, please, would you go get Lucy? I'll tell her here."

"And ask her – "

"Yes, if she can handle it. But you've been with her more in the past weeks than I have, so I can't give you any assurances, since I'm not sure what she'll say," Richard told him.

"I'll go now," Johnston nodded again, then left the prison.

Lucy opened the door of her room and stepped softly out. She had just been praying, and felt quite at rest inside. She was about to go downstairs when she saw Lieutenant Stephens leaning against the railing at the head of them. Startled, she turned and was about to reenter her room when he spoke.

"Miss Wilson."

She almost ignored him, but he continued.

"Have you heard the news about your brother?"

Lucy turned sharply. "What news?" she asked eagerly, quickly moving two steps closer to him.

He crossed his arms, "Only that Colonel Martin has finally decided what will be done to him."

"And what is that?" she asked, her breath coming in quick gasps.

~   ~   ~

Johnston opened the door and stepped into the hotel just in time to hear his brother lieutenant's loud, rough tones at the head of the stairs, then a short cry from Lucy Wilson and the sound of a heavy fall.

Stephens bounded down the stairs to be met by Johnston, who grasped his arm and exclaimed hoarsely, "What have you done now, Stephens?"

Lieutenant Stephens laughed. "I was just having a little chat with Miss Wilson up there," he said, shaking free from Johnston's grasp and going out the door.

Johnston threw a quick glance at the manager, who was coming out from behind his desk, and then leaped up the stairs. Lucy was crumpled on the floor in a faint. Turning around, he saw the manager's wife moving as quickly up the stairs as her large body would permit.

"What should I do?" he asked.

"Carry her into her room and put her on the bed," she told him, "I will take care of her."

Johnston obeyed, then went downstairs to wait. A few minutes later Lucy came down, looking pale, but composed. She walked quickly up to him and asked, "Won't you please take me to my brother, Lieutenant Johnston?"

"Yes, certainly, Miss Wilson. That is really the reason I came here; your brother asked me to bring you to see him."

"Because of what Lieutenant Stephens told me?"

"What did he tell you?"

"That the colonel has decided – "

"What is to be done to him?"

"Yes. Is it true? He told me Richard will be shot."

"I am very sorry, Miss Wilson."

"I can't believe it. I *can't* believe it!" she said, wringing her hands. "Tell me it isn't true!"

"I am very sorry, Miss Wilson," he repeated, "shall I take you to your brother now? He sent me for you."

She sighed and followed him to the door, which he opened for her, and they went out.

~   ~   ~

"But why, Richard?" Lucy cried, "why does it have to end like this?"

"Lucy, darling, you know it is *not* the end, whatever happens to us on earth."

"But I can't bear it!"

"'Cast your burden upon the Lord,' Lucy. I know you can't bear it with your own strength, but He will help you. Oh, and I just remembered; besides that, I believe God has sent someone to assist you."

"What do you mean?" she straightened from where she had been leaning against him and looked him in the face, puzzled.

He hesitated, not sure exactly how to tell her what Johnston had said to him.

"Johnston and I were talking when he came to tell me what the colonel had decided," he began, "and he asked me if – "

"If what?" Lucy asked in bewilderment. She still couldn't see where Richard was going.

"If I would give you to him – give him the right to take care of you."

Her eyes widened, but she didn't say a word.

"I agreed, as long as you would consent. What do you say? Are you willing to be his wife?"

Lucy stood up and walked over to the cold prison wall, leaning one of her elbows on it, and bringing both hands up to cover her eyes. "He is – very kind," she faltered after a moment.

"He would make a good husband," Richard said slowly.

All was silent in the little cell for several minutes, then Lucy said, "Have you prayed about this?"

"Yes, I prayed almost the whole time from when he left to get you."

"Do you think it is the right thing to do?"

"I do."

"I will – miss you Richard," Lucy's voice broke and she quickly stepped back to him, leaning into his chest as he wrapped his arms around her.

"I'm sorry, Lucy," he whispered.

"Isn't there anything I can do?" she cried, "I can't just let them – murder you like this!"

"It isn't murder, sister. It is war. If we captured one of their spies, we would do the same, and you would not protest."

"Ah, but before I did not think of their mothers and sisters, Richard!" Lucy spoke in a low voice, "Now I wonder where this all is taking us. What is the use of war? All that has happened in these three years is that many men, old, young, and even boys, have been killed, and we have not gotten anywhere."

"That is the age-old cry of the women when their men go to war," Richard said, "But as long as mankind is persistent in doing evil, as indeed we must, being born with a sinful nature, there will be war."

"But isn't there anything I can do?"

"No. Only pray that I am able to meet my death bravely, and thank God that I am a Christian."

The girl sobbed for several minutes after this. Finally, after she was quieter, he lifted her chin and gazed into her face for a moment, then kissed her forehead and asked, "Well, what about the lieutenant's answer?"

"Oh. Oh, Richard, I – I suppose I'll say – yes."

"My poor little sister, that doesn't sound much like a girl giving an answer to her first proposal!" he chuckled softly.

"Oh – oh, but I can't think straight right now. I'm sorry Richard. If it hadn't been for the other news, I might have been more enthusiastic. Well! I will be. I'll show the lieutenant that I will be very happy to be his wife!"

"Do you mean that, Lucy? I don't want to force you into a marriage that will be unhappy simply because you are afraid of being alone. I am sure the servants at our house will take sufficient care of you if you do not wish to allow anyone else to."

"No, I do mean it. Your question shocked me at first; I had never even thought of the possibility of such a thing. But he is a good, kind man; a Christian who will care for me well. I will try to be happy even though – " she hesitated for a second, " – I am afraid it will be hard, but I am ready. Especially with God's help."

"My dear, brave sister! Well, shall I call him?"

"If you wish."

~   ~   ~

Johnston stood impatiently in the hall after he let Lucy in to see her brother. At first he had paced up and down the hall, but now he simply stood near enough to the door that it was easily seen, but far enough away that he wouldn't be eavesdropping on the conversation. He couldn't help, however, hearing Lucy's sobs, which carried through the heavy door several times.

His chest and throat constricted, and then he suddenly heard a rough voice behind him say, "Somethin' make yer mad, Loot'nint?"

Johnston whirled around, realizing his hands had been clenched at his sides. He saw a grimy face peering out of the bars on the door of the next cell down the hall.

He glared at the other man for a moment, then dropped his eyes. Controlling himself, and raising his eyes again, he said quietly, "yes, something did make me angry, but it wasn't you, and I'd rather you wouldn't add to it."

"Awright, it's of no 'count one way or t' other. I jus' think I kin make one leetle observation, and that's as how yer seem t' be oncommon fond o' th' pris'ner in th' next cell. Th' spy, yer know."

The face disappeared with a raucous laugh, and Lieutenant Johnston frowned. Had his frequent visits really been noticed? Well, if anyone asked him, he would just tell the truth. That he had been delivering letters from the prisoner's sister, who needed advice from her brother. The notes themselves he had no objection to showing the colonel, of course. He was sure Lucy wouldn't object either. Lucy! He had already begun to call her that to himself. What if she didn't accept his proposal? He supposed she would go home to be cared for only by her father's servants. But a girl so young shouldn't be left unprotected. He would be willing to visit her home once in a while in the place of her brother to make sure she was safe, but would she be comfortable with such an arrangement as that? He bowed his head and prayed that the Lord would give him wisdom, as well as Lucy and Richard.

The door was finally opened by Richard, who motioned for him to come in. Johnston tried to meet his eyes, but Wilson was looking away, so he got no answer to the question he had been waiting to ask.

Lucy was sitting on the bed, her hands clasped tightly in her lap, and her eyes down. Her smooth black hair looked beautiful, even in the dim light of the prison cell, and her cheeks were flushed slightly. Richard turned back to face the soldier, and stretched out his hand to clasp Johnston's, resting his other hand on his shoulder. He nodded to the question in the lieutenant's eyes, and then said aloud, but in in a hushed voice, "Yes, she says she is willing to marry you." He smiled as a glad light began to show in Johnston's eyes, then continued, "so are you going to ask her now, or do you want me to just – " he paused, because Johnston wasn't looking at him anymore. He had turned to look at the girl, who was still sitting on the bed, in the same position as before.

"Lucy," Johnston's deep voice was gentle. It was the first time he had called her by that name. She looked up at him with wide eyes for a moment, then lowered them again shyly. Richard walked over to her and she stood up, moving within the circle of his right arm, but keeping her eyes cast down.

Johnston took a step nearer, then said softly, "Will you marry me, Lucy Wilson?"

"Yes, I will," she said in a low, sweet voice.

Her brother picked up her right hand, and took Johnston's. He placed his sister's little hand in his new friend's large one and said huskily, "She is yours, Johnston. Take care of her."

Johnston bent and kissed the trembling hand he held in his own, then nodded to Richard, "I will."

Lucy's brother turned abruptly and went to the wall, facing away from them. He leaned one shoulder against it, and bowed his head. Lucy watched his back for a moment, the looked up at the lieutenant and drew her hand away from his suddenly, stepping quickly to Richard's side. She looked up into his face and saw that his eyes were closed and two tears had escaped and were coursing down his face. His boyish face was creased with wrinkles, making him seem too old for his years.

"Richard!" she cried, throwing her arms around his neck. He automatically returned her embrace, then coming to himself and kissing her, said, "I'm sorry, Lucy. I don't know why – "

"Oh, Richard! I can't bear it!" she said, as she had before, sitting on the bed with her face in her hands. Suddenly she looked up with dry, painful eyes at her betrothed husband, "Oh, Lieutenant Johnston, can't *you* do something?"

He hesitated, "I can try. I know that Colonel Martin won't change his mind. But I might be able to find a way for Richard to – escape." He lowered his voice at the last word, then continued in quiet tones, "I know almost the whole town is on your side – or, I suppose I should say, *our* side, since I am convinced the Confederates are right now."

Lucy smiled, but Richard frowned and faced Johnston. "I can't let you do that, Johnston," he said.

"Why not?" Lucy exclaimed, "We've got to do *something* to get you out of here!"

"Because it's too big a risk, dear," her brother told her.

"I don't mind risking my life for a friend, Wilson."

"Yes, I believe you, Johnston, and thank you; but what you haven't considered is that you would not be risking just your life for me, but your wife also. Lucy needs you to take care of her. If you attempt to help me escape and are captured, she will be once again left without a protector, perhaps this time with no kind Union officer willing to help her," the last was spoken with a slightly detectable bitter sarcasm.

"But Richard – "

"No, Lucy. You must obey me. Your betrothed will be already suspected because of the fact that he, already known as a man from Georgia, is marrying a Southern girl. If I escape, they will be sure he has helped me. For your sake I cannot let him risk himself."

"Do not mind me, Richard, I am strong now."

"Lucy! I am ashamed of you!" Richard scolded half teasingly, "you say you do not care whether or not Johnston is arrested, when you have just now become engaged to be married to him?"

Lucy covered her face with her handkerchief to hide her blushes. "I did not mean that," she said quickly, "I didn't think."

"I know, dear, but you must realize that I do think, and I am sure this is the best way. I am sorry, but I will meet you in heaven. Now, it is getting late, and you haven't eaten your dinner yet."

"I don't know if I can."

"You must. But come and see me tomorrow, after you go to church."

"I will. Good-night, Richard."

"Good-bye, Wilson; thank you."

The hands of the two young men met in a warm clasp, "Good-bye, Johnston. Thank *you,* friend, for taking care of my sister."

Lucy sobbed, and Johnston took her arm, leading her out of the prison.

While they walked down the street, the girl kept her head down so that the blue-coated soldiers lining the streets wouldn't see the tear streaks on her face. But when they reached the hotel, she was met by the manager's wife, who stood waiting for them in the doorway. When Lucy saw the kind woman standing there, she broke down once again. This time there were no tears, but she clung to the woman and gave several shuddering sighs.

Johnston hated to see her go on like this, and tried to think of some way to stop it. Finally he said a similar thing to what Richard had said earlier, in a half teasing voice.

"Why Lucy, is this what young ladies do normally to announce their engagements?"

Lucy's cheeks were already flushed, but now they grew to an even deeper red as she lifted her head and looked at him. As the manager and his wife turned their eyes on her questioningly, she brought her hands up to her cheeks to hide her blushes, but she had to laugh. "I – I don't know, Lieutenant Johnston," she began, when he smilingly corrected her.

"Arthur."

"Oh, is that your name? I didn't know. Well – " she gave a little laugh, "I don't know – Arthur, if this is how girls usually act on their – engagement days, because as this is my first time, I haven't had any experience. Would you please tell me how you would like me to behave?"

"Oh, Miss Lucy, is it really so?"

"What?" Lucy asked, turning toward the manager's wife, who had asked the question.

"Why that you are engaged to the Lieutenant Johnston, of course?"

"Yes, it is. But please do not tell anyone yet," Lucy pleaded, "I am not sure whether it will be wise to let everyone know."

"Oh, I am so happy for you my dear child," the woman exclaimed, kissing Lucy on both cheeks, "I am sure that the lieutenant will make you a wonderful husband, even though he is," and she lowered her voice, "a Northerner."

Lucy laughed, "no, actually, he has changed his mind. But please don't tell anyone that either. We will discuss when it will be all right to let others know – or if it will be prudent to let anyone know at all. I know you will keep our secret."

"Of course we will, child. Don't you fret about that."

"Lucy, you need to eat, and then go to bed," Arthur Johnston told her, "you have had too much strain today."

Lucy laughed, "Yes, sir," she said, curtsying, "I will. Goodnight, Lieutenant – I mean, goodnight, Arthur."

She held out her hand and he pressed it, then she fled up the stairs, and he went back outside. The manager's wife turned to her husband.

"Well! What do you think of that?" she said, raising her hands expressively.

Chapter 25

The night passed slowly for Lucy, who tossed and turned in her bed. She couldn't sleep with all of the thoughts running through her head. She would try to think of Lieutenant Johnston – Arthur, now – and his kind words and actions, but when she did, her thoughts would always return to her brother.

If she closed her eyes, she would see visions of him lying on the ground, motionless, and rows of glittering-eyed blue-coated soldiers. Such sights made her shudder, so she tried to keep her eyes open as long as she could.

It was not until the "wee hours of the morning" that she dropped to sleep, dreamless, from sheer exhaustion, but she woke up at six, nonetheless, feeling weary and unhappy, but unable to sleep any longer.

"I can't, Oh! I can't let Richard be killed!" she cried aloud, "But do I have a right to take a chance of getting Lieutenant – Arthur into trouble? Richard says I don't, but what can I do?"

She thought back to the first day that she had arrived in this town with her brother. She recalled the strange town they had entered by mistake, and that Jackson brother and sister, who said such strange and confusing things.

Suddenly the words of a part of their conversation came flashing back to her, leaving her breathless with excitement and a new idea.

"Why did Richard ask Mr. Jackson if he knew the grocer?" she wondered, "and he was so mysterious about it too. He wouldn't say why. Could it possibly have been because – because the grocer was to be his – I suppose they would say – contact in this town? Maybe that is how I can help Richard! And even if I can't help him to escape, I could carry on the spy work he has begun!"

After the church services were over Lieutenant Johnston made his way through the crowd of churchgoers, aiming for one of his men, who had signaled to him. After listening to the sergeant's report, he turned, trying to get a glimpse of Lucy Wilson, but couldn't see her anywhere. He knew she had been in church; but she must have left immediately.

He had thought that she and he would go directly from church to see her brother, but he supposed she had not thought the same, and had gone home to wait for him there. So he started for the hotel.

He had almost reached that building when he saw the door open, and Lucy stepped out. The manager came out behind her and closed the door, then offered his arm to the girl. Johnston was astonished, but no more than was Lucy when she suddenly saw him. She started in surprise, and stepped back for a moment, then smiled and held out her hand.

"Good morning, Arthur."

"Where are you going?" he asked, after pressing and releasing her hand, "I thought we had planned to see your brother again right after the services."

"Oh! Oh, yes, we had. I almost had forgotten." She looked confused.

"What is the matter?" Johnston asked.

"Why – why n-nothing but the usual," she stammered.

He looked at her searchingly, but her eyes lowered, and she turned away.

The manager of the hotel touched Lucy on the arm and said quietly, "I don't believe you need me anymore, do you Miss Wilson?"

"N-no. I suppose not. Thank you, Mr. Atkins."

Johnston waited. Finally Lucy looked up and asked, "Well, are we going to my brother now?"

"Perhaps."

"W-why not?" she looked uncomfortable as he gazed at her silently.

Finally he said softly but firmly, "why do you not tell me, Lucy?"

"Tell you what?" she whispered.

"I do not know. But I do know there is something you want to tell me."

"Why should I want to tell you anything, Lieutenant Johnston?" she asked defiantly, throwing up her head.

He smiled slightly, but said firmly, "You don't believe you wish to tell me anything right now, but I think you will find everything will be better if you explain what is bothering you."

"I do not wish to speak to you, Lieutenant Johnston. Please do not speak to me. You may tell my brother I am not coming just now. I have no desire to walk with you. Adieu!" and she turned away with a swish of her full skirts.

Johnston took a step forward and caught both her hands. "Lucy," he said tensely, "Your brother has only two more days."

At this she collapsed, and he took hold of her arm to support her. Then, seeing that churchgoers were returning home, and the street was not as empty as it had been before, he led her around the hotel to a shaded spot behind a few trees.

"I'm sorry, Lucy," he whispered, "but I had to say it. It isn't as if you didn't know."

She shook her head and drew away from him, leaning an arm against the tree and bringing her handkerchief to her eyes. "I know that, Arthur," she said, "But now that you have said it, what do you want?"

He moved to where he could see her face, though it was shaded by her hat. "Lucy," he said gently, "Please tell me. I have a right to know now, remember."

"But you will not let me do it if I tell you."

He touched her shoulder and she looked up at him, pain in her eyes.

"If I do not allow you to do as you have planned, it will only be because I believe it would be wrong for me to do so. It is my duty to protect you. Now you are going to tell me what you are thinking of, and years from now, you will agree that it was all for the best."

"Years from now Richard will be dead!" she exclaimed passionately, "and you Northerners will have won the war."

He stepped back suddenly, dropping his hand from her shoulder. "If you do not believe me now when I tell you I am not a Northerner, I suppose you never will believe me," he said bitterly, turning to walk away.

She ran to him. "Arthur!" she gasped, sobbing as she took hold of his arm with both hands. "Oh! Arthur forgive me! I didn't mean it. I never did. Please – oh – please – " and she sank, weeping, on a bench nearby.

Arthur Johnston knelt beside her and took both her hands in his. Silently he waited for her to quiet down, then said, "Lucy, when I asked your brother to give you to me I meant it with all I am. I-I don't know how to explain it to you, but I love you. If you can ever care for me in the same way I will be very happy, but just now all I can ask is that you trust me, and that you know that whatever I do will be what I believe is best for you."

Lucy gave him a trembling smile and tried to free one of her hands, but he clung to both tightly.

"Just let me get my handkerchief!" she begged, half laughing and half embarrassed.

Smiling slightly, he released her hand and tucked into it his own square of white linen.

When she had dried her tears, she smiled at him. "You are right, Arthur," she said softly, "and you always were. I am a silly thing, and ought not to have given you all of this trouble. 'I am ashamed that women are so simple/To ask for war where we should kneel for peace./To seek for rule, supremacy, and sway/When we are bound to serve, love, and obey.'" The last of the quotation was spoken very softly, and she smiled again, "And I will, Arthur. I will help you in everything I can, though I'm afraid it won't be much, and I already – " she hesitated, "care for you very much. Now I will show you that I will obey you by telling you where I was going when I was leaving with the manager of the hotel. If I must not do as I had planned, I wish you would, but we must go to Richard soon," she spoke with a half sob, and Arthur's hands tightened on hers. He sat beside her on the bench now.

"Well," she continued, "I was very bothered last night, and didn't sleep well. No, I'm all right. Don't worry about that. Just let me speak. I went over and over in my mind the events of the past few weeks and came to a conclusion. I remembered something that Richard had said when we first came here that seemed to have something to do with his spying work. No, hush. I believe that if there is any one thing I can do for him it will be to continue his work. I think I know who the person he was to meet here is, and I was going to see him when you came. Now I have done; say what you will."

Johnston didn't answer for several minutes. His face was turned away, so she could not tell by it what he was thinking. Finally she shifted her position slightly, and put her hand on his arm.

"I'm sorry, Lucy," he paused, "I don't know what to say."

"Let's go to Richard now," she said, "We can talk about this later. But do you think it will do any good to ask Richard what he thinks, and find out if this man is truly the one he was to see?"

"Perhaps. That might be the best plan in any instance," he told her.

~ ~ ~

Tuesday afternoon, the two were talking behind the hotel again, and Arthur turned to look directly at his fiancé. "Lucy, would you mind marrying me tomorrow?"

"Tomorrow, Arthur! But tomorrow Richard – "

"I know. That's why I want to marry you then. So that I can be sure to have legal right to protect you."

Lucy raised her head and looked at him directly for a moment, her eyes shining through her tears. Finally she whispered, "You are so good, Arthur."

"There is none good but one, dear, and that is God; but I pray to Him that I will be good to you, and I believe this is right."

"If you really think so, then yes, I will marry you tomorrow. But – I do wish that our wedding anniversary and the anniversary of Richard's – death would not be on the same day. That is my only objection."

Arthur frowned. "That's true. Would today do as well? I was going to wait until tomorrow because I won't be able to get a marriage license until then, but we might get the pastor to perform the ceremony today, and then legalize it later."

"This is very sudden, but I am willing to do as you say."

"I am sorry, but," he suddenly laughed, "I am also glad. I do want to marry you as soon as possible. Shall we go ask the pastor then?"

"I suppose."

They had almost reached the pastor's house when Johnston asked, "Where do you want to be married? The pastor would do it in his house, I am sure, but Richard would be glad if he could see us."

"Yes. Can't we be married in his cell?" she asked eagerly.

"If the pastor will."

He knocked on the parsonage door. It was opened by the housekeeper, who welcomed them, and motioned them in to the sitting room. A minute later the pastor entered. He nodded, when he saw the two in the room, but seemed surprised.

"What can I do for you?" he asked.

"Sir, I believe you know of Miss Wilson's situation; at least, she has told me you do."

The pastor bowed.

Johnston continued, "Do you know, though, that her brother is to be shot tomorrow?"

The pastor turned compassionate eyes on Lucy. "My child, I am very sorry. I have praying for you, and so have many members of my congregation."

"Thank you, pastor," Lucy said quietly.

"We have come to you for help," Johnston spoke again.

"And what can I do?" the pastor asked.

Arthur Johnston reached out and took Lucy's hand. "We wish to be married," he said, "Miss Wilson will be left without a protector when her brother is gone, and I would like to be allowed by law to fill that place."

"But – how did this happen? Miss Wilson, are you sure you know what you are doing?"

"I am sure, Pastor," Lucy replied, "The lieutenant will be a good husband to me, I know. He is a Christian, and he is kind."

"This is not simply out of fear that you will be left without anyone to take care of you?"

"No, sir," she replied, "My father had a house to which I could go were there no one else for me. There are servants there, and they would have helped me, for they love me. Richard, my brother, gave his blessing to us; in fact, it was he who first asked me if I would agree to marry Lieutenant Johnston."

The pastor looked at her for a long moment, and realized she was telling the truth. "And you wish me to perform the ceremony?"

"Yes sir; today, if possible," Johnston answered.

"Today?"

"Today. Lucy's brother is to be shot tomorrow, and he ought to be present. Will you come to his cell and perform it there?"

"Yes. Do you have anyone who will act as witnesses?"

"Perhaps – Mr. and Mrs. Atkins?" Lucy suggested.

"The hotel manager and his wife? Certainly," the pastor said, "if you think they would agree."

Johnston nodded, "I'll ask them, but I know they'll come. We can't go together, or we'll be noticed, so Lucy and I'll leave earlier, and you will come separately. Be at the prison at suppertime, when most of the men will be off the streets. Come, Lucy, let's go back to the hotel."

So they were married.

Chapter 26

It was the day on which Richard was to be shot. He awoke early in the morning and prayed earnestly for himself, his sister, and his new brother-in-law. Then the soldiers came to take him away. They entered the cell and ordered him to come with them, which he did.

The Union soldiers were not rude, but he was a rebel, and a spy. He deserved his fate, and they felt little, if any pity. However, all this changed when he heard a voice call his name.

"Richard, oh Richard!" it was his sister. She and her husband were hurrying toward him. He looked at his guards. "May I? My sister."

The two soldiers looked at each other, then nodded. "Guess it won't do any harm," one of them said, "I wouldn't do it for him, but the young lady, poor girl. You know, I heard her pa's dead too. Besides that," he lowered his voice as the two came nearer, "the lieutenant seems taken with her. Wonder if there's anything in that? Strange, isn't it? A Confederate spy's sister and a Union lieutenant. But he's strong on duty, might be just that."

Richard knew his sister and Lieutenant Johnston had told no one of their marriage.

They came closer, and the guards stepped away, but kept their eyes on the prisoner.

Lucy flung herself into her brother's arms, mindless for once of the many eyes watching, though several men turned away, unwilling to gaze on this last parting of a brother and sister.

"Oh, Richard, Richard, why?"

"Darling, it must be. Forgive me for bringing you here when I knew there would be danger."

"Don't say it, Richard; of course I forgive you," she sobbed, "And I would have come anyhow, after Father had died. Pray for me once, Richard, before you go."

"Lord, our Heavenly Father, bless Lucy now, I pray. Help her to bear this new trial, and come through it strong in Thee. I know Thou art great and loving and able to help in times of distress. Bless my little sister, and guard her all the days of her life. Also," he murmured so no one else would hear, "bless Arthur Johnston, her husband, and keep them close together all of their days. In the name of Jesus Christ, through Whose blood we are free, I pray. Amen."

He grasped Johnston's hand, with one arm still around Lucy. "Take care of her," he whispered.

He kissed Lucy, and embraced her passionately once more, then handed her to her husband and nodded to the guards.

"I love you, Lucy!" he called, as they took him away.

"I've wondered sometimes, what it would be like to die," Richard thought, *"But I had thought I would have a few more years of my life first. Oh, well, I'm proud to die for the glorious Cause. Our Confederacy has need of many brave men. Thank God for giving me strength up to this point."*

Richard felt one of the guards pull his arm, "we're almost there. I must say, Reb, I'm sorry for your sister."

"Thank you," Richard nodded to him, "I believe she will be taken care of, though. I have made arrangements."

They walked up to a brick wall. Richard suddenly recalled the courageous words of a man who had been hanged by the British for spying during the American Revolution. 'I only regret that I have but one life to give for my country,' the man had said. "Am I able to say that?" Richard wondered, "I hope so. I can certainly be thankful for many things, though. That man was hanged, and I am to be shot. My sentence is much more honorable than his. Well, here it comes. God, help me."

His thoughts whirled in many different directions as they tied a blindfold around his head. He prayed earnestly, and waited for the shot he knew would come.

"Are you ready, Rebel?"

"I am."

His lips set firmly together, and he waited.

"Ready; aim; fire!" Lieutenant Stephens barked.

Richard heard the sound of a volley, felt a searing pain in his side, then something hurt his head, and all went black.

~ ~ ~

Richard groaned. *"I thought heaven was supposed to be painless,"* was the first that entered his mind. For he certainly felt pain. There was no question as to that. *"Where am I, then?"* he asked himself next, *"for this certainly cannot be heaven."*

His eyes were still closed, but he forced one of them open with a great effort. The other eye felt as though it were glued shut. Looking around, painfully, at the small circle he could see without turning his head, he saw a small patch of sky, a few trees, and a whole lot of dirt. Strange to say, he was lying in the dirt.

"What am I doing here?" he asked himself, trying to gather his muddled thoughts. Slowly he recalled the events of the day before. "I must be in my grave," he mumbled aloud.

"Yes, you are."

Richard would have been startled at the coarse, though quiet man's voice near his ear, did he not feel far beyond nerves. He lay there quietly, wondering what was to come next.

"You do not ask me who I am?" the grating voice inquired.

"Do you wish me to?" Richard was surprised at the sound of his own voice.

A rasping laugh was heard, and a bearded face came into his line of sight. Very much into his line of sight. In fact, now he could see nothing else. He was not startled to see the blue uniform the man wore, but only kept wondering vaguely what would happen next.

"You are the third man, or will be the third man, whom I have brought back from the edge of the grave – literally, of course," and the laugh was heard again. It hurt Richard's ears.

"I still have not introduced myself, have I?" that laugh again, "pardon me for my terrible manners. I am John Featherhead, or at least, that is who I am supposed to be. The Yanks think I am an idiot, and who can say I am not? But I work for them in return for this uniform and food. As you can see, one of my jobs is taking care of the bodies of dead men. Are you a dead man?"

"I do not know," Richard mumbled. He was very confused.

"Quite so, quite so. Well, we haven't much time. You must get out and go away. If you want to be a dead man, you will be one soon. If not – you may do your best to find help. I cannot help you any more than I already have. It was a miracle, I say, that you were not killed by the firing squad. You have a bullet in your stomach, and a big gash in your head. Another in your leg. Crawl away, if you wish, I will not stop you. I'll help you get out of this grave if you like, then I will go away. I must tell the Yankees that I put you in the grave, and they will be satisfied. They would expect nothing more from me, an idiot, hey?"

While talking, he pushed and pulled Richard out of the shallow grave which was obviously not intended to really hold anyone. Richard flopped over on his stomach, as the man gave a last heave, and groaned.

"Good-bye, and good luck!" the man left, leaving Richard feeling very much alone.

~   ~   ~

"Pa sent me to get you," Lily Mae heard her little brother's voice at the door.

"All right, Matthew, I'm coming."

She bid goodbye to the neighbor she had been visiting, and followed her brother out the door.

The two walked down the lane and onto the road in silence, then Matthew spoke.

"Promise you won't tell?"

"Won't tell what?"

"You've gotta promise first."

"Is it anything very bad?" Lily Mae was used to being her brother's confidante. Just two years older than he, the boy and girl had always done everything together. She was a pretty good judge of his feelings, as he was of hers. She could tell, even though she couldn't see his face in the dark, that whatever he was about to confide was extremely important to him.

"Not so terribly bad, but I'm afraid you'll think it is. Promise?"

"I won't tell, Matt, unless I'm sure there's a need."

He was disappointed, she could tell, from the way his arm loosened from hers and fell away, but a minute later he let out a big sigh, and said, "Promise one more thing, Lily Mae."

"Won't promise until I know what I'm promising. That's what got Solomon's mother into so much trouble in the Bible."

"Don't want to talk about the Bible right now. I want you to promise." Matthew was plainly out of sorts.

"Promise what now?"

"Promise you won't cry?" his voice was plaintive.

She linked her arm through his again, and said softly, "is it as bad as that? I'll try my best not to cry, whatever it is. Now tell me."

"I want to join the army."

"I know that, dear."

"No, you don't understand, Lily Mae. *I want to join the army!*"

"But I do understand, Matthew, I know you don't like to stay here all alone while our brothers are off fighting I know you've been hankering to go ever since the war began."

"You still don't understand, Lily Mae. I'm going to run off and join the army."

"No! No, Matthew, you can't! You promised Ma you wouldn't."

"I did not, and you know it. I remember exactly what happened. Ma said, 'you must not leave us,' and I said, 'I know you don't want me to, Ma.' That wasn't a promise."

"You can't do this, Matthew. Please don't do this to us. We need you here at home."

"You don't need me. You have Pa. He'd be fighting too, you know, if his leg wasn't all twisted so he can't march or ride. I love you all, Lily Mae, but you know that all the rest of the boys in town are gone, and I ought to go too."

Lily Mae caught her breath. Her brother seemed to have grown up when she wasn't looking.

"You're only thirteen years old," she reminded him desperately.

"Jed Lewis is only ten," he replied quietly.

"Did you ask Pa and Ma?"

"Sure! Been asking ever since the war started."

"No, I mean really ask them."

"Don't dast. They'll sure make me stay home. Ma'd have a conniption fit, and I'd start feeling so bad I couldn't leave. I'll just light out, and then I won't have to see her all sad like."

Lily Mae was silent. They had stopped walking and were standing at the edge of the woods. Matthew turned to her and took both her hands in his. He was a bit taller than she now, and she had to raise her head to see into his face.

"Look here, Lily Mae," he said pleadingly, "You know what I'm telling you is true. You know I can't stay here when the rest of the boys are helping our country."

"Oh, Matthew, don't *do* this to me!" she cried.

"Lily Mae, Lily Mae, *don't* cry!" he exclaimed in horror, "you promised you wouldn't."

"I didn't!" she looked up and smiled through her tears, "I said I'd *try* not to cry. What's the matter, anyway? You saw me cry dozens of times when we were kids."

"Yes, but about little things. This is real, big sister, and I wanted your help. You're hurting me."

"I'm sorry, Matt. But you are hurting me too. Won't you promise me you'll talk to Pa about this?"

"If you really want me to."

"Thank you so much! I won't cry anymore," she laughed, giving him a hug. Suddenly she clung closer to him. "Oh! What is that?"

"What?" he asked.

Then she heard it again. A groan. This time Matthew heard it too.

"Th-that's coming from the g-graveyard!" he stammered.

"Nonsense!" she exclaimed, recovering from her first fright, "where's my brave soldier brother now?"

But Matthew was right. They had almost gotten through the woods, and would pass the graveyard once they got out. It did sound as if the noise had come from the graveyard.

They heard it again.

"Someone's hurt," Lily Mae said, "so what are we going to do about it?"

They stood there for a couple of minutes, wondering what to do, when suddenly she gave a little shriek and jumped back. Matthew looked down, and they both saw a dark form moving slowly along the ground. It looked like a man, but why was he crawling? Was it he who had groaned?

An hour later, Matthew's plans for going to war were forgotten, at least for the time being, as the Maxwell family tried to make their guest as comfortable as possible. They had almost immediately guessed who he was, and were amazed at the miracle that he was still alive. He was obviously not well, though, and Mrs. Maxwell was unsure of whether or not he would stay alive for long. His wounds had become worse under the heat of the late spring sun, and he had lain at the edge of the woods all day with nothing to drink but a little water in a canteen that the Union "half-wit" had left him. He had been able to tell them that much of his story before fainting away. Now he lay on the bed in a stupor, barely seeming to breath. That night, during their family prayers, Matthew and Lily Mae's father prayed for the health of their unexpected, but welcome guest.

Chapter 27

Tuesday morning, Susanna found Thomas waiting for her in the library. He motioned her to come near, and to sit down, and she did, waiting for him to tell her what he needed. It was a long moment before he began to speak, and she wondered why he was looking worried.

Finally he looked up and said slowly, "Raymond and I talked last night right before he left. They were the last ones to leave, you know, beside Mr. and Mrs. Mandet, and so I got a chance to talk to him alone."

Susanna thought a moment, then nodded. On the next Sundays that the Vincents had spent with them, she had been relieved that most of her friends had seemed to forget Raymond was new, and so had not questioned her about him again. But now she wondered what he had said to her brother.

Thomas continued, "He was wondering if we could go through the time machine today."

Susanna nodded, "do you want to? I guess we could, if Mr. Elliot and Mr. Vincent don't think it's too dangerous. Have you talked to Daddy much about it?"

Thomas looked startled at her quiet acquiesce. He had expected shivers and silent pleading to stay home. He had dreaded asking his sister this, but now he found it much easier than he had expected.

Susanna had fought with herself and prayed the whole week, preparing for this moment. She saw that Thomas was surprised, but didn't let him know she knew. Instead, she asked him again, "Well?"

"Oh, oh, have I talked to Daddy? Yes, and he said that since we've waited a week, it should be long enough. We'll try to act inconspicuous at first, and see if the Yankee soldiers are still looking for us. If everything seems safe, we can explore again."

"Well, if Daddy thinks so, I'll go with you. I don't deny that I'll be nervous, but I trust you to protect me."

"Susanna!" her brother cried with boyish delight, "You are the best sister ever! But please don't go if you don't want to."

"But I do want to," Susanna made her voice light-hearted and cheery, "You know I've always wondered what it would be like to live back during the Civil War. Now I can find out. Just please don't go join the Confederate army!"

They both laughed.

~   ~   ~

A couple of hours later, the three young people, along with Mr. Elliot stepped through the door in the wall and entered the eighteen-sixties.

Once the door was closed again, they waited a moment, then walked back through it and into the little town of Laurelton. They neared the first houses and saw that there were still Union soldiers lining the streets, so they hesitated, and discussed the best course to take. They were talking intently among themselves when they suddenly heard a young voice nearby.

"Hello, got back?"

It was young Matthew Maxwell standing there grinning at them.

"Well, Matthew Maxwell! How are you today?" Raymond asked, punching the boy's arm.

"I'm just fine, but – say, are you Yanks, or Rebels?"

"If we've got to be one or the other, I guess we're rebels," Thomas laughed.

"I thought so, when that lieutenant attacked you couple o' weeks ago, but I wanted to make sure."

"Why?"

"Weeell, I just wanted to know if you have a good place where you can hide somebody pretty good."

"What do you want to know that for?"

"Will you promise not to let it out if I tell you a secret?"

"Sure. What is it?"

"I don't know if you'll believe me until I show you, but the truth is, there was a man who was killed, and didn't end up dead, and now he's in my house."

"I'm afraid you'll have to explain better than that, my boy, if you want us to understand," Mr. Elliot told him.

Matthew grinned, then explained his family's situation with their guest. As he finished, he told them, "The doctor isn't sure if he can save him. His wounds are pretty bad, and he hasn't waked up since we brought him to the house. Wisht there was something I could do. But Ma says nursing him is girl's work, and I wouldn't be any good."

"Can we come see him?" Raymond asked, after exchanging a look with Mr. Elliot.

"Guess so. But we can't keep him at our house much longer. There's no place to hide him, and if one of the neighbors drops in, don't know but they'll take him off to prison again. Of course, most of the neighbors are good secessionists, but you never know what to expect during war time, so it's better to keep an eye out and prepare for danger." Which bit of philosophy was unexpected from a boy of Matthew's age.

~   ~   ~

A few minutes later, they were in the Maxwells' home, Matthew having led them through the back streets, as he had on the first day of their acquaintance, so that they would not be seen by any soldiers.

Susanna was the only one of the group who really knew any of the rest of the family, so the others hung back a little while she greeted her friends. Bessie and Lily Mae looked tired, and Mrs. Maxwell looked worried, but Alice was almost as carefree as before.

"'Course he'll get well," she told them optimistically, "Doctor Parker always said that when his patients sleep, that's when he knows they're fine."

Little Alice didn't realize that the sleep Mr. Wilson was sleeping was not a natural one.

Mr. Elliot bent over the still form on the bed. "Well, he's certainly out," he nodded. He looked up at Mrs. Maxwell, "I've studied medicine, and I'd like to take a look at him, if you don't mind."

"Certainly," she agreed, motioning with her hand at her unconscious guest, "I'm sure it can't do any harm, and if you think you can help, we'll all be grateful. I do hope he gets well, and I'll nurse him as long as I'm needed. We're glad to do anything for the Cause."

She left the room, and Mr. Elliot pulled the sheet off Wilson's body. He let out a whistle of dismay as he saw the bloody bandages. "I don't know much about war wounds," he told the boys, "but this looks pretty bad. Let's see what's under those bandages."

The wound in his head and body didn't seem too bad, though they were pretty gruesome to the boys, who had never been associated with much worse than a mildly broken leg or a scratched hand. The leg wound made Mr. Elliot worried, though.

"I'm sure our doctors could save it," he told them, nodding thoughtfully, "but back in this time period, a wound like this would usually mean an amputation. I'm sure that's what the doctor means to do if it gets even a little worse."

"You said it's really not so bad that our modern doctors couldn't save it?" Raymond questioned.

"Yes – at least I'm pretty sure."

Raymond and Thomas looked at each other, then Raymond burst out, "Well, you've invented a time machine, haven't you? Why don't you use it?"

"I have been using it, or we wouldn't be here right now," Mr. Elliot looked at his young friend in confusion.

"No, I mean let's take him through the time machine to a modern hospital. Then we can save his leg."

"Or his life," Thomas said, "you heard Mrs. Maxwell say the doctor told her there's not much chance for him, because there isn't much good medicine here. You've got a great idea, Raymond! Let's take him to our world and let him live!"

Mr. Elliot looked at the young men in surprise. "I never thought of that," he said slowly, "but I guess it wouldn't hurt to try. However, what do you two think the doctors are going to say when we bring in a man with three bullet wounds?"

"That's right," Thomas said thoughtfully, "don't you have to write some paperwork about how the patient got hurt?"

"Well, it won't hurt to try, anyway," Raymond protested, "it's life or death for this guy, and what are we going to do about it?"

Part Two

United States Spy

Chapter 28

A soft cooing was heard as the man drew nearer the small barn that had been put up a few months before. He entered the building and nodded as he saw that there was the new arrival they had been expecting. He picked up the little bird and examined it carefully, noting the tracking device attached to its back. The other homing pigeons continued about their own business of eating, sleeping, and pecking at each other.

It was barely a second before the man shook his head in surprise. "I thought this one wasn't supposed to be carrying any messages," he said aloud, "it was just a test."

Nevertheless, he carefully undid the strap which attached the little capsule to the bird's leg. After letting the bird go, he pulled the rolled scrap of paper out of the capsule and opened it. Then he whistled in surprise. "Whew! What kind of a code is this? Time-travel machine – hospital – Civil War – pray – this doesn't make any sense!"

He left the barn and drove to a large building just inside a small town. On the third floor, he made his way past security and placed his fingerprints on a small pad by a pair of large glass doors which slid open when the computer recognized him. As he reached into his breast pocket for the slip of paper he accidentally knocked out a small booklet shaped somewhat like a passport and dropped it to the ground. It fluttered open, and if anyone had been there to see, they would have noticed the badge of the FBI before he quickly snapped it shut and placed it back in his pocket.

A moment later he was in his boss's office, explaining what had happened at the barn.

"Let me see that note."

"Yes, sir."

His boss looked down at the piece of paper and read aloud, "'Dear Margret, I'm still a little confused about what is going on. It just doesn't seem real. The man we brought through the time travel machine to the hospital is doing better, and the boys want to go back through again. I still am afraid of going back through the machine to the War Between the States time, because of the risks we were involved in when we went through before. Thomas wants to go, though, and I will go with him. Please pray that I will have peace. Your Cousin, Susanna.' Hmm, this does sound strange. And the bird wasn't supposed to be carrying any messages either. The plans might have changed, but I should have been notified. Pickard, report to headquarters the reception of the note, and ask why plans were changed without my being notified. Also ask for the key to this code. Go now."

"Yes, sir." Pickard left the office.

~   ~   ~

The Sunday a week after they had brought Richard Wilson through the time machine and to a hospital in the modern world, Susanna and Thomas and their family prepared for church. The Vincents had begun to come regularly to the services both at the Jacksons' morning church, and to worship at their house in the evening.

Susanna was tired of having to guard her conversation so as not to let her friends know what had been happening. She was not used to keeping deep secrets from the girls she associated with. Adele and Margaret, her two most intimate friends, had already questioned her too closely for comfort, and the other girls, Ann and Crystal Starr, and Kitty McKeith had seemed suspicious of her confused answers to some of their questions and her quick change of subject. Jennie too, her sweet and bubbly younger sister, had seemed on the verge of bursting into a volley of questions on several occasions, and this worried Susanna more than the others, for the girl had a way of finding things out for herself with her quick mind.

As they drove to church, Susanna kept the conversation merry – and it was not hard to do so. Edward and Jennie, the twins, were quite apt with their tongues, and had no trouble keeping up a sharp repartee to Susanna and Thomas's remarks. Danny also had ready wit, for he had learned from his older siblings.

Later that day, after the preparations for dinner and evening services had been completed and guests had started to arrive, Susanna opened the door for Raymond and his father. Raymond greeted her with a smile, then, after looking hastily around to see that no one was listening, he spoke quickly and quietly, "He's doing better, the doctors say. They are sure they'll be able to save his leg now, but – "

"But what?" she asked anxiously, "is there anything wrong?"

"Not exactly," he told her, "but the doctors have been asking awkward questions."

Susanna clasped her hands tightly in front of her and looked down. "Such as?" she asked.

"Oh, just how he got hurt, why someone would be fooling around enough to shoot him three times, and stuff like that. You know if it was an accident, usually it would just be that someone had hit him by mistake while they were out hunting or something, but three times?" he shook his head, "Dad and I really don't know how to explain. So far, we've just said that we found him somewhere and are helping him for no reason but that we're Christians and always want to help anyone who is hurt."

Susanna nodded, "And did they accept that as an answer?"

"I think so, at least mostly. You know we got rid of all his articles of clothing that were too obviously Civil War era, but I don't know what they'll do if he starts talking. They might shut him up in an insane asylum, like Thomas almost did when you first met him." He chuckled.

Susanna laughed with him, "How awful that was! I guess you have found out by now that Thomas is not what he seemed on that day? I don't know what made him so fiery then, but he's usually much nicer. You do know that don't you?"

"Of course!" Raymond laughed again, "but where is he? I've got to tell him what I just told you. I was going to tell him first, and then let him tell you, but when you opened the door, and no one else could hear, I just had to tell you."

Susanna laughed again, "I'm glad to know Richard Wilson is better, anyway," she said, "Thomas is downstairs with the rest of the boys, I think."

"See you later, then!" and Raymond swung open the door to the basement and clattered down the stairs.

His father followed Susanna into the kitchen where several of the adults were sitting discussing the latest news reports and wondering just what it would take to get the country back on the right track. Perhaps it was a strange subject for a Sunday afternoon, but one that was often brought up, nonetheless. It was not all politics, however, for often they would quote verses which had to do with what they were discussing, and the whole conversation was based on what the Bible had to say about different happenings around the world.

Susanna passed through the kitchen and out the door, where several girls were sitting on the screened porch. They greeted her with smiles and made room for her in one of the cushioned chairs that were on the porch.

"Is it time for dinner?" one of them asked.

"Not quite," Susanna answered, "there's still another half hour, I think."

A moment later the girls heard terrified screams coming from below them in the back yard. They hurried to the screens and looked out giving startled exclamations.

~   ~   ~

Raymond hurried through the large, finished basement and entered a room in the back from which could be heard shouts and laughter. He saw the boys and young men grouped around the ping-pong table eagerly watching the two competitors.

"Come on, Jack! Beat him! I know you can!"

"No way! Frank can beat Jack anytime, I think!"

"Let's go, Frank, hit it hard!"

"There you go, Jack!"

"That's right!"

"Whew! Where'd that ball go? Somebody catch it!"

Raymond swiped the air and caught the tiny plastic ball. He tossed it back to Frank Garrold, who was one of the two rivals, and greeted the couple of boys near him before nodding to Thomas, who quickly came over.

"How is he?" Thomas asked, following Raymond out of the crowded game room and into the empty room outside.

"Much better," and Raymond began to repeat what he had told Susanna a few minutes before. When he was only halfway through, however, Thomas, who had been looking out of the window at intervals suddenly gasped, and held out a hand for his friend to stop.

"Wait! Oh, no! I've got to –"

"What in the world!" Raymond exclaimed, "where are you going?"

Thomas didn't stop to answer. He dashed to the door and pulled it open, then flung himself through, not even waiting to close it.

"Where are you going?" Raymond called again, then he saw what Thomas had seen. Florence, who had gotten over her shyness pretty quickly, as Edward had predicted, was running for her life, it seemed, and screaming. At her heels was a large goose!

"Oh – my – goodness!" Raymond shouted, not realizing how loud his voice was. Several of the boys heard his shout and came running out of the other room. They watched as Thomas ran up to the goose – or actually, the gander, and grabbed it by the neck. Florence ran on a few yards, and then fell into her sister Susanna's arms. The older girl had come running down the porch stairs as she saw what was happening.

Thomas flung the gander from him and chased it back to its pen. It flew gracefully over the fence in spite of its ungraceful encounter with Thomas a moment before.

"Huh," said Thomas, "I guess they need their wings clipped again. You all right, Florrie?"

"I guess so, but I was so afraid it would bite me and make my legs bleed like it did Charles last week."

"It bit Charles last week?" Thomas exclaimed in surprise, "why didn't he tell me?"

"Because he's a boy," Susanna told him, leading her sister up the steps. She turned and looked over her shoulder, "It happened when he was in the pen feeding them. He told me, and thought there was enough fuss about it. He wasn't hurt, so I guess he thought you didn't need to know."

"Well," Thomas said, giving a chuckle, "that one ended just fine. Ever live on a farm, Raymond?"

"No, seems interesting."

"Sure enough!" Noah McKeith agreed, "Never calm for long. But this wasn't very compared to some things that happen on a place like ours."

"Really!" Raymond hoped they would explain what they meant, and they did. By the time they got back inside, there had been three stories told already and another was starting, but soon Thomas looked at his phone and realized it was time to gather in the kitchen to pray.

~   ~   ~

"Headquarters says there was no message sent, sir, and there was no code. They wish the exact wording of the message to be sent for analysis."

"Do as ordered, Pickard."

"Yes, sir."

A few minutes later he was back. "Headquarters says stand by for orders. The message was not authorized, and the code has not been found. They're not sure how the message came to be attached to the pigeon, because everyone associated with the project has denied writing the message."

"Thank you, Pickard. Let me know as soon as more information is obtained."

A little while later, Pickard again entered his boss's office. "News from headquarters, sir," he said, "in following the path recorded by the pigeon's tracking device, they have found it is probable that the pigeon stopped for rest at a house somewhere near here before finishing it's flight. I'm not sure where."

"And they think someone in that house attached the message to the pigeon?"

"That is the best guess right now, sir."

The boss looked directly at Pickard. "You understand that this is a very important project we are working on here, don't you? If the country is struck by an EM pulse, this may be the only way we will be able to communicate with anyone. Several of the other main powers in the world have had this operation going on for years already, and we're just starting. We can't let anything get in the way of this business."

"I understand, sir," Pickard answered, "If an EMP is sent through the U.S., all electronic communication will be cut off. But these homing pigeons will still be able to fly and carry messages."

"So since you understand how important our project is, you must understand how important it is that nothing else interferes. We've got to get to the bottom of the message you found as soon as possible." [1]

---

[1] See Author's Notes at the back.

~   ~   ~

"Hey, Raymond, how's it going?" Thomas answered the phone call from his friend.

"Pretty well; he's much better. The doctors think he'll be awake and talking by tomorrow."

"That's good – I think. I mean, do you think he's going to say something strange that'll make them shut him up?"

"I don't know. I hope not," Raymond answered.

"Well, we'll pray for him, and that he keeps quiet for as long as possible. What do you think we should do if he does start talking?"

"I don't know. Let's take things as they come, okay?"

"Yes, that's fine with me, but you know we're supposed to 'prepare for the worst and hope for the best.'"

"That's right. I'll talk to Dad and Mr. Elliot, and you ask your parents if there's anything they can think of that would have a chance of getting him back home safely."

"Will do; 'bye, Raymond."

"Goodbye."

~   ~   ~

Pickard hung up the telephone and hurried back to the office of his boss.

"More news," he said, "headquarters has traced the exact house where the pigeon stopped. It is believed that it ate there and rested for a while. They also have found that someone in that house owns homing pigeons of almost the same type we are using, so it is possible he or she picked one of the pigeons at random to send a message with, and it happened to be ours. Unfortunately for that person, the message was not sent where it was intended."

"Are there any further steps being taken?"

"They have not decided whether to notify the owner of what happened or not. First they want to find out if the message is really coded."

"That is all."

"Yes, sir."

Chapter 29

A couple of days later, Pickard and his boss received more news from headquarters. Pickard brought the news immediately to his boss as soon as he had finished the conversation over the phone. Now they had something to work toward, instead of simply waiting for word from headquarters. Now they would be the ones *sending* the information to headquarters.

He entered the office and explained: "Here is the information about the Jacksons – those are the people who own the homing pigeons, and who we believe sent out the message."

"Hmm," the boss said, scanning the paper Pickard had printed out from the email he had gotten, "What is this here? 'Oldest daughter, Susanna,' that would be the one who wrote the note, right?" he asked, looking up.

"Yes, here is the note. It is signed Susanna."

"Well, let's see, 'Christian family' what does that have to do with it?"

"Quite a lot, I believe. Christians always seem to get the best of any government they're living under for some reason. We can't let that happen this time, but we've got to be aware of the fact, and be careful."

"Hmm, never thought of that. Are you sure?"

"Certain, sir."

"Well, well, let's go on."

They read through the list of information on the Jackson family, and then decided on a plan. If all went well, they would know a lot more within a few days.

"He's awake, Thomas!"

"What?"

"Richard Wilson's awake. I asked the staff at the hospital to call me as soon as he was conscious, and they called just now."

"But – what are we going to do?"

"I would think he's well enough to be moved. We'd better get him out of there before he starts talking."

"But how? They always take years to let people out of the hospital."

"Well, goodness! We can't wait years," Raymond was half laughing and half serious.

"Figure of speech, Raymond. What did your dad say, anyway?"

"He isn't sure, General. We've just got to pray a while longer, I guess."

"Are you going to try to see him?"

"Sure, and I'll tell him not to talk, if I can."

"Call me back, or text me afterward, okay?"

"Okay! Goodbye!"

~   ~   ~

Raymond asked his father if he wanted to come along, but Mr. Vincent had a previous engagement, so the young man drove to the hospital alone. When he entered and asked to see the patient, there was a bit of discussion, but he was allowed in. Richard Wilson was awake, but did not seem fully conscious. Raymond stepped over to the bed and looked at him, then back at the nurse. She had turned and was doing something at the other side of the room, and didn't seem to be paying much attention, so he took Richard's hand and squeezed it, looking directly into the man's eyes.

"Wilson, Wilson, can you hear me?" he whispered.

There was a barely perceptible nod.

"Do you understand what I'm saying?"

Again a nod.

"Here's to test, if you have a sister named Lucy, squeeze my hand twice."

Two squeezes. He was definitely awake, and hopefully able to remember what Raymond was about to tell him.

Raymond looked back at the nurse again, but saw she was still occupied. He whispered again, "There is something important I have to tell you, Richard Wilson, and you must make sure to remember it." the patient nodded again, this time whispering back, "Yes?"

"You must be careful not to talk to these people at the hospital. We are going to try to get you out of here and back to your sister as soon as possible, but we are afraid they might lock you up if they know who you are. If they say anything you don't understand, just pretend that you don't feel like talking, or something like that. There will be a lot of strange things going on, probably, but remember that I am a friend, and – you remember the Jacksons?"

"Yes."

"They are friends also. Don't forget that. I don't know what is going to happen over the next few days, but it's better to be prepared. Do you know where your sister is?"

"No – yes – I think so. If I can get out of here and get my bearings, I think I can find her."

"Good. We'll try to get you out of here."

Another quick look and Raymond saw the nurse was turning around, so he nodded to Richard and asked cheerfully, "so is your leg feeling better?"

Richard nodded, then Raymond left.

~   ~   ~

"We have found that there is person in the hospital with bullet wounds supposed to be from a Civil War era gun, but he was not placed in the care of the hospital by the Jackson family or by any of their known friends. His name is unknown, as he was unconscious when brought to the doors of the hospital. However, the people who placed him in the hospital were Christians."

"Interesting, Pickard, interesting. Let's follow this clue and see where it takes us. What is the name of the people who brought this man to the hospital?"

"Vincent. They run a moving company in a town a few miles south of where the Jackson family lives. Neither the Vincents nor the Jacksons are much on Facebook or other lines of communication, but in what is on there, I can't find a single picture which has people from both families in it."

"Okay, keep working. I'm sure we'll find something."

"That's right, sir."

~   ~   ~

A week later, Raymond made a quick, unexpected visit to the Jacksons' house. He turned into the driveway and saw a couple of the kids out front pulling weeds.

"Hey there, Danny, Florence, Charles. How's it going?"

"Fine! Just fine! I didn't know you were coming over today, Raymond," Danny said.

"Neither did I, until just a few minutes ago. I have something I need to talk to your big brother about."

"Which one?"

Raymond laughed, "Thomas, of course. Who did you think?"

"You got to remember that we have four boys in this family," Florence told him, "And all of 'em are older than me."

"Oh, I remember all right. You couldn't miss them!" Raymond laughed, "there are so many of you that I can hardly keep track, though."

All the children laughed, and Raymond closed the car door and went up to the house.

The door was opened by Edward, "Hello, Raymond. I didn't know you were coming. Did you just drop by?"

"Sort of. I need to talk to Thomas. Is he here?"

"He will be in a couple of minutes. Are you staying for lunch?"

"Oh – no, I can't stay. I just have something to say to Thomas, then I'll leave."

"I guess you can take a plate with you then. Or, is what you have to say to Thomas private?"

"Yes."

"Well, then, you two can take your lunch and eat it in the library while you're talking."

"Oh – but I, uh, okay, I guess so."

Edward laughed, "come on in. Sit down in the library while I tell Susanna you're here, and I'll be right back."

The boy was gone like a flash, and Raymond waited for a moment, then unsuspecting, Jennie walked in.

She stared at him, startled, and exclaimed, "I didn't know you were here!"

"Well, now you do," Edward laughed as he returned and seated himself on the sofa. Jennie disappeared for a moment, then came back and sat beside him.

Raymond looked the twins over carefully. They didn't look much alike, though they were twins. Edward was light haired; almost as blond as his sister Susanna with dark blue eyes, but Jennie's hair was of a dark brown color, like Thomas, and her eyes were brown to match.

"What have you two been up to today?" Raymond asked them as a way to start a conversation.

The twins looked at each other. Then Edward began to sing with a twinkle in his eye, "What did we do today, sis, what did we do today?"

Jennie paused hardly a second, then sang back at him, "Anything from scrub the floors to put the toys away!" She continued, "I would spy a little work and say 'this must be done,'"

"Oh joy, oh boy! We would have so much fun!" Edward finished.

Raymond laughed, "did you make that up?"

"Some, but not exactly. The tune is an old one, and some of the words are too. We just improvised to make it fit," said Jennie.

"What song is it?"

"The original was written during World War I and was called *Where do We Go from Here, Boys, Where do We Go from Here?*" Edward replied, "Not all of the verses from the original are good, but we like the tune."

"Do you do that often?" Raymond asked, "I mean, improvise on old songs with new words?"

"Yes. In fact we do it so much that a lot of our friends call us the 'singing twins!'" Edward laughed.

At that moment Thomas opened the front door and walked in. He looked at Raymond in surprise, but came over and shook his hand after putting down the computer bag he had taken to work with him.

"Hello, Raymond. Came over for lunch?"

"I needed to talk to you, Thomas, and Edward here told me we could do it over lunch."

"Sure we can. Is the food ready, Jennie?"

"Yes, Mommy said to call everyone as soon as you got home. Daddy's not coming for lunch."

"Okay, go ahead then. Call everyone to come in here, or does Mommy want to pray upstairs?"

"No, she said you can pray in the library. She told us to bring her food upstairs for her."

Raymond wanted to ask if and why their mother was not feeling well, but wasn't sure if it would be polite. Before he could frame an appropriate question, the twins had left and Thomas was asking, "Something about that Wilson guy?"

"Yes."

"We can eat in here and talk. The kids will leave us alone."

"That's what Edward said," then to change the conversation, as the other members of the family were beginning to gather in the library, Raymond asked,

"How many books do you have anyway?" He looked around at the walls covered with bookshelves.

"Let's see," Jennie began with mock seriousness, counting off on her fingers, "we have eighty-six G. A. Henty books, seventy-two Christian Heroes and Heroes of History published by YWAM, two series by Robert Elmer containing eight books each, the American Adventure series has forty-eight books in it,"

Edward continued in a sing-song chant, "Four books by Elizabeth Yates, eight books by Isabella Alden – *girls'* books!" he shook his head in pretended disgust, then went on, "Three-four-five books by Margaret Sidney, about twenty in the Tom Swift series,"

Jennie took up the line again, "thirty-two of the Trailblazer series, and about a hundred missionary biographies besides what we've already said – "

"Okay! Hold it, hold it," Thomas exclaimed, laughing, "Raymond didn't want a literal account of every book in our library!"

"We didn't give him an account of every book in our library," Jennie protested, shaking her brown locks away from her face, "not even half! We have a couple thousand books in our library other than those we already spoke of, not counting the picture books and the – oh – did you say to stop, Thomas?" and she looked up with a great deal of pretended surprise.

"Yes! I did," he shook his head at her, still laughing, "leave our poor guest with his senses, won't you? There is no need for him to memorize the exact number of books we have, when I haven't the least idea of the amount myself."

"Neither have I," Jennie confessed with a laugh, "but I could find out."

"No, thank you. Is everyone here? Let's pray," Thomas said, "Dear Lord, You are awesome and wonderful and all-powerful. We ask that You protect us from harm, and take care of Mommy as she is not feeling well. Please help me and Raymond as we discuss our question and let us find the best answer. Bless this food we are about to eat, Lord. In the name of Jesus I pray, Amen."

Susanna explained what they would be eating, and which pots contained what, then they all trooped into the kitchen to serve themselves. When Raymond and Thomas had gotten their plates, they went into the library and sat down. Then Raymond told his friend what had happened at the hospital.

"Hmm. Any ideas?" Thomas asked, "do you think they'll let him out anytime soon?"

"No. The only thing I can think of is storming the hospital and carrying him off by force!"

The two young men laughed together, and Thomas asked with a chuckle, "but what would you do about later? Of course we would be arrested for such a thing."

"Oh, we'd be in disguise, of course. Then the next day I'd go in and ask to see him. When they told me what happened, I'd act very surprised and angry, and ask what kind of security service they had anyway?"

He got up and set his plate down, and pretended to be annoyed, "What do you mean he's gone? Kidnapped under the very noses of the hospital guards? Huh! I thought you were supposed to be safe. I guess I'll have to find a better hospital next time I need one! This is ridiculous! I wanted to speak to that man my father and I have placed here! Now how can I find him? What have you done with him, you incompetent unreliable – " he broke off as he saw Susanna leaning against one of the pillars and watching him in amusement.

Thomas and Raymond both burst into laughter, and Susanna looked from one to the other in astonishment.

"Who in the world were you talking to or about?" she asked, "my brother? This almost reminds me of what Richard Wilson said about him the first day we met," and she laughed.

"Thomas and I were discussing ways to get that guy out of the hospital, and this was one of them."

"To go and rail and storm at the hospital guards? I don't think that'll get you very far!" she laughed again.

"No! This one was just a joke. I didn't really plan to do that. But we can't think of anything better, can you?" he asked her.

"I? I don't know, I'm sure. What kind of an idea do you need?" she questioned, seating herself beside her brother.

"We just need a really simple way to get Richard Wilson out of the hospital very soon, even though they haven't given him leave yet. We don't want to take the chance of his talking, and ending up in an insane asylum."

"I see. How do you propose to do this? And what was the plan you were just discussing – or rather, ranting about – when I came in?"

"Oh, that?" the boys laughed, "Raymond suggested storming the place in disguise, kidnapping our man, and going back the next day to complain."

"Complain of what?" she asked.

"Complain of the incompetence of the hospital security that would let a man be taken away right under their noses."

"Goodness, but that *is* a ridiculous plan! It all makes sense except the storming the hospital and carrying off your man part. How in the world do you think you can do that?"

"We don't think we could do it. It was all a joke. But if you can't think of anything better, we might just have to try it."

"Well then I guess I'd better start thinking hard," she exclaimed, "because I'm sure I *don't* want you two coming home all broken and bruised and maybe shot just because you tried to break into a hospital. You are *not* accomplished criminals, and I am *sure* you would not be able to act like ones, even for only one night. I've got to go back to the kids now, but I will be thinking. You can count on that!" and she left with a little laugh and a wave of her hand.

"I guess she's right," Raymond said in pretended dejection, "my beautiful plan wouldn't work so well after all."

"It sure wouldn't! But we might as well give up and wait for him to get better. You said he told you he'd try to hold his tongue, didn't you?"

"I did, but you never know if he'll be able to or not."

"But what can we do?" Thomas protested, "Those people at the hospital hardly ever let anyone out early."

"That's true. I wonder if your sister will be able to think of anything."

"I don't know. She's pretty imaginative, and can think up solutions to almost any problem, but this one is so strange I'm not sure she'll be able to find an answer. I don't think anyone will be able to. Talked to your dad and Mr. Elliot yet?"

"Of course, but neither of them can think of anything."

~   ~   ~

Pickard knocked on the door to the boss's office.

"Come in. Hello, Pickard. Found anything out?"

"Yes, sir. Something very interesting, and if I'd been watching more carefully I might have even more information."

"Well, go on."

"Raymond Vincent, the son of the man who has placed the wounded man in the hospital – you remember?"

"Yes."

"You know it's been much easier to track people since the government started requiring GPS in every cellphone. I looked up Raymond's phone and found that he was just leaving the Jacksons' house."

"Really!"

"Yes. If I had only noticed he was there a few minutes earlier, I might have listened to the conversation and found something out, but I didn't. I'll set the computer to notify me if he goes into that house again."

"That's right. Do that, and tell me if you hear anything important. But that we are sure now the Vincents and the Jacksons are acquainted is very important."

"Yes, sir."

Susanna came to Thomas on Saturday night looking excited. "Thomas, I want to talk to you," she whispered, ignoring the interested eyes of Charles, who was nearby.

"All right. Come into Daddy's office after the kids are in bed."

"I'll do that."

A few minutes later they were sitting facing each other in chairs behind the glass doors of their father's office.

"What is it?" Thomas asked.

"I have an idea about what you and Raymond were talking about a couple of days ago."

"How to get Richard Wilson out of the hospital?"

"Yes."

"Well, what is it?" he asked again.

"Frank Garrold is in governmental service, isn't he?"

"I think so. You know some government people can't talk much about their jobs. I don't know exactly what he does. But what does he have to do with it?"

"I thought we could let him in on the secret, and he could use his authority to get Mr. Wilson out of the hospital."

"Hmm! That might work. Good idea. I'll ask him on Sunday, if I can get a chance, if he is allowed to use his authority for something like that. You know they might only be allowed to use their authority for things they are commissioned to do by the government."

"I didn't think of that. But we can try anyway. Please do ask him, but you probably don't want to tell him why you want to know unless he answers 'yes' because Mr. Elliot doesn't want anyone to know about the time machine."

"That's right. Okay, I'll ask him tomorrow if I can. Now we should go to bed."

As they stood up and opened the door to leave, Thomas suddenly put a hand on his sister's shoulder.

"You're not worrying about the machine anymore, are you?" he asked.

"N-no. Not much. I think I'm doing a lot better."

"That's good. I don't want you to feel bad, but I really would like to keep going through the machine."

"I know, Thomas. And I'll go with you whenever you go. It's getting a lot easier. I wouldn't be able to stay here by myself, though. If you go, I'll have to go with you, or I definitely *will* worry."

"Okay, whatever you say," he answered, giving her a one-armed hug. They went upstairs together.

Chapter 30

Sunday was a bright and cheerful day. Susanna noticed that as soon as she awoke and got out of bed. Later, as she was brushing her long blond waves of hair, she thought, *"I hope Thomas gets a chance to ask Frank about getting Richard Wilson out of the hospital. I keep remembering Lucy Wilson's face – her eyes filled with tears and her lips trembling – as she told us that her brother was in prison. I hope we can save him for her. Oh! I wonder what she is doing now? I mean, what she did after he was taken from her, because it happened a hundred fifty years ago! That feels so strange. I guess she thought he was dead. Maybe she went back home. I guess she would have had a father and mother. Well, when we get him out of the hospital and take him back to his world, he'll know where to find her."*

She rolled the sides of her hair back and slipped a clip in. Then she straightened her shirt and skirt and went downstairs.

At breakfast she caught her older brother's eye. A nod assured her he had not forgotten their conversation of the night before. When she was finished eating, Nancy needed help with her own hair. Soon the family was in the car and driving to church.

~ ~ ~

Thomas signaled for Frank Garrold to come over to where he was standing.

"Need me, Thomas?" Frank asked, when he reached his side.

"I have a question for you," Thomas told him.

"Ask away. I hope I know the answer."

Thomas moved farther away from the crowd of boys and into the other room. Frank followed.

"Frank, I want to know how much authority you have with that government position of yours."

"Whew, that's hard to explain. What exactly do you need to know for?"

"Can you get someone out of somewhere that they're supposed to stay?"

"Again, you'll have to be more particular for me to answer, Thomas."

"All right," Thomas said, "what about a police station, a hospital, or an insane asylum?"

"Mmm, let me think."

~   ~   ~

"Well, Pickard, what have you found out now?" the boss asked.

"I tried to call the hospital and ask the name of the man with the bullet wounds, but they wanted to know my reason for calling. I couldn't think up a good excuse. What should I tell them?"

"Tell them you think the man might be a relative you've been trying to trace."

"I'll do that. They won't know the difference."

A while later he was back, "He is conscious, they said, and has told them his name. It is Richard Wilson."

"Were they able to get any more out of him?"

"No, when they asked if any of his family were to be contacted and for their phone numbers, they say he looked around wildly for a moment, then dropped back in a faint. They believe it is just the after effects of the wounds, maybe a bit of a problem from the one on his head, but if this time machine stuff is true, it could be he just didn't know what a 'phone' was!"

"That's true. Here's what you can do to get more information. Have the computer notify you if either the Vincents or the Jacksons speak his name."

"Okay."

"And how's our other work going? You've been so busy with this lately I'm afraid the pigeons are going to be neglected."

"Oh!" I just thought of something. What if the girl who sent the message on the pigeon wonders why she never got an acknowledgment from her cousin?"

"That's true. We could find out who her cousin is, and put the message on one of the pigeons there, pretending the pigeon was just delayed, but if that girl counts her pigeons she'll find there aren't any missing."

"She might think she imagined that she sent the message."

"She might, but that all depends on what kind of a girl she is. We don't know enough about her to take the chance. The best thing to do would be to take one of her pigeons and attach the message to it, sending it to her cousin."

"How would we do that?"

"Oh, you'll find away. Someone can sneak into the yard, get into the barn, and take one of the pigeons. It probably won't fly at night, but we could bring it here and let it go in the daytime."

"How would we get into the yard without being seen?"

"If criminals can do it, we can too. Just look up on the records whether they have a burglar alarm or not."

"So I'm going to enter that yard in the middle of the night, trying not to set off the burglar alarm, break into the barn or whatever they have the pigeons in, and steal a bird?"

"Pickard!"

"Yes sir!"

"Anyway, you don't have to do it yourself. You can get someone to do it for you."

"I know what I can do," Pickard grinned, "I'll go to the jail, find a housebreaker, and pay him to do the job."

"Good idea. Why don't you do that. Now go away and let me finish this work."

Pickard stared at his boss for a minute, but receiving no returning glance from the man whose head was bent over his paperwork, he turned and walked out the door, muttering, "That was supposed to be a joke."

~   ~   ~

When Lucy had watched the guards take her brother away on that awful day she had felt as if her heart was breaking. Arthur had not dared put his arm around her on the streets, but as soon as he had reached that quiet garden behind the hotel, he had pulled her close and let her cry her heart out.

After she was done, he quietly took her into the hotel and told her to get some rest while he went out to make arrangements. A while later, on the stage going home, he had informed her, "I told the Colonel that I'd promised Richard I'd take you home. I don't think he suspected anything, as he has long been aware of what he calls my 'soft heart' and though he thinks it ridiculous, he knows he can't change me. He gave me leave for a week, but I don't know what he'll do when I don't come back. Once I'm in the Confederate army, I think I'll be safe enough, though what will happen if they capture me, I can't say. But don't worry about that dear, I'm taking you to your home first to make arrangements, then you'll go to my mother."

"Will she receive you again?" Lucy had asked, "will they believe you when you tell them you've changed your mind?"

"I don't know, but I believe that the fact that you are a Southerner will help them so they might not doubt me."

"I hope so, Arthur."

~   ~   ~

A couple of weeks later, Arthur Johnston alighted from the train and helped his wife to the platform beside him. He was no longer wearing the hated blue

230

uniform. That had been discarded while at Lucy's house. No longer either would he be called "Lieutenant" until he joined the Confederate army.

There was no carriage waiting to meet them, as he had not notified his parents of his marriage or that he was coming, but there was a farmer with his wagon at the station, and he was easily hired to take them to the Johnston estates.

As they arrived, Arthur watched Lucy for her reaction. His family's house was not what it had been before the war, but the grounds were still beautiful, for as yet there had been no battles nearby.

She smiled up at him, "It's beautiful, Arthur, and I'm certain it will be a pleasure to stay here. I do hope your mother will – "

"She is sure to, dear," he told her, "I know it. But come in. You must not mind if they don't notice you at first, for I will be kept busy answering their questions. Now I almost wish I had given them word I was coming."

"It is too late for regrets," she whispered, "let us go in, and we will see what happens."

They had descended from the wagon, and the farmer had driven off. Then they walked up to the door of the house.

It was opened by a servant, whose eyes widened at the sight of her former master.

"Oh, Mistah Arthuh! You come back? What's yo' pa goin' to say?"

"Thank you for your kind welcome, Hattie, and yes, I'm glad to be home," Arthur said with a laugh, as he took the woman's hand in his.

"An' dere's yo' own laugh again! Yo' jus' wait till I tell yo' ma you'se here."

"Don't tell her, Hattie. Just say there's a gentleman to see her and he wouldn't give his name."

"Yas, suh. I will. Yo' jus' wait till she sees you, dat's what I say."

"Thank you, Hattie. Now go tell Mother. I'll go into the parlor."

It was a few minutes later, that a lady stepped into the doorway. She hesitated, took a couple of quick steps forward, then stopped short.

"Arthur? What are you doing here?" she asked uncertainly, her eyes filling with tears.

He held out his arms, "Mother!"

She took a breath, seemed to hesitate a little longer, then uttered a sob, half of joy and half of fright, and ran to him.

A minute later, she said, "But Arthur, my son, your father – "

"I hope my father will receive me again when he hears I have changed my views on certain things and am about to join the Confederate army."

"Oh! Oh, Arthur!" and she threw her arms around his neck, "I never dreamed this would happen, though I prayed for you every day. But oh, I am so glad."

"So am I, Mother, but you do not ask how my mind was changed, after it was made up so firmly."

"Well? I supposed you would tell me soon."

"I will," and he drew Lucy forward, "this is the woman who has convinced me that the South is right. She is now my wife, and I hope you will take her as your daughter. She has no one in the world but myself, her father and brother having just died."

"My dear," Mrs. Johnston said softly, "I trust my son that he has chosen wisely. Will you let me be a mother to you?"

"Oh, Mrs. Johnston – Mother!" Lucy faltered, and was in the lady's arms.

The door was flung open and a tall man strode into the room. "What are you doing here?" he thundered, "Did I not tell you to stay away from this house?"

Arthur stood up and faced his father.

"You did, sir, but there was a condition. You said that I was not to come into this house until I had changed my views as to who was right in this war. Now that I have, I believe I have a right to come back."

"Arthur. Arthur, my son, are you speaking the truth?"

"Never more in earnest, Father."

"Then come here." And the son and father were clasped in a warm embrace.

"Now Father, I wish to present my wife, Lucy."

"You are married? And you did not send us word?"

"We have been married only a little over two weeks. There was much haste, as Lucy's brother was in prison about to be shot because he had been spying for the Confederacy. The marriage was a private one."

Johnston ignored the fact that his father himself had been the one to tell him not to send word whatever happened.

"And it is you who has brought my son back to me?" Mr. Johnston asked, holding out his hand to the girl.

She looked at her husband, how *was* she to answer that? But he answered for her as she took his father's hand, "Yes, Father, it was she whose arguments convinced me to come back to your side."

~   ~   ~

"Well, what did Frank say?" Raymond asked, when he called Thomas on Monday morning.

"He isn't sure. He needs more information than I was able to tell him under my promise to Mr. Elliot. I'll have to ask Mr. Elliot if it will be all right to explain the whole situation to Frank Garrold, and ask him to promise not to tell, or how much of it I will be allowed to say."

"You want to ask him yourself, or should I ask him?" Raymond questioned, "He's coming to our house for dinner tonight."

"Then you go ahead and do the asking. I need to know the answer soon, though, because we want that Wilson guy out of the hospital as soon as possible."

"That's right. Well, I've got things to do, so I'll say 'bye now, but I'll get back to you as soon as possible," Raymond said.

"Thanks."

That night Raymond texted Thomas, "He said yes. Tell Frank Garrold whatever you need to tell him, as long as he is safe."

~ ~ ~

As inconspicuously as possible Susanna eyed the glass doors behind which Thomas and Frank were closeted. They were sitting in Mr. Jackson's office, as she and Thomas had done when she had suggested he ask Frank Garrold for help. "I do hope he is able to do it," she whispered under her breath, then hurried away before they had a chance to notice her.

"Susanna, what's Frank Garrold here for?" she felt a tug on her arm and found Jennie standing at her side.

"He had something to talk over with Thomas," the older girl replied offhandedly, hoping her sister wouldn't keep asking questions. But Jennie had no intention of being put off that way.

"What do they have to talk over?" Jennie asked, "Is Thomas trying to do business with him?"

"Not exactly. It's something more private, I think." Finally Susanna stopped trying to get around the point and spoke plainly, "Jennie, you'd better just leave them alone and forget about it. I'm sorry, but this time your curiosity can't be satisfied. I know you like to know everything that goes on here, and we tell you as much as we can, but there are some things that can't be told. I'm sorry," she repeated.

Jennie nodded, "I know. I won't ask any more questions if I can help it," she said, "Is Frank staying for dinner?"

"You said you wouldn't ask any more questions!" Susanna teased.

"Aw, Susanna!" the younger girl laughed.

Susanna answered, "Yes, I know, that isn't what you or I meant. Probably he will stay for dinner. We'll see when they come out."

The two sisters went into the kitchen to finish the dinner preparations.

Chapter 31

Frank Garrold stared at his friend. This was much more than he had expected – not that he had had the slightest idea of what to expect, though. This was harder to answer than he had expected too. His job in the FBI did give him a certain authority, but should he use it in the way Thomas wanted him to?

"I'll have to think about it," he said slowly, "I don't know if I can. But then," he thought for a moment, "why not? I'm just taking one man out of the hospital. As far as anyone knows, he's just someone who was out shooting with a friend and got shot up by accident. Well, let me have a day to think, and I'll tell you tomorrow whether I'll do it or not. I realize you can't wait too long, or he'll have to start talking, which could be damaging to that Mr. Elliot."

"That's true. So please do hurry. If you decide you can't do it, we'll have to think of another way to get him out, and that might take a while. Now we're done, though, can you stay for dinner?"

"I guess so. Let me text Mom that I won't be there."

~   ~   ~

A man in a dark suit with his hat pulled over his eyes strode up to the front desk in the lobby of the hospital. As the woman sitting behind it looked up, he opened his coat and pulled out a badge which he flashed in front of her face.

"Y-yes, sir?" she asked, startled.

"There is a patient here that I want removed," he said gruffly, "I have a place I need to take him. I have been informed that he is well enough to be moved now, and he will receive all further care that he will need at his destination."

"Which patient, sir?" she asked, staring at his coat, under which he had again hidden the badge.

"This is highly classified business. Get me the manager."

"Yes, sir."

She picked up the telephone on the desk and hurriedly called the manager.

"There's an FBI agent here, and he wants to see you," she said, trying to control the shaking in her voice. She had been startled greatly.

A moment later a man came striding up to the desk. He held out his hand to the FBI agent, and asked, "How can I help you?"

"Take me somewhere we can speak privately," came in the gruff tones of the dark-suited man.

"This way," the manager nodded, and led the man into a room where he closed the door after them. It was not until then that he noticed two more men, wearing sunglasses and moustaches, who were close behind the FBI agent. He couldn't tell if they were in the FBI also, but it didn't really matter. They took their places outside the door when he closed it, and waited while their leader talked to the hospital manager.

He flashed his badge before the manager to prove who he was, and then said, "You have a patient here named Richard Wilson."

"I – I believe so," the manager said hesitantly, "I can't keep track of all the patients we have here, but his case was so strange, talk of him has gone all over the hospital."

The FBI agent frowned – at least what could be seen of his face was in a frown – the manager felt it was very disturbing to speak to a man whose eyes were hidden.

"That is not good," the agent said sternly, "he was not to be talked about. It is too late now, but I am getting him out of here, and you need to give me his room number and the information on how to care for him."

"Should I get you his doctor?" the manager asked.

"That would be fine. But fast. I am in a hurry."

"Yes, sir. I will. If you'll just wait here a moment, I'll be back with the doctor as soon as possible."

The agent took a seat, and the manager hurried out the door, nearly bumping into the two men who were waiting outside. These two entered the office when the manager was gone, and the younger one spoke to the FBI agent, lifting his dark glasses to see him better.

"Wow, that was great, Frank! You made it seem so real."

"Thanks, Raymond. But it's not done yet."

Raymond nodded, then lowered his glasses, and the two again went out the door as the manager came back with the doctor.

"Is there anything special that needs to be done for the patient?" the FBI agent asked the doctor.

"Here is the information on him," the doctor answered, handing the man a sheaf of papers, which he took and placed inside his coat.

"Now take me to him," he ordered, "and how easily can he be moved?"

They began walking down the aisle towards an elevator.

"If you have a big enough vehicle to fit a stretcher in the back – "

"I do."

"Then we can have to orderlies take him out – if that will be all right."

"Fine, but my men can carry him."

"That could be dangerous for the patient – I mean – that will be fine," the doctor finished confusedly. Though he couldn't see the agent's eyes, he felt the fierce glare directed toward him.

"How much does a stretcher cost?" the FBI agent asked.

The doctor named an amount.

"There's the money. We'll keep the stretcher and the patient, and you can forget about both. That's an order."

"Okay," the doctor said softly, "okay."

A few minutes later they walked into Richard Wilson's room. He was sleeping. The agent signaled for one of the men behind him to wake the patient up.

"He's not drugged, is he?" the FBI agent asked.

"No, he should wake up easily," was the answer.

"Hmm. We might want to drug him, so he won't make a fuss, but there's no time. You, wake him up and tell him not to make any arguments."

One of the men in sunglasses – the younger one – bent over the bed and touched the shoulder of the patient. He awoke, and looked up with a start.

~ ~ ~

Raymond looked into Richard Wilson's face. "Shh, do you know me?" he whispered, barely moving his lips, "I'm Raymond Vincent. You were a spy, so you should know how to act. Pretend you're confused, and maybe a little worried. We're trying to help you, and we need to get you out of here."

Wilson gave a barely perceptible nod, and Raymond turned back to Frank, "he's awake, sir. Let's get him out now. He'd better not make a fuss," and he turned to look at Richard with a little frown.

"Get a stretcher and someone to move him onto it," Frank said to the doctor.

~ ~ ~

A few minutes later, an orderly and a nurse entered the room. The three strange men stepped back while the patient was moved to the stretcher, which was on wheels.

"Where are you taking me?" Richard Wilson asked in a confused voice.

None of the men answered, and he groaned as the nurse adjusted him in the stretcher.

"You may go now," the FBI agent said to the doctor. "These people can take the patient downstairs, and then my men can take him outside."

The doctor nodded and left, after one last worried look back at the patient.

A few minutes later, the FBI agent walked toward a large black SUV, his two men following behind with the stretcher. They laid both sets of back seats down, and carefully slid the stretcher in. "Good thing I got one of the larger SUV's, the FBI agent said with a laugh, "Or we might not have been able to fit him in here. There's barely enough room as it is. You two will have to sit on top of the seats."

~   ~   ~

"Now Frank's done his job, it's going to be your turn, Raymond," the older man said, swiping a shock of silver-gray hair off his forehead.

Raymond nodded, "I hope I can do as well as Frank did," he said with a grin, "wasn't he great, Dad?"

"Sure was. It wasn't as hard as I was expecting. Wherever did you learn to act like that?" he asked the driver.

"It's really not the complicated," Frank told him with a chuckle, "All I have to do is watch the other men at work and imitate them. I think Raymond's part is harder, because his face will be uncovered, while mine was disguised."

Raymond nodded, "I'll shave my moustache off so I'll look like I normally do, and they'll recognize me. But I've got to convince them that I don't know what happened to our friend here." And he nodded towards Richard Wilson.

This seemed a signal for the man to talk. He lifted his head and looked at Mr. Vincent, "Now where are you taking me? You told me to act confused," he turned back to Raymond, "but there wasn't much acting that needed to be done. I really was confused."

The other three men laughed.

Mr. Vincent answered, "we're going to try to take you somewhere that you're safe, and where you can get back to your sister once you're better. Are you sure she is being taken care of?"

"Yes. She's – married."

"Really! I hadn't thought she was married. You told us she was *Miss* Wilson."

"Yes, and it's a long story. Maybe I can tell you sometime, but right now – I'm feeling – not so – " and his head fell back in a faint.

~ ~ ~

Raymond walked up to the hospital alone, feeling more than a little nervous. *"Why is it so important to hide our trail like this?"* he asked himself; but he knew the answer. If anyone had any idea that there might be a time travel machine, and word reached the government, they would probably stop at nothing to find it. Such a machine could be used in many ways to serve governmental purposes. Mr. Elliot wanted to make sure that didn't happen.

He entered the doors and walked up to the desk. The woman there looked startled on seeing him. She stared at him for a moment, then said, "How can I help you?"

"As usual, I want to see the patient I and my father placed here," he said calmly.

"Oh . . ." she hesitated a second, then said quickly, "I'll call the manager."

"What do you mean, you'll call the manager? Is there something wrong with the patient? Why can't I just see him like I usually do?" he asked impatiently.

"Uh . . . just a minute," and she picked up the phone, "hello, yes. Please come to the desk, one of the Vincents is here. He wants to see Richard Wilson." She put the phone down and looked back at Raymond, "He'll be here in a minute. Will you have a seat?"

Raymond shook his head, "what's wrong? Is he worse? I thought he was getting better."

"Please wait until the manager gets here," she told him, more self-possessed now that the matter was out of her hands, "he'll take care of any problems you have."

Raymond shook his head again, "what's wrong?" he mumbled; then he sat down on one of the chairs in the lobby.

A few minutes later the manager came in and signaled for Raymond a little nervously.

Raymond looked at him accusatorily, "why can't I see Richard Wilson? He was much better just a couple of days ago. Has he had a relapse?"

"Well, yes."

Raymond moved closer to the manager and said impatiently, "why can't I see him? Is it really that bad?"

"Yes," the manager turned away for a moment, and said, "he's dead. That's why you can't see him. I don't know what happened. He suddenly had some complications that we weren't able to take care of."

Raymond was surprised. This was not exactly what he had been expecting. But he kept up the game he was playing, "What do you mean he's dead? I guess you'll have to give the body to us for burial. We can at least do that much for him."

"We have already disposed of the body. We knew you were not related to him, so we took care of what needed to be done as quickly as possible."

Raymond wanted to keep playing the game, and worry the manager into telling the truth, but he decided to leave it at that. After all, the manager believed that he knew nothing about the happening a couple of days before, and that was what was wanted. So he nodded solemnly and left. Was it his imagination, or did the manager blow out a sigh of relief behind his back?

A tall man in a dark suit walked into the hospital and strode quickly to the front desk. The woman behind the desk was startled as he flashed a badge before her eyes.

"Get me the manager. I want to talk to him," he ordered.

"Y-yes, sir," she stammered, reaching for the phone.

A few minutes later the manager came hurrying up. The dark-suited man said quickly, "Take me to a place where I can speak with you privately."

The manager saw the badge the FBI agent was holding, and hurriedly showed him to the same room into which he had taken the other FBI agent a week before.

"I understand you have a patient here named Richard Wilson. A man with gunshot wounds."

"No we don't," the manager said positively, but with nervousness. What in the world was going on?

"What? I can assure you that my information is reliable. You have a patient here named Richard Wilson, and I want him removed into my care as soon as he is well enough to move."

The manager licked his lips. "I'm afraid that will not be possible, sir," he began quietly, "the patient you refer to is – "

"What do you mean it won't be possible!" the agent stormed, "I've given you orders, and you must comply! Do you know what this means?" and he waved his badge before the manager's face.

"Yes, yes I know what it means," the manager stammered. What was going on here? he wondered, didn't the FBI work together? Why did this agent not realize that the problem had been taken care of a week ago. Well, since there seemed to be something wrong, he would just keep up with his plan to tell everyone the patient had died.

"Well, are you going to take me to the patient, or will I have to take other measures?" the agent threatened.

"I'm sorry, sir. The patient you are speaking of is dead. I would take you to him if I could."

"What! Why was I not told of this?" the agent fumed.

"I'm sure I don't kn – "

"Stop that! What did you do with the body? Is it still here?"

"No. I don't know what happened to it. My job here is to manage things, not take care of dead bodies."

"Then tell me who does take care of things like that."

"I would have to look it up. I don't keep things like that on the top of my head. But it would be impossible to trace the body now, sir. It was probably either used for dissection in a medical school, or cremated."

"And his clothing? Can I trace that?"

"Doubtful. It most likely disappeared with the body. We don't keep track of such things."

"Impossible! You ought to take better care of things around here. I think I'll have to report you."

"Go ahead and report," the manager laughed, "I'm not one who goes searching through dead men's pockets."

"Are you sure there's no use trying to trace his clothes?"

"Well, I wouldn't waste the time," the manager replied, "but you can try if you want. I don't think there's any evidence of what happened to the body."

The FBI agent paced impatiently up and down the small room. Then he suddenly turned and looked straight into the eyes of the manager, catching him off guard. "You're lying to me." He said in a deep stern voice.

The manager started, and stammered, "What – what do you mean? Who said I was lying?"

"*I* said you were lying. Now tell me the truth! That man is not dead."

"If he's not, that's the first I've heard of it," the manger laughed, trying to regain his assurance.

"Stop that!" the agent shouted, "What's wrong with you?"

"Nothing's wrong with me. But I'm beginning to think something's wrong with you."

The FBI agent stood very still for a moment, then said in a cool, but still fierce voice, "You are lying to me. No more jokes; no more games. Do you see this badge? I expect an answer, and I expect it now."

"Okay, here's your answer. A week ago an FBI agent came and took away the patient. He told me to keep it a secret, so I fixed everything to make it seem as if the man had died."

"You're lying to me! Tell me the truth! He's dead, isn't he?"

It took a while to sort things out. Finally the man left the manager's office and hurried out of the hospital.

~   ~   ~

Pickard rushed up to his boss's door and pounded it, though he knew he shouldn't. The boss called for him to come in, though somewhat impatiently.

"What's wrong, Pickard? Don't you know better than to bang on the door like that?" he demanded.

"Yes, sir, I'm sorry," said Pickard, "but our man has disappeared."

"What?"

"I went to the hospital, as you told me to, and they told me Richard Wilson was dead."

"So? Did you examine the body?"

"No. They told me the body was irrecoverable. That it was impossible to trace."

"Don't they know the FBI better than that? We could trace a hair clip back to the right woman."

"Yes, sir. I argued with him for a while, and tripped him up until he finally admitted that the man wasn't dead."

"So? What else?"

"You won't believe this. The manager of the hospital told me that a week ago an FBI agent marched into the hospital and removed the patient, without leaving a bit of information."

"What! This can't be possible!"

Chapter 32

Frank Garrold slammed closed the door of his little Acura and hurried towards the new office which had only been built recently. A business woman in a trim brown suit reached the door at the same time as he did, so he opened it and motioned for her to enter. Her eyebrows pressed together and she said sharply, "I can take care of myself, thank you very much!" then pulled the door out of his grasp, jerking her chin for him to enter first.

Frank shrugged. He should have known better. None of the women he had had contact with while working here had ever allowed him to help with anything – not even the smallest gentlemanly services. He proceeded into the office and found a note waiting on his desk, and picked it up, reading its contents. It was short, terse and to the point.

Go to the boss's office as soon as you arrive.

So he did. "You wanted me, sir?" he questioned, as he stepped inside.

"I did, Garrold. I have a new job for you."

"Yes? What is it?"

"Take this information to your desk and look it over. This is the hard copy. Would you rather have me email it to you?"

"No, thanks. This is fine." Frank took the papers and went back to his desk.

He read through the first page and his eyes widened. "What in the world?" he asked himself, "how did they – " he dropped the paper back to the desk and leaned his forehead on his hand. "What do I do now?" he wondered, "I can't betray my friends, but if I refuse to take this case – I'll be in big trouble. Is there any way I can get out of it?" he thought for a long time, but came up with no answer. Finally he read through the rest of the papers and then gathered them up to take back to the boss's office.

"Come in," he heard, a second after he knocked on the door.

"I've read the papers, sir," he said.

"And?"

"What do you want me to do?"

"I want you to get to the bottom of the case," the boss told him.

"Well, I might be able to do that, but why is it so important? Would you mind telling me?" asked Frank.

"Do you realize what a wonderful discovery it would be for our US government if we were able to find this time travel machine?"

"Well, no. But I can understand that the government would be glad to know of such a machine."

"That's for sure. Well, how soon can you start? You aren't in the middle of anything, are you?"

"No, not really. But this doesn't sound like something I would like to do. Is there anyone else who could take this one?"

"What does it matter whether you like it or not? It's not your job to *like* things; only to *do* them. And besides, we have a reason that we want you to take this case."

"Yes?"

"You know the people who are involved."

"What! I thought I recognized the names, but there are a lot of people named Jackson. Is it really the ones I know?" Frank argued in his head, *"That wasn't really a lie. I didn't say anything untrue. Anyway, in this job, I can't always tell the truth. That's just the way it is."*

"Yes, they are the family who I would guess you know, since your family goes to the same church."

"I see."

"So they'll talk to you, and you can get information out of them easily."

"But I can't betray my friends like that!"

The boss laughed, "what did you get into this job for then, boy?"

"I-I don't know. Can't someone else take the case?"

"No. You would be best."

"Listen, sir, Thomas Jackson is one of my best friends. I've known him since I was a kid."

"And how long ago was that, sonny? You don't look much more than a kid now!" the boss grinned.

Frank reddened at this thrust, but shook his head in pain and confusion, "But if they find out that I've been spying on them, they'll never speak to me again!"

"So don't let them find out."

"I just can't do it, sir," Frank shook his head doggedly.

"You can, and you will!" the boss said sternly, "Don't give me any more of that 'family and friends, can't betray them' talk. It won't go here. In this job you work for the government, not your friends."

"I thought the government was supposed to be of the people."

"Don't be ridiculous! I'm not in this position just because a lot of people thought I should be here. It's hard work and brains that got me where I am! I don't worry myself about the *people*, of all things! Now forget about all that family loyalty stuff and do as I tell you."

Frank hesitated, his face still wearing a confused and hurt frown.

The boss leaned forward. He knew how to deal with this.

"As I said, that's one reason why we picked you. The Jacksons know you and trust you," Frank choked, but the older man took no notice of it, "so they'll be much more free in speaking with you than they would with a stranger. We have been listening in on a few of their conversations through their cell phones, but so far, they have been very careful about what they say, and have not said anything we can catch. I don't know why, but it's obvious that they're trying to keep the machine a secret. So again, in answer to your question, no, we can't send anyone else. You are the one for the job. Besides," he leaned forward, a little flattery wouldn't hurt. Young men had a lot of pride and would succumb easily to such arguments, "you have done some wonderful work for us since you joined. I don't know what we would do without you. Even if you were not chosen for this case because of other reasons, you have been so amazing in your work that we would have picked you just for that."

Frank wasn't sure how much of that to believe; he hadn't thought he had done so very much. But it was nice to hear – and then, thinking about it – there had been a couple of times when he had found out some pretty remarkable things for the FBI. Well, if they thought he was that good, he wouldn't be one to argue. He thought a moment more, then let out a short sigh, squared his shoulders, and lifted his chin, rising from his chair. "I'll do it." He nodded once, shortly, "I know I've got to obey orders, and I understand why you think I'm the best man for the job. I'll do it." and he clenched his jaw, wheeled, and headed out of the room, scooping up the papers of information on the case as he went.

After the young man left, the boss rubbed his hands together and chuckled, "He's all right. Garrold is just one more young man who needs to learn that his work is more important than friends or family. But he'll get over it pretty soon. I saw his face right before he left, and I've seen others like him. They all have to give in sooner or later, but when I see a face look like that, I know it won't be long."

He chuckled again, then turned back to his computer.

~   ~   ~

"Raymond wants to know if we're free on Saturday afternoon."

"What for?" Susanna asked, looking up at her brother.

"Can't you guess? He wants to take Richard Wilson back through the machine and hand him over to the Maxwells."

"Oh." Susanna drew a deep breath, but forced a controlled smile, "That sounds good. Will they take him?"

"Who, the Maxwells? Sure they will. They'd do anything for the 'Glorious Cause' with their two sons in the army."

"Mm-hm."

"So is Saturday fine with you?" he asked.

"I guess so. I can't think of anything else we have to do then," answered Susanna.

"Okay. I'll tell him then."

After Thomas left, Susanna argued with herself, "I've got to stop this! Why does my stomach turn over at every mention of the time-travel machine? I thought I'd gotten over it a long time ago, but it keeps coming back."

Thomas returned suddenly, making her jump, "Are you sure you want to come too, Susanna? I know you don't like the machine; it makes you nervous."

"Nervous! Does he realize how terrified I am that something will happen to us every time we step through that door?" she exclaimed inwardly.

"I could go by myself, you know, with Raymond and Mr. Elliot or Mr. Vincent."

"We've already talked about that," Susanna reminded him, "the second time we went. I couldn't stand the waiting without knowing what was happening to you. If you go, I'm coming too."

"Okay, whatever you say."

He left her then, and she leaned her chin on her hand, gazing off into space.

~ ~ ~

"Ma, there's one of those strangely dressed men at the door again. I wonder if they have something to tell us about Mr. Wilson," Bessie called.

Mrs. Maxwell hurried out of the back room, "well, and why don't you open the door, girl? Don't keep a guest standing outside!"

She pulled open the door and let Raymond Vincent into the house. The Maxwells weren't too surprised to see that Susanna was with him.

"Mrs. Maxwell, can you take your patient back now?" he asked, "we can't keep him any longer."

"Of course we can. When can you bring him?" she queried.

"Well actually, we brought him here on the chance. My father and friend are outside holding him in a stretcher."

"Goodness me! Why didn't you say so before?" she exclaimed, bustling past him to the door and flinging it wide. She stepped outside and beckoned for the stretcher-bearers to come in. Susanna moved to the back corner of the room so as not to be in the way.

"Bessie, bring those two chairs over here to lay the stretcher on, so we can roll him onto the bed easier."

Her daughter obeyed, with Raymond's assistance, and soon Richard was transferred to the bed.

"Alice can sleep with you, Bessie," Mrs. Maxwell said briskly, "but Lily Mae will have to sleep on the floor. We'll roll out a mat for her during the night."

"You could bring Matthew's mattress down here and let him sleep on the hay in the attic," Bessie suggested.

"Yes, that'd be best. I'll tell him to fix it up how he likes when he comes in tonight. Where's Lily Mae now?"

"She's over visiting Lydia," Bessie answered, "and she took Alice with her to see Zach."

"Fine. I'm going to take your pa his dinner. When they get back, give them theirs."

"Okay, Ma."

Mrs. Maxwell turned to the four visitors who were still standing in the middle of the room, "Will you have some dinner?" she asked.

"No thanks, we already ate," Mr. Vincent answered, "we'll be going now."

"Goodbye, and thank you for taking care of Mr. Wilson. I can't hardly believe they didn't take his leg off, it looked so bad, but I'm glad they didn't."

~   ~   ~

Richard opened his eyes, trying not to groan. How many times had he done the same thing over the past few weeks? Now as he awoke, he found himself in a place he didn't recognize in the least. He supposed it was the house of a family called Maxwell, because Raymond Vincent had told him that was where they were taking him. Raymond had also told him that he had been here once before, the day after he had faced the firing squad, but he didn't remember any of it. He must have been unconscious most of the time.

Now as he looked around, he saw a girl sitting by the bed, knitting. She looked up and met his eye, gave a start of surprise, then a faint smile.

"I'm glad you're awake. How do you feel?" She put her knitting in a basket at her feet and rose, resting a hand on the back of her chair.

"I feel as if I could get up and walk out of here if I had a little food," he said with a smile.

"Good! I'll call Ma, then I'll get you something to eat." She left.

A large woman came bustling into the room a minute later, "Hello, young man. I'm Mrs. Maxwell. I've told you that before, but I don't guess you remember anything that happened on the couple of days you were here."

"No, I don't. But thank you, Mrs. Maxwell, for letting me stay here and use your bed."

"That there's Lily Mae and Alice's bed. But they've got places to sleep elsewhere, and you need the bed for now."

She sat down in the chair her daughter had vacated, and smiled at him, "Lily Mae said you feel fine, but hungry. She's getting you some food."

"That sounds good. *Didn't she say that this is Lily Mae's bed? It must be that girl,"* he thought.

"I'm going to take a look at that leg in a bit," Mrs. Maxwell told him, "And maybe change the bandages. The one on your head looks fine now. It seems to have healed pretty quick."

"Yes. They took good care of me at the hospital, but it was a very strange place. As long as they made me better, and saved my leg, which Raymond said the doctor here was going to cut off, I don't mind not understanding what it was all about."

"There's some things on this earth as is not meant for us to know," Mrs. Maxwell said with a wise nod, "but one thing I do want to know is when Lily Mae is coming back with that soup she was getting."

"If all our wishes could be granted so easily, Ma, it'd be a care-free world," came in Lily Mae's voice as she entered the room with a steaming wooden bowl.

"Perhaps so," Mrs. Maxwell answered tersely, propping the pillow higher behind Richard's head so he could eat, "but it ain't good for anyone to get everything they want. If 'twere so, the world would be full of a whole lot of spoiled rotten screaming babies."

Lily Mae laughed. "That's so. Whenever I see that horrid Lew Acton I just wish his ma had smacked him good a coupla times when he was a kid. If she had, he mightn't be so detestable now."

"And getting what he wants is what's done it," Mrs. Maxwell agreed. She looked at the patient who was listening, amused, "This'll be a warning to you, young man, we'll humor you because you're a sick man, but if you start acting like you own everything, you'll learn better!"

Richard let out a hearty laugh, then groaned, placing a hand on his side, "I forgot that I wasn't to laugh until this gets better," he gingerly felt the bandages covering his wound, "Sure hurts to laugh with a broken rib, even if it's almost well." He smiled at Mrs. Maxwell, "But if I start acting like a spoiled baby you have my full permission to 'smack me good,' as your daughter says."

There was a stifled gasp from Lily Mae, but Mrs. Maxwell chuckled, "I don't think we'll have to worry about that," she said, "You don't seem to be that kind of man."

"I hope not," he grinned.

~   ~   ~

"Is it all right if we look around for a little bit before going back?" Thomas asked his sister.

She shrugged, "I guess so. But why didn't we get you some clothes that look a little more old-timey? You boys could at least have worn button-downs, but your polo shirts look so strange around here."

"That's right, we should have," Raymond agreed, looking at himself and his friend ruefully, "I don't know why we didn't think."

Mr. Vincent nodded, "You're probably right, Susanna. It's not really safe to walk around in these clothes after already being noticed for them. What do you boys say we come back in a couple of days and wear button-downs then?"

"Sure," the boys agreed.

"That's the best plan," Thomas said, "Now we've got Richard back to the Maxwells, there's no real need for us to be here. It won't hurt to wait a few days before coming back. It's just that we haven't been here in weeks, and I'd like to look around some more."

"You'll get your looking around time," Mr. Vincent assured him, "The time-travel machine always stands over that door, you know."

Chapter 33

Listening and paying attention to the sermon had never been so hard for Frank Garrold since he a little boy of five. He tried. He tried really hard, but his mind kept turning to what he had been commissioned to do that afternoon. *Commanded* was more like it.

"How could they ask me to do such a thing?" his brain kept on screaming, *"After a while, no matter how long I'm able to hide it, the news will get out and I'll be hated by everyone in the church. But I can't disobey orders. I've got to do it, and that's all there is to it. Stop it!"* he screamed inwardly, *"Stop thinking about it! – But my Dad and Mom taught me to think for myself,"* a little voice inside his head reminded him, *"No, now that I've got a job, I've got to do what my boss says,"* he shook his head, one quick little jerk, *"That's what they tried to tell me: the government doesn't like people to think for themselves. Stop it! It's too late! I'm going to do it and that's all there is to it!"* he repeated.

Frank was so deep in his thoughts that he was startled and jumped when he felt a little hand rest on his leg. He looked down at his little eight-year-old sister. Ellen turned her dark eyes up to him questioningly. Frank shook his head, patted her hand, and smiled at her. It was a forced smile, but she seemed satisfied for the moment, and nestled closer to him. Frank put his arm around her shoulder, but his muscles tensed again at the thought, "I wonder if she'll ever allow me to do this again after she and everyone else find out what I'm about to do?"

When the service was over, Frank took hold of Ellen's hand and drew her to his side. After waiting until almost everyone had left the church building, he knelt down in front of his sister so as to be able to look her in the eye and said, "Ellen."

"Yes, Frank?"

"Would you please not tell anyone what happened in church today?" he begged.

"What do you mean?" she asked in surprise, "I can't tell Dad and Mom?"

"They – well, listen. I was just thinking about something I didn't want to think about, and I was trying to get it out of my head and listen to the sermon. Haven't you ever had that happen to you?"

"Oh yes, all of the time," Ellen answered, nodding her head.

"So that's why I asked you not to tell Mom and Dad," he told her, "I don't want them to be worried that something's wrong, because everything's fine now, and I'm not upset anymore. Okay?"

"Okay," she nodded again, seriously, then gave him a one-armed hug. "I'm sorry you were thinking about something you didn't want to think about," she said, "can I go play with Florence now?"

"You certainly *can*," he teased, "unless I grab you like this," he caught one of her wrists in his hand and held on while she squealed and laughed, trying to get away, "Then you *can't!*"

"Oh!" the little girl giggled, "I meant *may I?*"

"Yes, you may," Frank said, releasing his sister to run off and join her friend.

The smile faded from his face as he stood and watched her leave. "I just lied to my baby sister," he whispered, "I've never done that before. Well, it was just a little lie, and it made her feel better," he argued with his conscience, "No! I know there are no such things as big or little lies. Why did I do it? I had to. No, I didn't. I'm done with this! It's too late to change it now. I can't stay here any longer. I'm going to go home and read or something until it's time to go to the Jacksons' house. *If* I can make myself go."

Frank had moved out into the aisle when he realized he wasn't alone. There were two men about his father's age standing talking near the pulpit, and near them was the daughter of one of the men. She was keeping an eye on her baby brother, who was playing on the floor.

At first Frank only saw that it was a young lady, but then he looked straight at her and saw that it was Ann Starr, the girl who had been his sister Sara's closest friend. It seemed strange to see Ann without Sara at her side, but his sister had married and moved away a few months before. He had played with the two younger girls often when he had been a little boy, since their parents were good friends and had visited often, but as they grew older, he stayed with the young men and his sister and her friends had stayed with the other girls. He had not spoken with Ann other than a few pleasantries in several years.

Frank saw to his embarrassment that she had watching him talk to himself, and had most likely noticed his serious conversation with Ellen also. Ann seemed a bit embarrassed too, but she held his gaze for a second, as if she wanted to tell him something. He shook his head slightly. There was no way he was going over there and talking to her. Not with everything that was going on in his head and his life at that moment. Her hands moved, and he broke his gaze at her face to look down at them. She clasped them together, and raised them to her chest, then released her clasp and raised one hand to point toward the ceiling.

The young man understood immediately. She could tell, he supposed, that there was something wrong – how? He never had been able to understand a girl's thoughts, in his slight experience with only two sisters, but he knew that somehow she did know he had a problem he didn't know how to solve, and she thought he should pray about it.

Frank lifted his eyes to her face again, and stared blankly at her for what seemed a long moment to him. His head was whirling again, and he once more screamed at himself, "It's too late!"

Ann continued to watch him, and he didn't know what to do. Finally he shook his head fiercely, tearing his gaze from her face, and hurried out of the church, trying to keep from breaking into a run.

"Let's go upstairs," Adele suggested, "we sat down here almost the whole time last week. I'd like a change," and she laughed.

"All right," Susanna agreed, "Is that fine with the rest of you girls?"

"Sure," Crystal laughed, "then we won't need to worry the boys will come in while we're talking, because they aren't allowed upstairs!"

Then everyone laughed, and the half a dozen older girls went upstairs together. Their younger sisters were out back watching the soccer game the boys were playing.

"Oh, Susanna! May I do your hair?" Margaret exclaimed, sinking to the floor of the Jackson girls' dressing room, "I haven't done it in so long!"

"Yes, Susanna! Let Margaret do your hair," Adele nodded, "She's so good with hair, and yours is so beautiful."

"Thank you, Adele," Susanna said, unclasping her hair clip and letting her blond waves to fall past her waist, "I guess I will let Margaret do my hair – if you will let me do yours. Yours is really nice too, you know."

Adele laughed, "Well, since I want to see what Margaret will do to your hair, I guess I'll have to let you do mine. But please, *please* try not to pull too much. Some of you girls can stand it and not even feel it, but my head is verrrry tender!"

"I'll try," Susanna agreed. She moved a low stool behind Adele, who was sitting on the floor, and sat on it. Then Margaret came to stand behind her, and it became a hair-doing staircase.

There was a lot of girlish chatter and giggling going on when the young ladies heard a voice speak from the doorway, "Children, would it be fine for an old married lady to come in and chaperone your activities?"

There was a burst of laughter and three of the girls made a rush for the one who had just come in, dragging her into the dressing room and seating her right in the midst of them on the daybed.

"Now Angie Davis!" Ann Starr exclaimed, shaking a finger in her face, "I'm a whole year older than you are, and just because you got married first doesn't mean you can treat us like we're a bunch of toddlers!"

Angie laughed, and said, "be careful, girls! You're smashing me to pieces, and if you do that, there'll be no one left to take care of Luke and the baby."

"The baby! Where is she? Tell us this minute and let us get her!"

Angie shook her head, "I'm not going to tell you unless you promise to be careful. The way you're acting right now, if I tell you where Esther is you'll hurt her by trying to grab her from each other. You've got to remember she's only three months old."

"Yes, ma'am," Kitty McKeith laughed, "Maybe you girls don't think so, but I know my sister, and she means what she says. If you don't listen to her, you'll never get to see that baby."

Angie had been a McKeith before marrying Luke Davis.

"Oh! We'll be good, won't we girls?" Adele turned her head to look at the laughing group and got a teasing reprimand from Susanna for it, "How can I possibly do your hair, Adele Hostler, if you keep looking every which way?"

"Oops! Sorry."

"Now, since Kitty gets more chances to hold Esther than the rest of you do, we'll leave her till last," Angie said, "I think I'll let − " she held her sentence suspensefully in the air, while the girls waited impatiently. Then she finished, " − Crystal go first, because she's the youngest."

There were good-natured groans from the other girls, and an excited squeal from Crystal. "Where is she? Where is she?" she asked.

"Remember, girls, let Crystal get her," Angie said warningly, with a pretty motherly air. Then turning to Crystal, "she's on Jennie's bed."

Crystal ran out of the dressing room and appeared a moment later with the baby in her arms.

"I'm done," Susanna announced, giving a final smooth and pat to Adele's hair.

"I'll be done in a minute," Margaret promised, pulling another lock of Susanna's hair into place.

"How do you like it, Adele?" Susanna asked.

Adele surveyed her brown hair in the full-length mirror which hung on the door to the bathroom. "It's very good, Susanna. I like it a lot. I think I might do it myself sometime, if I can."

"It's not that hard," Susanna assured her, "You should be able to do it yourself pretty easily."

"There!" Margaret exclaimed, lifting her hands from Susanna's head, "There! It's done."

Susanna stepped up to the mirror and looked at herself. Margaret waited nervously, wondering how she would like it.

Kitty slipped a large hand mirror into Susanna's hand so she could survey the back. She did, and gave a soft giggle of appreciation. Then she turned to Margaret, who was still waiting anxiously.

"It's very nice," Susanna began, and a couple of the girls gave muffled groans and exclamations.

"Nice!" Crystal exclaimed, "Margaret, it's magnificent!"

"A masterpiece," Angie agreed.

There was a commotion somewhere out in the hall, and the several younger girls came trooping in, Jennie among them. She whistled at the sight of her sister's wonderful coiffure.

Susanna turned around to look at the younger girl teasingly, "'Whistling girls and crowing hens – '" she began.

Jennie ran to her and pulling on her arm, swung her in a circle, "'Always come to some bad ends!'" she laughed, then gasped, "Oh, no!" as Susanna's hair came tumbling down, hairpins flying, "Just like that, I guess," she said ruefully, "I'm sorry, Susanna. Is it all because of the whistling?"

Susanna laughed. "It saves me the trouble of taking it down, anyway," she said.

"What! You were going to take it down?" several of the girls gave surprised exclamations.

"Yes," Susanna nodded, "You know the rule. If the model doesn't want to keep the hairdo, she may take it down."

"So you didn't like it?"

"Oh, I did. But it's far too elaborate for a simple occasion like this. If we went down there our parents and the boys might notice, and I don't like being the center of attention for something like this. I don't mind going on stage and singing or acting, as you all know, but having people comment on my dress several times in a row would be pretty embarrassing."

Jennie laughed, and then lived up to her nickname as a "singing twin" by singing to the tune of *The Campbells are Coming,*

> *The big boys are coming, oho, oho.*
> *The big boys are coming, oho, oho,*
> *The big boys are coming, they're coming to see,*
> *Susanna must run away now; she must flee!*

There was a burst of giggles from all corners of the room as she finished, and Susanna shook her finger at her younger sister making a clucking sound with her tongue. "Not so bad as that!" she exclaimed.

The soccer ball flew through the air. The boys watched it, and three of them ran to where they could reach it when it came down. When it did come down, it bounced once, then after an awkward kick from Steve's foot, it flew out of bounds.

"Our throw!" Thomas yelled, "You'll take it, Joshua?"

Joshua Hostler picked up ball and threw it in. A few seconds later, Harold Davis was dribbling down the field with his brother Carter at his heels.

"Come on, Wagon, you can get it away from him!" Alan Hostler shouted.

Harold felt Carter closing in, and quickly looked around, calling, "Who's open?"

Thomas, who was captain of his team, quickly shouted out orders, "Hey! Watch Jack, Alan! Josiah, get on Danny!"

"I protest!" Danny cried, "I object to being jumped on, Thomas! I know that is illegal."

All of the boys and young men that were close enough to hear turned and regarded Danny with amazement. "What in the world?" Thomas exclaimed.

"You told Josiah to get on me," Danny said in a hurt voice that would have done credit to Jennie, the actress, "I know you won't find anywhere in the rule book that soccer players are allowed to pile on top of each other like football players do."

After a few more seconds of startled astonishment, Thomas burst out laughing, "Danny! You know very well that 'get on him' is soccer slang for 'watch him.' Come on, boys! Danny's just up to his tricks again. Don't pay attention to him."

"Goal!" shouted "Wagon" Davis.

While the discussion had been going on, Harold had reached the goal and taken a shot. There were cheers, and a few groans, but everyone was good-natured, and while each wanted their team to win, there were smiles on all faces as Harold was congratulated for his shot.

"How in the world did you get it past Luke all by yourself?" Noah McKeith demanded, "He's the best goalie we have!"

Harold shrugged, then accepted the high-five the older boy offered him.

~ ~ ~

A few hours later, after the evening service, and when everyone was fellowshipping once more, Frank made his way over to Thomas. He tried to act as if nothing was wrong, and succeeded pretty well.

"You like sci-fi, don't you?" he asked carelessly, "Have you read the *Robot Wars* by Sigmund Brouwer? I read those when I was just a little kid, and liked them a lot, but they're interesting to older people too."

"Yes, we have them in our library. I did like them. Susanna liked them too, even though she doesn't really like sci-fi stories. Some of the other books by that author aren't so wonderful, though."

"Yeah, I never found any I liked so well as the *Robot Wars*," Frank agreed. Then he asked, "Do you know of any good books on time travel?

Thomas shot him a knowing look. He thought Frank was interested because he had helped them get Richard Wilson out of the hospital.

"No, I haven't read much science fiction," he said, "even though it's one of my favorite genres. There's a lot of sci-fi out there, but most of it's by non-Christian authors, and I try not to read too much of that."

"How's the time-travel thing going?" Frank whispered.

Thomas looked at him with a laugh, "Temporal Prime Directive. I can't talk about that."

Chapter 34

When Frank Garrold walked into the office building on Monday morning, he was feeling a little better than he had at church the day before, because he wasn't surrounded by reminders of what he would miss if he was found out. But he still felt more than a little sick at the thought of what he was doing and how he was planning to betray his friends. A few names such as Judas and Delilah entered his head, but he resolutely pushed them behind him and sat down to work. A little while later the boss called him into the office.

"So did you learn anything?" he asked.

"I've decided to go slow on this one. But he seems to be willing to talk about it," Frank answered.

"That's good. We're still trying to find out what happened to Richard Wilson, the man who was taken from the hospital."

Frank put his hand into his pocket and fiddled with his key ring, trying to overcome the nervousness that suddenly washed over him. What if they found out he was the man who had done it? *"Impossible,"* he told himself, *"I covered my tracks. I took the rental SUV back to the rental agency up in North Carolina. There's no way they can trace me."* He nodded, and said, "Well, I'll try to find more information as quickly as possible, but I don't want to speed things up too much, because the Jacksons might suspect something if I did. I don't want them to realize I know more than they tell me."

"That's right. Just keep on as you have been doing," said the boss. "Dismissed."

~   ~   ~

"Come in," the boss called.

Pickard opened the door and entered the office.

"Any news?" the boss asked.

"Yes. I have traced one of the bills used to pay for the stretcher."

"Really! That's good. What denomination?"

"It's a hundred dollar bill. I decided that one would be easier to trace because it was larger, and wouldn't be as likely to be given in change for anything."

"Yes. Do you have it now?" the boss asked.

"Yes. Here it is," Pickard handed it to him.

"So next you want to trace the number on this bill, and see whose hands it passed from last before being given to the hospital manager."

"That's right, sir. I'll start that tomorrow," Pickard answered.

"I like Raymond Vincent," Susanna heard Edward say in the next room, midway through the week, "Don't you, Jennie?"

"He's pretty nice," Jennie replied. "I haven't talked with him much, though, because he's a boy, you know. If you say you like him, I'll like him too." At this they both giggled.

Susanna heard the twins' feet thump on the floor, and then the door slammed. She thought back over the conversation and wondered, *"Do I like Raymond? Yes, he's nice, but I can't believe how mean he was on the first day we met."*

She pounded the dough she was kneading down onto the counter hard, and paused a moment before resuming her task.

"They used us for a test! If they had asked first, I would have said no, but they should have asked anyway!" she ignored the fact that the test wouldn't have worked if they had known they were being tested.

She punched the bread dough hard, "The Bible says we have to love everyone," she said aloud, but finished vindictively, "But it *doesn't* say we have to *like* everybody!"

When Susanna realized she had been speaking aloud, she looked around quickly to see if she had been heard. Seeing no one, she breathed a sigh of relief and gave the dough a few last pats before dropping it into a greased bowl to rise.

"And there is a big difference," she said in a whisper, "between loving someone and liking them. I can be friendly to Raymond, but I *don't* know if I can be friends with him."

She scrubbed her hands in the kitchen sink to get the sticky scraps of dough off of them. "Mr. Elliot actually apologized. Mr. Vincent didn't do anything much to apologize for. Raymond was there watching us. He could easily have told us before what the problem was. He watched us search for our house, getting more and more worried, and he probably just stood there *laughing* at us! Oh!" she whirled around, clenching her fists together, "How unkind can he be?" She felt she must do something with her hands, now that she couldn't take her anger out on the bread dough, so after wiping them thoroughly on a towel, she hurried to the piano and sat down, played several crashing chords, then started playing a piece of Beethoven much faster than it was supposed to be played.

After a few minutes, she had calmed down a bit, and began playing a hymn. After she had gone through it once, she began to sing.

"Trials dark on every hand,
And we cannot understand
All the ways that God would lead us
To that blessed Promised Land"

When she reached the end of the chorus, she choked a moment before finishing,

"We will understand it better by and by."

She sang through the second verse automatically, her thoughts elsewhere, but suddenly jerked back into reality when she heard a car door slam in the driveway. Her father was home. She continued singing with her mind on the actual meaning of the words in the third verse.

"Our hearts are made to bleed
For some thoughtless word or deed,
And we wonder why the test"

Her voice broke, but she continued,

"When we've tried to do our best,
But we'll understand it better by and by."

Susanna's hands moved slower and slower until she was only playing simple chords, one note for several words, and finally she stopped. She finished the chorus softly, her hands dropping into her lap,

"We'll understand it better by and by."

Her eyes were filled with tears that she refused to let fall, and there was a choking sensation in her throat. *"Maybe I will 'understand it better by and by,'"* she thought, *"But I can't understand a bit now."*

Though the song had moved her, there was still bitterness in her heart. *"If Raymond had said one word of apology,"* she said to herself, *"it would be all right. But how can I trust someone who is so insensitive? Thomas would never have done anything like that in the first place, but if he had, he would have realized immediately that he had done wrong and would have apologized."*

Susanna realized that Thomas had some faults, but whenever she compared him to other young men or boys, he came out on top. She realized that perhaps she was a little biased, but there was no one she would rather have had for a brother than he.

The door opened, and Mr. Jackson entered. Susanna tried to slip from the piano and through the door of the playroom, which was only a few feet away, but it was too late.

"Hello, Susanna!"

"Hi, Daddy," she answered, without looking at him. She placed her hands on the keyboard again and began playing an upbeat tune. Her father put down his computer bag and came to stand behind her.

"Where's everyone else?" he asked.

"The twins are outside," she told him, "And I think Nancy is with Florence in the playroom. I don't know where the little boys are. Thomas isn't home yet. Mommy's upstairs, and the baby's inside her."

Mr. Jackson laughed heartily, and Susanna continued playing. Suddenly she stopped and jumped up from the piano bench. "I'm going to check on the food," she said, "It's cooking, and I just took a break for a few minutes."

Her father squeezed one of her shoulders with his hand before she left, then as she walked away, he called after her, "I forgot to ask how you were doing, Susanna!"

She laughed, "I'm fine, Daddy."

She opened the pot lid without remembering to be careful, and got a burst of steam in her face. "Ooh!" she squealed.

Her father came up behind her, "Are you sure you're all right?"

"Yes. A little steam won't hurt me," she laughed.

"No, Susanna. That's not what I'm talking about. You sounded funny a minute ago when you were talking to me; over at the piano."

"Oh! Did I? I was just thinking. Wondering about something."

"Can I help," he asked, "Maybe I can give you an answer."

"Well – the Bible says to love everyone, but it doesn't say to like everyone, does it? I mean, you can always show someone Christian love by being kind to them, and helping them if they need help, but that doesn't mean you have to like them, does it?"

"Hmm, I think I understand what you mean," he said thoughtfully, "And it does seem as if you're right. For instance, if I saw a drunkard one day on my way home from work, I could help him get back home, and love him as Christ tells us to, but since he's not a Christian and someone that I would associate with or let my family be friends with, I wouldn't have to like him. In fact, it would be very hard to even think about liking him until he had changed."

Susanna nodded, "yes, that's what I mean. So you think it's all right?"

"It all depends on the circumstances," her father looked at her quizzically, wondering where this was coming from, "You have to make sure there's a very good reason not to like someone."

"What do you mean?" she asked.

"Let's see. Once when I was about Edward's age I had a very good friend that I played a lot with. He was a Christian, and so was his family, and our families would get together often. Well, one day we had an argument. I don't remember what it was about, but I know we were both pretty worked up about it. Then, since we couldn't agree, I said some mean things, and he said some mean things, and we got so angry with each other that we parted that day, each with the belief that we could never be friends again."

His daughter was listening intently.

"A couple of days later, I got to thinking. Why should we make such a big deal over a little thing like that? And now that I had thought, though I hated to admit it, I had been half wrong myself. I realized that since we'd liked each other so much, and there was no real reason why we should break up the friendship over something like that. So I thought I'd just like him anyway, whether I got mad at him again or not. Apparently he had been thinking the same things, because when our families got together again, he reached for my hand and said, 'Still friends?' and I answered, 'Still friends.'"

Susanna shook her head, "I don't understand what you mean."

"I mean that if there are lots of good reasons why you should like someone, a little thing you don't like about them shouldn't stop you from liking them altogether. If they're a Christian, and their family is nice, you should think about the good things about them and not the bad, so it's easier to like them."

"Mm-hm. I think I get it now. Thanks, Daddy."

"Do you mind telling me who it is you're having trouble liking?" Mr. Jackson asked.

Susanna looked up at him quickly, then shook her head, "Not right now," she murmured.

She turned back to her cooking, and her father said, "I'll pray for you anyway," then left.

A few minutes later Susanna heard the front door open again, and she knew Thomas was home. She heard the thump of his computer bag as he set it on the floor, and two softer thumps as he dropped his shoes onto the shoe shelf. A few minutes later he entered the kitchen.

"Smells good!" Thomas exclaimed, "what is it?"

"This is dinner," she told him, "you won't be able to smell lunch. It's tuna salad, and it's in the 'fridge."

"Why in the world did you have to make that?" he teased.

"Thomas, you and Florence are the only ones in the whole family that don't like it."

"I know," he laughed, "And since all of the rest of you like it, I guess I'll have to eat it. But quick, tell me what's for dinner. Please say it's something I like."

"Do you like meatloaf and mashed potatoes with gravy and steamed squash?"

"Mmm! I certainly do. Can't we use the time machine to make dinner come more quickly?"

"No!" Susanna exclaimed, her body stiffening, "I don't think that's a good idea. We shouldn't use the time machine to take us to the future because God has a plan for everything, and we ought to be content to wait for His timing."

"You're right, little sister," Thomas's hand rested on her shoulder, "I was just joking, but I shouldn't have teased you about that. I know you're not comfortable with this time-travel thing yet."

"That's all right," she shook her head. "How did work go today?"

"Pretty well. One of our biggest clients is still undecided about whether to work with us or not, though. Hopefully he will decide soon. Here, let me help with that!" as Susanna began to lift a five-gallon pot of boiling water toward the sink.

Thomas quickly washed his hands in the kitchen sink, the took the hot pads from her and lifted the heavy pot to rest on the edge of the sink.

"This is the potatoes?" he asked.

"Yes. If you could drain it, that would make it a lot easier for me."

Thomas held the lid of the pot partially on to keep the potatoes in and let the water out at the same time. While the water was pouring out, he turned his face away so the steam wouldn't hit his face as hard, "Raymond texted me on my way home. He said he and his dad want to have a get-together with just the two of our families, because it's harder to get to know us on Sunday, when there are so many other people here."

Susanna looked at the clock, then pulled the towel off the bowl of rising dough and punched it down before turning it out onto the counter. "And?" she asked.

"And I told him it was a good idea, but I didn't know for sure which days we were free, so I'd talk with Mommy and Daddy and find out when would be a good time to do that."

Susanna nodded. She cut the dough into three even pieces and formed them into balls. "What exactly does he mean by a get-together? Does he want to have dinner with us, or would we go to the park for an afternoon, or what?"

"I don't know. Going to the park sounds like fun. We haven't done that in several weeks."

"Yes," remember that last time we went?" she asked, trying to change the conversation, "Danny fell into the creek when he was trying to get the football and got soaking wet. We had to put a towel under him so he wouldn't soak the car seat."

"That was funny," he agreed, "Do you think Danny would like the time machine? Maybe we can go through it again soon, and take some of the other kids with us. If we boys just remember to wear button-downs, we won't look so strange hopefully. Raymond can't wait to go either."

Susanna sighed in exasperation, "Can't you think or talk of anything but Raymond Vincent and the time machine lately? There was always plenty to talk about before, but now you push the subject of the time machine into every conversation we have together! I'm just sick and tired of the whole thing."

Thomas had finished draining the potatoes, and he moved the pot back to the stove, then came to stand close to his sister. "I'm sorry, Susanna. I didn't mean to annoy you."

She sighed again, "And I'm terribly sorry for speaking to you that way, Thomas. I don't know what's wrong with me lately." She fiercely smashed one of the balls of dough, then shook her head and formed it back into shape again before covering it to let it rise again.

"Is there something you would like to talk about?" Thomas asked softly.

"No! There's nothing I want to talk about, because you'll always bring the conversation back to Raymond and the time machine."

"I know you don't like the time machine," Thomas said, "And I'll try not to talk about it so often now I realize what I've been doing. Why don't you like Raymond though?"

"Who said I don't like Raymond?" his sister demanded, "He's nice enough. I don't know him as well as you do because you're a boy."

"Then why do you get annoyed when I talk about him?"

"Thomas," whispered Susanna, "you used to talk about me, and you used to talk about yourself. We used to talk about what happened in our family, and things that concerned ourselves. Now you don't. If I start to tell you something, or ask you something, you turn the conversation somehow back to Raymond. Is he more important to you than I am?" she caught her breath on a sob.

"Susanna," Thomas hugged her tightly, "You are my sister. No outsider can be more important to me than you are until I get married. I am afraid I have gotten caught up in the excitement of the time machine and forgotten to pay attention to things that are more important, but I'm sorry. However much I like the time machine, you are much, much more important to me. Do you believe me?"

"Yes. I believe you," she whispered, wiping her eyes on her sleeve. "I'm sorry for storming at you like that, Thomas. I really don't know what's wrong with me. All day I've been out of sorts."

Frank Garrold felt sicker and sicker with every sentence he heard. Finally he turned off the speaker with a pound of his finger. "I can't listen to this!" he exclaimed under his breath, "A private conversation between two of my best friends. This is more than a private conversation. This is confidential. Anyway, they're not talking about the time machine; only about the fact that Susanna doesn't like it. Oh! I feel so ashamed of myself for even listening to this much."

He rubbed his forehead with his hand and turned back to his computer, "but it's too late to change anything now. I'm in this business, and I've got to put my best into it. Anyway, I won't listen to that conversation anymore. All it does is make me sick, and there's no information to be gained from it, though the boss would say keep it up just in case if he were here."

~   ~   ~

"I'll be praying for you," Thomas told Susanna, "Is there anything else you want to talk about?"

"No," she shook her head and backed away, "I've got to finish cooking."

"I'm sure the cooking can wait if there's something we need to discuss," he told her gently.

"Maybe the cooking could wait," she laughed shakily, "but the children couldn't. If I don't have lunch ready by one o'clock, Edward and Danny especially will be starved."

"I'll help you," he told her, "there are only fifteen minutes left until then. What can I do?"

"I'm going to mash the potatoes for dinner," she said, "if you could wash those lettuce leaves before those fifteen minutes are up, that would be nice."

"Okay, I'll do that," he said, "Want to play a game while we work?"

"Like what?" she asked.

"I don't know, what about our story game? The one where each of us can only say one word at a time, and as quickly as possible, while making real sentences and stories."

"Sure, let's do that," Susanna agreed, "it's fun. You go first."

"Once," Thomas began.

"there" Susanna continued.

"was"

"a"

"little"

"alligator"

"who"

"liked"

"to"

"play"

"tennis!" Thomas finished with a laugh.

"One" Susanna went on.

"day,"

"he"

"found"

"a"

"rat"

"who," the game continued for several minutes. When one story came to a doubtful or crazy conclusion, they started another. Though the game didn't sound difficult when they talked about it, the action was hilarious, and it was challenging to quickly find a word that could work with the rest of the sentence when it came to each person's turn.

Chapter 35

The Frisbee whistled through the air. Edward caught it, and sent it on to Charles, who whirled it in Raymond's direction. The two families had decided to have a sort of picnic barbecue in the Jacksons' backyard on Friday. Now, after lunch was over, the boys had begun to play Frisbee.

The girls decided to go for a walk, and the adults were sitting in chairs under the porch, watching the boys play.

A while later, the girls were sitting on the grass at the top of a big hill when the boys came upon them.

"Look out, girls, we've come to stay!" Edward said, dropping down beside his twin sister.

"Why should that make us look out?" Florence asked with a giggle.

"Well, you can't very well look *in*, can you?" called Danny from where he had dropped a few yards away.

Susanna picked a dandelion leaf from near where she sat, and nibbled on the end of it.

Edward gave an exclamation of disgust, "I don't see how you like those bitter things!"

"*I* don't think they're bitter!" Jennie said, defiantly picking a dandelion leaf herself and biting a large piece of it,

"Anyway, I don't mind that you don't like them," she continued, "that just leaves more of them for us."

"It leaves more leaves for you!" Danny called.

There were a couple of chuckles, then Thomas asked, "can't you make a song about that, twins?"

"I don't know, probably," Jennie answered. She thought for a moment, then said, *"Goober Peas,* Edward."

He nodded, and Jennie began, "Sittin' on a hill, eating dandelion leaves,"

Edward continued, "Jennie thinks they're tasty, she's happy as you please. *But* her brother Edward, would pass the chance to try,"

Jennie finished, "But never does she mind it; she'll give a grin and cry:

They both sang the chorus together, "Leaves, leaves, leaves, leaves, dandelion leaves!"

Edward finished, "If you will leave the leaves alone, that leaves more leaves for me!"

The rest of the family laughed, and joined in as they sang the chorus again,

"Leaves, leaves, leaves, leaves,

Dandelion leaves!

If you will leave the leaves alone,

That leaves more leaves for me!"

A few minutes later, Danny, who had brought a football along, asked if anyone would join him. The boys immediately jumped up, and Susanna said, "I'll join in just a minute." Nancy was picking a bouquet of dandelions a few yards away.

Jennie leaned closer to Susanna as the boys took up their positions, "Are you ever going to tell me what happened?"

"What do you mean?" the older girl asked.

"That day, when you came home wearing that old-fashioned dress. You and Thomas have acted funny ever since, and that was the day you met Raymond. Is there something wrong with him?"

"With Raymond? No," Susanna shook her head, but then she caught sight of Florence, who was listening intently, and turning her head so only Jennie could see, Susanna mouthed, "Later," nodding her head toward the little girl.

Jennie looked at Florence, and back at Susanna, and mumbled, barely moving her lips, "Tonight?"

Susanna shook her head again, "Soon. I'll tell you. But not yet."

The boss called, "Come in!" in answer to Pickard's knock.

"You won't believe what I just found out!" the agent exclaimed.

"I won't? Why don't you tell me, and see what I believe."

"I have found out who removed Richard Wilson from the hospital," Pickard said, speaking slowly, "It was – Frank Garrold."

"Do you really mean it?" the boss jumped up, "Is it possible that you made a mistake?"

"No, I'm sure."

The boss sat back down again. "In that case – "

"What?"

"We'll not do anything to him yet," the boss said, "but we'll watch him very closely. In a little while we can arrest him, but we'll have to do it quietly, so they don't realize why he was arrested, or it will be harder than ever to get information out of them."

"Yes, sir. So you want us to watch him?"

"Yes."

~   ~   ~

Frank had argued with himself more than ever over the past few days after listening to that conversation between Thomas and Susanna. Though he had thought he had given up and let himself be trapped in his job with the FBI, he found that it was just as bad as ever. "I can't pray about it anymore," he said to himself, even though he knew that God would listen no matter what he had done. Unconsciously, he was praying, but there were no focused attempts to talk over his problems with the Heavenly Father.

Finally, though, he decided that he was going to tell Thomas and Susanna what he had done and warn them of further attempts to find the time-travel machine. He had thought he would feel better once he had decided something for certain, but he felt just as bad as before. As he made his way to the Jacksons' house, with every step he felt something arguing that this was not a good idea.

"They'll hate me, for sure," he said to himself, "they can't do anything else. But I have to do it. The weight of this thing is driving me crazy. At least I can warn them to be careful. I don't know how to get out of it at work though. I guess I'll have to keep on doing as I have been. I could pretend to try to get information for them."

He turned into the Jacksons' driveway, and saw that there was another car there already.

"Oh, no!" he exclaimed, and again he felt the urging to turn back, but he fought it, and told himself that he'd just ask to see Thomas alone for a minute.

He saw Thomas and Susanna sitting on the porch, however, with Raymond Vincent, and decided he might as well tell all of them at once.

"Hello, Frank! Came over for a talk?" Thomas called as Frank came up the walk.

"Yes. Are the kids anywhere around?" Frank asked nervously, "This is something private. You can tell them later if you want to – and you probably will."

"Do you want me to go inside?" Raymond asked, half standing up.

"No. You'll hear soon anyway. I was going to tell Thomas to tell you," Frank licked his lips and leaned against the railing. Then he remembered something suddenly.

Frank pulled his phone out of his pocket and placed a finger on his lips. "Give me yours," he whispered, holding out his hand to each in turn.

There were questioning looks on their faces, but they did as he said. When he had all four phones in his hand, he opened the door of the Jacksons' house and placed them on a chair in the entryway, then came back outside.

"Now," he said with relief, "they can't hear us."

"What in the world is going on, Frank?" Thomas demanded.

"The FBI is trying to find the time-travel machine," Frank answered.

"What! How do they know there is one?" Raymond exploded.

"No, no," Frank held out his hand, "I didn't tell them that. I did do a whole lot of other things, and I'll tell you what I did. But they found out that there was a time machine and that it's somewhere around here from another source. Then they put me on the case."

"And you took it?" Thomas asked in disbelief. Susanna clasped her hands together tightly in her lap and closed her eyes.

"I didn't want to. I had a long argument with the boss about it, but he told me I'd have to do it," Frank sighed. "I didn't tell them about helping you get that Wilson guy out of the hospital. But I did search for information for them after that. I'll tell you I did do it half-heartedly, but I don't know if you'll believe me. I'm sorry."

"What else?" asked Thomas, staring at him.

"I told the boss I didn't want to do it because you were my friends, but he said that since you were my friends you would trust me, and I could get more information out of you."

"Trust you is right," Thomas growled, "I can't believe you would do this to us! How much information did you give them?"

"I – oh – I can't tell you!" Frank had all he could do to keep from breaking into sobs. *"Stop it!"* he told himself fiercely, *"You're a man. Face the problems you've made for yourself without acting like a little kid."*

Thomas stood up and faced him, "You will tell us, and you will tell us everything!" he said menacingly.

Susanna gasped, and pulled on his arm, "Thomas, please sit down." He paid no heed.

Frank took a deep breath, "I told them that you had met Raymond under very mysterious circumstances, and I repeated the conversation we had a couple of months ago on the first Sunday that the Vincents started coming, about how you met him."

"Go on," Thomas said sternly.

Susanna had given up pulling on her brother's arm. She looked at Raymond. Though she had only a few days before been so angry with him, now that Frank had seemed to betray Raymond, she wanted to defend their new friend against the old one.

Raymond met her eyes with a serious gaze, then both turned their faces back to the two young men who were standing.

"I told them some other inconsequential stuff: that you were interested in sci-fi, and what you said about not being able to talk about it. Oh! I don't know why I ever took that job in the first place."

"We're very sorry," Thomas said sarcastically. He was angry, that much was obvious. "Now hurry up and tell us what else you told them," motioning impatiently for him to go on.

"One more thing. I-I don't really want to tell this, but I guess I have to."

"Yes, you have to," Thomas assured him.

"Thomas! *Please* sit down again!" Susanna begged.

"Leave me alone, Susanna," he said roughly, shaking off her hand; she sank back in her chair, covering her face.

Raymond pressed his lips together. Thomas certainly had a reason to be angry with Frank Garrold, but he had no right to be unkind to his sister. *"I guess he isn't thinking very clearly right now,"* he thought, *"like the time he got so mad at Richard Wilson."* He couldn't think of anything to say to the shrinking girl beside him, so he turned his attention back to Thomas and Frank.

Frank leaned on the railing heavily. Thomas had backed up one step in response to his sister's urging, but stood facing him fiercely, waiting for Frank to continue.

"We have our computers set to signal us whenever one of your phones picks up the words 'time machine,'" he began, "So a couple of days ago I saw that signal, and obeying orders, I turned up the volume to listen to your conversation."

Frank paused for a second, then finished, "It was you and Susanna talking, Thomas. You were talking about how she doesn't like the time-travel machine – and – and other things," he said with a glance at Raymond.

Susanna gasped, and Frank looked at her. She was leaning forward in her chair, her breast heaving, and her eyes wide and staring. "You did what?" she exclaimed.

"Yes," he answered simply.

"Oh! Oh, Frank!" she cried, "how could you?"

Susanna sank back down into her chair and bent her head, sobbing. The shame of having her confidences with Thomas cast abroad for Frank to hear was coupled with the fact that he, a close friend of the family, had betrayed them so far as to listen. Her sobs shook her shoulders, and Raymond, watching her, suddenly exclaimed, "Thomas, I'll handle the rest of this. You take care of your sister!" he stood up and pushed Thomas out of the way, taking a hold on Frank's arm and drawing him along the porch until they were several feet away from the other two.

"I don't know what to say to you," he began, looking at Frank cautiously, "So why don't you just get in your car and leave. You have told us everything, haven't you?"

Frank nodded miserably, "I'm sorry," he said.

Raymond opened the door and reached inside for Frank's phone, handed it to him, and waved him away.

"I must say I am sorry for you," he called, just before Frank disappeared down the walk. The other young man gave no sign of hearing.

Raymond wondered whether he should go back to where Thomas and Susanna were to talk it over, of he should wait until later. A sudden shriek from the girl decided him. He ran the couple of steps back to where they sat as quickly as he could and exclaimed, "What happened?"

Susanna gasped out, "Thomas, Thomas!"

"What?" he asked quickly.

She held out her hand, which was tightly closed, "I saw a fly on your shoulder, Thomas, and I grabbed it. I don't know why I did, since we're outside, but – oooh! Take it," and she pushed her closed hand closer to him.

"What in the world?" he exclaimed in astonishment, "Is there anything wrong with the fly?"

Susanna nodded, gasping and sobbing with every breath, "It's not a fly, Thomas. Tell me if it is what I think it is."

He pushed his thumb and forefinger into her fist and came out with the "fly" held between them. He caught his breath, "Oh no. Please, no Lord."

"Then it is! It is!" Susanna cried, and she clutched her hands to her throat in horror.

"What is it, General?" Raymond asked in a low voice.

"Let's go inside," Thomas said quietly, his voice hoarse.

"Hold it tightly, Thomas," Susanna said.

"I am," he answered.

Raymond stared, looking from one to the other, what was going on?

They entered the house, a strange hush surrounding them. Everyone else was still outside. Raymond scooped up the three phones that Frank had put inside earlier and gave each to its owner. They entered Mr. Jackson's office, and Susanna and Raymond took the two chairs, Thomas standing at the desk.

"See anything really heavy?" Thomas asked.

"Are you going to tell me what is going on?" Raymond demanded.

Thomas picked up a hammer that had been left in there the day before when someone had been fixing a bookshelf. He lifted it, and Susanna exclaimed, "try not to smash it too hard, Thomas, just break it."

"Okay," he said, and let the hammer fall gently on the "fly," which was still held between his fingers. "We'll call that the 'stun blow,'" he said, "Now it should stay down without me trying to hold it, so I won't hurt my fingers with the hammer when I hit harder."

The "fly" lay on the desk without moving, and Thomas brought the hammer down. There was a sound as if the hammer had contacted with metal, and Thomas said dryly, "this 'fly' has a stronger exoskeleton than most flies do."

Susanna took a deep breath and said, "so you're sure, Thomas?"

"Yes. It's no fly. It's a drone."

"What!" Raymond exploded, jumping from his chair and picking up the smashed metal pieces, "Is it possible?"

"Oh, it's possible, all right," Thomas mumbled, running a hand over his hair.

"I'll never feel safe again, Thomas!" Susanna cried, "To think that Frank Garrold, of all people, the one of you boys whom we all looked up to, turned traitor and listened to that conversation we had on Wednesday – one that I wouldn't have had anyone hear for the world, and now there's a drone no bigger than a fly on our front porch!"

Thomas patted her shoulder, "We'll have to keep the doors closed so nothing can get in," he said.

"But that doesn't make a difference! I'll always feel as if someone is watching me!" she shivered.

Raymond gave a sudden exclamation, "Oh! If the FBI heard our conversation with Frank, they know he turned traitor on them. What do you think they'll do to him?"

"Oh, no!" Thomas groaned, "we'll have to warn him. I'll call him right now."

"Do you think his phone's bugged?" Raymond suggested.

"I don't know, but we'll have to take the chance."

"Yes, no matter what he's done, he did say he's sorry," Susanna said, "and he has been our friend. We can't let him just drive into a trap they've set for him. But what will he do?"

"Why don't we ask him that question," Thomas suggested, picking up his phone.

"I'll record the conversation," Raymond said, taking out his own phone, "We might want to review later."

Turning it on speaker so all three of them could hear, Thomas placed the phone on the desk and seated himself on the arm of Susanna's chair.

"Brrring, brrring!" the phone rang, then Frank Garrold answered, "Hello, Thomas?"

"Frank, we need to warn you."

"About what? I doubt I'm coming to church anymore, if that's what you mean."

"Frank! Frank, don't give up God, no matter what else you have to give up!" Susanna cried.

"I – don't know, Susanna, I'll try," Frank answered.

"No, that's not what I meant," Thomas said, "Listen, right after you left Susanna found a drone shaped like a fly sitting on my shoulder. We have smashed it, but whatever it heard was probably sent back to the FBI office. If they heard your confession, they know you've turned traitor on them and you're in danger!"

Frank blew out a long breath, "You're right. That is a problem. Thanks for calling, Thomas. I'm glad you still care enough about what happens to me to do so."

Thomas's fists clenched. For the first time he realized how harsh he had been with his friend, even though some would say Frank deserved it.

"Frank," he said steadily, "I want to tell you that you're still our friend. We will always care about what happens to you. I'm sorry I was so angry with you earlier that I couldn't tell you that before you left."

"Thanks, Thomas," Frank's voice broke, then suddenly they heard him exclaim under his breath, "Oh no, Lord, please no!" as Thomas had a few minutes earlier when he had found the drone.

"What's the matter, Frank?" Raymond asked.

"There's a police car behind me, and he's flashing his lights. I've got to turn off. For once, I hope I was speeding."

"We're praying, Frank."

"There are a couple of vehicles that could be FBI in front of me."

"We're still praying. You should pray too."

"Okay, Thomas, I'll try. But I'm not doing too well. If anything happens, tell my family I love them, because I might not be able to get word for a while."

Susanna crossed her arms on the desk and laid her head down on top of them. She couldn't cry anymore, but several shuddering sighs shook her.

"Lord, protect Frank. Let him know that You are there and that You love him," Thomas prayed, "We'll trust You to do what's best. But, oh, Lord keep him safe!"

"I've pulled my car off the road now," Frank murmured, "the policeman is getting out and – I was right! – I see several other men, not police, coming too."

The three young people, feeling helpless shut in Mr. Jackson's office, continued to pray, but silently now.

"I'm putting my phone down on the seat, on speaker," Frank said, "that way you can hear if you want to. If you don't just turn your phone off."

"No, turn it on video chat, and put it up on your holder," Thomas told him, "I'll put a piece of black paper over the camera on my phone so they can't see us. Then we can see what happens too."

"Okay," Frank said, breathing heavily. A minute later the two phones were connected on video chat, and Thomas showed his face once, quickly to smile at Frank, "We're praying for you," then Thomas covered the camera with a paper. They could see Frank, but Frank couldn't see them. Frank angled the phone in the holder so that they could see the men getting closer to his car. He was speaking faster now, trying to get it all in before the men who were surrounding him closed in, "They'll take my phone away as soon as they find it anyway. Don't talk, then they won't know you're listening so soon."

"We love you, Frank," Thomas said.

Frank seemed to choke, but he didn't reply. A few seconds later, Frank rolled down the window, and they saw a policeman standing there with a gun. He spoke with a rough voice. "Frank Garrold?"

"Yes."

The recording lines on Raymond's phone moved up and down with each rise and fall of the voices. Thomas suddenly took a screenshot of Frank talking to the policeman. Thankfully, the officer had not noticed the phone.

"Hand over your license, your badge, and your gun," he demanded.

"Here they are," Frank surrendered without any fuss.

"We've got you covered," the officer said as he took the gun quickly.

"I can see that. Four, five, six men?"

"And more you can't see. Get out of the car."

Susanna pressed her hand to her lips to keep from screaming. She had read of things like this for years, but now it was far too real. Thomas reached over absently and patted her shoulder. She took his hand and held on as if her life depended on it, gazing at the small view the phone showed them, and wishing she could see more, but dreading what it would look like if she could.

"You know why we're arresting you?" they heard a voice demand, more faintly now, since Frank had gotten out of the car, but since the window was open, they could still hear.

"Yes; at least, I have a good idea," Frank answered.

They could only see part of Frank's body now that he was out of the car, but they saw a black-coated man next to him jerk his arms behind him, and another snapped on handcuffs.

"Thomas!" Susanna whispered desperately, "What are they doing to him? What are they *going* to do to him?"

Thomas shook his head at her and placed a finger on his lips. "I don't know."

Frank's voice came over the phone again, "Where are you taking me? Will I be able to contact my parents? They will be worried."

"Let them worry. You should have thought of that first – *traitor!*" a rough voice told him.

"Oof! Ouch! I can walk myself, can't I?" he exclaimed, as the two men beside him pushed him back into the view of the camera. Thomas took a couple more screenshots, his jaw clenched.

Obviously Frank was speaking louder so the ones listening over the phone could hear, and he wasn't hurt enough for him to exclaim quite that much, but Thomas lifted Susanna from her seat. "You don't need to watch this, Susanna," he whispered so the people on the other end wouldn't hear, "Go to Mommy. You can tell them what happened if you want, or you can wait for us. It'll soon be over, because they'll find the phone and turn it off."

Susanna turned an anguished, pleading face toward him, "Oh! Can't we do something?"

"It's too late. If we had called him earlier – but it's not time for this right now. Go!" and he pushed her toward the doors.

She looked back at him one last time, then at Raymond, then she opened the door softly and left.

Raymond and Thomas looked at each other for a moment, then back at the phones, Thomas's showing what was happening, and Raymond's recording the sounds that carried over the phone.

Suddenly a man opened the car door and looked around. He pulled the phone from its holder, "Hey, you guys! Someone's been listening! The phone's on a call - video chat!"

"What!"

"Really!"

"Who is it?"

Thomas quickly took a couple of screenshots of the closest men's faces before the man holding the phone covered the camera with his thumb. The sounds were clearer and louder now, but they couldn't see anything anymore.

"Who are you, and why are you listening?" one of the men demanded.

"If it were any use, I wouldn't tell you," Thomas answered, motioning Raymond to be quiet, "but since you can find out anyway, I'm Thomas Jackson."

"Uh-huh. Guessed it would be something like that," a second man spoke.

"What are you going to do to Frank?" Thomas demanded.

"We're going to take him on a vacation. He's been working too hard and seems worried. He should have plenty of peace and quiet where he's going," the men laughed.

"You'd better tell me now – or else!" Thomas exclaimed, "We're on your trail. We know where you are. If you don't let him go soon, we'll get him back somehow!"

The men laughed once more, "Guess again, mister!" one of them said, "You don't seem to be thinking straight."

"Can I talk to Frank for a minute?" Thomas asked.

"Hey, Garrold! Have anything you need to say to your friend?"

"May I?" Frank asked.

"Guess so. Just a few words, then we're hanging up."

Frank's voice sounded closer now. He spoke hurriedly, "Tell everyone I'm sorry," he began, "and tell Ann Starr that she was right, and I wish I'd done what she said. I'll do it now."

The two boys listening looked at each other with wondering eyes, but Frank was speaking again, "Tell Mom and Dad I love them, and my sisters too. I don't know if it'll be possible for you to forgive me, Thomas, but –"

Thomas broke in, "I forgive you, Frank. So will everyone else," but the call was ended before he had finished the last word.

Chapter 36

Raymond ended the recording on his phone, and he and Thomas sat looking at each other for a long time. Then they got up and went outside. Susanna was sitting in her father's lap, her head pillowed on his shoulder. He was speaking softly to her.

Thomas and Raymond sat down on the grass in front of their parents and waited for someone to speak.

Mrs. Jackson looked at them silently for a moment, then said, "Won't one of you please tell us the whole story from the beginning? Susanna came out a few minutes ago and tried to tell us, but she was – incoherent."

"What we thought she said," Mr. Vincent told them, "Was that Frank Garrold has been spying on someone, and the FBI have arrested him, and that you found a drone somewhere. How much of that is true, and what does it mean?"

Thomas and Raymond told the story as clearly as possible. When they were finished, Mrs. Jackson closed her eyes, "Lord, help us," she murmured, "this is more complicated than I thought."

"Are you sure it was a drone?" Mr. Jackson asked.

"Positive. It couldn't be anything else. Metal flies don't normally fly around here," Thomas answered.

"What do we do about Frank?" Raymond asked, "I wonder where they've taken him."

"I wish I'd been in there when you were listening through the phone," Mr. Vincent said.

"I recorded the whole conversation," Raymond told him, pulling his phone from his pocket, "So you can hear it now, even though you weren't there when it happened."

"And since it was on video chat, I was able to get a couple of screenshots, so I have pictures of what happened," said Thomas.

"Not right now, boys," Mrs. Jackson said softly, "The children are coming."

Susanna jumped off her father's knee. "I'm going inside, so they won't ask questions," she said, "I'll be in your room, Mommy."

Mrs. Jackson squeezed her hand as she passed her, and then looked back at the others. "We've got to talk about something unimportant," she said, "I don't want the children asking questions. I especially don't want them questioning Susanna. As far as they are concerned, she just went inside for a few minutes, all right?"

The others nodded. Susanna was certainly not in the mood for questioning now, and if she was questioned later, she might break down again. Listening to an old friend's confession, and then watching him be arrested would be a difficult experience for any girl.

~   ~   ~

An hour later, Mr. Jackson sent a call down the prayer chain. First he called one of the elders, who was at the head of it. This is the message he gave.

"Mr. Harley? Hello, I have an urgent prayer request."

"Yes, Philip? Is it for the prayer chain, or is it private?"

"For the prayer chain."

"What is it?" Mr. Harley asked.

"Frank Garrold was just arrested, and we don't know where he was taken. My son and Raymond Vincent just went over and told the Garrolds, who sent back word for me to send out the prayer request."

"Can you tell me what he was arrested for, or is that private?" Mr. Harley asked.

"Here's all the information I can give you right now: Tell the parents to keep the news from their younger children. Ellen Garrold has not been told yet either. They may tell only those older children who will be discreet in what they say. Frank was doing something wrong, but he was arrested for trying to fix it. I can't explain right now; it's a long story. Call a church meeting for tomorrow at five o'clock. Any of the older children who want to come may, but the younger ones need to stay at home. The parents may make the decision about who is mature enough to come. We will explain what happened as far as possible then."

"Okay, got it, Philip."

"Good. Goodbye."

~   ~   ~

Saturday evening, the church was filled even before it was five o'clock. Everyone was eager to hear just exactly what had happened in connection with Frank Garrold.

The Vincents had brought Mr. Elliot with them, and he stood up to speak first, "We are going to tell the story from the beginning," he said, "and since I was the one who started it, I will tell my part first."

There were surprised looks around the congregation, since he was a stranger to everyone there.

"I invented a machine," he said, "and I'm not going to tell you what it is; but I'll tell you that it was fun to use, but could be dangerous if it got into governmental hands. We used the machine several times, I myself, the Vincents, and the Jacksons. A few weeks ago we had something in connection with the machine that needed to be taken care of – really almost a life or death situation – but it was almost impossible to do it without proper authority, so Frank agreed to use his position as an FBI agent to do it for us. He promised not to divulge our secret."

Thomas stepped up to the front, "The Vincents were at our house yesterday, and while the kids were playing out back and our parents were watching them,

Susanna, Raymond and I were sitting on the front porch. Frank drove up, and we were a little surprised, because we hadn't expected him, but you all know you can drop in whenever you want, so that was all right. He came up to the front porch where we were sitting, and took our phones away, putting them inside the house, so the speakers on them couldn't be tapped. Then he began to talk. He told us that he works for the FBI, as we, and most of you already knew, and they had told him to spy on us and find Mr. Elliot's machine. He says he argued with them, but finally gave in. He didn't tell them about helping us, but pretended he'd never heard of the machine before, and started he says half-heartedly spying on us, using only the information they gave him."

The congregation was shocked, to say the least. But no one spoke aloud, and Thomas went on, "Frank told us he was feeling so bad about it he finally decided to come to us and confess the whole thing. He wasn't sure what he was going to do after that. I guess he would have had to quit his job, or pretend to keep spying. But after he left, Susanna put her hand over what she thought was a fly on my shoulder, and caught it. Why she caught it instead of just brushing it away, since we were outside, I'll never know, but I'm so thankful she did. It was not a fly. It was a drone. Through it, we think, the FBI had been listening to our conversation with Frank, in spite of the precaution of moving our phones inside. So they knew he had turned traitor on them."

Thomas took a deep breath, then told how they had talked to Frank over the phone, and watched him be arrested.

"We're going to play the recording Raymond took, and put my screenshots up on this screen here," he finished, and the lights dimmed so they could see the screen more easily.

There was a picture of Frank as he watched the men close in on him, and a picture of him talking to the policeman through the window. Several of the girls who had come closed their eyes when the pictures of him wearing handcuffs came on, and a couple of them put their hands over their ears.

Thomas had a couple of close-ups of the FBI agents, but after that the man had put his thumb over the camera, so there were no more pictures. Raymond shut off the recording before it was done. Just before Frank had begun to say his last words.

"The rest is personal messages," Raymond said, "and I'll only show those to the ones they were meant for."

~ ~ ~

"Ann! Thomas Jackson and Raymond Vincent and their dads are here," Elizabeth Starr called, looking out the window in surprise.

"Really! Well, let them in. Tell them to sit in the living room, and I'll be there in a minute."

"Okay!" and the younger girl opened the door even before they knocked.

A few minutes later Ann Starr entered the room and asked, "Are you here to talk with Dad? He'll be home in a few minutes." She wondered what they had to say. She couldn't get out of her head the story they had told two days before.

Sunday had been a hard day for almost everyone in the church. The younger children, of course, didn't know what was wrong. The Garrolds left right after services, but Ann had time to catch a glimpse of little Ellen's face. She seemed to be having a hard time. Half of the church didn't go to the Jacksons' house and the other half didn't stay long after services. The conversations had been carefully kept away from the subject of Frank Garrold, but everyone had it at the top of their minds.

Now Ann wondered if what the visitors had to say was about Frank, but she didn't say it aloud. She just waited for an answer to her question.

"Yes, we want to see your father," Mr. Jackson answered, "Actually, we want to see both your mother and father, and you."

"Me? Uh, okay. I'll be back in a minute," and she hurriedly left the room. What in the world could they have to say to her? Maybe it was just that they were talking to the parents and the oldest child of each family they visited, and Ann was the oldest in her family.

She could do nothing but wait and see. She quickly found her mother, who was outside on the back porch, "Mom,"

"Yes?"

"Mr. Vincent, Mr. Jackson, and Thomas and Raymond are here. They want to talk to you and Dad and me."

"Okay. Tell them I'll be inside in a minute. Is it a private conversation? Do we need to be somewhere that the other kids can't hear?"

"I don't know. I'll ask. If it is, I guess we could come out here, right?"

"Sure. Is Dad home yet?" her mother asked.

"No. He should be home any minute, though."

When they were all on the back porch, Mr. and Mrs. Starr, Ann, and their guests, and the other children had been warned away, Mr. Jackson spoke, "You were all there on Saturday, right?"

The Starrs nodded.

"Raymond stopped the recording before it was done because the rest of it was personal messages that he would deliver privately."

Again the Starrs nodded. They couldn't see where he was going.

Mr. Jackson nodded to Raymond, who had taken out his phone and was holding it in front of him.

"We don't know what this message means, but we're thinking that you will," Raymond said, looking at Ann. She was startled. How could she translate a message Frank had sent to someone?

"Here's the recording of it," Raymond went on, and he tapped his finger on the "play" button.

" – Everyone that I'm sorry," came Frank's well-known voice, "and tell Ann Starr that she was right."

Chapter 37

Ann jumped when she heard her name, and her parents looked at her questioningly.

Frank's voice continued, "and I wish I'd done what she said. I'll do it now."

"Oh!" Ann exclaimed, "oh, that's why – " and she burst into tears. Mr. Starr stood up, and the guests stood up with him. He motioned for them to leave, and whispered as they entered the house, "Thank you. I don't know what it means yet, but it looks like Ann does. Now, please don't discuss this with anyone."

"We were never planning to," Mr. Vincent assured him, "that's why we stopped the recording early. There was also a message for his family, of course. We just took that to them."

"Goodbye," Mr. Starr said, as he closed the door behind them.

"What does this mean, Ann?" Mrs. Starr asked gently.

"One – minute, Mom," Ann wiped her eyes on her sleeve, "I'll tell you as – soon as I can – stop crying."

"Okay."

It only took minute for the girl to calm down, then she looked straight at her mother. Her father had not returned. He had thought it would be best to let his wife handle this. She would tell him everything later.

"One Sunday, a few weeks ago," Ann began, "I saw Frank talking with Ellen. I didn't listen, but I saw that it was a very serious conversation. Then he teased her for a minute before letting her run away to play. I wouldn't have paid any attention to it, because that looked normal enough, but then I saw him start talking to himself. His lips moved, but I don't know what he said. I didn't try to figure out, anyway."

Ann bent her head for a minute, then looked back at her mother and shook her head, "He looked very upset and angry about something, and his fists kept clenching, and – well, I should have stopped watching him, I know, and I tried, but I kept glancing back at him until he finally saw me. That made me embarrassed, of course, but suddenly I felt strongly as if I should tell him to pray. He looked very embarrassed himself that I was looking at him, but he didn't stop looking at me. So I just moved my hands like this," she showed her mother the motions she had used on that day, "and he looked startled. Finally he shook his head, and almost ran out of the church building. I thought he was shaking his head because he didn't want to pray, and I guess I was right. Oh, Mom!"

"But he said he'd do what you said now," her mother reminded her, "so that means he will pray now."

Ann nodded, "I kind of forgot by the end of the day, and it didn't seem too important. I guess it's one of those things that you realize are vital only when it's too late. Why did Frank do it, Mom, why did he?" the tears were falling again.

Mrs. Starr pulled her daughter close, "I don't know why he did it, Ann. Sometimes the government makes me think of a deep pool of water. Whenever someone gets involved in its work, they will eventually sink to the bottom, unless they have a life jacket, which in this case, would be Christ."

"But wasn't – isn't Frank a Christian?" Ann asked, "I thought he was."

"I don't know, honey, I thought he was too."

"Then why?"

"Maybe his life jacket was thin, and didn't hold him up for very long. Let's pray he'll get a thicker one soon."

Ann sniffed, and wiped her eyes again, "He did say he was sorry," she whispered.

"And we'll need to pray for him really hard," said Mrs. Starr, "because if you remember, he thinks that he has no friends. He betrayed his friends at church, and for some reason he thinks we aren't as forgiving as we should be, and then he turned traitor on the FBI, so they're not on his side anymore. I think Thomas made him understand that we still all love him, but he must feel very alone."

Ann choked on a sob, and forced her tears back, "Poor Frank. Are you going to tell the younger children what happened?'"

"No. Just that Frank had to leave for a while. We don't want the children discussing it among themselves at church. When they get older, they might have to be told, but we'll take that when it comes."

~   ~   ~

A week later Raymond went up the front walk to the Jacksons' house. He had been a regular guest for so long that he almost felt as if he belonged to the family. When he knocked, little Nancy opened the door. "Hello, Raymond," the bubbly child said eagerly, "You want to see Thomas and Susanna, or are you going to talk to me?"

"I think I'll talk to you," he laughed, catching up her hands and swinging her in a circle in the large entryway.

A laugh was heard from up above, and he saw the twins looking down at him from the balcony, "Hi!" they called, and came rushing down the stairs.

Raymond was quite entertained by Nancy's chatter, as they stood in the foyer talking. Susanna came in a little while later, and Jennie asked, "How's Mommy doing?"

"She's much better," the older girl answered, "And she says she probably won't feel very bad for another several months."

Raymond was confused. Was this a regular illness that Mrs. Jackson had? Did she know how to predict her bad spells? She had not seemed to be doing well since he had met them, which was a couple of months ago.

Nancy tugged on his hand, "Mommy's sick 'cause she's going to have a baby," she told him, "I can't wait until she's born. At least," she grinned, "I hope it's a girl."

It was a sudden revelation to Raymond. He had been an only child, and he had no experience with pregnant women. "So that's why your mother hasn't been feeling well?" he asked, looking at Susanna.

She was surprised, "haven't we told you? I thought you knew."

"No, I didn't know. But that sounds like fun. When is the due date?"

"She's only three months pregnant right now," Susanna said, wondering why Raymond looked so relieved, "so the baby will be born sometime around the end of November or the beginning of December."

"A sister for Christmas?" he said.

"Well, boy or girl, the little one won't stay in as long as that," Susanna laughed, "But we'll still have a newborn at Christmastime."

~   ~   ~

"Dad, where are you?" Raymond called, as he entered his house.

"Upstairs!" Mr. Vincent called back.

Raymond bounded up the stairs. "Dad!" he said eagerly when he saw his father, "I found out what's wrong with Mrs. Jackson. I mean, there's nothing wrong at all! She's just pregnant, and that's why she was feeling sick!"

Mr. Vincent laughed, "I'm glad you finally found out, son. You didn't know? I knew long ago."

"No," Raymond turned serious, "I didn't know. I thought there was something really wrong with her – like Mom."

"I'm sorry, Raymond. If I had known you were still worried about that, I would have told you."

"It's all right now!" Raymond exclaimed, "But I sure am glad to know."

Thomas came up softly behind Susanna and caught her around the waist, swinging her around, "You've been too quiet lately," he laughed as she squealed, "What're you thinking about?"

Susanna faced him with a pensive frown, "I was wondering how we could get Frank Garrold back," she said.

"I know, I've been wondering about that too. The only way I can think of is to tell the FBI we'll show them where the machine is if they'll let Frank go and never arrest him again."

"Yes, but we can't let them know where the machine is."

"Frank's much more important than any old machine," Thomas said.

"Yes, but the government could hurt a lot of people with the time machine, while Frank is only one, and besides, what do we know but that he's as comfortable and happy as can be?"

"You're arguing with yourself, Susanna," Thomas told her, "One minute you say you want to get him out, and then the next you give a reason why we shouldn't even try."

"I know," she sighed, "and that's what I've been doing for the past several days. I wish Mr. Elliot had never invented that silly machine!"

"We wouldn't have been able to save Richard Wilson," Thomas reminded her.

"Yes, but I'd rather have Frank safe than Richard Wilson," she said impatiently.

"I know. But there's not much we can do about it."

Susanna nodded.

"How's your grudge at Raymond coming along?" Thomas asked, half teasing and half serious.

She shook herself, "I've tried to get rid of it, but it keeps coming back. I've prayed, and I've thought of all the nice things I can about him, but nothing works. I still keep thinking about how mean he was to let me get so upset before he told us what was wrong." She had started off thoughtfully, but was becoming angry now, "I can hardly bear it when I think of him standing there laughing at us because he knew what was wrong and we didn't!"

"That was pretty mean," Thomas agreed, "but you can't let it form your opinion of him. Just forget about it and be friends like you would if nothing had happened."

"Leave me alone, Thomas! You're being no help at all! Go away. I can choose my own friends, if you let me!"

"I thought you asked me to pray for you," he said quietly.

"Oh, just – I'm so sorry! That was so disrespectful. You're right, and I'm wrong, but I can't seem to do anything about it."

"I'll keep praying."

"Oh, Thomas?"

"Yes?" he had been about to leave, but he turned back.

"About Raymond. Today he said he hadn't known that Mommy was pregnant. He looked so relieved when he found out that was why she was feeling sick. I wonder why?"

"Maybe he was afraid she had some bad illness," her brother suggested.

"Maybe, but he doesn't know her well enough to be so worried about that, does he?"

"I don't know. He's been over here a lot lately."

~   ~   ~

Thomas called to Susanna, "Raymond has an idea!"

"An idea about what?" she called back, leaning over the railing of the balcony to see him as he stood in the foyer.

"Come down here and I'll tell you."

"Coming!" and with a swish of her skirts, Susanna was down the stairs and standing beside him.

"He has an idea about how to get Frank back from wherever he is," Thomas said.

"Really! What is it?"

"Oh, he couldn't text it to me, of course! Our phones are probably being watched."

Susanna shivered, "Yes, I know. So is he coming here to talk to you?"

"Yes. Tomorrow."

~   ~   ~

The next day Raymond arrived at the Jacksons' house. When Charles answered the door, he told Raymond that Thomas hadn't arrived yet, so Raymond went outside to wait. He saw Susanna walking in the backyard, and she waved, but didn't come any closer.

Thomas arrived soon, and greeted Raymond excitedly. "So you have an idea," he whispered, just in case there were any more drones around.

Raymond nodded, and Thomas said, "I'll ask Susanna if she wants to hear it now, or wait until I tell her."

"Okay," Raymond agreed.

He watched as Thomas went over to where Susanna was walking, and stood talking with her for a minute. She shook her head, and said something. Thomas nodded, and came back.

"She says I can tell her later," Thomas said.

"But she's not in the middle of anything," Raymond commented, looking at her.

Thomas shrugged, "It won't hurt to tell her later. Maybe she doesn't want to go inside and talk, which is what we'll have to do to be safe."

"Maybe. But wouldn't it be safer to tell it once and have it done? The more times we have to talk about it, the more chance there is of the FBI getting word," Raymond murmured quietly.

"Mm-hm. I'll ask her again if you like."

Susanna shook her head when Thomas reached her, but when he started talking, she looked thoughtful. Finally she shrugged and started to shake her head, but Thomas suddenly picked her up like a baby and began to carry her back toward where Raymond was standing. At that, she gave in and began to laugh, struggling to get down.

"Put me down, Thomas!" Raymond heard her say between giggles, "I'll come."

"You bet you will!" he exclaimed, doing as she said.

~   ~   ~

Instead of going into Mr. Jackson's office this time, the three went downstairs. They spoke in low voices, even though they were pretty sure they were safe, because a drone the size of the one they had found before could crawl under doors easily.

"We need to try to get Frank Garrold back from wherever they've taken him," Raymond began, and the others nodded, "Well, there's only one thing I think will work."

"And that is?" Thomas asked. Susanna was sitting on the edge of the pool table, and he was standing on the floor beside her.

Raymond faced them, "I am afraid that Mr. Elliot won't do it. But what would have to be done is we would send word to the FBI that if Frank Garrold is given to us, we will show them the time-travel machine."

"But we can't do that!" Thomas began.

Raymond held up his hand, "Wait just a minute. Let me finish. We would destroy the plans for the machine. Then, we would place some sort of bomb or self-destruction thing in the time-travel machine. We would show it to them, but before they got close enough to get hurt, we would destroy it. Then we could keep our promise, and show them the time machine, without letting them get it."

"Yes! That's a good idea. But would Mr. Elliot agree to it?"

"I don't know, but as far as I can see, it's the only way."

~   ~   ~

"Dad, I asked Mr. Elliot to come over this evening," Raymond stuck his head in the door of his father's room.

"You did? Why?"

"I have an idea about how to get Frank Garrold back. I need to discuss it with Mr. Elliot."

"Okay. Is he going to be here for dinner?" Mr. Vincent asked.

"No. He'll come around seven o'clock."

~   ~   ~

And when Mr. Elliot did come, Raymond explained his plan and asked, "Would you be willing? I know you've worked on this a long time, but there's no real reason to keep it, as far as I know, especially if you don't want the government to get it."

Mr. Elliot looked thoughtful, and a little sad. He *had* put a lot of effort into his project, and he hadn't thought it would end this way.

Raymond continued, "Frank is more important than the machine. I know you believe that."

Mr. Elliot nodded, but remained quiet.

"Have you seen the Jacksons recently? Susanna was extremely upset about the drone she found, and I couldn't really say that Thomas was any too happy about it either."

Mr. Elliot nodded again.

"I've been reviewing the past few months over and over these last few days, and I've been thinking that we've put the Jacksons – especially Susanna – under a lot of pressure. I guess I really am not the one to be saying this, but I kind of wish we hadn't."

Once more, Mr. Elliot nodded.

Raymond felt that he wasn't good at explaining things, and tried to go into more detail, though with much nervousness as to how the older man would take it, "I'm not sure we should have used the Jacksons as an experiment in the first place. It just doesn't seem right, and I'd like to try to make it up to them now, by putting things back as far as we can into the way they were before. To do that we'd have to get Frank Garrold back, and get rid of the time machine, and convince the FBI that all the records of it have been destroyed."

Mr. Elliot nodded one last time, and then spoke, "Raymond, you're taking too much on yourself. You don't want to blame me, I guess, and that is very good and respectful of you, but to blame yourself just doesn't make sense. You are right, though. I shouldn't have used them for a test, and I apologized for that long ago. It's too late to correct that error, but I'll do whatever I can to solve the problems I've created."

As Mr. Elliot was leaving, he suddenly stumbled a bit, and put his hand on the doorframe.

"Are you all right?" Raymond asked anxiously.

"Yes. It's only that I'm not as young as I used to be," Mr. Elliot said, and left quickly.

Chapter 38

Richard Wilson was much better. He could walk from his bed to the back door and outside, to sit for a while each day in the warm summer air. Soon he would be able to go to find his sister. This morning he was sitting on a chair that was set under a tree behind the Maxwells' house. No one was around, since there was plenty of work to be done.

Richard wished he could do something to repay the Maxwells for their wonderful care of him, but he didn't know what he could do. Of course they wouldn't accept money, since they had taken him as a guest, but what else was there?

He sat thinking, pondering this question for a long time, then opened the Bible which was on his lap and began to read it. After flipping through the pages, he suddenly thought of a plan, which made him close the Book once more and sit silently thinking. A little while later Bessie and Lily Mae came outside.

"Mr. Wilson! You must be very tired of sitting out here by yourself," Bessie exclaimed, "I'm sorry we haven't anyone to entertain you regularly, but the only one of us who doesn't have any chores to do is Carter, and though he might be entertaining, I'm sure he'd wear you out in a minute!"

Richard laughed, "You're right about that, Miss Maxwell. I don't think I'm ready quite yet to try to keep up with a two-year-old."

"We have everything taken care of just now," Bessie continued, "so we can sit out here with you and talk while we knit if you don't mind."

"Mind! Certainly not. Please do. Sitting here thinking one's own thoughts does become wearying after a while," he replied.

Lily Mae laughed, "I should think it would."

The two girls sat down on a bench that was set against the outside of their house and began knitting. Richard watched them quietly for a while, then asked if they would like him to read to them.

"That would be lovely!" Bessie exclaimed.

So Richard opened his Bible again, and turned to the book of Esther, chapter five. Clearing his throat, he began, "'Now it came to pass on the third day, that Esther put on her royal apparel, and stood in the inner court of the king's house.'"

The two girls looked up, a little surprised at this unusual selection, but he continued reading. When he reached verse three, he read it with especial emphasis: "'What is thy request? it shall be even given thee to the half of the kingdom.'"

Bessie and Lily Mae did not seem enlightened, so the young man continued to read. Again, when he reached verse six, he read with added emphasis, "'What is thy petition? and it shall be granted thee: and what is thy request? even to the half of the kingdom it shall be performed.'"

He ended after verse eight, in which Esther only asked the king to come to another banquet, promising that then she would tell him what she wanted.

Then, looking up, he smiled whimsically at the two girls sitting before him, "I feel as though I were the king in the story," he said, "I want to find some way to serve you, but when I ask, all you want is to serve me another meal!"

Lily Mae blushed at the compliment, though it was given half in annoyance.

"Oh, Mr. Wilson!" Bessie laughed, but then turned serious, "You know very well, sir, that we don't want you to repay us."

Richard shook his head in despair, "I know that. You have made that very clear. But please tell me if ever there is any way in which I can serve you."

The two girls nodded. Then talk turned to other things.

~   ~   ~

"I'd like to go use the feather bed once more before you burn it," Thomas said.

"I loved feather beds when I was a boy," Mr. Elliot told him, with a reminiscent nod, "but recently the one I have has become pretty uncomfortable. Maybe it's because I'm growing older."

"I don't like feather beds at all," Susanna told them. "Even though I never used one until recently, I always thought they would be uncomfortable. But since Thomas likes them, I'll tolerate them."

Mr. Elliot laughed, and nodded, "I saw that from the second day I knew you, Susanna. You like me, though, even though you don't like my feather bed?"

Feather bed was the phrase they had chosen to use instead of time machine, since Frank had warned them that the computers were set to pick up the latter phrase.

Susanna smiled, "Yes. And I'll go with Thomas one more time if he likes. It can't be too bad."

"No," Raymond laughed, "But leave your phones at home, so they can't use them to show where you went. If they suddenly stopped being able to track them, they would know that they had passed through it, and they would look for the exact place where they were lost, so that they – "

Susanna held up her hands in pretended terror, "Please, Raymond, please! You are using way too many pronouns! What in the world do you mean?"

Raymond looked blank for a minute, then laughed and explained, "If you leave your phones at home, the trackers will think you're there – at home – too. Whoever heard of someone leaving without their – the persons own – phone in this modern world? Then they – the ones who are searching for the feather beds – will not try to follow us to the site where we'll try them – the feather beds – out one more time before burning them – the feather beds, not the searchers."

Everyone laughed.

"That was almost as confusing as your last speech, Raymond," Mr. Elliot told him.

"I've figured it out, boss," Pickard exclaimed, as the boss came to stand behind his chair while he was listening to the conversation between the Jacksons, Raymond, and another man.

"What have you figured out?" the boss asked.

"The code word they're using instead of 'time machine' so that the computer isn't picking it up."

"Really? What is it?"

"Feather bed!" Pickard said. "It was a bit challenging, because at first they styled their conversation in a way that would just sound like they were talking about normal feather beds, but that young guy, Raymond Vincent gave it away. They're planning to visit the time machine again soon, but they're going to leave their phones at home this time so we can't track them that way. We'll have to go back to the old-fashioned method of assigning someone to watch them. Shadowing them."

The boss nodded, "Do it."

"I will, but let me listen to the rest of this conversation. I hope I haven't missed too much." Pickard turned back to his computer and turned up the volume button which he had lowered at the arrival of the boss.

~   ~   ~

"See you later, General," Pickard heard Raymond say, presumably to Thomas.

"Hmm, that might mean that Thomas Jackson is in charge of this project!" Pickard thought.

"Bye, Raymond, and don't forget to try out the feather bed," Thomas said.

Pickard laughed grimly, "They don't know that I've decoded their little ruse," he said to himself, "But that only makes it easier for us. But I wonder about that 'General' thing. Thomas Jackson must be the one in charge. I'll follow that up."

It was only five minutes after Raymond and Mr. Elliot left the house that Thomas and Susanna set out too. They left their phones at home, as had been arranged, and told their mother not to worry if they didn't respond to her calls.

"Goodbye, Thomas, goodbye Susanna. I'll try not to worry, but I don't like not knowing where you are, and not being able to contact you."

"I'm sorry, Mommy. This is the last time, you know."

"Yes. I hope so. I'm glad you've been having fun with this, Thomas, but remember, if you hadn't ever used it, we wouldn't have lost Frank Garrold."

Susanna's face stiffened. She didn't like being reminded of what had happened, especially since she was trying to forgive Raymond, and every time she thought of Frank, she became more hurt and angry.

"See you later, Mommy!" Thomas said, catching his sister's hand and pulling her with a laugh out the door of their parents' room.

Nancy stopped them on their way out the door, "You're going away *again*, Thomas? Why do you have to go?"

"I'm sorry, Nancy. Susanna and I are going for a walk."

"Can't I come with you?" the little girl asked.

"No," Thomas laughed, "you stay at home this time. But I'll play with you when I get back, okay?"

"Okay."

Thomas picked Nancy up for a hug, then set her down to run back into the house.

~   ~   ~

"Here we go. This is your last chance, Dad. You sure you don't want me to stay while you go through?" Raymond asked the question with such an obvious desire to receive a negative answer that all the others laughed.

Mr. Vincent shook his head, "No. We've already discussed that. Mr. Elliot's going because he is the one who invented the machine. You kids are going to have a good time. I've already been through several times, so I don't need to go now. Just go, son, and don't worry about me."

Raymond smiled in a relieved way. He did want to go through, but he was glad his father didn't seem to care much to go himself.

Chapter 39

After Arthur left to join the Confederate Army, Lucy fell naturally into the family life of his parents' home. Mrs. Johnston was a very sweet lady, she discovered, and while Mr. Johnston was fiery and apt to blast off at the slightest provocation, Lucy soon made him love her, and he would do almost anything for her.

Before Arthur had left she had discussed the possibility of carrying on Richard's spying activities, and they had agreed if any opportunity came her way she would take it.

Lucy was sitting on the back porch, enjoying the sunshine when Hattie stepped out of the house and said, "Miss Lucy, a gen'man to see you."

"Arthur?" Lucy asked eagerly, jumping up.

"No, not Mistah Arthuh. Anodder gen'man."

Hattie held out the card tray, and Lucy read the card on it, "Mr. William Beckett. I wonder who he is?"

"I dunno, Miss Lucy. I nebber seen him before."

"Well, I'll go in. You stay near please, Hattie, in case we want tea."

"Yes'm."

Lucy entered the parlor and bowed to the man who was waiting there. He was dressed like a gentleman, as Hattie had said, and his face seemed good. Not exactly kind, or good-natured, Lucy thought, but one that she could trust.

She held out her hand, saying, "Mr. Beckett?"

He shook her hand, and nodded, then asked, "And you are Mrs. Johnston?"

"I am," she replied.

"Shall we sit down?" he asked, "I have a sort of business to discuss with you."

"Surely. What is it, Mr. Beckett?"

"I have recently seen your husband," he began, "He is well, and sends his love. I have a letter of introduction from him," he handed it to her. It was a simple letter briefly explaining that Mr. Beckett was to be trusted, and ending with a declaration of Arthur's continuing love. Mr. Beckett continued as she looked back up at him, "In our conversation it came out that you are eager to help the Southern Cause as much as you can; spying if necessary."

Lucy nodded eagerly, "Not only if necessary, sir," she corrected, "I would dearly like to be allowed to help with any spying work I can."

"Well, then we have just the job for you," he told her.

~ ~ ~

After visiting the Maxwells' house, where, following a little incident with a neighbor, they asked after Richard's health and then said goodbye to everyone, the group from the modern side of the time machine didn't stay long in the past. As they neared the door over which the time-travel machine was placed, they remembered that, according to the plan, this would be their last time visiting the past.

"I guess we won't see this place again," Thomas said thoughtfully.

"That's right. Too bad. We've had some fun here," Raymond shook his head.

"It is really hard to believe we'll be destroying what I've worked on for decades," said Mr. Elliot sadly.

They opened the door and went through, then waited for Mr. Vincent to turn the machine back on and let them know they could come back.

When they had left the time machine and were walking down the street, Raymond said suddenly, "Race you to that tree over there, Thomas!"

Thomas laughed, and sprinted ahead. He beat Raymond, but only by a close margin. Raymond laughed, saying good-naturedly, "Good job, General, I guess I'll have to do some more practicing before I can beat you." Suddenly a couple of black-coated men appeared and walked up to the two boys. Susanna and the older men had been left a ways behind.

"Thomas Jackson and Raymond Vincent, correct?" one of the men said abruptly.

The boys nodded in surprise. Then Raymond recognized that the man who had spoken was the man they had talked to over the phone on the day that Frank Garrold had been arrested. Looking at Thomas, he couldn't be certain the other boy had realized the same thing, but Raymond was beginning to get worried.

"Tell us where the time machine is," the man demanded.

The boys shook their heads, "We can't do that," Raymond said.

"I have a gun."

The boys looked at each other, then back at the man. Thomas answered this time, "We just can't tell you."

"You want your friend back safe?" the man demanded.

"Sure we do. But we can't let you have the machine."

"Then you're coming with me, *General*, for further questioning," the man said, and his partner took Thomas's arm.

"Hey, wait a minute!" Raymond exclaimed, "what are you doing?"

"We're taking your friend in for questioning," the man answered.

"Why?"

"We want to know where the time machine is, and he seems to be in charge of this operation. Goodbye."

Thomas gave Raymond a meaningful look, "Now you'll have to get two of us out of there," he told him.

Raymond understood immediately. They were to go on with the plan he had thought of, but instead of negotiating for only Frank's freedom, they might have to get Thomas out too, depending on how long they kept him prisoner.

"You don't understand," Raymond tried once more, "He isn't in charge. I just call him that as a nickname. It's because of his real – "

"And you think we're going to believe that?" the man scoffed. He took hold of Thomas's other arm and the two men walked off at a moderate pace with Thomas between them.

~   ~   ~

Susanna made a move to run forward when she saw the man grab Thomas, but Mr. Vincent caught her arm. "Wait, Susanna!" he said, "What are they doing?"

"They're arresting Thomas!" she cried, "that's the same man who arrested Frank. We saw him over the phone, remember?"

Mr. Elliot drew in a breath, then he nodded, and the three tried to hurry to where the boys were standing, but by the time they reached the tree Raymond and Thomas had raced to, it was too late. Thomas was walking off with the two men, and Raymond was staring after him in dismay.

"Raymond! What happened?" Susanna gasped.

He turned quickly to look at her, "Isn't it obvious?" he growled, "they've taken Thomas in for questioning."

"Raymond!" Mr. Vincent warned.

Instantly Raymond was apologetic, "Oh, I'm sorry, Susanna! I was just so upset – you see – it's my fault!"

"What?" the others exclaimed.

Raymond shook his head, "They've heard me calling him 'General' and they think it meant that he was in charge. So they think he can tell them more than the rest of us."

Susanna's breath was coming quick and fast. She walked over to a nearby fence and crossed her arms on the top rail, facing away from the others. They stared at her back silently for a minute, then Mr. Elliot whispered, "This is too much. I should have gotten rid of the machine long ago."

"Well, now it's too late to change that. We'll just have to get them back as fast as possible," Mr. Vincent told him.

Raymond put his hand on his hip and it bumped into his holster. "Aw, I had a gun," he exclaimed, "Why didn't I use it to stop them?"

"That would only have gotten us all arrested, son," Mr. Vincent told him. "We have to do this legally. You can't fight the law with anything but words."

The two men continued talking, guardedly, in case any drones were nearby.

Raymond walked over to the fence Susanna was leaning on, and placed one of his arms atop it, turning to face her. The side view of her face showed that she was staring off into space. He wasn't sure she knew he was even there.

It seemed like a long time before she turned and looked at him. He was startled at the expression in her eyes. It was one he had only seen once before: the very first day the machine had been used, when they had come back through to modern times, and she had been angry that she and her brother had been used as a test. Now it was even more fierce, however, and he was more afraid of this than the tears she had shed when Frank had been arrested.

Seeing he said nothing, Susanna turned away from him and looked back into the empty field again. "Go away," she whispered.

Raymond looked steadily at her, "I will if you really mean that, but do you really want me to?" he asked.

She whirled on him, "Yes! Everything has gone wrong since we met you! That very first day we saw you, it was because you were so unfeeling as to use us as a test. Everything that has had to do with you has had something bad in it for us. If we had never met you, our lives would be going on as before. Thomas would be here, and so would Frank Garrold. We wouldn't even know of the existence of a time machine, and my heart would not be – falling – to – pieces –" and she broke her gaze from his face and looked off into the open field again.

"I'm sorry," Raymond began.

"Are you? Are you really? I don't think you even can feel anything."

"What do you mean?" he questioned in astonishment.

She took a shuddering breath, then said quietly, but with strain in her voice, "The very first day, when you hid and watched us, laughing at our difficulties; knowing what was wrong, but not willing to help us – since then I have not known whether you were to be trusted. If you had gotten us out of there before we had started to worry, I believe I might have forgiven even the fact that you used us for a test, but – oh, what am I saying?"

"But, Susanna, " Raymond began, knowing he had been wrong, but still wanting to defend himself, "It wasn't my idea to – "

She cut him off, "I know it wasn't your idea to trick us in the first place, but Mr. Elliot apologized. You could have saved us all the stress of not being able to find our home if you had only been able to think about how we felt instead of just laughing at our confusion. That's why I don't think you can have any real feelings, or care what is happening to me."

She was still angry; her eyes flashing as she turned back to him. Raymond was shocked. This was a different Susanna than he had ever seen before.

He said quietly, "Whether you believe it or not, I am sorry about what I did then, and I was planning to apologize, but hadn't had the chance yet."

"Hadn't had the chance yet," she said scornfully, "you could've said it any time today, or yesterday, or last week! What about when we went to the Maxwells' house? If you were embarrassed to say it aloud, we were alone for a minute in front of the door. The others could see us, but they couldn't hear us."

"How about I say it now?" he asked, "Susanna, I'm really sorry for waiting so long before telling you what was wrong and why you couldn't get home the first day we met."

Susanna looked away again, "I'd like to believe you," she said softly, "but I don't know if I can. Right now I'm just worried about Thomas," and her face hardened with anger again.

"I'm so sorry about that. Terribly sorry," Raymond said gently, "We're going to try to get him back as soon as we can. I can't tell you how I wish it had never happened. I'm sorry."

"Yes, you're sorry." Susanna. said vengefully. "but you can't feel what I'm feeling right now. You can't make yourself feel what another person's feeling; you can't know what it's like to lose someone you depended on like this. Wait till you do, then say you're sorry, and mean it."

"Susanna," he began, steadily gazing at her. She looked at him wonderingly.

"I lost my mother a year ago," he said slowly, pronouncing each word as if it gave him pain, "We thought she had just a little sickness, then suddenly it worsened, and she died. I know even better than you what it means to lose someone I love."

Susanna's eyes were wide. "Oh, what have I said," she breathed, "How cruel of me." She suddenly looked off into the field again, and said, "Now you will hate me just as much as I – " and hesitated.

"As you hate me?" Raymond finished for her, "Do you really hate me, Susanna? And all because of that mistake I made – that wrong I did you on the first day we met?"

She shook her head slowly, "No, I don't hate you. That's not what I meant, but it was easier to say that way."

"Then what did you mean?"

"I don't know," she whispered.

"Please tell me. I think I have a right to know if there's something I still need to do to clear away the wrong I did you then."

"Nothing," she shook her head.

"So you aren't angry with me anymore?"

"Not really."

"Then what's the matter?"

"I want my brother back!" she cried desperately.

"We'll try to get him back as soon as possible," Raymond said soothingly, "Anyway, maybe they just took him in for questioning, and aren't going to keep him for long."

She nodded dismally, her face she kept turned away. She still had not shed a single tear.

"Don't you think we should go tell your parents what happened?" he asked softly.

Susanna looked up at him then, and he saw her lips had begun to tremble. "Tell Mommy and Daddy that Thomas is gone?" she said quaveringly.

She looked so young and vulnerable, and he had a sudden feeling that he wanted to protect her from any more of this terrible business they had gotten into. Impulsively, he reached forward and placed his hand on hers, which still rested on the fence. "No, he's not gone," he told her firmly, "He's just going to be away from home a little while. We'll get him back."

"How can you know?" she asked.

"I don't know, but I do know that God will take care of him wherever he is. We'll pray for him, just like we did for Frank, and I'm sure we'll get him back."

Susanna looked down, took a deep breath, then suddenly laid her head down on top of their hands and began to sob. Raymond turned and motioned frantically for his father. This was something he wasn't ready to deal with.

Mr. Vincent hurried over to the fence, and patted Susanna on the shoulder. She straightened, and Raymond drew his hand away, escaping to Mr. Elliot.

A minute later, Mr. Vincent and Susanna came over to the others. Susanna was calm and composed. "We're ready to go to the Jacksons' house now," Mr. Vincent said.

On the way home, Mr. Elliot suddenly staggered, and put a hand to his chest, catching Raymond's arm with his other hand. He shook his head when the others asked if anything was wrong, "No, I'm just growing older. I have these spells every once in a while."

Chapter 40

When they reached the Jacksons house, Susanna told the others to leave, and let her go in alone.

"I'm going to ask Mommy if she wants to tell all of the children the whole truth, or if she wants to keep it a secret," she said, "We usually tell the children everything, but this is an unusual situation." Other than her one burst of sobs by the fence, Susanna had not shed a tear since Thomas was arrested. Instead, she seemed to be strangely braced up somehow.

"Please do not tell anyone what happened," she begged, "I just want to talk to my parents first."

"Okay," Mr. Vincent agreed. The other two men nodded.

Susanna lifted a hand in farewell, "Thank you. Good-bye. Umm – how about one or two of you come tomorrow? We can't talk over the phone, you know."

"All right," Raymond's father agreed, and the girl ran around the house to the basement door, hoping she wouldn't be noticed if she entered this way.

But her family was too large to let that happen. When she was halfway up the stairs to her mother's room, Nancy came running into the hallway, and seeing Susanna, called, "Where's Thomas?"

"I don't know," her big sister answered truthfully.

Nancy left, and Susanna hurried up to find her mother folding clothes by her bed.

"Mommy, I have something to tell you," she said slowly, closing the door behind her.

They decided they might let the twins know, but the younger children would not be told everything. At the dinner table, Mrs. Jackson announced that Thomas had found that he needed to leave for a few days; they weren't sure how long. The younger children groaned, because Thomas was always willing to do anything for them, so they would miss him, but Jennie looked thoughtful.

After dinner, Jennie silently helped Edward with the dishes. He looked at her sideways a couple of times, then asked, "What's the matter?"

"Just thinking," she said.

"Oh. About what?"

"Tell you later, if I can. Hey, Edward, can I go for a minute, I want to ask Susanna something."

"Sure. We're almost done anyway. Don't worry about coming back."

"Thanks!" and she ran out of the kitchen.

"Susanna," Jennie called, running into their room and jumping onto the bed beside her older sister.

"Is there something you need?" Susanna asked.

"Well – not exactly. I have a question."

"What?"

"How much does Thomas's disappearance have to do with Frank Garrold's?"

"What!" Susanna exclaimed, looking her little sister full in the face.

"You promised you'd tell me some time," Jennie said, "What about now?"

Susanna sighed, "We were planning to tell you anyway. Why don't you call Edward, and I'll explain everything I can."

"Then it's true!" Jennie exclaimed.

"Yes, it's true," her older sister nodded tiredly.

A little while later, Susanna, Jennie, and their father went out for a walk. After walking for a few minutes, Jennie tucked her hand into her father's and squeezed tightly, whispering, "Someone's following us."

"What!" he exclaimed, "Are you sure?"

"Sure."

"I guess they found out that we don't take our phones with us everywhere we go," Susanna said softly, "so they decided to shadow us, hoping to find the machine that way instead."

"Let's go home, Daddy," Jennie whispered nervously.

~   ~   ~

The next day Susanna drove Thomas's car to the grocery store with the twins. She read off the grocery list, and each of them went to a separate part of the store to find different items.

Jennie was picking her way through the cold isle of refrigerators, looking for frozen peas, when she almost bumped into Jack and Harold Davis.

"Hey, Jennie! How are you today?" Jack called out, bringing the grocery cart he was pushing up to her side, "here, let me get that!" as she found that the shelf the peas were sitting on was too high for her to reach.

"Hello, Jack, Harold. I'm fine, thanks."

"How many do you need?" Jack asked, his hand still up on the pea shelf.

"Just three bags," she answered, taking them from him.

"Who else is here?" asked Harold, "Unless you drove yourself?" he asked teasingly.

"Susanna brought me and Edward," Jennie answered with a laugh and a shake of her head.

"How's Thomas doing?" Jack questioned.

Jennie frowned suddenly, "I don't know," she blurted out, caught off guard, then stammered, "I-I mean, he's fine, I think."

"Is something wrong?" Jack frowned.

"Hey, Jack, Harold!" Edward suddenly came up and Jennie breathed a sigh of relief. She hadn't wanted to lie, but how to get out of the situation had been beyond her.

"Hello, Edward," Harold said, "Jennie told us you were here."

"She told you!" Edward pretended to be angry, "how could she?"

Everyone laughed.

"We were asking about your family," Jack told him, "and your sister must have been thinking about something else, because when we asked how Thomas was, she said she didn't know!" he laughed, but stopped quickly when he saw Edward's face was serious.

"Come on, Edward," Jennie said, "I've got everything I was supposed to get, and you do too, don't you?" he nodded, and she finished, "then let's go find Susanna. She's probably waiting for us."

"Hey, wait a minute," Jack ran a couple of steps to catch up with them, "Is there anything wrong with Thomas? Is he hurt or something?"

"I – we've got to go," Jennie said desperately, but the Davis boys saw that her lip was quivering.

"If there's anything wrong – if he's hurt, or sick – you might as well tell us so we can pray for him," Jack said quickly. He wondered if he should just leave them alone, but he was an old family friend, and felt he ought to at least see if there was anything he could do.

Susanna joined them at this moment, and the Davis boys noticed a line between her brows.

"Where's Thomas?" Jack asked.

"He's away for a few days. I'm not sure how long he'll be gone, but hopefully not more than a day or two. Maybe he'll be back tomorrow," she answered quickly, "come on, Edward, Jennie. Let's get our things on the counter."

"Susanna, is there anything wrong with Thomas?" Jack asked.

She spoke carelessly, "Not that I know of, why?"

"Is that the problem? You don't know where he is?" Jack questioned quickly.

Susanna gasped and turned swiftly to look at him, "How did you – I mean – oh, I don't know!"

Jack stepped a little closer, but Jennie was quicker. She whispered in her sister's ear, "Maybe he can help us – the bomb, you know. If we have people shadowing us, it'll be hard to set it, but he can do it, since they don't know him. Oh! And besides, doesn't he work for some kind of a – a demolition company or something?"

Susanna nodded, and then looked back at Jack, "Can you come over right after lunch?" she asked.

"Sure, I can."

"Hey, you two, what's the matter?" Harold demanded in a whisper, helping the twins take the articles out of their cart and put them on the counter.

They didn't answer.

"Well, I guess we'll be praying for you guys," Harold said slowly. He punched Edward on the shoulder, and smiled at Jennie, noting the boy's compressed lips, and the girl's tear-filled eyes, which she quickly averted.

"You can just bet I'll get Jack to tell me what's what when he comes home from their house!" he said inwardly, waving a goodbye.

~   ~   ~

Mr. Jackson opened the door for Jack Davis and before the young man could say anything whispered, "When you get inside, ask about Thomas as if you don't know anything. That'll put them off the scent."

Jack was completely confused, but did as he was told. When he sat down in the library, Susanna came in and he said, "Hello, Susanna! Where's Thomas?"

"Oh, he's not here right now," she answered as if nothing were wrong, "he had somewhere he needed to go for a few days."

"Oh! How's your mom doing?"

"She's fine. We can't wait until the baby's born!"

Edward came running in, "Hi, Jack. You want to play ping-pong?"

Jack looked at Susanna and she nodded, so he said, "sure! Let's go downstairs."

As they turned to leave the room, Mr. Jackson motioned for him to wait. He made the hand sign for "phone," then held out his hand.

Jack understood, and pulled his phone out of his pocket, handing it to Mr. Jackson, who set it on a nearby bookshelf. Then all four went downstairs.

~   ~   ~

"That Jackson boy hasn't told us anything," Pickard said, stepping into the boss's office. "Garrold can't tell us anything, because he says he never saw the machine itself, only heard it talked about. I think his story is believable. But Thomas Jackson knows everything, and he won't talk."

"We've got to find out somehow. Keep on tracking the movements of the others, and maybe they'll lead us to it," the boss said.

~   ~   ~

"I'll get that bomb for you," Jack assured them, "I know what door you're talking about, so I can find the machine easily, I think. Did Mr. Elliot destroy his computer yet, and any papers he might have had printed out?"

"I think so," Mr. Jackson answered, "If not, he'll do it soon."

A sudden step was heard on the stairs, and the conversation ceased, everyone waiting to see who it was.

Raymond entered the room, "Hi! Jennie told me you were down here. Am I interrupting something? Susanna told me to come over this afternoon."

"No, you're not interrupting," Mr. Jackson answered.

"What's going on? Why is Jack here?"

"He's going to get the bomb for us, because we're being watched, and can't," Edward said.

"Watched! That's why that car seemed to be following me as I drove here!" Raymond exclaimed.

"Yes, so we can't do anything that might lead them to the machine," Susanna said.

"I'm in demolitions," Jack said, "I'll have to look around the area, but the Jacksons have told me there's a shed nearby and a few trees. If I could get a contract drawn up with Mr. Elliot to get rid of some of the stuff on his property, I could 'accidentally' blow up the time machine along with it."

"Great! That should work. It's a good thing you thought of him, Susanna."

"Oh, I didn't!" Susanna laughed, "Jennie did."

"Yes, I sort of pushed to find out what had happened to Thomas, and since I was about to have to be told anyway, Jennie thought they might as well make me work for the information," Jack laughed. "But seriously, I'm really thankful I bumped into you this morning at the grocery store. If you had tried to blow up anything yourselves, you could have gotten into worse trouble than ever with the law. Since I actually can get demolition supplies legally, it'll be much safer for your plan."

~   ~   ~

"They've given in!" Pickard exclaimed.

"What do you mean?"

"I heard them talking, through their phones. They were a little ways away, so it was hard to hear, but I could hear enough to understand what they meant.

The Jackson girl, the sister of the one we arrested for questioning, sounded like she was crying, which is perfectly normal, since she doesn't know what we've done with her brother, to whom she seems much attached."

"Well?"

"Well, she said, 'Can't we just let them have the machine? Maybe if we do, they'll give us Thomas and Frank back.'"

"And what did the other people say?" the boss asked.

"The Elliot guy, who we think invented the time machine, said, 'I don't want to lose it! And it's too dangerous to give it to the government.' Then Raymond Vincent said something like, 'but we've got to get our friends back,' and after a while Elliot gave in."

"So you think they'll let us have the machine if they can get those two young men back?" the boss asked.

"I think so."

"Well, let's try them. Go to the Jacksons' house and offer an exchange. I don't really care if we keep Garrold, and of course Thomas Jackson is no use to us."

"All right, I'll do it," Pickard nodded.

~   ~   ~

"Mommy, there's someone at the door," Susanna called softly.

"Who?" her mother asked, coming out of the school room where she had been helping Frances with her math, "Is it the mail?"

"No. I don't know who it is. It's some man."

"Okay. I'll answer it."

Mrs. Jackson opened the door, "Yes? Hello."

"Mrs. Jackson?"

"Yes."

"I have a letter for you. Please read it now."

"Okay," she took the paper, read it through, and showed it to her daughter, who was standing behind her.

"Do you work with the people who sent this letter?" Mrs. Jackson asked.

"Yes," the man answered.

"So you say you'll give my son and our friend Frank Garrold back if we show you where the time-travel machine is?" asked Mrs. Jackson.

"Yes. What is your answer?"

"I'll have to discuss it with the others," she told him, "but I'll do almost anything to get my son back. How can I get word to you when we decide what our answer will be?"

"I'll come back tomorrow for the answer." And he left.

Susanna turned to her mother and whispered joyfully, "It worked! When we staged that little conversation in front of our phones, hoping they would hear, and I pretended to cry, and demand that we give up the machine so that we could get Thomas back! Oh, I'm so glad!"

Chapter 41

Two vehicles drove up in front of the Jacksons' house. Susanna gazed eagerly out of the window where she, Raymond, and Mr. Vincent were watching, for a glimpse of her brother. Mr. Elliot and Susanna's parents were watching from another window.

A man and a woman got out of one of the cars and walked up to the door, ringing the doorbell. Mr. Jackson answered it.

The woman spoke first, "Mr. Jackson?" he nodded, so she kept on, "Mr. Elliot has agreed to take us to the Time-Travel Machine if we release your son and Frank Garrold."

"That is true," Mr. Jackson nodded.

"Is Mr. Elliot here?"

"Yes, he is."

Mr. Jackson stepped aside to let Mr. Elliot in front of him.

"Take us to your machine, Mr. Elliot," the woman commanded, "as soon as we are in possession of it, we will hand over the prisoners."

"No, I won't take you to the machine until the prisoners are free," Mr. Elliot protested.

"How can we trust that you'll show us where the machine is if we set the young men free first?" the woman demanded.

"How can I trust that you'll set the boys free if I show you the machine first?" Mr. Elliot asked, "besides, my argument is better. Since we both know that the FBI can find anyone they want to find, if I didn't show you the machine after they were released, you could always take them back."

The woman nodded, and her partner spoke this time, "let's do it. How far away from us is the machine?"

"Not very far. We can walk to it, if you will," Mr. Elliot answered.

"Then we'll let our prisoners go now, and they can walk with us to the machine," the woman told him.

~   ~   ~

"Raymond, Raymond, Thomas is getting out of the car!" Susanna exclaimed.

"Yes, he is. I think it worked," Raymond said, "now let's just hope they won't be too mad when they find out how we tricked them."

Susanna shivered, but hurried to the door. Now both Frank and Thomas were out of the vehicles, and were standing in the driveway.

"Mommy, may I go out?" Susanna begged.

Mrs. Jackson looked at her husband, and he nodded. Susanna and the Vincents followed Mr. Elliot out the door slowly, but once they were outside, Susanna couldn't keep still any longer, and broke from the group to throw herself into her brother's arms, "Oh, Thomas!" she exclaimed, "I'm so glad you're back!"

"So am I," Thomas said, hugging her, "they told me that you agreed to show them the time-travel machine if they would let us go."

Susanna nodded, "We did. We just couldn't bear to have you gone."

"Well, I'm glad to be back," he told her, keeping up the ruse, "but are you sure this is the right thing to do?"

"You're more important than any machine!" she said.

Thomas and Frank walked with their friends, while the group of FBI agents followed. When they neared the door in the brick wall, Mr. Elliot said, "Wait just a minute."

He motioned for the man and woman who seemed to be in charge and said, "You see that door over there?"

"I'm not blind," the woman informed him tersely.

Mr. Elliot nodded politely, "Well, wait here, and I'll show you something," he said. He walked up to the door and turned off the button that made the machine invisible. There were a few gasps from the group of FBI agents.

He walked back to where the others were standing. "There's your time machine," he told them, "we can keep the boys now? We did our part and showed you the machine like we said we would."

The woman nodded, "that's right. The boys are yours, and the time machine's ours."

"As much as is – " Mr. Elliot paused as an explosion rent the air, " – left of it!" he finished, "as much as is left of it!"

"What did you just do!" the woman yelled as a large section of the brick wall collapsed, taking the machine with it.

"We showed you the time machine," Mr. Elliot told her calmly, nodding, "we never promised we'd let you have it."

"Where are your plans?" she demanded, "where are the blueprints for the machine?"

"I destroyed my computer several days ago," he said, "so there's no way for you to recover your files."

"Then you will have to rewrite them for us!" the woman said angrily. She pointed to two of the agents, "you, go and examine the ruins for any information you can find."

They came back a little later and shook their heads, "There's nothing. The explosion ruined it all. There are only a few tiny pieces of metal left among the bricks."

One of the men stepped forward with a triumphant look on his face, "You are all under arrest for public endangerment by the unauthorized use of explosives!"

Jack stepped out from behind a tree and came forward with a confused look on his face. "Say, what's going on here?" he asked. "Hello, Mr. Elliot! I finished that demolition job you gave me. You should be able to make your driveway through that wall now." Turning to the federal agents, he said, "I'm sorry if you were startled by the explosion. I am a licensed demolitions expert, and I had a contract with this gentlemen to remove the old brick wall so he can put in a new driveway."

Not to be foiled so easily, the woman grabbed Mr. Elliot's arm, "You've done this!" she screamed at him, "you just ruined our chance to make a wonderful discovery! Now you'd better get busy and write us another copy of those plans, or else!"

Mr. Vincent stepped to Mr. Elliot's side, "Ma'am, that machine took him a very long time to build. I don't think he could rewrite the plans in just a few short days."

Mr. Elliot suddenly stumbled backward and fell to the ground. Thomas and Raymond tried to catch him, but were too late.

"What's wrong with him!" the woman shrieked.

"I don't know," Mr. Vincent said, "but it looks like he needs a doctor – and fast!" He took out his phone and quickly dialed 911, ordering an ambulance.

Chapter 42

Mr. Elliot died that night in the hospital. It was heart trouble, the doctor said, along with the fact that the man was simply very old, and it was impossible to save him.

The FBI didn't give up their search for a long time, though. They took possession of Mr. Elliot's house and examined it from top to bottom. But finally they had to admit defeat. As the old man had said, he had destroyed all the evidence. So a few months later, everything settled down once more for the Jacksons and their friends.

"I can't wish it had never happened," Thomas told Raymond afterwards, "but I'm glad it's over."

"I feel the same way," Raymond answered thoughtfully. "Because you know, if it hadn't happened, I'd probably have never met you. And knowing your family has been wonderful."

Susanna entered the room in time to hear the last few sentences. "Yes, I think it is nice that we met you, Raymond, but oh, the cost! Couldn't we have met in an easier way?" she laughed.

"I don't know, but I'd much rather have met you this way, than not met at all," Raymond told her.

"Besides, if we hadn't had the time machine," Thomas reminded them, "Richard Wilson would have died long ago."

"He did die long ago," Raymond informed him, "It's been about a hundred fifty years since we rescued him."

"Right," Thomas shook his head.

"Ugh!" Susanna exclaimed with a short laugh, "I think maybe in ten years I'll be willing to hear the words 'time travel' mentioned again! Can we just forget about the whole thing and be normal?"

"I doubt we'll ever forget," Thomas assured her, "but we can simply not discuss it. What do you two say we go downstairs and play some ping-pong?"

Epilogue

Jennie hurriedly searched through the bag she kept her hair accessories in. Not finding what she was looking for, she searched more frantically. "I've got to find it!" she exclaimed.

She sat down on the floor and emptied the contents of her bag into her lap, shaking her head in dismay as she ascertained that what she was looking for was not there.

"What's the matter, Jennie?" Edward asked, entering the room dressed spic and span in his suit and tie.

"I can't find my hair clip!" she told him, smoothing her ruffled skirt and sifting through the many hair accessories in her lap.

"Which one?" he asked, squatting down beside her, "you have a whole lot there."

"My favorite," she explained, "the gold one, with clear beads in the center and on the dangles – you know, right?"

"Uh-huh. And you can't find it?"

"Mm-mm. I can't." Jennie heaved a great sigh.

Suddenly Edward laughed and began singing in a rollicking voice,

> *Oh, my darling, oh my darling,*
> *Oh, my darling gold hair clip,*
> *You are lost, and gone forever*
> *Oh, my darling gold hair clip!*

Jennie pouted, "You know Mommy told us not to sing 'Clementine.'"

"Yes, I do!" he laughed, "but she didn't say we couldn't sing about hair clips! *You* know the tune is fine, and she just doesn't like the words."

"Edward, this is serious! I really wanted to wear that hair clip to the wedding, but now I can't."

"I guess Frank and Ann can get married whether you have your hair clip or not!" he teased, continuing,

> *In the girls' room, in her bedroom*
> *Getting ready for a trip;*
> *Jennie Jackson started axin'*
> *"Where's my darling gold hair clip?"*

Jennie turned away, and Edward quickly put a hand on her arm, "I'm sorry, Jennie. That was pretty mean – but look – stand up and turn around, will you?"

Jennie did as she was told, then suddenly knelt down again and pounced on something that glittered on the floor. "Oh, Edward! That's why I couldn't find it in my bag, I'd already dropped it!"

Then she burst into song,

> *Edward laughed, and Jennie cried, so*
> *Edward gave his sis a tip,*
> *Said, "just stand, and turn around, and*
> *You will find that gold hair clip!"*

They sang the chorus together, while scooping the hair accessories back into Jennie's bag, but with a little different twist:

> *Oh, my darling, oh my darling,*
> *Oh, my darling gold hair clip,*
> *You're **not** lost, and gone forever*
> *Oh, my darling gold hair clip!*

"Will you get your hair done quickly, please?" Edward asked, "I want you to help me with something before we leave."

"Okay," Jennie nodded, standing up and moving toward the bathroom, "but I can't wait to see Frank and Ann get married!"

"Uh-huh. I guess girls would like that kind of stuff," Edward shrugged. "Hey, you know what, Jennie?"

"What?"

"I wish we had had a chance to go through that time-travel machine too. Susanna and Thomas didn't seem to have much fun, but I bet we would."

"Yes, I'm sure. We'd have to be careful, though, so that no one was hurt with it. Do you think someone else might invent a machine like that sometime?" she asked.

He shook his head, "who knows? But it does sound like a lot of fun. You could know just what it was like to live back in the old days. Well, see you downstairs!"

The End

Author's Notes

Pigeons: This has become a real problem in today's world. An EM pulse may be dreaded almost as much as a nuclear attack, and is actually more likely. If an EMP were directed toward the USA, and stopped all electronic communications, it would be virtually impossible for people to survive. The Chinese government has addressed this issue by beginning to train carrier pigeons so that if an EMP were directed toward them, it would be possible to communicate, though at a far lesser rate than normal. So far, the United States has not released any information about how we are preparing for such an attack or not.

Take a sneak peek inside the next book in this series: Jennie and Edward's story.

Chapter 1

Jennie Jackson climbed over a couple of rotted boards, her twin brother Edward staring after her. "I really don't think we should do this, Jennie!" he called, looking up at her, several feet above him.

"It's okay, Edward! Nobody owns this property," She called back, "I'm just looking at this old building. I wonder how long ago it fell apart?"

"There's no way of knowing," he grumbled, "We've never been over here before. Come on, let's go home."

"Aw, Edward. Just a few more minutes."

"Okay," he sighed, shaking his head, "I'm coming too, though. What if you fell through something and broke your leg and I'd have to – Oh, great! Now what have you done!" he leaped forward as Jennie disappeared suddenly with a little squeal and a crash.

"Jennie! Are you all right?"

"Sure I am," she shouted, poking her head out of a hole between boards with a big grin, "but you ought to come down here, Edward! My goodness!"

"What is it?" Edward was beginning to get interested too. He clambered up over the last shaky boards, and lowered himself down beside his sister.

"Whoo-ee, look at this!" Jennie whistled, gazing around in fascination.

They were in a little room, whose walls had stood up even when the roof had caved in. The walls were bare, but there was a little bench on one wall, and a table by another. The table was covered with broken boards, parts of the roof, but under it was something that made Edward look twice.

He jumped forward and knelt by the side of the table, reaching under and pulling out a large old-fashioned computer. The keyboard came along with it, attached by some cords.

"Cool," Jennie breathed, "Think you can make it work, Edward?"

"I don't know. It seems to have been smashed for some reason."

"When the roof caved in?" she asked.

"I don't think so. This table saved it from that. I think someone or something destroyed the computer before that, and then left it here until the roof caved in."

"Well, I don't know a thing about it, but you are majoring in computer science, so you should know how to fix it if anyone can," she told him confidently.

"I'll try. I don't think I can actually make this computer work, but I might be able to get the information out of it and onto another computer," said Edward.

"Let's do it. I'll help you if I can, even though I don't know much about it, but it ought to be a whole lot of fun!"

The twins had been exploring an old building on an empty acre of property in the country near the town they lived in. They had gone on a drive just for fun, and Jennie had wanted to examine the ruined structure when she saw it. They had knocked on the door of one of the houses nearby and had been informed that no one had been on the property in years.

~   ~   ~

"How's it going, Edward?" Jennie asked, peeking around him to look at his computer screen, and the machinery he had laying all over his desk.

"Fine. I haven't quite gotten the files to work out yet; this computer we found is so out of date that it won't work well with my computer. But I'm getting closer."

Jennie fingered the tiny silver earing dangling from her right ear, and Edward looked up, "I've been wondering why Susanna didn't get her ears pierced a couple of months ago when you did," he told her, "She likes fancy things just as much as you do."

Jennie threw back her head and laughed.

"What?" he asked.

"Oh, you silly!" she teased, "don't you know Raymond hates earrings?"

"What does that have to do with it?" he asked, confused.

"Silly!" she said again, "they're going to start courting in a couple of weeks. He's already asked if they can, but she hasn't answered yet. She's going to say yes, of course."

Edward's brow wrinkled, "How do you know this?" he asked, "I haven't heard a word."

"Well, neither have I – exactly," she told him, "There are some things a girl can just tell."

Edward shook his head in despair, "I used to know everything you did. I could tell what you were thinking most of the time just because we are twins, but now? I guess it must be because you're a girl and I'm a boy."

"Oh, we're still close enough," she assured him, "And it was only last week that you told me you knew I didn't like Mrs. Davis's potato salad, when no one else could tell. But yes, you are right, there are some things that boys can't understand about girls!" and she threw him a teasing glance, tossed her hair over her shoulder, and flung herself out of the room.

~   ~   ~

"Jennie!" Edward called, sticking his head out of the door to his office.

"Yes?" his twin hurried up the stairs.

"Oh, I just wanted to tell you that I've figured something out. I've got some of the information from that old computer onto my computer, and I think I can read it pretty easily!"

"Really!" Jennie burst through the door and into the room, "Anything interesting?"

"Oh, yes! You won't believe it." He spoke in rather a strange voice, "Come here;" he took her hand and drew her over to his desk.

Leaning over her shoulder he pointed to the words on the screen. Jennie gasped, then read aloud,

Elliot's Time Travel Machine Plans